THE
TIN
COLLECTORS

STEPHEN J. CANNELL

THE

TIN

COLLECTORS

COMPASS PRESS

AN IMPRINT OF WHEELER PUBLISHING, INC.

Published in Large Print by arrangement with St. Martin's Press in the United States and Canada.

Compass Press Large Print book series;
an imprint of Wheeler Publishing Inc., USA

Set in 16 pt Plantin.

Library of Congress Cataloging-in-Publication Data

Cannell, Stephen J.
    The tin collectors / Stephen J. Cannell.
        p. (large print) cm.(Compass Press large print book series)
    ISBN 1-58724-080-7 (hardcover)
    1. Police—California—Los Angeles—Fiction. 2. Los Angeles (Calif.)—
Fiction. 3. Police corruption—Fiction. 4. Large type books.
I. Title. II. Series

[PS3553.A4995 T56   2001b]
813'.54—dc21   2001026356
                                                                      CIP

For Roy Huggins:
colleague, mentor, godfather,
and friend

ACKNOWLEDGMENTS

A S ALWAYS, there are many people to thank in connection with this book. First of all, my team of regulars: Grace Curcio, who was always there, weekends or holidays, retyping my penciled-in first draft, encouraging me when I asked about a rough chapter— "It's great, but you'll fix it"; Kathy Ezso, at the computer, doing change after change with bulletproof efficiency, contributing encouragement and opinion; and my noodge, Wayne Williams, who reads with a sharp eye and sharper pencil, correcting details and phraseology.

To Sally Richardson at St. Martin Press, who has been a supporter and fan since the beginning of my novel-writing career and who with this, my sixth novel, has at last become my publisher. We're going to be a team for the new millennium. To Charles Spicer, my new editor at St. Martin's, who has made huge contributions in the publication of this, our first book together.

Many thanks to my Los Angeles Police Department technical advisers, who let me see the inside of the Internal Affairs Division, starting with Captain Michael Downing, who gave me hours of help. Special thanks to all of the advocates and defense reps at Internal Affairs who shared their process and work habits with me, especially Sergeant Dianne Burns, Sergeant Horace Frank, and Defense Rep Sergeant Thomas Dawson, Ph.D., as well as many others. They are real heroes who are charged with the awesome responsibility of seeking truth, often in the face of extreme pressure.

Thanks to Jo Swerling, again a stellar critic, who read the manuscript in hot-off-the-computer chunks and contributed in so many ways.

To Roy Huggins, who earned the dedication on this novel with thirty years of friendship and mentoring.

To Eric Simonoff, valued agent and friend, who along with Mort Janklow looks over me with protective determination, helping me grow.

And finally, but most important, to my wife, Marcia, and to my children, Tawnia, Chelsea, and Cody, who shine a bright light on my life so I can swim unafraid in the dark waters of my imagination.

Principles serve to govern conduct when there are no rules.

—LAPD MANAGEMENT GUIDE TO DISCIPLINE

THE "CHOOCH" LETTER

Dear Dad:

Charles Sandoval, who everybody calls Chooch, arrived this afternoon as planned (actually, I picked him up). This is already shaping up as one of my biggest boners. I pulled up at the fancy private school Sandy's got him enrolled in and I had to go to the principal's office to sign the pickup permission slip. The principal, John St. John, is a wheezing, hollow-chested geek who seems to honestly hate Chooch. The way he put it was: "That child is from the ninth circle." I had to ask, too. It's from Dante's Inferno. *Apparently, the ninth circle is the circle closest to hell. Now that I've met Chooch, not an entirely inappropriate analogy. Then, this pale erection with ears hands me a packet of teacher evaluation slips. For a fifteen-year-old, his rap sheet is impressive...pulled fire alarms, and fights in the school cafeteria (food as well as fists). Mr. St. John informs me that they have notified Sandy that Chooch is not to return to the Harvard Westlake School next semester and that I need to get him enrolled elsewhere (like this is all of a sudden supposed to be my problem). But it's not as if this boy doesn't have a good reason to be angry. I think I wrote you, he's a love child with one of Sandy's old clients. Making matters worse, Sandy doesn't want him to know how she makes her living, so she's been shipping him off to boarding schools since third grade.*

Needless to say, I had no idea what I was getting into here. Maybe I can last the month until Sandy takes him back or sends him to the next sucker on her list. One way or another, I'll work it out.

I'm planning to get out to Florida again sometime next year. I was thinking you and I could rent one of those fishing boats like we did last time, drink some beer and cook what we catch over a beach fire. Those memories are treasures in my life.

I know, I know, cut the mush, blah…blah…blah. I miss you, Dad. That's all for now.

> *Love,*
> *Your son,*
> *Shane*

1
USE OF FORCE

SHANE WAS IN deep REM black. Way down there, but still he heard the telephone's electronic urgency. The sound hung over him, a vague shimmer, way above, up on the surface. Slowly he made his way to it, breaking consciousness, washed in confusion and anger. His bedroom was dark. The digital clock stung his eyeballs with a neon greeting: 2:16 A.M. He found the receiver and pressed it against his ear.

"Yeah," he said, his voice a croak and a whisper.

"Shane, he's trying to kill me," a woman hissed urgently.

"What...who is this?"

"It's Barbara." She was whispering, but he could also hear a loud banging coming over the receiver on her end, as if somebody was trying to break down a door.

"He's trying to kill you?" he repeated, buying time so his mind could focus.

Barbara Molar. He hadn't seen her in over two months, and then just for a moment at a police department ceremony, last year's Medal of Valor Awards. Her husband, Ray, had been one of three recipients.

A crash, then: "Jesus, get over here, Shane. Please. He'll listen to you. He's nuts, worse than ever."

Shane heard another crash. Barbara started screaming. He couldn't make out her next words, then: "Don't, please..." She was whimpering, the phone was dropped on a hard floor, clattering, bouncing, getting kicked in some desperate struggle.

"Barbara? Barbara?" She didn't answer. He heard a distant, guttural grunting like a man sometimes makes during sex, or a fight.

Shane got out of bed and started gathering up clothes. He slipped into his pants and grabbed his faded LAPD sweatshirt. He snapped up his ankle gun, hesitated for a moment, then pulled it out, chambered it, and strapped it on. He ran out of his bedroom toward the garage without even looking for his shoes. He was already behind the wheel when he realized he had forgotten that Chooch Sandoval was asleep in the other bedroom. He wasn't used to having fifteen-year-old houseguests. He knew he shouldn't leave Chooch alone. The garage door was going up as he backed out his black Acura. Grabbing for his cell phone, he dialed a number from memory. He streaked down the back alley away from his Venice, California, canal house, as cold beach air slipstreamed past the side window onto his face.

Brian "Longboard" Kelly, his boned-out next-door neighbor, picked up the phone. "Whoever this is, fuck you" was the way he came on the line.

"Sorry, Brian, it's Shane. I got called out, and Chooch is still asleep in the guest bedroom."

6

"Chooch? Who the hell..."

"The kid I told you I was taking for the month. Sandy's kid. He came yesterday."

"Ohhh, man..."

"Look, Brian, just go over and sleep on my couch. The key is in the pot by the back door."

"Good place, dickbrain. Who would ever think to look there?"

"Just do it, will ya? I'll owe ya."

"Fuckin' A." Longboard slammed the phone down in Shane's ear.

Shane was now at Washington Boulevard. He hung a left and headed the short distance to the Molar house. When they'd still been partners, he'd made this trip at least once a day to pick up Ray, heading across Washington to South Venice Boulevard, through Gangbang Circle, where, once it got dark, the V-Thirteens and Shoreside Crips staged their useless, life-ending street actions, occasionally killing or wounding a tourist from Minnesota by mistake.

He shot across Abbot Kinney Boulevard and turned right onto California, finally coming to Shell Avenue. All the way there, he wondered why Barbara would call him. Why not dial 911? Of course, the answer was sort of obvious after he thought about it. Even though she was scared spitless, she still didn't want another domestic-violence beef in Ray's LAPD Internal Affairs jacket. He was a thirty-year veteran with a big pension, which another DV complaint would jeopardize. That pension was an asset that was half hers.

7

Still, Shane Scully was the last guy Ray Molar would want to see coming through his door, quoting departmental spousal-abuse regulations at two A.M. *So why Shane? Why not Ray's current partner?* He guessed he knew that answer, too. She called him because she thought she could control him, use him for protection, then keep him from talking. Also he was handy, only five miles away.... Just like before, he had turned up as the double zero on her slow-turning roulette wheel.

When he got to Ray's small, wood-sided house, he pulled into the driveway behind Ray's car and jumped out. The hood was warm on the dark blue Cadillac Brougham; the lights were on in the house. Then he heard muffled screaming.

"Shit, I hate this," he mumbled softly, feeling the cold grass on his bare feet. He moved toward the house, tried the front door and, to his surprise, found it was open. Reluctantly, he stepped into his ex-partner's living room.

Ray's house always seemed delicate and overdecorated. Too much French fleur-de-lis upholstery, too many knickknacks and hanging lamps. It was Barbara's doing and definitely didn't seem like the lair of a street monster like Ray Molar. Ray should live in a cave, cooking over an open fire, throwing the gnawed bones over his shoulder.

Shane could hear Barbara's screams coming from the back of the house, so he moved in that direction. He came through the bedroom door just in time to see Ray Molar hit his slender, blond wife in the solar plexus with the butt end of his black metal street baton. Then, as she doubled over, he expertly swung the nightstick sideways, catching her in the side of the head with a "two from the ring" combat move...a baton-fighting tactic taught to every recruit at the Police Academy. Shane stood frozen, as Barbara, her head bleeding badly, slumped to the floor, almost unconscious.

"Ray..." Shane's voice, a raspy whisper, cut the temporary silence like a sickle slashing dry wheat. "What's the story here, buddy?"

Ray Molar swung around. He was at least six-four and weighed over two-forty, with huge shoulders and long arms. He had bristly blond hair and a corded, muscled neck. Adding to these Blutoesque dimensions was a huge jutting jaw and almost total lack of a forehead. "Get the fuck outta here, Scully. We don't need the Boy Scouts," Molar growled, his pupils round points of focused hatred.

Shane had seen that look in the street many times before and had come to fear it. "Let's just back off, slow down, and give it a rest, Ray." Shane was moving slowly toward him, not wanting any part of the fury and craziness he saw on his ex-partner, but feeling compelled to get close enough to protect Barbara if he swung on her again. When Ray lost control, he could turn instantly murderous. He spewed white rage without thought, violence without reason.

"You got anything to eat?" Shane said, trying to refocus the energy in the room. "I'm

9

starved. Missed dinner. How 'bout I get us a beer and a sandwich, something.... We chill out a little... Cool out... Talk it down... Get solid..."

"You wanna eat somethin'? Eat shit, Scully!" He was halfway between Shane and Barbara, still brandishing the black metal police baton.

"Ray, I don't want trouble, but you can't go hitting Barbara with the nightstick, man. You're gonna fuck her up bad."

Then Ray started toward Shane, swinging the metal stick in a lose arc in front of him. "Yeah? Who's gonna stop me, dickwad?"

"Come on, let's stay frosty here, Ray. Let's...let's—" And he stopped talking because he had to duck.

Ray swung the nightstick. It zipped through the air an inch from Shane's ear. As he was coming back up, Ray swung a fist, hitting him with a left hook that landed on Shane's right temple, exploding like a pipe bomb, sending him to the floor, ears ringing. Then Ray yanked a small-caliber snubby out of his waistband. It looked to Shane like an off-brand piece, a European handgun of some kind, maybe a Titan Tiger or an Arminus .38, definitely not standard police issue. Ray always kept a "throw-down gun" on him to drop by a body if some street character got funky and had to take a seat on the sky bus.

"Put it away, Ray."

"You fucking this bitch, too? You fucking her? 'Cause if you ain't, you should get in line—everybody else is."

10

"Come on, Ray, that's crazy. I never touched your wife; nobody's messin' with Barb, and you know it. Why're you doin' this?"

"She's been getting snaked by half the fuckin' department." He turned back and glowered at her. "Am I right, baby? Tell him 'bout all the wall jobs you been doin' in the division garage."

Barbara groaned. Ray, turning now, aimed the gun at Shane, pulling the hammer back. Shane watched the cylinder begin to rotate on the center post as Ray applied pressure on the trigger. He was strangely mesmerized by the hole in the barrel; a dark eye of damnation, freezing his stomach, dulling his reactions. He was seconds from death.... Almost without realizing it, his right hand slipped down to his ankle, fingers encircling the wood-checked grip of his 9mm automatic. He slid the weapon free.

Shane dove sideways just as Ray fired. The bullet thunked into the wooden doorframe behind him. Shane was operating on instinct now, with no control over what happened next, going with it, not questioning, rolling, coming up prone, his Beretta Mini-Cougar gripped in both hands.

As Ray turned to fire again, Shane squeezed the trigger. The bullet hit Ray Molar in the middle of his simian brow.

Huge head jerking back violently.

Brainpan exploding, catching the 9mm slug.

Then Ray looked directly at Shane as the gun slipped from his meaty paw and thumped

11

onto the carpet. Ray's pig eyes, bright in that instant, registered hatred and surprise, or maybe Shane was just looking for something human in all that animal ferocity.

Ray Molar took one uncertain step backward and sat on the edge of the bed. Even though his heart was probably still beating, Shane knew that his ex-partner was already dead. But the street monster sat down anyway, almost as if he needed a moment to consider what he should do next or where he should go, momentum and gravity making the decision for him, toppling him forward, thudding him hard, face first, onto the carpet.

Shane looked over at Barbara, who was staring at her dead husband, her mouth agape, her puffed lip split and bleeding.

"Whatta we do now, Shane?" she finally asked.

IN THE SECONDS after the shots were fired, the bedroom seemed so quiet that he could almost hear dust settle. Then the sharp smell of cordite, mixed with the coppery smell of blood, began to fill his nostrils. Barbara was still on the floor not ten feet from Ray's body. Shane moved first. He stood slowly, feeling his knees shake as he rose. He stumbled to the dresser and leaned on it heavily, propping himself up for support. They were both trying to digest it, understand what had just happened and comprehend how it would alter, in a ghastly way, events stretching before them. Then, from the floor, Ray Molar farted. Shit ran into his pants as his bowels let loose. The perfect punctuation mark for the past few minutes.

"We need to get a story, Barbara," Shane said. "This isn't going to go down smooth. You know how they all feel about Ray."

"I don't know... I don't know... He just..."

"Barbara..."

Her eyes were darting around the room in a desperate escape dance. Her face was also beginning to swell where Ray had hit her on the right side, distorting her natural beauty.

"Tell me," he prodded softly, "what set him off?"

Somewhere in the distance they could hear the faint wail of a police car.

"Already?" she said, referring to the sirens.

"You were screaming, shots were fired, you've got neighbors. Nine-one-one response time is supposed to be less than five minutes. If something more is going on here, I need to know, Babs. You and I, we're not completely clean, if you know what I mean."

"I know." She pulled herself up on the bed and sat. He could see that her hands were shaking as she brought the back of her wrist up to wipe the blood oozing from the corner of her mouth. Her hand came away with an ugly red streak on the back. "He...he just...I don't know."

"He just what? Let's go, there isn't much time. What set him off?"

"I got a call yesterday from a woman. She asked me if I'd seen the videotape yet."

"What videotape?"

"I don't know. That's the whole point. I haven't got any tape, and I told her. She sounded like she was crying. Then she said it was coming in the mail, and it will show me what a cheating bastard Ray was."

"Who was she?"

"Didn't say. I didn't recognize the voice. She just hung up."

The sirens were now less than a block away as Barbara Molar looked at Shane in desperation. "What're they gonna do?"

"They're gonna separate us. Take statements. This is our only chance to coordi-

14

nate. We need the same story. Stay with me here, Babs. Keep goin'. What happened next?"

"Ray hasn't been home much since he got his new assignment. He's been away days at a time, so when he got home tonight, I asked him where he was all the time. I told him what the woman said and he...he just...went nuts. You know his temper, how he gets. You worked patrol with him. He accused me of sleeping with his friends. He called me a whore. He started beating me. I can't take any more beatings. I can't. I told him I was going to leave him, and then he chased me into the bathroom. I locked the door and called you. Then he just—"

The sirens growled to the curb outside, and Shane quickly looked around the bedroom, taking mental pictures of the crime scene, filing them in his memory for later. Oddly enough, it was Ray who had schooled him in this technique, quizzing him at "end of watch" on what he remembered. They'd sit in some bar at EOW, betting drinks on the answers. Ray would ask questions: What was on the dresser? How many windows in the kitchen? Were there screens? Ray was violent and unpredictable, but he sure knew how to police a crime scene.

"They're gonna take me downtown," Shane said. "They'll take your statement here, then probably transport you to the ER. Just say exactly what happened. He would have killed you, Barbara. He fired first. This was self-defense. Just leave out you and me. Whatever you do, stay tight on that."

They could hear cops coming into the house through the open front door.

"We're back here, LAPD!" Shane yelled. Then, as an afterthought, he whispered to Barbara, "Call the phone company and see if you can get an AT&T printout of calls to your phone so we can try and find out who that woman is."

Barbara nodded just as a uniformed South Bureau "dog and cat" team came through the door, guns drawn. Shane had his hands in the air and his Beretta Mini-Cougar hanging down, dangling uselessly from his right thumb. "LAPD," he said again.

The cops didn't know him, and not seeing a badge, the male officer rushed him, disarmed him, and threw him down onto the floor right next to a puddle of Ray's blood. The female kept her Smith & Wesson trained on him until her partner had Shane cuffed. Then they both roughly yanked him up.

"Where's your shield?" the lady cop said. Her nameplate read S. Riley.

"On my dresser, at home. I was asleep. She called for help. I live four miles from here. I'm Sergeant Shane Scully, Southwest RHD. My serial number is 50867."

They looked down at Shane's now-bloody bare feet, then at Ray. The male cop was a policeman III; his nameplate read P. Applegate. He knelt down and looked closely at the body. "Shit. This is Steeltooth. You shot Lieutenant Molar."

Shane stood quietly as Applegate fingered

his shoulder mike. "This is X-ray Twelve. We're Code Six at 2387 Shell Avenue. We have a police officer down. We need a sergeant on the scene and the coroner. Notify South Bureau Detectives we have the shooter in custody. He claims to be Southwest Robbery/Homicide Sergeant Shane Scully." Then he turned to Shane. "Gimme that serial number again."

"It's 50867," Shane said into the officer's open shoulder mike.

"You get that?" Applegate asked. The female radio-transmission officer answered quickly.

"Roger, X-ray Twelve. That's 50867. You're Code Six Adam at Shell Avenue, requesting a supervisor and a Homicide unit. Stand by." There was static, and in less than thirty seconds, the RTO came back on. "X-ray Twelve, on your suspect ident: that badge number is confirmed to Southwest RHD Sergeant Shane Scully, 143 East Channel Road, Venice, California."

"Roger. We're locking down this crime scene for Homicide and moving outside." The officer then turned to Shane. "Who's your direct supervisor?"

"Captain Bud Halley, Southwest Division Robbery/Homicide."

"You got his call-out number?"

"Just call the squad. I can do it myself if you take these cuffs off."

"Hey, Scully, you done enough already. You just croaked the best fucking cop on the force." Then he unlocked the handcuffs. "Shannon, take Mrs. Molar into the kitchen. I'll hold Sergeant Scully in the living room." They left Raymond Molar in an expanding pool of his own blood to wait for the Homicide team and lab techs.

On every unnatural death in L.A., the RHD assigns a fresh homicide number and the next team up on the division rotation gets the squeal. The numbers start on January 1 and continue sequentially until the last day of December. If the body is a male, the number is proceeded by an *M*; if female, by an *F*. On that chilly April morning, Lieutenant Raymond George Molar became M-417-00.

The RHD team got there a little after three-thirty A.M. as the crime lab was just finishing photographing the scene. The two lab techs had already done their preliminary workup. They'd bagged the lieutenant's hands, outlined the DB in tape, and were standing around, waiting for the detectives to show before rolling the body.

Both Homicide dicks were veterans and had been notified before they got there that the officer down was the legendary LAPD Lt. Ray "Steeltooth" Molar. They had both signed Patrolman Applegate's crime-scene attendance sheet and now stood in the bedroom looking down at the body with stone-cut expressions as the lab techs flopped Ray over. His face had already begun to fill with blood, causing a darkening of the skin, known as lividity. More post-mortem renal jettisoning had occurred, and the smell of feces in the room was getting strong as the two detectives from Robbery/Homicide silently policed the area, making their preliminary notes and observations. They graphed the location of the body and marked the bullet in the doorjamb that Ray had fired, then instructed the lab techs to dig the slug out and get it to the Investigative Analysis Section for a ballistics comparison. They bagged Shane's 9mm Beretta; it would be booked as evidence.

Shane was waiting in the living room with Patrolman Applegate. After half an hour the lead Homicide dick, an old, wheezing department warhorse with a basset-hound jawline, came out and sat on the sofa opposite Shane. His name was Garson Welch; he and Shane had shared a few easy grounders back when Shane was still working uniform in Southwest. One case had been so simple, they solved it in less than ten minutes when Shane arrested the perp half a block away as he was trying to stuff the murder weapon down into a Dumpster. The man had confessed on the spot. Shane and Welch had gone EOW at the jail and had had a few beers in a cop bar on Central known as the Billy Club. They didn't have what you'd call a friendship, but they were at least friendly—better than nothing.

"This ain't gonna go down too good at Parker Center, Shane," the old detective said, rubbing his ample forehead with a big, liver-spotted hand.

"Yeah, Gar, you're right. I should've just stood there and let him kill her with his nightstick."

"Calm down and listen," Welch went on. "What we got here is a brown shit waffle. Lieutenant Molar had big juice with the Super Chief. People you and I only read about in the *L.A. Times* are getting phone calls right now over this piece of work. I just got a call and found out he's been Mayor Clark Crispin's police driver for the past two months. So there's gonna be big interest at the city level. We're gonna go slow and get it right."

"The mayor's driver? Shit," Shane said. He hadn't known that was Ray's new assignment.

"I'm gonna take your preliminary here, then send you to the Glass House and let your captain do the DFAR," Welch said, referring to the Division Field Activity Report that had to be filed after any incident involving violence or death at the hands of a police officer.

"I got my car. I can meet you there," Shane volunteered.

"I'll have one of the blues drive it in and park it for you in the underground garage, but you're gonna go downtown in the back of a detective car. By the book. That way, nobody gets days off for bullshit nitpicks."

"Yeah, sure, if that's the way you want it." Shane was beginning to get a premonition of disaster. Then he followed Detective Welch out of the house for the long drive to Parker Center.

DFAR

THE TRIP DOWNTOWN at four A.M. on deserted freeways took only twenty-two minutes. The black-and-white slickback that the RHD dicks were forced to drive now finally made a wide turn off Broadway, its headlights sweeping the south side of the Glass House. It pulled up to the security station. Sergeant Welch showed his badge, signed them all in, and drove into the huge underground parking garage that adjoined Parker Center.

The building was known as "the Glass House" to everybody on the job because of the excessive amount of plate glass that draped its huge boxy shape. The otherwise nondescript building had been designed in the fifties, which had proved to be a decade of architectural blight. The parking garage next door went down nine stories underground. The detectives found a spot on U-3, and both led Shane out of the parking complex, through a security door, and into the third basement of police headquarters. They took the elevator to six and got off at the Robbery/Homicide Division, which took up half the floor and was fronted by a thick glass partition.

Garson Welch buzzed them through and found the OOD, a thin-faced sergeant in uniform, sitting at a computer just inside the squad room. "Is Captain Halley around? He was supposed to get a call out on this activity report."

The sergeant nodded and pointed down the hall. "Interview room Three," he said.

They moved single file down the linoleum-floored corridor and turned into a small, windowless interrogation room that contained a scarred desk, two wooden chairs, and Robbery/Homicide Captain Bud Halley. Halley had his jacket off and was showing the beginnings of a twelve-hour beard, having missed his shave at four A.M. He had also missed two belt loops. Other than that, he was a remarkably handsome, fit, prematurely gray man in his mid-forties. He was Shane's Southwest Homicide Bureau commander. They had a good professional relationship. In the two years Shane had been assigned to Southwest Detectives, Halley had given him two excellent evaluation reports. As Shane came through the door, Captain Halley motioned him to a chair. "You guys don't have to stick around unless you need him. I'm gonna send him home after the activity report," he said to the two detectives.

"Thanks, Cap, check you later," Welch said as they left the room and closed the door behind them.

"We only have a few minutes and then God knows what happens," Halley said.

"A few minutes? What're you talking about? You're doing the DFAR. What's the rush?"

" 'Cept I'm not doing it. Deputy Chief Thomas Mayweather is on his way in. He's doing it."

"The head of Special Investigations Division is doing my activity report? You can't be serious. Why him?"

"Chief Brewer ordered it," Halley said.

"Same question, then."

"Don't you know what Ray Molar's assignment was?"

"Yeah...he was Mayor Clark Crispin's bodyguard and driver. He was also killing his wife with a nightstick. He fired a shot at me. Barbara Molar is my wit. This should be a slam dunk. So what's the deal?"

"Lemme give you the secret to survival around here." Shane waited for the punch line. "Everything that's not department history is department politics. Chief Brewer was awakened by Mayor Crispin, who called the Big Kahuna from the Dark Side, who got rousted off his sailboat at the marina. He was planning to sail across the channel for a long weekend in Avalon. Now, instead of salt air and sea chanteys, Deputy Chief Mayweather is coming here, in his fucking yacht attire, looking to tear you a new asshole."

"Cap, let me say this again, so none of us miss it. Steeltooth was killing his wife. He shot first. If I hadn't returned fire, we'd both be in the county icebox bleeding from the ears. I know for a fact Ray has two spousal-abuse beefs in his IAD package. He's a regular at rage-management counseling. Aside from that, we both know he was a head thumper from way back. You don't get the nickname Steeltooth just because your last name's Molar."

"Don't convince me. Make Mayweather believe it," Halley said softly.

Shane's hands started to shake. He was coming down from a two-hour adrenaline rush. He had killed Ray Molar, his ex-partner, a man he had once respected, then came to fear, and then finally to hate. His emotions hovered just below consciousness. He knew he couldn't afford a mistake, so he pushed personal feelings aside and concentrated on his plight, his survival instincts taking precedence.

Deputy Chief Mayweather was six three and ebony black. He had a shaved head and always carried himself with the athletic grace he had shown as a first-string point guard on the UCLA basketball team in the seventies.

He moved through the predawn stillness of the Robbery/Homicide Division and looked at the tired collection of swing-shift detectives who were manning their desks, sneaking glances at the clock, waiting for the day-watch to show up and relieve them. Mayweather stuck his gleaming black head into the interrogation room containing Scully and Halley.

"Let's do this upstairs." Mayweather's voice was cold and smooth, Vaseline on ice. "We'll use the conference room on nine. Bud, see if they got some coffee down here and bring it up." Then, without even looking at Shane, he moved out of the room, leaving them there.

"Good luck," Halley said as Shane got up off his hardwood chair and followed Mayweather, who was already halfway down the hall, striding toward the elevators with a Yul Brynner elegance, his arms swinging freely, his hips slightly forward. He was not in yachting attire. He'd dressed for this gig. The suit he wore was charcoal gray, creaseless, and fit him like a second skin. Tom Mayweather could easily have made a nice living on the pages of *GQ*.

Shane moved along behind him like a barefoot, dark-haired, brown-eyed shadow, his own gait more the shuffling stride of a street fighter. Although Shane had always been able to attract women, he found his own looks pugnacious and off-putting. In his mirror, he saw a face marred by cynicism and loneliness. He was always surprised when he heard someone describe him as attractive.

He caught Mayweather at the elevator. Both men remained silent as they waited for the stainless-steel doors to open and take them to the ninth floor, where Tom Mayweather and the other deputy chiefs had their offices down the hall from Chief Burleigh Brewer.

"Sorry about the Avalon trip, sir," Shane said, going for a little pre-interview suck.

"Let's save everything for when we get the tape running, okay?"

"Sure," Shane said.

The door opened and they stepped in and rode the humming metal box to the light-paneled, green-carpeted executive floor. All the way up, Deputy Chief Mayweather said nothing, but he was staring at Shane's blood-stained bare feet.

Shane had been on nine only once before. He had been in Chief Brewer's office three years ago when he received a Meritorious Service Medal. He had risked his life, the citation said, freeing two children from a burning car wreck on the San Pedro Freeway.

They moved down the hall. Shane glanced out the plate-glass windows and could see the morning sun beginning to light the corners of the buildings across Sixth Street, throwing a fiery glow on the stone roofs and concrete balconies of the old brown buildings that surrounded the huge police monstrosity like tattered memories.

Mayweather opened the door to the conference room, turned on the lights, and left him there.

The room was paneled in the same light-colored wood. It was huge and windowless, being part of the interior structure of the building. On the walls were portraits of all of L.A.'s past police chiefs. The father of the new department, Chief William H. Parker, was hanging in a place of honor on the wall at the head of the table.

They had all learned about Bill Parker in the Academy. In 1934 then-Lieutenant Parker, a law school graduate, was assistant to L.A.

police chief James E. Davis. From that post, Parker saw the workings of L.A. city government close-up. The Shaw brothers presided over a corrupt city, and Chief Davis was beholden to the Shaws. Mayor Shaw's brother controlled the Vice Squad and was selling sergeant's tests for five hundred dollars apiece. Working with Lieutenant Earl Cook, Bill Parker campaigned for the passage of the city charter amendment that contained Section 202, which provided for a Police Bill of Rights and administrative reviews to protect police officers from inappropriate charges of wrongdoing. That section of the city charter set the model of police disciplinary review that the LAPD still uses today. Portraits of Chiefs Davis, Reddin, Gates, Williams, Parks, and Brewer hung on the walls of the conference room and seemed to glower down at him, silently reproaching him for killing one of L.A.'s finest.

"Guy was murdering his wife," Shane muttered to himself and to the stone-faced gallery of disapproving ex-police chiefs.

Mayweather returned with a tape recorder and plugged it in. He chose the seat at the far end of the table, under the recently hung painting of Burl Brewer.

Mayweather glanced at Sergeant Scully. "You're a sergeant one, is that right?"

"Yes, sir."

"Okay, Shane, you and I don't know each other. I guess we've probably met once or twice, but we're not really acquainted. It's

27

important you know that I'm just here to take your statement. I'm going to try and determine what happened and then make a recommendation to the department as to what our next step should be. A police officer died at your hands. His death may have been completely unavoidable, but either way, we're into a mandatory use-of-force review. I'm not here to hurt you, take advantage of you, or trap you in any way. Okay?"

"I appreciate that, sir."

The door opened and Bud Halley entered with a pot of coffee and three mugs. He poured. They each took one, blew across the steaming surface, then sipped gratefully.

"What goes on here is subject to the Police Bill of Rights under Title One," Mayweather continued, "so this pre-interview will not preempt any of your Skelly rights or privileges guaranteed by Section 202 of the city charter." The Skelly hearing was his chance to answer the charges against him before his case went to a Board of Rights, if it got that far.

"This is an administrative review and is subject to the provisions laid down in Section 202. I'm going to record the interview." Mayweather turned the tape on. "Raise your right hand." Shane did as he was instructed. "Do you, Sergeant Shane Scully, swear that all information given by you during this interview is the truth, the whole truth, and nothing but the truth, so help you God?"

"I do."

"This tape-recorded interview is for use in

an Internal Affairs investigation only. For purposes of department statute-of-limitations requirements, today, April sixteenth, will be the due date of this inquiry. If no action is taken within a year of this date, the investigation will officially be determined to be closed. Is this interview being conducted at a convenient time and under circumstances you find acceptable?"

"Yes, sir."

"Are you aware that the nature of this interview is to determine if the escalated force that resulted in Lieutenant Molar's death was within departmental use-of-force guidelines?"

"Yes, sir."

"It is April sixteenth, at five-seventeen A.M. We are in the main conference room, on the ninth floor of Parker Center. Present is the interviewer, Deputy Chief Thomas Clark Mayweather. Also present is the officer being interviewed, Sergeant One Shane Scully. Witnessing the interview is Captain Bud Halley. In accordance with departmental guidelines, it is noted that no more than two interrogators are present. Okay"—Mayweather paused and glanced at a crib card in front of him—"Section 202 governs this part of the administrative process and establishes procedures for the completion of a chronological log. If you could take care of that, Captain Halley? And then if you could get us a fresh DR number to file the case under." A DR number was a Division of Records number, issued in all nonarrest reports.

Bud Halley nodded then took out a pad and pen to begin a chronology.

"Shane, if you could just start at the beginning and tell us what happened this morning... Don't leave anything out. Give us approximate times if you can. I want to get it all down on tape because the preliminary interview will be an important part of the record, if anything more comes of this later."

"Okay." Shane cleared his throat and began to tell exactly what had happened, starting with the wake-up call from Barbara at 2:16 A.M., followed by his call to Longboard Kelly. He told how he drove to Shell Avenue, found the front door open, saw Molar beating his wife. He related the conversation that ensued, telling how he tried to settle it down. Then how Molar, moving toward him, swung the baton at his head, hit him with his fist, pulled his gun, and fired. Shane explained how he returned fire, killing the huge LAPD lieutenant with his 9mm Beretta Mini-Cougar, just moments before Unit X-ray Twelve arrived.

When he finished, he looked up at Mayweather, who was making notes on a pad, a puzzled expression on his face.

"That's everything," Shane finished.

"Tell me about your relationship with Raymond Molar."

"Uh...well, he was sort of a mentor, I guess you'd call it. I met him when I went through the Academy. He was conducting a self-defense lecture. He and I were at the same table for lunch. We sort of hit it off, gravitated to each other. He did three street-combat classes while I was there, and we became friends. After I graduated, I ended up in Southwest, in the Seventy-seventh Division. He was a sergeant there. I was still just a probationer, and since we were friends, he got himself assigned as my training officer. He was my partner for the first six months of my tour. After I finished probation, we rode together for six more months."

"Sergeants don't usually ride with partners."

"Well, in the Seventy-seventh, a lot of the sergeants took a shotgun rider. It's pretty hairy down there. Anyway, we rode together for that last six months, and then I got reassigned. I went to the West Valley Division for four years, then spent six in Metro. I've been back at Southwest for the past six years and in RHD down there for twenty-eight months. Ray was in Central, then Newton, so we didn't see much of each other after that."

"I see." Mayweather made some more notes on his pad. "You see him socially during that first tour in Southwest when you were partnered?"

"Yes, sir, we were friends."

"Right about then you had an Internal Affairs complaint that wasn't sustained, isn't that correct?"

"Excuse me, sir, but I thought I had immunity from background on unsustained IAD complaints." Shane knew that since Mayweather was head of the Special Investigations Division, which supervised IAD, he had access to those old Internal Affairs records. Obviously, the deputy chief had done more than change clothes before coming in for this interview.

Mayweather looked up and lay down his pen. "I'm just trying to determine if, when you were before that Board of Rights in March of '84, you were still partnered with Ray Molar."

"Yes. That was just before we stopped working together."

"Okay." Mayweather picked up his pen. "You say Lieutenant Molar pulled a gun. Did you see it clearly?"

"I was only a few feet away."

"What kind of gun was it?"

"I think it was a European handgun, a Titan Tiger snub-nose thirty-eight is what it looked like."

"That's not a department-approved hand-gun."

"Well, he was at home. I suppose he can have any kind of weapon he wants at home."

"And then, after you shot him with your Beretta, what happened to his gun?"

"I guess he dropped it. I don't know, I was kind of jacked up after the shooting."

"Sergeant Scully, do you mind taking a urine test? As you know, you can refuse under the Police Bill of Rights, but I should warn you that in an administrative hearing, unlike a criminal case, your refusal can be viewed by the department as insubordination. You could be brought up on charges. If you *do* refuse, I'll have to send for a DRE to examine you anyway, and his opinion will go in the record and carry the same weight." A DRE was a drug recognition expert who would make a judgment on sobriety by observation, checking vision and reflexes.

"That won't be necessary. I'll take the test, sir," Shane said.

"I'll get the paperwork ready." He leaned over and picked up the phone. "This is Mayweather. Send somebody up from the lab for a urine sample and have whoever's on the duty desk out there dig around and get me an authorization form." He hung up the phone, having never shifted his gaze from Shane. Then he leaned back in his chair and templed his fingers under his chin.

"Barbara Molar is quite an attractive woman."

"Yes, sir, she is. The lieutenant was very lucky."

"Until tonight."

"Well, yes, that's what I meant, sir.

"Right."

They sat in silence for a few moments.

"Did you and Lieutenant Molar retain a friendly relationship after you were reassigned to the Valley Division?"

"Well, sir...no. Like I said, we sort of drifted our separate ways."

"I heard you and he got into some kind of scuffle one night, back in '84, just before you were separated as partners."

Shane looked over at Captain Halley for help, but the captain only nodded slightly, encouraging him to keep answering. It was now painfully obvious that Mayweather had someone in the IA Administration Section open his sealed jacket in violation of his rights under Section 202. The fight with Steeltooth had been logged because Shane had needed medical attention for his injuries. However, neither he nor Molar had pressed for a hearing, so it went into his sealed record as an unsustained incident. He couldn't prove that Mayweather had opened his file. The deputy chief could claim he had heard about the fight secondhand. Now Shane had to answer the question or face insubordination charges. He felt used and double-crossed.

"I need an answer," Mayweather said. "Was there an altercation?"

"I guess you could say that. We had a kinda problem once."

"What was that all about?"

"Shit, it was nothing.... I mean, shoot... we...we'd been working long hours and I was nervous, facing that Internal Affairs board. I was stressed. Molar was fucking around. We were in the detective squad room in Southwest. He threw ice water on me, so I pushed him and he went down over a chair. If you knew Ray at all, you wouldn't have to ask what happened next."

"What happened next?"

"We went down into the parking garage, and while six or seven guys from the squad stood around and watched, Ray punched out two of my teeth, broke my nose, and pretty much destroyed me."

34

"And you're not mad about that?"

"Well, for a while I guess, but that was Ray. He and I had just about ended our tour by then, so we unhooked. I was rotating out. He was on the lieutenant's list back then. Pretty high up. The sixth band, I think, so he was going to get his bar in a month or two anyway. We both just moved on."

"And you didn't harbor any resentment? I find that hard to believe."

"Chief, if I could ask...has anybody looked at the damage on Barbara Molar's face? Has anybody seen what he did to her? 'Cause if all these questions strike to some other possible motive, that's why I went over there. I tried to break it up. He fired first, and I was forced to return fire. He was seconds from killing both of us. I hope you photograph those injuries because all I was trying to do was keep us off Forest Lawn Drive."

"We'll get photographs, don't worry about that."

There was another charged silence in the room that lasted for almost a minute.

"Anything else you want to say for this record?" Mayweather said.

"No, sir. That's what happened. I'm sorry he's dead, but he gave me no choice."

"Okay, then." Mayweather looked at his watch. "This interview is concluded. It is five thirty-five A.M. This tape recording has been continuous, with no shutoffs, and it has been witnessed throughout by Captain Bud Halley." Then he snapped the machine off and rubbed his eyes. "That's it, Sergeant. I'm going to forward this transcript to the Officer Involved Shooting Section of the Robbery/Homicide Division, and they will schedule your Shooting Review Board. Don't sweat it. That board is mandatory with any incident involving firearms."

"I know, sir."

"Then get outta here. Go give the lab tech his sample and go home."

"Yes, sir."

Shane got up and moved past Captain Halley, into the hall. He waited for his CO to come out, thinking they would ride down together and Shane could get a performance critique, but Captain Halley didn't come out. The door was slightly ajar, and he could hear Mayweather and Halley talking. Then suddenly the door was kicked shut, cutting off the conversation and leaving him alone in the hall.

STREET DIVORCE

SHANE WAS FORCED to wander in the Parker Center garage, looking for his car. It was six A.M. He had started on the top level, which was aboveground, and had moved slowly through the garage, heading down, deeper into the bowels of the parking structure. He had his keys in his right hand. They had been left for him at the OOD's desk in Robbery/Homicide, but the uniform who had driven his car in didn't tell the duty sergeant where in the garage it was parked. The structure was huge, and his bare feet were cold on the concrete floor. As he walked, he could occasionally see flashes of red on his feet—Ray's blood. He had stood in it, and it had seeped up, between his toes, staining his skin. After giving his urine sample, he'd been in such a hurry to get out of there and get home, he hadn't remained in the rest room to wash it off.

"Sergeant Scully. Over here," a voice yelled at him; he turned around and looked back. He could see two uniformed officers standing by the elevator. He was six stories down, and the garage was dimly lit by the neon overheads. The two policemen moved out of the darkness toward him. The overhead lighting threw long shadows under their visors, and he could not make out who they were. As they got closer, he realized he had not seen either of them before. It was not unusual for members of the LAPD not to know one another. There were over nine thousand sworn members of the department sprawled over a huge geographic area. From the markings on their uniforms, he could tell that they were both first-year officers—policemen I's.

"What is it?" he asked.

They were close enough now for him to see that they were both in their early twenties. Their silver nameplates indicated that the shorter one was Officer K. Kono, the other, Officer D. Drucker. Kono had a wide, flat face and the complexion of a native Hawaiian. Drucker was a bodybuilder. His arms bulged the short sleeves of his Class C uniform shirt. They stood in front of Shane, studying him as if he were roadkill that one of them would eventually be forced to scrape up.

"Whatta you want, Officer?" Shane asked Drucker. "I've had a long night. I wanna get home."

"That Ray's blood on yer feet?" Kono asked. He had no Hawaiian accent. He was pure West Valley, but his voice was shaking with emotion.

"Whatta you guys want?" Shane repeated.

"Why'd you have t'butt in?" Drucker asked. "Who asked you?"

Shane could now see that they were both extremely emotional. They had obviously heard about Ray's death, which was spreading through the department like a raging virus. He speculated that Drucker and Kono must have come in and waited for him in the garage.

"He was killing his wife. He was taking batting practice on her with a baton."

"So you butt in and give him a fucking street divorce," Drucker hissed. A "street divorce" was police slang for any domestic argument that turned into a murder.

"Get outta my way." Shane tried to push past the two cops, but they held their ground and he found himself bumping shoulders with them violently. They weren't about to let him through, so Shane backed up and reevaluated the situation. He didn't have his gun. It had been booked by Homicide as evidence. He was alone in an empty garage. He was barefoot and tired, and his head still ached from where Ray had hit him. The two cops in front of him were jacked up on anger and out of control emotionally. In that moment, he had a flash of how it must feel to run up against enraged, violent cops in a desolate part of the city with no witnesses and no way to prove what really happened. Here he was, a sworn officer, standing in the police garage, yet he was beginning to pump adrenaline and fear for his safety.

"Is this about to turn into something?" he asked softly, glaring at both of them.

"Ray was the real deal, asswipe," Drucker hissed. "You're department afterbirth. Ray knew we had to take this fucking town back a street at a time. Since Rodney King, we've been eating shit and smiling about it. Ray

39

knew that had to change. He knew the war was on, knew what we had to do out there. He understood you can't just stand around while a buncha freeway-dancers put it to ya."

"If you believe that, both you guys need to take a swing through the Academy retraining program."

"Swing on my dick, Tarzan," Kono hissed.

Shane shook his head and smiled. "Okay," he said, "I guess that ends this discussion. Your move."

"This is police headquarters," Drucker said. "This is the Glass House, man. Nothing happens here. But stick around, Scully. There's gonna be some payback."

"Now you're threatening me, Drucker?"

"You killed the best cop to ever ride in this department," Kono said. "Shot him just 'cause he was straightening out his old lady? Okay, it's done. Ray's gone. But we loved him, man, we—" He stopped, and Shane thought he saw moisture in the young Hawaiian cop's eyes.

"You two guys need to go home and think this out," Scully said.

"We don't need to think nothin' out," Drucker snapped. "You think it out. We've got someone pulling your card right now. From now on, nobody's gonna take your side. Nobody's got your back, Scully. You're a walk-alone."

"I'm putting you both in for this."

"Have fun," Drucker said, touching the brim of his visor. "Your word against ours. Have a nice morning, asshole." They both turned and walked away. He could hear their footsteps echoing in the concrete darkness. Then a car started, headlights went on, and they pulled past him, going fast. The wind from their black-and-white flapped his sweatshirt as they sped away.

Shane stood alone in the garage; he suddenly felt a shiver of dread come over him. Then he turned and again started looking for his car. He found it way down on U-9, at the back of the garage, on the bottom level. When he looked at the car, something seemed wrong, it seemed lower. He knelt down in the dim light and saw that all four of his tires had been slashed. The black Acura was squatting sadly on its rims.

"Shit," he said, looking at the car. Then he suddenly remembered Chooch. He wondered how he would ever get home in time to get the boy to school.

CHOOCH

SHANE ARRIVED HOME at a little past seven, driving a slickback he'd checked out of the motor pool. He parked the black-and-white detective's car in the driveway and entered the back door. As he walked into the kitchen, Chooch was bent over with his head deep in the refrigerator. Startled, he jerked around and glowered.

"It's fucking bleak in there, Chuck. Don't you got nothin' to eat?" Chooch was dressed in baggy jeans pulled down low, gang-style, exposing two inches of his red plaid boxer shorts. His white T-shirt read EAT ME.

"There's some strawberry Pop-Tarts in that cupboard," Shane said as he quickly headed through the kitchen, hoping Chooch wouldn't see his bloodstained feet and put him through a description of the early-morning shooting. Shane moved into the master bedroom, which was furnished in "relationship-eclectic." Nothing matched. All the furniture in his house was salvaged from broken love affairs. It had gotten to the point where every time he and a new female roommate went furniture shopping, there was some cynical side of him that would wonder which of the new bedroom or living-room ensemble pieces would become his in the post-relationship

42

settlement. The result was a depressing mixture of colors and styles.

He stripped off his blood-spattered sweatshirt and pants, then got into a hot shower, scrubbing Ray's blood off his feet with his shower nailbrush, rubbing so hard that he was afraid his toes would bleed.

Shoot it; frame it; hang it in his gallery of defining moments. The Lady Macbeth Exhibit. He finished with his feet and then stood under the hot spray, trying with less result to cleanse his spirit. Finally he got out of the shower, wrapped himself in a towel, and looked in the foggy bathroom mirror. The face was angular and rugged. Dark eyes wore a raccoon's mask of sleeplessness. His hair hung black and limp on his forehead. He stared at himself for a long time, trying to see if he looked as different as he felt. In his thirty-seven years Shane had never killed anyone before; on the drive home from the department, that change in his life experience had started to weigh on him. Now, as he stood in his bathroom, it was plunging him into a fit of depression, which, according to the self-help psych books he had started reading recently, was self-hatred turned inward, driving his spirit down. He turned away from the mirror and dressed in slacks, white shirt, maroon tie, and a blue blazer. He slipped on socks and loafers, clipped his backup gun onto his belt, grabbed his pager, badge, and handcuffs, then went into the living room, where Longboard Kelly was snoring on the sofa.

Shane shook the twenty-eight-year-old blond-haired surfboard shaper's shoulder to wake him. Brian had turned out to be a surprisingly good friend. In the two years since Kelly had moved in next door and had started running his surfboard business out of his garage, the resinhead and the cop had surprised themselves with their unlikely friendship.

"I'm back, Brian. Thanks, man."

"Mmmmsaaakjjjjaaaawww," Longboard said, and rolled over, turning his back on Shane.

Shane smiled and headed into the kitchen, where Chooch was now seated at the small wooden table. Chooch had one of the strawberry Pop-Tarts in his hand, nibbling at the edges. He had struck an insolent go-fuck-yourself pose with one hand jammed deep down in his pants pocket. His bare feet were up on the table.

"So, how much is the upslice bitch paying you?" Chooch started, unexpectedly.

Shane knew, from years on the street busting gangbangers and pavement princesses, that *upslice* meant a cheap woman and referred to the vagina. It pissed him off that this kid would refer to his own mother that way.

"She's not paying me anything."

"So what's the deal, then? She carving you some beef?" Another gangbang sexual reference.

"I'm not sleeping with your mother, Chooch. I've got other reasons. Now get your feet off the table, we've gotta eat off a' there." He

44

slapped Chooch's feet hard, knocking them off the wooden tabletop. Chooch exploded out of the chair, anger and violence seething.

"Don't fuckin' hit me," Chooch said, breathing through his mouth, his right hand balled into a fist at his side.

"Go on...take your best shot," Shane said softly, "but you better tell me where you want your body sent first."

"Oh, you're gonna swing on a fifteen-year-old?"

"Hey, son, I've seen fifteen-year-olds roll pipe bombs under taxis and peel a clip-a'-nines at a passing squad car. Being fifteen gets you nothing."

Chooch unclenched his fist and stood there for a long moment.

"Gee, look't this. I think we're really beginning to communicate," Shane said sarcastically, then moved over and grabbed a second strawberry Pop-Tart out of the box on the counter. He dropped it in the toaster and pushed the lever down. "You do your homework last night?" Shane asked, not really knowing what to say to the hostile Hispanic youth across the kitchen, glowering at him with smoldering eyes. At six feet, he was almost Shane's height, and already Shane could see he'd been hitting the weights. He had Sandy's dark good looks.

"I don't do homework. I got fly bitches do it for me."

Shane could see why Sandy had begged him to take Chooch. *"Do whatever it takes,"* she had said. *"He needs a male authority figure. He's got to see where this path he's on is headed."*

"Chooch, you and I have to get along for a month. Let's try and keep from peeling the skin off each other. Now get your stuff together, we gotta get you to school."

"I ain't goin' to school. I quit. Where's the TV? I can't find it. What kinda jerkoff ain't got a TV?"

Shane didn't answer. He moved out of the kitchen and into the guest bedroom. The house was on one of the Venice, California, grand canals, and through the side window he could see the morning sun glinting off the still water. It was 7:10; he figured if he hurried and there wasn't much traffic, he could still get Chooch across town to the Harvard Westlake School by 8:15. The school was located on Coldwater, in the Valley.

As he started to grab Chooch's book bag, he saw that there was a stash of tobacco tucked into the side pocket. He took the Baggie out and held it up. Two ounces of marijuana. He carried the book bag into the kitchen, where Chooch was standing, looking out the back door, his arms folded across his chest. He pretended not to be watching as Shane emptied the Baggie of Mexican chronic down the kitchen sink and turned on the disposal. It finally dawned on Chooch what was happening. He exploded away from the wall and made a grab for the Baggie.

"Hey, what you be doing with my bale, man?"

46

Shane grabbed Chooch by the collar, spun him, and backed him up, slamming him hard against the refrigerator, pinning him there.

"Hey, asshole, take this to the bank. Rule one: You're not gonna smoke grass in my house. Not today, not ever!"

"That shit was hydro, man."

"And you can stow the rap dictionary, okay? We're talking English in this house."

"Fuck you."

They were nose to nose, breathing hard. Shane was close to the edge, focusing his frayed nerves and growing depression on this angry fifteen-year-old. He took a deep breath to calm down. Then he let go and took a step back. "I don't know whether you get away with stuff like this at school, but it won't work here," he said in a calmer voice.

"I don't wanna stay here. I'm leaving," Chooch said softly.

"Okay, here's the deal.... One: Use any dope in this house, you're gonna get a chin-check from me. Two: You do what I tell you, when I tell you. Three: Knock off the Hoover Street attitude. Four: You're gonna do your own homework and not farm it out to girlfriends. If you live up to those four rules, here's what you get from me in return. You get room and board. You get my friendship and respect. You get a fair deal; I'll lay it out straight. I won't ever lie."

"Like I give a shit."

"And clean up your mouth."

"You think I wanna stick around and go to your bullshit white-slice Gumby boot camp?"

47

"You take off, I'll put the LAPD Runaway Squad on you. You'll go to juvie detention and then to a CYA camp, where you won't have to worry about some private-school geek in a bow tie who teaches chemistry. You'll be slappin' skin with the heavy lifters from south of Hawthorn."

The two of them held gazes. Even though Shane was tired and mad, he had to admit that Chooch Sandoval had been dealt a bad hand. Sandy had made a bunch of horrible choices when it came to her son. Now Chooch was full of anger and resentment. His hormones were raging, and he was looking for a place to park all that frustrated hostility. On the plus side, Chooch had not whimpered. He didn't feel sorry for himself, and he was no cupcake. Somewhere deep down inside, Shane had already begun to respect him.

"I'm through going to that school," Chooch said. "I got no friends there. It's not what I'm about."

"That's one of the best private schools in California. You're throwing away the chance of a lifetime, and for what? So you can hang with a bunch a' street characters?"

"They're my brown brothers. My home slice."

"They don't care about you, Chooch."

"And you do? Or Sandy? I ain't for sale, asshole. You can't buy me with clothes or a school or this crummy deal you got here. You ain't got what I need, Mr. Policeman."

"Get your shoes on. Where are they?" Shane

asked. "And change out of that shirt." Chooch snorted but didn't move, so Shane went into the guest room, found another T-shirt and Chooch's tennis shoes. He reentered the kitchen and handed them over. "Let's go.... Put 'em on, or face the consequences." Chooch changed shirts, then slipped his shoes on without bothering to tie them. Then he exited the back door, insolently brushing Shane with his shoulder as he went past.

Shane followed him out into the alley behind the house, where the department Plymouth was parked. It was a detective car but looked exactly like a regular black-and-white minus the Mars-bar light on the roof.

Back in 1997, Chief Willy Williams had started making sergeants drive them instead of the preferred plainwraps. In the old days, before Chief Gates, one of the perks of being a detective had always been driving an unmarked car, but now nobody bothered to check out a department car off duty except in extreme circumstances. Trying to work a stakeout or surveillance in a slickback was absurd, so detectives ended up using their POVs—personally owned vehicles.

"I ain't gonna show up at school in this," Chooch said, looking at the car, appalled.

Shane opened the passenger door, then spun Chooch around, took out his cuffs, and slapped them on, cuffing his hands in front of him.

"What you doin', man? What's this for?"

"Comin' to school handcuffed in a squad

car oughta harden your rep. You'll be chasing the fly bitches away for a week." He pushed Chooch into the front seat of the car, and he could see the boy smile slightly as he walked around and got behind the wheel.

It was 7:45 A.M. before Shane finally caught his first minor break of the day. Traffic on the 405 was unusually light. It took him only forty-five minutes to get over the hill, into the Valley. Harvard Westlake was half a mile up Coldwater Canyon, on the left side. All the way there, Chooch had remained silent. He had pulled his CD player out of his book bag and plugged himself in.

Even with the break on the traffic, Shane arrived at Harvard Westlake fifteen minutes late. He pulled past the Zanuck Swimming Stadium and the Amelia and Mark Taper Athletic Pavilion. He let Chooch off at the Feldman Horn Fine Arts Building, where his first-period class had already convened. The intended image-enhancing uncuffing ceremony passed without audience.

"I'll pick you up at three-thirty," Shane said, putting his handcuffs away.

"Whatever," Chooch growled. Then with his book bag over his shoulder, he did a gangsta lean into the building.

Shane watched him go, feeling a sense of frustration and uselessness. What on earth was he ever going to be able to give this boy? It had seemed like a good idea two weeks ago when he'd told Sandy yes.... A chance to contribute to Chooch Sandoval's life in an important way. Shane had been fighting recent bouts of intense loneliness and had seen himself helping Chooch sort out his adolescent problems. Shane hadn't expected him to be such a hard case. Now that he had him, he doubted he would be able to make any deposits in Chooch Sandoval's adult experience account. This boy was already molded by the strange circumstances of his life. And now, in the harsh reality of Chooch's anger, it occurred to Shane that maybe he had just planned to use Chooch to find meaning in his own life. While Shane was pondering these thoughts, his cell phone rang and dropped him back onto an even more distressing playing field.

"Yeah."

"Shane, Captain Halley."

"What's up, Skipper?"

"I don't exactly know how to tell you this, but the Molar shooting is turning into a red ball." A red ball was any department case with such a high priority that failure to succeed threatened career advancement. "They're not going to take it to a Shooting Review Board."

"Whatta you mean, they're not gonna? They have to."

"Your case is jumping the Officer Involved Shooting Section and going directly to a full Internal Affairs Board of Rights."

"It's what?" Shane couldn't believe what he was hearing. "How can they send it to a Board of Rights without first giving me a shooting review?"

"The chief can send any case he wants to a full board on his sole discretion. He doesn't have to give any reason. Look, Shane, I don't know why this is happening, but you can't stop it. It's inside departmental guidelines."

"Sir, you gotta talk to them. I mean, I don't wanna go through another BOR. I'm gonna get time off without pay. It's career poison. It's gonna be in my jacket. This is nuts. Anybody would've done what I did. For God's sake, he fired on me. It was self-defense."

"It's what the chief wants."

"I don't even know Chief Brewer. I only met him once. He gave me a Citation of Merit."

"I've gotta go. You'd better get in touch with a defense rep. Who handled your case last time?"

"DeMarco Saint."

"You like him?"

"I guess. He got me off," Shane said dully.

"I think he's retired, but because of IAD crowding, there's a new provision for using retired officers. If you want, I can get you his address and give him a call."

"Sure, check and see if he's still living at the beach." Shane waited on the line for a few seconds. His head throbbed. His stomach churned. The captain came back on.

"He still lives in Santa Monica, on the Strand—3467 Coast Highway. I'll let him know you're coming."

Shane put his car in gear and pulled away

from the shaded, tree-lined splendor of the private school, then made his way back toward the beach and the shrewd counsel of DeMarco Saint.

All the way there, he kept trying to figure it out. Ray Molar had been a black hole in his life from the day he first met him seventeen years ago. In the beginning, he'd been too green to see it. Eventually he recognized Ray for what he was and had gotten away from him. Last night, with Barbara's call, he'd been pulled back into Ray's sinister orbit. In one second he'd ended Ray's life and opened some kind of evil vortex that now threatened to destroy him as well.

DEFENSE REP

ANY POLICE OFFICER facing an administrative review gets to choose a defense rep to defend him. According to Section 202 in the Police Bill of Rights, that representative can be anyone in the department below the rank of captain. The charter provides that the chosen officer *must* serve as the accused's defense representative unless such service would cause undue hardship or unless the chosen officer has a current duty assignment of such a sensitive nature as to prohibit the time commitment.

Over the years, several officers had become very adept at winning Internal Affairs cases and, as a result, got chosen as defense reps time and time again. They became schooled in the legal vagaries of the department disciplinary system, and most of them viewed Internal Affairs as a black hole of intrigue that they referred to as "the Dark Side." In a way, these men and women were mavericks inside the department, seeing themselves as an important demarcation line between the accused officers and the meat-eating "politicians" who worked at Internal Affairs.

Such a man was retired Sergeant DeMarco Saint. He lived on the beach in Santa Monica. His house was run-down and desperately in need of a new roof and paint. He had made his place a hangout for a young, breezy beach crowd: everybody from surf bums and Rollerbladers to volleyball players and sidewalk musicians. They hung in clusters in front of his wood-shingled bungalow. DeMarco Saint presided over this collection of party animals like a wise, bearded guru. He had been a police officer for thirty years and had pulled the pin just last December. Then he had made an almost seamless transition from maverick cop to New Age swami.

Shane pulled his slickback into the public parking lot two doors down from DeMarco's house and showed his badge to the attendant, who greeted the free-parking move with a frown. Shane locked the car and walked to the beach bike path. He could hear loud rap music pounding before he even got on the pavement. As he got closer, he saw several young girls in string bikinis and some tanned surfers in boxer shorts sitting on DeMarco's low brick wall like prizes in a game of beach Jeopardy being played all day at high energy under a synthetic drumbeat.

Of course, Shane looked like a cop to them right off, and the conversation shriveled up like rose petals in a hot summer wind. By the time he got to DeMarco's wall, only the recorded rap of Snoop Doggy Dogg managed to ignore his presence.

"DeMarco around?" he asked the closest girl, a tall brunette in her mid-twenties.

"Inside," she said, arching a pierced eyebrow and clicking her silver tongue stud against her teeth to see if it would piss him off.

"That's nothing." He smiled. "I've got mine through my dick."

She laughed as he moved past her and through the front door of DeMarco's house.

He found the fifty-eight-year-old defense rep on his hands and knees, trying to adjust one of the blasting speakers while a teenage boy watched.

"Fucking bass is vibrating. Sounds like shit," the young surfer with bleached blond hair and black roots said sullenly.

DeMarco kept fiddling and finally took some of the low end out. He leaned back on his knees to listen. "Whatta you think?" he asked. "Better?"

Snoop Doggy Dogg's staccato voice was bouncing ghetto hatred off the walls while DeMarco leaned forward again to screw with his woofers and tweeters.

"Gotta fuck the pigs. Gotta make da man die, if he come passin' by da pork's gotta fry," the Snoopster rapped violently.

"You got a minute?" Shane yelled.

DeMarco turned and saw him, grinned, and stood up. He was over six feet tall, and since Shane had last seen him, he'd let his gray hair grow. It was now tied in a ponytail that hung a quarter of the way down his back. He was wearing a tank top and had added a few tattoos that Shane thought looked ridiculous on his spindly arms, but not anywhere near as ridiculous as the silver cross that dangled from a chain in his left ear.

"Halley called. Been expecting you." He turned to the fifteen-year-old surfer. "You tinker with it for a while."

As the rap banged against their ears, he led Shane through the kitchen, where he grabbed two cold Miller Lites out of the refrigerator, and then out the back along the side of the house, onto Santa Monica's long, sandy beach. The waves were unusually high that morning because of a storm in Mexico. They broke energetically forty yards away, shaking the sand under the two men's feet.

"I must be getting really old," Shane said. "That shit pisses me off."

"I like having the kids around. So what're you gonna do?" He smiled, then reached into his ears and pulled out some cotton balls.

Shane couldn't help himself, he started laughing. "You're tuning your speakers with cotton in your ears. No wonder your low end is vibrating."

Shane and DeMarco sat in the warm sand and ripped the tabs off. The beer cans chirped and hissed foam. They clinked aluminum, and both took long swallows.

"I need help," Shane said.

"I know. Captain Halley already filled me in. He thinks you're being schmucked."

Shane looked at DeMarco. Sixteen years ago, a much younger DeMarco had saved him at a BOR. He was praying the newly ponytailed defense rep could do it again.

"Alexa Hamilton is back down there," DeMarco continued. "I figured she'd've transferred to some cushy job in administration by now."

"She's still there after sixteen years? I thought an average tour at Internal Affairs was only five years."

"She used to be their number one tin collector," DeMarco said. "They brought her back just to get you." A tin collector was an advocate who got convictions that resulted in an officer losing his badge. Sergeant Alexa Hamilton was the department prosecutor who tried him all those years ago, only she had failed to get his tin.

"They're all a bunch a' ladder-climbing

suck-ups," DeMarco said, his hatred for the Dark Side spewing out of him unchecked. "Everybody in the fucking division is looking to get to the top floor of the Glass House. It sucks, the way it's set up."

Shane had heard DeMarco's complaints before and knew the old defense rep was talking about the fact that most of the captains and deputy chiefs on the ninth floor at Parker Center had also spent time as tin collectors in Internal Affairs. That made assignment as an IAD advocate a coveted post. It was a club. Lieutenants and below were selected by virtue of their test scores and oral boards, but to make captain, you had to be picked by the chief of police. The fact was, it was hard to be picked if you hadn't spent some time on the Dark Side. This phenomenon had the effect of making Internal Affairs a catcher's mitt for every hot dog and ladder-climbing politician in the department.

"Why did you mention Alexa Hamilton? What's she got to do with this?" Shane asked, thinking of the attractive but overly severe woman who sixteen years back had prosecuted him with such fanatical enthusiasm. She had quite a reputation, both personally and professionally, leaving a long trail of busted careers and broken hearts. More than one Parker Center Romeo had moved in with her, only to discover that her personal demands matched her professional compulsions. Shane wondered if her apartment was furnished in relationship failures as his was.

He had grown to despise her in the few months that his case was going through the division. One of his best moments on the job was seconds after his not-guilty verdict had come in. He looked over and saw such distress on Alexa's face that it gave him a moment of pure, soul-cleansing vengeance. When she caught him looking, he smiled and surreptitiously flipped her the bird.

"I thought you knew," DeMarco said, interrupting his thoughts. "She's got your case. She put in for it."

"You can't be serious," Shane groaned.

"Yeah. If at first you don't succeed, and all that good shit." DeMarco took another long pull on his beer and let out a deep belch. "Maybe you shouldn't've flipped her off."

"Wouldn't matter, she hates me anyway."

DeMarco went on. "It's not good that they hopped over your Shooting Review Board and went straight to a BOR. It shows the department is going to war."

"Why? Barbara Molar is my witness. She'll say what happened."

"I made a few calls down to my old crew at the Representation Section in Parker Center. The rumor down there is, this whole railroad train is coming right out of Mayor Crispin's office. He wants your balls in his trophy case."

"Why?"

"Lemme take a wild guess...." He drained his beer. "How 'bout 'cause you lit up his bodyguard. Blew his arithmetic all over that bedroom wall."

"You gotta help me, Dee. You gotta get me off."

"I'd like to, Shane. I really would. But frankly, I can't get into that rat race again. Alexa Hamilton is one tough, nail-chewing piece of business. I faced her fifteen or twenty times. Lost more than I won. I don't like it one bit that she's volunteering for this case. That tells me there's a big political payoff somewhere. Maybe lieutenant's bars and a transfer to something sexy like Organized Crime or Special Investigations. Mayweather could set that up for her, no sweat."

"You're telling me I'm cooked before we even get a hearing?"

"Tell you what...you know Rags Whitman? He's a good defense rep, smarter than me. I used to ram my dick up their asses and piss on their hearts. Ragland, he's mellow, he plays the game—Mr. Wheel of Fortune. They like him at Parker Center. I was you, I'd get him to take your case. Ask him to plead you out, see what kinda deal he can get. My bet: maybe he gets you a six-month suspension without pay and no termination."

"For defending myself from that crazy bastard? What kinda deal is that?"

"You shot Ray Molar. Not a good move, but you got an eyewitness who, we hope, backs you up. You got Ray's bullet in the wall, proving he fired before you got him. You also got Molar's record of spousal abuse. All this is good. On the bad side, you got the fuckin' mayor of L.A. tail-gunning you. You got Chief Brewer with his ears back, and you got some tricky 'undue use of force' statutes that could go against you. Your best bet is to see if Rags can spin the big wheel and plead it down."

"You won't help me? Come on, Dee, you're off the department. They can't threaten you; they can't get to your pension. What's the problem?"

"I'd do it if I could, man. I just can't. I've got no stomach for it anymore. I go down there, and my guts start churning. I'd choke. I hate those pricks worse than the National Anthem. You wanna know why I pulled the pin? It wasn't 'cause I had my thirty in. It was ulcers. My stomach lining looks like a Mexican highway. I can't put myself back in that mess. Go talk to Rags. Get him to negotiate a kick-down."

Shane stood up and handed DeMarco his half-empty beer. "Okay," he finally said. "Sorry to take up your morning." Then he turned and walked away, his shoes filling with warm sand as he went.

"Hey, Scully," DeMarco called, and Shane turned around. "Whatever you do, don't volunteer to take a polygraph. I think the IA poly is rigged. They use it to get confessions. I've had more than one case where I think I got a bum test."

"Okay," Shane answered. "Thanks for the warning."

Shane pulled out of the parking lot and back onto the Coast Highway. As he started toward the Santa Monica Freeway, his stomach was churning and he could taste bile in his throat. Then he heard a siren growl and saw a black-and-white behind him with its red lights on. Since he was in a black-and-white slickback, it surprised him that he was being flashed to the curb like a civilian. He pulled over and got out.

A young uniformed cop with two stripes on his sleeve moved up to him.

"What's up, Officer?" Shane asked.

"You Sergeant Scully?" the man asked.

"Yeah."

"I'm Joe Church. I was ordered to accompany you to Parker Center forthwith. Apparently your mobile data terminal is turned off."

"They get the gallows up already?" Shane quipped.

"I'm sorry, what, sir?" Officer Church said, deadpan, maybe with a tinge of cold anger.

"Why?" Shane asked. "What do they want?"

"Chief Brewer wants to see you immediately." He sort of barked it at Shane.

"Did I do something to piss you off?" Shane asked.

"You wanna follow me?"

"I can make it. You afraid I'll get lost?"

"Why don't you wait till I pull around.

Since you haven't got a bar light, I'll put on the flashers and siren. It gets us there faster."

"You got a siren, how cool. I can hardly wait."

Shane got back into his unit and waited until the squad car pulled around in front of him. Joe Church growled his siren once, then raced out into the fast lane with Shane behind him.

The two police cars shot up onto the Santa Monica Freeway, heading back to downtown L.A. and Parker Center, Code Three.

7
SUPER CHIEF

TRAFFIC WAS JAMMED up because some jackass had issued a motion-picture permit to an Arnold Schwarzenegger movie that was now shooting on Wilshire at Spring Street. The film crew had moved in downtown, parking their honey wagons, dressing rooms, and sixteen-wheelers up and down the curb on Third, laying out barricades and blocking traffic for ten city blocks. Shane couldn't believe that some dummy in city government had signed a film-location permit that would tie up all of downtown L.A. Twice, Patrolman Church had to get out of his car and talk to an off-duty policeman working for the movie company so they could get through.

After struggling for over forty minutes, they finally drove into the parking structure next to Parker Center. They both found a spot on the top level. Shane got out of his car, and Joe Church immediately joined him.

"Damn movie has this town tied up worse than my colon," Church growled as they looked at a low-flying helicopter that was hovering half a block away. There was a cameraman hanging out of the side door in a harness. Suddenly the rotors changed pitch, and the silver-and-red Bell Jet Ranger took off after a car that was speeding down barricaded Main Street after a motorcycle, Arnold Schwarzenegger kicking ass on celluloid.

"Let's go," Church said, getting back to business, taking Shane by the arm.

"I can make it. Even go to the bathroom now without Mommy's help."

"Don't be an asshole, Scully. I've got orders."

Shane decided not to push it, but he pulled his arm free and followed Church into the building.

For the second time in four hours, he found himself back on the ninth floor. They moved off the elevator, onto the thick, seafoam green carpet, past the blond paneling and executive furniture, until he was finally standing in front of a massive woman who sat behind an oak desk the approximate size and shape of a Nimitz class carrier. She was parked directly outside Chief Burleigh Brewer's office.

Joe Church had shifted gears. No longer the stern centurion, he was now wearing an ingratiating, apple-polisher's smile. "Patrolman Church," he effused. "I was called specifically by Chief Brewer for this assignment. I've brought Sergeant Scully in. It was a 'forthwith.'"

"Thank you, Officer," the linebacker-sized woman said. Her heavy body wasn't helped by the shoulder pads in her tan suit coat. The name on her desk plate read CARLA MILLER. "You can sit down over there, Sergeant," she said to Shane, pointing to a chair. Joe Church took a position of advantage, guarding the exit.

"Jeez, Church," Shane growled, "I'm not Clyde Barrow. I'm not gonna shoot my way outta here. Try giving it a rest."

Carla Miller nodded to Church. "We'll be okay."

Church shuffled his feet, flashed a gee-whiz smile, and a few seconds later backed out of the office and was gone.

Carla buzzed Chief Brewer and talked to him softly for a second, then hung up the phone.

Shane waited in the chair for almost thirty minutes, watching the efficiency with which Carla Miller fended off appointments and people. She was a tough, competent goalie, crouching in the net, deflecting problems. She never looked at him once. Outside, he could hear the distant drone of the movie helicopter as it whirled and turned, its rotors whining above the streets of L.A.

Suddenly the intercom buzzed. Carla picked up the phone, listened, then looked at Shane. "You can go in now."

He got up and moved into Chief Brewer's office. The first thing that struck him was that the movie helicopter seemed to be almost inside the office. The chief had a huge expanse of glass. You could see all the way down Main Street to the Financial Center. The Bell Jet Ranger was hovering loudly only fifty feet from the chief's plate-glass window. It was a startlingly eerie effect.

Chief Brewer's back was to him. He was looking out the window at the chopper and the movie company in the street below. The camera ship hovered, stirring air gusts against the window. The rotor sound inside the office was almost deafening. Shane could see the pilot's features clearly. The cameraman hanging from straps inside the open side door was still hunched over the eyepiece. It occurred to Shane that while he had been outside, waiting with his heart in his throat, his police commander had been watching them shoot this fucking movie.

Then Chief Brewer turned. Making it worse, he was holding a pair of field glasses. He set them down on his desk and motioned to Shane to come forward.

"You wanted to see me, sir." Shane's voice was lost in the noise from the helicopter. Somewhere in the pit of his stomach he knew that what he was about to be told was not going to be good. Sergeants get summoned to the COP's office for only two reasons, and Shane was pretty sure he wasn't about to get another Meritorious Service commendation.

Then the chopper turned and flew away abruptly, photographing some part of the movie in the street below. The silence that ensued was a blessing.

"Sergeant Scully, you've had a busy morning," the chief said. He was a stout forty-five-year-old red-haired man with cheeks that always seemed to have a ruby blush. He had his suits carefully tailored to hide a growing midsection. Recently he had added rimless glasses that blended a touch of severity into an otherwise unremarkable face.

"Yes, sir. Busy morning, sir," Shane said, trying to read where this was going.

"Movies," the chief said. "Boy, they use a fuck of a lot of equipment. They've got four whole blocks tied up down there. Three helicopters. That one there is the camera bird. God knows what the other two are for. We let 'em use one of the police choppers for a picture ship."

"That's very generous, sir. I'm sure they're grateful."

"It's a Schwarzenegger flick called *Silver and Lead*. He plays a cop who breaks up an armored-car robbery. It's a silver shipment, but it turns out the robbery is just a decoy to pull the cops away from a presidential assassination. Arnold signed a copy of the script for me," Chief Brewer bragged.

"Bet that'll be worth a few bucks." Shane felt like a moron, standing there with his asshole puckered, talking about the movie business.

"People would feel a lot better about you, Sergeant, if you were more of a team player."

No segue. One moment it's show biz, the next it's team ball.

"Oh?" Shane said. "I think I'm a good team player, sir. Check with my captain, my watch commanders."

"I'm not talking about your field performance, Scully. I'm sure you're a good detective. That's not what this is about. What I'm talking about is attitudinal."

"Attitudinal?" Shane was lost. He didn't have a clue.

"Sometimes a guy will find himself in a position where he thinks maybe he's got an advantage. He thinks maybe he got lucky, stumbled into a piece of good fortune, but the fact is, he's not lucky at all. Fact is, he's stepped in a vat of shit and doesn't even know it. Then he's isolated—a marked man. That's not a good thing. It's better if you're a part of the team."

"Exactly what is it we're talking about, sir? I'm kinda lost."

"Are you? How come I knew that's what you were going to say?" Chief Brewer stood there, looking at Shane as if he were a grease spot on one of his new silk suits. Then he let out some more line. "Sergeant, there are items missing from Lieutenant Molar's case files. According to his duty logs, they were in his house before you shot him. They are no longer there. We questioned his wife. We believe she knows nothing. That leaves you. You were in a position, after you killed him, to remove those items."

"And you think I have them?"

"These items might appear to you to be some kind of windfall or perhaps something an ambitious person might think he could use to his advantage. They aren't what they appear to be. Lieutenant Molar was involved in something very sensitive, and he had the full cooperation of this office. This material could easily be misinterpreted if it got into the wrong hands. It needs to be returned now!"

"Sir, I don't have anything of Ray's. *Nothing*."

"I fully expected you to deny this because we both know it's against departmental regs to remove another officer's case material. You could be terminated if you admit you took it. However, Sergeant, there are things in this life that are worse than job termination. I expect that you're going to continue to deny it until the full gravity of the situation becomes clear to you, but by then it may be too late. There may be nothing I can do to help you."

"What items?" Shane's heart was pounding now. He was feeling as if he were trapped in a nightmare and couldn't find a way to wake up. "I didn't take anything," he repeated.

"In which case, you probably wouldn't object to taking a polygraph test."

"A polygraph? I... I don't even have a defense rep yet. I... I'm not sure I want to submit to a lie detector test without legal advice."

"Again, exactly what I thought you would

say. Believe me, Scully, you're making a horrible mistake."

"Sir, I'm not saying I won't take a polygraph. It's just... I'm having a hard time figuring out what's going on. I shot a man who was trying to kill me. He'd been beating his wife with a nightstick. Since that happened, my shooting review was canceled. I understand my case is being directed to a full administrative hearing, and now you're telling me I'm supposed to have stolen something from Lieutenant Molar's house? I took nothing, sir. I'll swear an affidavit to that fact."

The chief made a waving motion, brushing all this aside. "Here's my deal, Scully—and if you know what's good for you, you better take it. You've got four hours to turn over what you took. Drop the material off here. If you think you can use it to extract either money or career advantage, then you're going to find out that the entire city of Los Angeles, from Police to Sanitation, will go to war against you. It won't end well. By way of example, the district attorney, right now, is seriously considering filing murder charges against you for killing Lieutenant Molar."

"What?" Shane couldn't believe what he was hearing.

"Sergeant, do yourself a big favor and turn the material over."

Shane stood across from Chief Brewer with his knees shaking. He tried to collect his thoughts, then he took a breath to calm down.

"Let's suppose I have what you want and I

70

turn it over," he said. "What happens to the charge of removing case materials and my Internal Affairs Board of Rights?"

"Maybe something gets worked out there. We look the other way on the case material. Your undue-use-of-force gets sent back to the Officer Involved Shooting Section, they look it over. Maybe it gets disposed of in a few hours, the district attorney decides there's no case."

"So you're using the BOR and this murder charge to try and scare me into doing what you want?"

There was an awkward silence, then the chief took a step toward him and changed the subject.

"Sergeant, there are only three places that material can be, and we've already looked in the other two. You've got four hours. Your career, and maybe the way you spend the rest of your life, depends on your decision. That's all I have to tell you." Then he turned his generous backside on Shane and looked out the window again, at the movie company.

Shane hesitated, wanting to continue to try convincing him, but it was obvious he had been firmly dismissed. Shane turned and walked out of Burl Brewer's office, closing the door behind him.

When he got into the waiting room, Alexa Hamilton was sitting in the same chair he had been warming a few minutes before. She stood when she saw him. Alexa Hamilton was in her mid-to late thirties and was beautiful in a severe, hard-charging way. Coal-black hair was pinned up on the back of her head. High cheekbones and slanted eyes gave her an exotic look that Shane didn't think fit her no-nonsense, ball-busting personality. She had a tight, gym-trained body. He thought her beauty was badly overpowered by a raw will to succeed that made her sexually unattractive to him. He saw her as one of the new breed of LAPD ladder-monkeys, moving fast through the department, eating her dead, leaving a high-octane vapor trail behind her.

"We meet again," she said, arching a tapered brow and smiling without humor.

"This isn't a meeting, it's an ambush."

"Call it what you like, I'm ready. I don't usually have to take two swings at such a slow pitch."

"I'll try and put a few more rpms in my routine." He looked down at the folder in her hand. "That my package?" he asked. "My sealed background records seem to be making the rounds. Will I be reading about my confidential history in next month's newsletter, or is it just going up on the division bulletin board?"

"I'm not reading secure files, Scully. I don't need to cheat to hammer you in. The infield fly rule's on. We have a play at any base."

"If you say so." He walked out of the office and was heading down the hall when she stuck her head out and called to him.

"Hey, Scully."

He turned and faced her.

"I didn't 'peel the nine' at Ray Molar, you

did. You go around shooting your ex-partners, you're bound to pick up a little grief."

"Lemme file that under 'shit to remember.'"

He stabbed hard at the elevator button, missed, and stabbed again. Thankfully, it opened almost immediately and he got on, stepping out of her black-eyed stare. It whisked him mercifully away, down to the traffic-jammed reality of downtown Los Angeles and Arnold Schwarzenegger.

8

TOKING

AFTER PICKING UP his Acura at the Spring Street Tire Center, Shane got back to the Harvard Westlake School at three-thirty to retrieve Chooch. He waited in a long line of British and German cars driven by Beverly Hills soccer moms. When he finally pulled to the curb where the students waited to be picked up, there was no Chooch. Then he saw him, off to the side of the crowd, sitting on a curb by himself. His CD player was hooked in his ears; he was lost in the music. Shane tapped on the horn to get his attention. Chooch picked up his book bag and ambled over to the newly shod black Acura now sporting four Michelin radials that Shane couldn't afford at a hundred dollars a tire.

As Chooch was sliding into the front seat, a tall, reed-thin man with a lipless mouth, curly hair, and heavy, dark-rimmed glasses stuck his head into the car. "Mr. Sandoval, I'm Brad Thackery, head of the Latin department and high-school assistant dean of admissions."

"I'm not his father," Shane said.

"Oh…uh, well, I'm sorry. I just got the job two months ago, and I'm still trying to get all the names and faces straight. Will you be talking to Chooch's parents today?"

"Whatta you need, Mr. Thackery?"

"We need to schedule a teacher's conference immediately. Chooch has some severe problems that need to be addressed, *ad summum bonum*."

Off Shane's puzzled expression, he translated, "For everyone's good."

Shane looked at Chooch, who seemed not to be hearing any of it as he bobbed his head to the beat of some alternative rock leaking at high decibels from his earphones.

"I'll call his mother. Thanks."

Parents behind him were beginning to tap their horns impatiently, so Shane put the car in gear and pulled out onto Coldwater.

Shane said nothing until they were on the Ventura Freeway. "Hey, Chooch," he said, looking over at the boy slumped down in the seat beside him. "Chooch, you wanna take off the headset for a minute!? We need to talk."

Chooch paid no attention. He was bobbing his head to the music, oblivious.

Shane suddenly reached over and ripped the jack out of the CD.

74

That got his attention. Chooch spun around and glared. "What!" he said angrily.

"They want a teacher's meeting."

"I heard him. Thackery's a dick. Who the fuck cares? I hope they kick me out."

"Whatta they wanna talk about?" Shane asked. "I've gotta call and tell your mother."

"Whatta they wanna talk about? They wanna accuse me of dealin' drugs at school."

"Of what!?"

"You heard me. They think I'm dealin' drugs."

"Are you?"

Chooch didn't say anything, he just shrugged.

"You're not gonna tell me?"

"You're a fuckin' cop. Don't I get a lawyer and my Miranda rights first?"

Shane pulled the car off the freeway, down the Sepulveda ramp, and parked on the busy cross street. Then he turned to face Chooch. "Listen, Chooch, I'm not a cop where you're concerned. I'm your..." Shane couldn't think of the right word. What was he?

"My what?" Chooch challenged. "My fuckin' guardian? My baby-sitter? My spiritual coach? What the fuck are you?"

"How 'bout your friend," Shane finally said.

"You're not my friend. I don't have any friends. Not one."

"Chooch, if you're selling drugs to kids at school, we've got a big problem. They could go to the LAPD. They could file criminal charges against you."

Chooch leaned back in the seat, not sure what to do.

"I'm not gonna bust you," Shane continued, "but I've gotta know what the deal is if I'm going to help."

"Not gonna bust me, huh? Where'd I hear that before?"

"Tell me. Were you selling drugs?"

"No. I didn't sell nothin'." He leaned back and closed his eyes. "Once or twice, maybe... I loaned some Rasta weed to somebody. And then maybe once or twice I found some cash in my locker that I don't know where it came from...."

"Shit," Shane said, not sure how extreme his response to this should be. "You're in deep shit if they can prove it. Is anybody there gonna talk?"

"You mean, will my dickhead clients roll over and give me up?" Chooch asked. "In a fuckin' heartbeat. You want my opinion? They're not gonna go to the cops. That school doesn't want some newspaper story about drugs on campus. Since I'm Mexican, they're also probably scared shitless somebody will charge 'em with race discrimination. They're just gonna demand I go quietly, something I'm real prepared to do."

Shane looked hard at the teenager, still sitting with his head back on the seat, his eyes closed.

"It isn't your problem anyway," Chooch said. "You're just this month's paid jerkoff."

"Right. That's me." Shane put the car in gear

and headed back up onto the freeway. They didn't speak all the way back to Venice.

Finally, Shane pulled into his house at 143 East Channel Road. He parked in the garage and got out. Chooch grabbed his book bag and slouched along after him as they opened the back door. The two of them walked into the kitchen, and Chooch slung his book bag angrily onto the counter.

"Take that into your room and start doing your homework."

"Homework? Ain't that a little off the point?"

"Do it anyway," Shane said. Then he moved out of the house into his small backyard, which looked out onto one of the narrow channels of Venice. What had been a cold April morning was now turning into a surprisingly pleasant California afternoon.

From Shane's small backyard on Venice's East Channel, he could see all the way down the intersecting Howland Canal.

Venice, California, had been the brain-child of Abbot Kinney in 1904. Kinney had wanted to create a luxury community in the style of Venice, Italy. He supervised the design of channels to carry water in from the ocean two blocks away. He designed his development around four long canals, intersected by a series of concrete, arched Venice-like driving bridges that spanned each canal. He added small walking bridges and brought some scaled-down gondolas over from Italy. It had been quite a place in the early 1900s but had seen hard times ever since. The canals still had a sort of rustic charm, but the once-grand houses of the thirties had been knocked down or subdivided and in their place were smaller, cheaper structures. The architectural style ranged from antebellum to trailer-park modern. The people who now lived on the canals were an even more interesting mix. Young doctors who smoked dope lived next door to disapproving retirees. New Age musicians and mimes competed for hat tips on the boardwalk, while four blocks inland, on Fifteenth Street, gangbangers and unaware tourists fought and died over wallets and watches. Jammed in with all of this confusion, next to a longhaired surfboard shaper, was LAPD Sergeant Shane Scully. There was something about the canal blocks of Venice, California, that suited him; something offbeat and sad. Venice seemed as misplaced as her residents.

Less than half a mile to the south were the yuppified environs of Marina del Rey, where young ad executives and airline flight attendants took sexual aim at one another in the crowded waterside bars and fish houses. A mile to the north was Santa Monica, with its population of trendy superagents, junk bond salesmen, and Hollywood power brokers. Halfway in between, sitting on its silly three-foot-deep canals, trying to be something it could never duplicate, was the other Venice, sinking into the mud of social indifference as surely as Venice, Italy, was sinking into the sea.

But Shane Scully was at home there, like no place else on earth. Venice, California, defined him.

As he watched a hummingbird hang energetically over the still East Channel, he opened his cell phone and dialed Sandy.

She answered after the tenth ring and seemed out of breath. "Yes," she said. "Hello." She also sounded angry and impatient.

"Catch you at a bad time?" he asked sarcastically.

"Shane, I can't talk now. I was already out the door. I'm late."

"Then let me make it quick. I think they're going to throw Chooch out of Harvard Westlake for dealing grass. Some guy named Thackery wants a teacher's meeting with you. I told him I'd let you know. That's the whole message. Nice talking to you."

"Wait a minute. He's dealing what?"

"Grass... Mary Jane, Aunt Hazel, African bush, bambalacha. You pick the cool name. He's selling shit to his classmates, and Mr. Thackery ain't one little bit amused about it."

"Well, what am I supposed to do? I can't... I mean, can't we...?"

"Unfortunately, I don't think there's much *we* can do. But *you've* gotta call and set something up. As Thackery says, 'It's for everybody's good.' *Ad mumble bubble gum.* And before you ask, lemme say that as this month's paid jerkoff, I'm not up for the teacher's conference."

"Come on, Shane, it can't be that bad."

"Sandy, I'm in some very big trouble myself

79

right now. Big enough that I could end up getting fired or, worse still, even prosecuted by the DA."

"But—"

"No. Listen. I can't handle this problem. I didn't know what I was getting into with Chooch."

"He sounds worse than he is. He's not that bad. You just have to be patient with him."

"You're sure about that? 'Cause I think he's one very confused, very angry kid. I think he's in the diamond lane to Juvenile Hall, and not that you care, Sandy, but I think you need to pay more attention to him. This kid is being passed around like a hot rock. Nobody's giving him what he needs."

"Including you?" she said darkly. "I thought you told me you *were* up for it, that you wanted to make a one-on-one investment in something with lasting dividends."

"What the fuck were we drinking, anyway?"

"Shane, look, I hear you. Unfortunately, I'm working for the DEA right now. I'm up to my ass in a dangerous sting that is days from going down. You know from the jobs we've pulled together that my biggest jeopardy is right before I drop the dime. If I get made now, I could end up the captain of a fifty-gallon oil drum at the bottom of the Catalina Channel. I can't take Chooch. I can't take a chance he'll get hurt, and I can't divert my energies or my concentration at this point in the sting. You said you'd take him. You promised. Otherwise, I wouldn't have left him there."

"Okay, Sandy. I'll do the best I can. But you wanna know something...?"

"Not if it's gonna be a lecture."

"It's an opinion, baby. This boy is hurting bad. He's on fire. He's so self-destructive, I'm heartsick for him. But I'm up to my ass in department bullshit. I shot my ex-partner."

"That was you? It was on the news." Shane didn't answer. "Well, good," Sandy finished. "Ray was a son of a bitch. He deserved to die."

"No, he didn't. But if this goes like it's been going, I'm not going to be available for Chooch, either. So start figuring what you're gonna do and call this prick Thackery and get him off my ass."

"Okay, okay, sugar. I'll call him. Gotta run. Bye." And she was gone.

He slumped down in his rusting metal lawn chair, and then someone cleared his throat. Shane turned and realized that Chooch had come out the side door and had been sitting in one of the other metal chairs at the side of the house.

"Well, she's probably got a lot more important shit on her mind," Chooch said. "Want me to roll you a number? It's pretty fine Jamaican ganja."

Chooch had some Zig-Zag papers and a small cloth drawstring bag in his hand. Shane hadn't had a hit of marijuana since the Marine Corps, but he was so tight, so frayed, that he was worried about his imploding psyche. "Yeah, sure, roll me up one."

"No shit?" Chooch said, "What about Rule

One: No smoking grass in my house, not now, not ever?"

"I gotta do something to bend the energy in this day. Rule One is temporarily suspended."

Chooch rolled a bud, fat and short. Then he handed it over. Shane sat there, holding the jay, wondering what kind of example it was going to be for him to blast a joint in front of Chooch or, worse still, get high with him. But then he thought of the events of the day, starting with his shooting Ray Molar at 2:30 A.M., all the way through to his disastrous meeting with Chief Brewer. Somehow, in the light of all that, passing grass with an angry fifteen-year-old just didn't seem all that important.

"Fuck it," he said, then reached back and grabbed one of Chooch's matches, fired up, took a hit, and passed it to Chooch.

The two of them sat in metal chairs in the small, green-brown garden behind Shane's house, sharing the joint and trying to unwind their separate but equally devastating problems.

THE
"FUNERAL" LETTER

Dear Dad,

Boy, do I wish you were here so we could sit down and talk this one out like the old days. I'm really in the shit this time, Pop, and no matter which way I turn, I'm faced with a new set of terrible options.

Where to begin?

I guess Ray's funeral is my biggest unanswerable right now. The department is going to give him a full-dress good-bye: honor guard, speeches, everybody wearing black ribbons across their badges. Today we got a department directive demanding that all officers not on day watch attend in dress blues. There's going to be a parade led by two hundred Mary units (motorcycle cops), followed by a hundred black-and-whites. The damn thing forms up at the Academy training field and will wend its way out of the foothills to Forest Lawn. Full TV and press coverage, of course.

Part of me wants to go. I feel like hell, and going to Ray's funeral might help me through it. Another part of me is scared to death. They're going to have this giant turnout of my brother officers: a twenty-gun send-off, with everybody mourning Ray Molar, "the Policeman's Policeman" and double Medal of Valor winner.

My problem, of course, is I'm the asshole who shot him.

I don't know if I can bear to stand there under all the hatred I know will be directed at me.

What would you do, Dad? I could really use the advice. I remember you told me once that, in matters of the soul, the thing that is the most difficult to do is generally the thing that you must do. You said that in order to grow spiritually, one must not turn away from emotional hardships. But, still, I feel so isolated, so alone, so out of the loop.

Having you so far away has made things difficult. I know you can't get around much and having emphysema makes flying difficult, but I need help, Dad.

I guess one of my problems is I always tried to make the department my second family. All that bullshit they preach up at the Academy...the long blue line, fraternity of police, brothers in blue... I wanted to believe all that. I think maybe it's why I decided to become a cop. And now, despite almost seventeen years on the job, I've found a way to fuck it up. I'm alone again.

If you have any thoughts, gimme a ring. I'm still undecided about Ray's funeral.

I wish I had your strength, willpower, and sense of honor. I'm trying to do what I think would make you proud but, damn it, I'm panicked to go to that funeral.

You're probably saying I should just bite the bullet and go. So, that's the answer. You always did know what was best.

I miss you and love you. I know, enough already, blah, blah, blah.

Your loving son,
Shane

WARRANT

SHANE DIDN'T GO to the funeral.
He put in for a sick day and, mercifully, it was approved. He hated himself for not having enough guts, but he just couldn't make himself attend. Chooch, showing more backbone, had not objected that morning when Shane loaded him into the car, took him across town to Harvard Westlake, and dropped him at school. They barely exchanged words as Chooch got out of the car.

Shane drove back to Venice, trying hard not to think about his emotional cowardice. He arrived home and busied himself cleaning the small house. He did some deferred maintenance, fixing a sprung hinge on the back screen door, then managed some idle conversation with Longboard Kelly, both of them talking over the back fence. But he couldn't keep his mind on what Kelly was saying...something about Hawaiian North Shore supersets and the merits of a stubby board compared with a nine-foot Hawaiian classic. As he walked back inside, his recollection of the conversation hovered over him like a dream barely remembered. Then he checked his answering machine, something he hadn't done for almost ten hours. There was only one message:

"Shane, it's Barbara. I know it might be dan-

gerous, but we need to meet. I assume you'll be at the funeral, but obviously we can't talk there. How about 'our spot'? I could be there by one. The funeral is scheduled to be over by twelve-thirty. Don't contact me, I'm worried about my phone. I'm calling from a pay booth. Just be there. I have news. I love you."
Beep.

Their "spot" was the outdoor restaurant at Shutters Hotel on the beach in Santa Monica. Once or twice, when they'd been dating, they'd taken a room there. The place was picturesque, and most of the units overlooked the water. Back then they'd both been in their early twenties and single. Having lunch together on an open patio before going up to a rented love nest was fine. Now, after shooting Ray, the last thing he needed was to be seen hunched over a table, in whispered conversation with his widow. Still, Shane was drawn to her in a way he couldn't describe. Maybe it was guilt, or maybe the feeling that she had been the one, and he had lost her through bullheaded pride, or maybe she had become just a fantasy in his memory. He had saved her from Ray, setting up, God help him, possibilities for some sort of future together. Or maybe it was just that he hadn't been laid in almost three weeks. Whatever the reason, he decided to take the chance and meet her there. After all, he rationalized, she said she had "news."

He dressed with more care than usual and even used the hair dryer on his dark, unruly mop. Then he got in the Acura and drove the short distance up the coast to Santa Monica.

He arrived at Shutters at about quarter to one and selected a table near the back of the patio. He ordered her favorite bottle of wine, a French Montrachet. While he waited, he tried to justify the meeting in his guilt-ridden conscience. Maybe her "news" would shed light on his problems. Maybe it would be something that would help dig him out of the mess he was in. Of course, lingering always, like a sour aftertaste, was his desire for her and the knowledge that he wanted to sleep with her again. It was another picture for his gallery: guilt-ridden lust...presenting a portrait of carnal self-hate. Hang it in the Virginia Woolf exhibit.

She arrived at 1:25 and stood in the doorway of the patio restaurant, wearing a black dress with a single strand of pearls. She wore large dark glasses to cover a black eye. The swelling from the nightstick was gone, and miraculously she no longer appeared to have any bruises. Her blond hair shimmered in the bright afternoon sunlight. She looked around the patio, spotted him, waved off the maître d', and walked toward him with her athletic dancer's step. She had once performed in the chorus of several musicals at the Dorothy Chandler Pavilion. She slipped gracefully into the vacant chair, puckered her lips, kissed the air, and smiled. Now that she was across the table from him, he could see that she had expertly covered the effects of the beating with Dermaplec, an over-the-counter makeup that is the best product available for hiding bruises. Every patrolman answering a spousal-abuse complaint quickly learned to check the medicine cabinet for Dermaplec. If it was there, it was almost as good as a confession by the husband that he had engaged in wife battering before.

"Hard day," she said sadly. "I thought you'd be at the funeral."

"Truth is, I chickened out."

"I can hardly blame you. It was a real Hollywood layout. Chief Brewer made a speech. Said Ray exemplified commitment to community and police honor. Mayor Crispin talked about his courage. Said he set a new standard for police excellence. They had a twenty-one-gun salute, gave me the flag off his coffin. There was a helicopter flyby, the whole police air unit."

"I'm surprised Schwarzenegger could spare the bird."

She cocked her head.

"Nothing," he said, not wanting to go into it.

"Anyway, Ray's in the ground. Lots of ceremony, lots of news crews and crocodile tears. Jeez, you wouldn't believe what a big deal it was."

Shane poured her a glass of Montrachet. She sipped the wine and looked out over the sandy beach and the ocean a hundred yards beyond. A light wind ruffled her perfectly streaked blond hair. She seemed to be working up to something. He waited and let her get at it in her own way. Finally she turned back to him, a small, sad smile on her face. "This is strange, sitting here again after all these years, isn't it?" He nodded his agreement. "God only knows why I chose to marry him, Shane. All day I've been trying to figure what was going through my mind. You were always the one."

"You don't have to explain it," he said, shifting awkwardly under the weight of the conversation and her penetrating stare.

"You were what I was looking for, but Ray told me *you* had beat that kid half to death in Southwest Division. He told me horrible things about you and I just...got mixed up. It wasn't until after we got married that he told me one night when he was drunk that he did it and that you had just taken the blame so IA wouldn't kick him off the job. He thought it was funny. 'Scully's just a dumb fuck,' he said."

"It's okay. It's done. Forget it." He felt his self-respect washing away like water rushing back to the sea, taking the sand beneath his feet, altering his stance, threatening his balance. It seemed wrong to be discussing this on the day that Ray went into the ground. Wrong to feel desire for his widow, wrong not to have found the courage to go to the funeral.

Barbara went on, in a hurry to rid herself of her own painful memories. "Back then, when I told you not to call me anymore, I cried for a whole night. I thought you had done what Ray said, you were on trial at Internal Affairs for it...and I..." She stopped and shook her head. "Ray started coming around a month later, and he seemed so strong. At first he could be so sweet, so tender. It was sort of touching, a huge brutish guy like that with an inner softness. I was looking for something, I don't know what. Then he kept at me...calling... gifts...it went on for years before I said yes. My dancing career was going nowhere, and I just thought..." She shook her head in exasperation. "Whatta mistake, huh?"

"Barbara, you don't have to explain it to me. Please. I understand."

"I want to, Shane. I need to. I know this is a shitty day for it, but frankly, in the twelve years we were married, I'd come to despise Ray, and I had come to despise myself for getting into such a mess with him. He drank, he cheated, he didn't come home sometimes for a week. Then a few years ago, he started hitting me. At the end, I was so frightened of him. I swear, it was a relief to see that casket go into the ground, almost like his grave was the doorway to my future." She took a deep breath. "If that seems coldhearted, I'm sorry. It's how I feel."

Shane looked at her for a long time. Under the dark glasses he knew she had beautiful aqua-blue eyes, the exact color of tropical reef water. She had a luscious body and chiseled features. More than once, in the old days, he had walked into rooms with her and felt the gaze of every man in the place undressing her. She was a physical trophy, but it went beyond that. He thought she had intense feelings and a depth of personality that this conversation betrayed. God help him, Shane still desperately wanted her, wanted to hold her and make love to her, but the feeling diminished him. Making it worse, he could tell that she was reaching out to him, asking him for forgiveness and inviting him to try again.

"Barbara, I think, no matter what eventually happens between us later, this needs to wait."

"I know. I know. It's just... I've been thinking about what it would have been like if things had been different. Sounds like a sad Barbra Streisand flick, doesn't it?"

He sat there looking at her, afraid to mention the number of times he had lain awake with the same thought. They'd really fucked it up. Ray had given it a nudge, but it had been the two of them, accelerated by Shane's pride and anger, who had pushed something special over the cliff. Now any future relationship was destined to be a reclamation project. Ray's memory would forever be between them.

"You said you had news," Shane said, changing the subject.

"I got the phone printout like you asked, from AT&T. I got the number that woman called in on."

"Great. Lemme see it."

She handed over a slip of paper and he frowned. "This is a Venice exchange."

"I know."

"Why would somebody send an important

package through the mail, where it might get lost, when they could just drive by at midnight and stuff it into your mailbox?"

"I don't know. Doesn't make much sense."

He pulled out his cell phone and dialed the number. He got a recording. "Disconnected," he said as he snapped the phone closed. "When you gave your statement, did you tell the police about the woman who called and the videotape she said was coming?"

"Yeah. I told them everything." Then she added with a strange smile, "I told them Ray fired first, that it was self-defense."

Shane sat, thinking for a long moment. "We need to take a look through your house. I want to do a thorough search."

"There's nothing there. Robbery/Homicide looked already when they did the crime-scene investigation."

"I wanna look anyway. Maybe they missed it. I think that tape the woman was talking about may be what this is all about. Can we skip lunch and go there now?"

"What if they have someone watching the house? They'd see us together."

"With two-thirds of the department taking the day off for Ray's funeral, I doubt there's any spare manpower for a stakeout. Now is the best time. Let's go. If it's there, maybe we can find it."

He paid for the wine, and they walked out of the restaurant. On the way through the lobby, Shane had another thought. "Barbara, do you know Ray's cell phone number?"

"No. It was strictly a business phone. He told me never to use it, but I think he had it written down somewhere. Why?"

"When we get there, see if you can find it."

"Okay." She got into her red Ford Mustang convertible. The parking attendant stared openly as she pulled away, her blond hair streaming in the wind. Invisible in her wake, Shane got into his Acura and followed.

When they got to Barbara's house on Shell Avenue, the front door was ajar. Shane pulled up to the curb as Barbara pulled into her driveway. They both got out of their cars and looked at the half-open door with concern. Shane pulled his gun and handed Barbara his cell phone.

"Call nine-one-one if I'm not out in two minutes," he said. Then he moved up the steps and onto the front porch. He could see that the front-door lock had been drilled. Part of the tumbler mechanism was lying on the porch at his feet. With his toe, he edged the door open, staying to one side, out of sight. Then, when he had determined it was clear, he slipped into the house.

He could hear drawers being opened and closed in the back. He moved silently in that direction, finally looking into the bedroom where, seemingly a lifetime ago, he had killed Ray Molar.

There were two uniformed police officers

going through dressers and closets. Shane decided to retreat. He didn't want to be caught in this house with Barbara standing outside. As he took a step back, the floor squeaked; both policemen spun and saw him standing there, gun in hand.

"What the fuck're you doing going through Ray's house?" Shane snarled, switching to offense and glaring at the two officers.

They were both first-year patrolmen. One of them he recognized as John Samansky, Ray's last probation partner. He was almost too short to be a cop, probably barely reaching the LAPD five-seven male height requirement. He had made up for his short stature by lifting weights. His wide trapezius muscles were straining his uniform shirt collar. The other police officer Shane had never seen before. He was also young but prematurely balding, with a narrow, pockmarked face. His nameplate read L. AYERS.

"Whatta you doing here, Scully?" Samansky asked. He had the blown voice of a pack-a-day saloon singer or a throat-punched club fighter.

"You got a warrant?" Shane asked, ignoring the question.

"Show him, Lee," Samansky said. Patrolman Ayers pulled a folded slip of paper out of his pocket and waved it under Shane's nose. "Not that you got any rights in this house, least not that we know about."

Shane ignored the comment, turned, and moved out of the bedroom, back to the front door. He waved to Barbara, who closed the cell phone and walked into her house. He didn't need more cops added to this party.

"Give her the warrant," Shane demanded as she entered the living room.

Lee Ayers handed it to Barbara.

"Why?" she asked. "Why are you searching my house?"

"That's none of your business, ma'am," Samansky said, his sandpaper voice gruff and irritating.

"You two are patrol officers," Shane said. "Long as I've been on the job, it's always detectives who administer warrants and paw through the dressers. Shouldn't you guys be parked on a corner somewhere, writing greenies?"

"You're the asshole who's headed for Traffic Division," Ayers said with a smirk. " 'Sides, we got this squeal direct from the top of the Glass House. You got a problem with that, take it up with the warrant control officer at Parker Center."

Shane took the warrant out of Barbara's hands and looked at it. It had been signed by Judge Jos;aae Hernandez, known by police and trial attorneys around the municipal courthouse as "Papier-M;afach;aae Jos;aae" because he was willing to hang all the paper the cops wanted: subpoenas, arrest warrants, wiretaps. If they wrote it up, Hernandez signed it. Defendants had their own moniker: "The Time Machine," because the judge was infamous for passing out maximum sentences. He was a Mayor Crispin ally.

Shane handed the warrant back to Barbara. "You guys about through?" he asked.

"Yeah, we did the whole place," Ayers said. "You need to vacuum behind the furniture, lady. You got a fuckin' butterfly collection back there."

The two cops moved out the side door. Samansky had Barbara's garage-door clicker, and he opened her garage, exposing their black-and-white. They had parked it there to avoid calling attention to their presence.

While Lee Ayers got into the patrol car and backed it out of the garage, Samansky turned to Barbara. "You should be ashamed of yourself. Scully is the guy who shot your husband."

"That's none of your business," she said weakly.

" 'Cept it is my business. Ray was my friend, my partner. He was special. A guy like Ray comes along once in a lifetime. You had the best, lady. I'm fuckin' dyin' here…can't even believe he's really gone. You're his wife, and you're walking around with the shitwrap who dropped him. You should be ashamed." Then he turned, moved to the squad car, and got in. He glowered at them from the passenger seat. "I wonder what Robbery/Homicide's gonna say about you two bein' together. Wonder how that's gonna play downtown." Samansky cleared his raspy throat, hawked up a spitball, and shot it in their direction. It landed two feet from the step they were on. Then he threw the garage-door opener at Shane, who snatched it out of the air.

They backed out of the driveway, around Barbara's Mustang convertible, and onto the grass. The squad car bounced over the curb, banging hard into Shane's black Acura, caving in the front fender with its pipe bumper, knocking Shane's car away from the curb. Then Lee Ayers cranked the patrol car's wheels and sped off up the street.

"It just keeps getting better," Shane said softly. "I can hardly wait till the tin collectors find out you and I were spending time together."

They turned and walked back into the house. Shane stood in the living room. It was probably a waste of time, but he decided to make his own search anyway. He checked the living-room furniture first. The carpet indentations were exposed, proving that the two cops had moved the sofa as promised. He pulled off some of the seat cushions and saw that they had all been stabbed with a kitchen knife that had been left on the floor under the sofa. That meant they had been looking for something that was small enough to be hidden inside a seat cushion. Something about the size of a videotape, he thought.

As he moved through the house, it was obvious that Samansky and Ayers had done a thorough job. It was also obvious that whatever was missing was still missing. The whole house had been searched. If they had found what they were looking for, they would have stopped when they recovered it.

Shane kept looking anyway, but he was getting dispirited. He ended up in the bedroom closet. He carefully went through the top shelf. Nothing. He checked the shoeboxes. Nothing. As he was getting set to close the closet doors, something caught his eye. He looked again and saw that there were half a dozen white shirts in plastic cleaner bags. What stopped him was that several of the shirts were on white hangers with printed plastic that read BAYSIDE CLEANERS, while two others were on plain hangers with light green cellophane over them. He took all the shirts off the rod and held them up.

"What is it?" Barbara asked.

"I don't know. Why do you use two different dry cleaners?"

"I don't. I just use Bayside, here in Venice."

Shane held up the Bayside Cleaners shirts. The covers indicated that Bayside was located at 201 South Venice Boulevard. He put them on the bed, then examined the other shirts with the plain hangers and greenish cellophane covers. There was no printing to indicate the name and address of this second cleaner. He pulled the laundry tag off one of the Bayside shirt collars. It was a small yellow strip with a number and bar code. Then he found the laundry strip for the unknown cleaner: a purple square stapled through the bottom buttonhole.

"You say Ray was away a lot. Maybe he had these cleaned somewhere else." Shane took the shirts with the purple square strips and folded them over his arm. "We have a database for laundry tags. Sometimes, when we get a John

Doe with no ID, the laundry mark helps us identify the body. I'll drop this at the Scientific Investigations Section and see what they come up with. I better get out of here. Did you find that cell phone number?" he asked.

She snapped her fingers. "Forgot," she said, and went digging around in one of Ray's drawers. She found the box the phone had come in. Inside, with the warranty and sales slip, Ray had written the number. She handed it to Shane.

"Same number as on the AT&T printout," he said, holding up both sheets of paper. "Whoever she is, she was using Ray's cell phone."

"So we can't trace it."

"Guess not."

Shane moved toward the front door but stopped in the entry as Barbara put a hand on his arm. She looked at him softly with her beautiful blue-green eyes.

"Can we see each other?"

"Barbara...that's gonna get us nothing but grief."

"Tell me you don't want to see me. Just say it, and I won't bring it up again."

"I can't say it, 'cause I do. It's just..."

"If we're careful?" she said. "I feel so lonely, so frightened."

Why is this happening this way? he wondered. Finally he put a hand up to her face and held it there for a moment. "I'll think about it. I guess if those two cops notify RHD, the damage is already done," he heard himself say

101

stupidly. Of course, he knew he could probably explain away one incident. He could say he'd come over to apologize or pay his respects. All he needed was to start seriously fooling around with Ray's widow in the wake of this shooting. A first-degree murder charge would probably be his reward for that behavior. *How could he even consider seeing her again?* His heart was beating fast, slamming in his chest like a broken cam shaft, his breath coming in rasping gasps. Loneliness swelled. He looked at her and wondered again how this had gotten so fucked up.

"Buy a cell phone," he said impulsively, "a new one. Leave the number on my home machine. You have mine. Since these cells aren't secure, don't use my name if you call me."

"Okay," she said. Then she reached up to kiss him, and he found his lips brushing against hers. He started to put an arm around her but then pulled away and quickly left her house without looking back.

Samansky was right. They should be ashamed, but a hard-on was stuffed sideways in his Jockey shorts. He reached down and adjusted it. Another work of art, *The Pagan Love God*; hang it with the others. The Shane Scully Gallery was filling fast.

He got to his car and knelt down to survey the bashed front fender. It was hard to tell whether he or his poor black Acura had been taking more hits recently. He reached over and tugged the fender slightly off the new radial front tire. Then he got behind the wheel, and with the front fender rubbing badly, he turned the car around and drove back to his house on the East Canal in Venice.

Two hours after he got home, another uniformed patrolman showed up. He hand-delivered the PERSONAL AND CONFIDENTIAL envelope Shane had been dreading. Inside was an LAPD Letter of Transmittal.

THE
LETTER OF
TRANSMITTAL

POLICE DEPARTMENT

LETTER OF TRANSMITTAL
APRIL 21, 2000

ADJUDICATION
Complaint filed by Robbery/Homicide and IAD. Place of Complaint: 2387 Shell Avenue, Venice, CA. Complaint Investigation CF no. 20-4567-56. This complaint form contains allegations of misconduct against Department employee:

SERGEANT I. SHANE SCULLY
Serial No. 8934867

SOUTHWEST DIVISION
RHD

Allegations are listed below with recommendations for classification and supporting rationales.

ALLEGATION ONE:
That on April 16, at approximately 2:30 A.M., Sergeant Scully inappropriately involved himself in an incident of domestic violence.

ALLEGATION TWO:
Sergeant Scully drove to the house of his ex-partner, Lieutenant Raymond Molar. He did not use his police radio to call uniformed police, instead electing to inject himself into a potentially dangerous incident where uniformed personnel would have been in a better position to contain the situation.

ALLEGATION THREE:
Sergeant Scully arrived on the scene and used inappropriate and out-of-policy escalating force. (Force may not be resorted to unless other reasonable alternatives have been thoroughly exhausted.)

ALLEGATION FOUR:
After engaging in an inappropriate escalation of force, Sergeant Scully fired his police weapon, which resulted in the death of Lieutenant Raymond Molar.

ALLEGATION FIVE:
Sergeant Scully removed from the Molar residence certain related case items that he believed would reflect badly on him in the subsequent investigation. (Note: The confidential nature of these materials prohibits notification and description of same in this letter of transmittal, but such notification will be made available to the accused upon discovery.)

CLASSIFICATION
It is recommended that all allegations be classified as *sustained*.

RATIONALE
It has been determined by investigating officers that Sergeant Scully had a prior relationship with the wife of the deceased. As a result, Sergeant Scully should have known that his involvement in this domestic dispute would not produce a favorable outcome. His reckless attempt to intervene in a family dispute where he had an emotional history, and his refusal to call for uniformed assistance, produced a situation that resulted in an undue escalation of force and the death of Lieutenant Molar. Further at issue is Sergeant Scully's prior relationships with both the deceased, Lieutenent Molar (ex-partner), and Molar's wife (former girlfriend). This throws doubt on his use of force and gives rise to questions of personal motive. It is also noted that on February 12, 1984, then-Patrolman Scully was involved in a physical altercation with the deceased in the underground parking structure at Southwest Division. This altercation resulted in the breakup of their partnership and Scully's transfer to West Valley Division.

COMPLAINT HISTORY ANALYSIS
Sergeant Scully's use-of-force history has been examined, and it has been determined that this officer has had six complaint investigations in ten years (none sustained). How-

ever, he has received one departmental admonishment due to a nonsustained Board of Rights involving the severe beating of a nineteen-year-old Hispanic gang member in Southwest Division. (It was determined by the board that some eyewitness accounts of the beating were perjurious, and this perjury resulted in the subsequent not-guilty verdict. However, in the estimation of Sergeant Scully's commander, some undue force had taken place.) In reviewing his complaint history, it has been decided that this officer has shown a pattern of failure to exercise good judgment. Additionally, he has received admonishments for two separate (preventable) traffic accidents. There are no negative-comment-card entries from his current commanding officer.

RELIEF FROM DUTY CONSIDERATION
It is recommended that this officer be relieved from his duty in Southwest Robbery/Homicide and that he be suspended without pay until further notice. Note: The complaint copy and Relief from Duty Suspension Form (1.61) issued by Internal Affairs Division and signed by Deputy Chief II Thomas Mayweather is being faxed to Sergeant Scully's CO, Captain Bud Halley, in accordance with departmental regulations. Upon receipt of same, Sergeant Scully shall surrender his gun, badge, and identification card to Captain Halley for safekeeping.

The chief of police has directed this case to a full Board of Rights, said board to commence ten days from the date of this letter.

COMMANDING OFFICER'S RESPONSE
None.

> Respectfully submitted,
> Alexa Hamilton
> Internal Affairs Division

10
PANEL

A LETTER OF TRANSMITTAL is always delivered to an accused officer and is, in essence, a summons and complaint. It gives the preliminary results of the IAD investigation and the determination by the department of the appropriate form of adjudication.

Shane had received the letter just before going out the door to pick up Chooch from school. He ripped open the brown envelope with trembling fingers. He had figured it would be bad, but this was even worse than he had expected. He shook with rage as he read the allegations. Then he stuffed the document into his side pocket and headed out the back door. *Fuck 'em,* he thought, *I'm not gonna plead this out. I'm gonna fight it.*

He pried the crushed front fender farther away from the tire, using the Acura's tire jack. Then as he took the 405 over the hill to Coldwater, he turned on his cell phone to call his new defense rep, Rags Whitman. He had talked with him once yesterday, but Rags was in the middle of defending another BOR, so they had agreed to meet at six that evening.

He punched the number into his cell phone.

Rags Whitman was on a break outside hearing room three when he answered the phone. Internal Affairs had rented the top three floors of the Bradbury Building in downtown L.A. It was a beautiful turn-of-the-century structure with a glassed-in courtyard and black wrought-iron banisters. Because Parker Center had become so overcrowded, the entire Advocate Section of IAD, as well as its four main hearing rooms, had been moved to this architectural treasure at the corner of Broadway and Third.

"Yeah," Rags answered in his surprising soprano voice.

"It's Shane. I just got the Letter of Transmittal."

"Bad?" Rags asked.

"They suspended me without pay. They're alleging I shot Ray because I used to date Barbara. It's total bullshit!"

"You'll probably do much better with

DeMarco, if that's the way they're going. He fights gladiator-style."

"DeMarco won't take the case."

"He changed his mind. Your machine was turned off. He's been trying to reach you all afternoon. He didn't have your mobile number, so I gave it to him. The way this is going, you better start leaving your cell phone on."

"Oh," Shane said. He'd turned his answering machine and cell phone off because he was afraid that Barbara would call. He'd been having second thoughts about seeing her and wanted to put some distance between them for the time being. "You got his number handy? I don't have it with me."

Rags Whitman gave it to him, and Shane dialed.

"Go," DeMarco said when he answered. Shane could hear a mellower brand of rap being played in the room behind the conversation. This time he thought it was L. L. Cool J.

"It's Shane."

"Where've you been? I changed my mind. I gotta get one more swing at that bitch advocate Alexa Hamilton. I've been trying to reach you all day."

"I had my cell off by mistake. I'm glad you reconsidered. I got this fucking Letter of Transmittal. It's a complete load a' shit. They're fuckin' me over, Dee."

"Meet me at the beach as soon as you can."

"I've gotta go pick up a friend's kid at school. I promised his mother. Okay if I bring him?"

113

"Sure, I'll meet you at the Silver Surfer. It's a bar-restaurant on the Strand, about six doors up from my place. How 'bout an hour?"

"How 'bout an hour and a half?"

"See ya then."

"Hey, Dee…thanks. I feel better with you on this. I wanna go to war. I don't wanna plead out this bullshit. I wanna fight it."

"We'll talk in an hour."

When he arrived at Harvard Westlake, Brad Thackery was waiting for him. Thackery followed Chooch to the car and immediately came around to the driver's side.

"We still haven't heard from Chooch's mother," he said angrily, shoving his thin, pinched features and wiry hair down into Shane's face.

Chooch got in the passenger side and pretended to pay no attention, looking out the side window at the football field.

"Whatta you want me to do about it?" Shane said sharply.

"I want you to have Mrs. Sandoval get in touch with my office."

"I told her to call you two days ago."

"Obviously, neither you nor she have any idea of the seriousness of Chooch's situation. This is about his future here at Harvard Westlake."

"I told Sandy. I can't do more than that."

"*Facta non verba*," Thackery said with a smirk, then added, "Actions speak louder than words."

"*Gobbelus feces*," Shane replied, and after a

114

second to figure it out, Chooch burst into laughter.

Shane put the car in gear and pulled out onto Coldwater. He was smoking mad. Of course, he knew it wasn't Thackery, it was his whole damn life that was pissing him off.

"*Gobbelus feces*. Eat shit—pretty fuckin' good," Chooch crowed.

"Calm down, will ya...it wasn't that funny."

Chooch looked at him carefully, then turned off his headset and put the rig back into his book bag.

"Don't worry about Thackery, okay? It doesn't matter that Sandy didn't call. They're gonna throw me out anyway. It's a done deal. I'm not even in regular classes anymore. I'm in detention. They don't care if I do my homework or not. They're just sitting on me till they can tell her I'm dust."

"Shit," Shane said. "Good goin'."

"I don't care, so don't sweat it."

"Yeah, that's right, I forgot. I'm just this month's paid jerkoff."

"That was before. You're not a paid jerkoff anymore. You've been promoted."

"To what?" Shane was barely paying attention. His mind was spinning, a kaleidoscope of horrible, career-ending problems.

"You're my doobie brother," Chooch said with a grin, "my ganja gangtsa and Rasta weed warrior."

"Listen, Chooch, you gotta forget about that. Okay? I'm having a rough time right now, I'm not thinking straight. That was a huge mistake."

"Shit, it was the first thing you did that I liked. Showed me some stones, man. No other cop I know would sit around with some kid and bogart a fatty."

"Chooch, if you tell anybody about that, I'm gonna kill ya."

"No sweat. I can keep a secret." He smiled, then put his headphones on again and cranked up the tunes. He stayed plugged in until Shane made the turn onto the Santa Monica Freeway. It was the wrong way home, so Chooch took off his headset and looked over. "Where we going?"

"I gotta go to a meeting down at the beach. It should only take an hour, maybe less. You can hang for a while, okay?"

Chooch cocked an eyebrow. "Something's going on, right? You're in the soup, just like me, aren't ya?" he said with surprising intuition.

"It's okay. I can handle it."

They shot off the end of the freeway, back onto the Coast Highway. Five minutes later Chooch and Shane were walking through the front door of an almost empty bar-restaurant with a sawdust floor and a neon sign that read SILVER SURFER.

It was 4:15 in the afternoon.

They found DeMarco seated at the bar. He was wearing cutoffs and a blue-jean vest with no shirt, working on his third beer. The other two empty brown glass longnecks were lined up on the bar beside him.

When Shane introduced DeMarco to Chooch, the teenager looked at the long-haired defense rep and smiled. "Cool fuckin' earring, dude."

"I like your friend, Scully. You're finally kicking." The defense rep smiled at Shane.

"Is it okay for him to be in here?" Shane asked, referring to the fact that they were in a bar that served hard liquor.

"Yeah, he can go play the video games over there. Technically, that's not in the bar area."

Shane dug into his pockets and gave Chooch some change. The boy moved over to a small alcove in sight of the bar, sat on a stool, and began feeding coins into one of the machines.

Shane slid the Letter of Transmittal over to DeMarco, who read it carefully, then set it on the bar between them. "Mark, gimme another Lone Star," he yelled. "How 'bout you?" he asked Shane.

"Slow down on the brewskies, will ya? I'm on fire here."

"Then you're in luck. With this bladder, I can piss it out for you," DeMarco quipped. "In your telephonic absence, I went ahead and covered some pro forma ground. Tell ya this much, Alexa Hamilton doesn't let much grass grow under her magnificent gym-trained ass. She already got the rotation list for your judging panel and faxed it to me. Seven names: four sworn members of the department above the rank of captain and three civilians. If you remember how it works from before, you get to throw off two of the cops and two of the civilians, leaving you a panel of three judges: two sworn, one civilian." He reached into his blue-jean vest pocket and pulled out two slips of paper. "This ain't much of a beauty contest," he said, sliding both slips over to Shane. "In my opinion, all of these department guys are douche bags. Tell me who you like. I hate the whole bunch." DeMarco read the names aloud while Shane studied the list. "Captain Donovan McNeil, West Division; Commander Mitchell Van Sickle, Ad Vice; Deputy Chief Laurence Gadsworth—he's the chief's administrative staff officer, so forget him; and Captain Bernard Cookson."

"Jesus," Shane said, "except for Donovan McNeil, who I used to go fishing with occasionally, aren't these guys all in Chief Brewer's golf foursome?"

"Yep. But it gets worse. Look't the civilians: all lawyers from South Temple Street; one's a retired judge, a Crispin crony, of course. I checked the others—all work at the municipal courthouse and all have strong political ties to Mayor Crispin. This guy here, Knox Pooly, actually chaired his committee to reelect."

"What's going on here, Dee? This isn't right."

"No shit. You're getting screwed without the Vaseline. If Donovan's an old friend, I'm surprised he made this list of suckfish."

"He figures. A year ago he was the chief's community affairs officer. They probably picked him not knowing he was a friend of mine."

"Okay, so we keep him on the list and hope that he'll at least have divided loyalties. Who else?"

"Not Deputy Chief Gadsworth, of course. I'll take Commander Van Sickle." Shane looked at the list of three civilians and cocked an eyebrow at DeMarco for help.

"Beats me," DeMarco said. "Throw 'em out alphabetically or just drop 'em over your shoulder and the one closest to the door stays. Good a way as any."

"I'll take Clifford Finch. At least he's a defense attorney."

"Okay, then your panel is Captain Donovan McNeil, Commander Van Sickle—he'll be the chairman, based on rank—and Cliff Finch. Good fuckin' luck. This bunch would convict Santa Claus of home invasion, but I'll notify Alexa that these are our choices."

Shane sat and brooded as DeMarco was served his fourth beer, then started to gulp it down. "Go easy, will ya?" Shane murmured.

"When I'm being fucked, it feels better if I get a little loaded first," DeMarco said dourly. He picked up the Letter of Transmittal and reread the Rationale Section. "Two things here; let's take 'em in order. One: they think you took something from Ray's home."

"It's bullshit. I don't know anything about it."

"You wouldn't hold back on me again, would you, Shane? You did last time."

119

"I don't know what they're talking about."

"Okay, so what's with this old fistfight in the garage at Southwest Division?"

"Nothin', just frayed nerves. It was way back in '84, for God's sake. You and I were just going through the BOR. I was uptight. I boiled over, that's all."

"Shane, you gotta tell me the truth, the whole truth, and nothing but the truth; otherwise, we're gonna get blackjacked at that board. I'm gonna ask you again. What the fuck was going on between you and Ray and Barbara? Why did you get into that fight?"

"We never talked about it, but you knew who really beat that Hispanic kid half to death."

"My guess—it was Ray."

"Right."

"So, not that it matters all these years later, but why don't you do me a favor and finally spit it out. Tell me what happened."

"I was in a gas station, taking a leak. I came back to where our patrol car was parked, and Ray was beating this kid with his baton. I broke it up. If I hadn't stopped it, Ray would have killed him. Then, after the complaint got filed by the boy's family, Ray begged me to take the blame. The kid's head injuries had him blank on the incident. He couldn't remember who hit him. Since I was just a probationer and had no complaints on my record, Ray convinced me I would probably get only a few weeks' suspension. He said he'd make up my lost pay out of his own pocket. I was his partner—real young, impressionable. Back then I was just like some of these rookies today. I thought he was the best cop on the streets of L.A. He had a way of getting to you, making you believe in him. And he was brave. More than once he risked his life for a brother officer. His two Medals of Valor were not bullshit. So I said okay. I took the complaint for him. But later, while you and I were going through the hearing, I started having nightmares. In those dreams, Molar and I would both be beating that kid. We'd be taking turns. I'd wake up sweating, hating myself. I was under a lot of stress back then, and I guess it was the beginning of my seeing Ray for what he really was—a vicious, violent son of a bitch who wasn't a cop so he could protect and serve. He was a cop so he could kick ass and hold court in the street....

"It boiled over that night in Southwest. Barbara had just broken up with me. I was under investigation at IAD, and I just snapped. I yelled at him. He went into the coffee room, got a pitcher of ice water out of the refrigerator, told me to cool off, and threw it on me. I pushed him; he fell; we ended up in the parking garage. It wasn't much of a fight."

"You were way out of your weight division," DeMarco said softly. "He had almost a hundred pounds on you."

"That's the whole story."

Again, DeMarco swigged on the beer. He put the bottle down and began making Olympic rings on the varnished bartop, stamping them out with the bottle's wet bottom. Finally he wiped his artwork away with his palm. " 'Nother longneck, Mark," he shouted.

"Listen, Dee... I hate seein'—"

"Give it a rest. Okay?" DeMarco said sharply. "Don't tell me how to lead my life. While you were running around with your cell phone turned off, I've been working this thing. I'm not through filling you in yet, so shut the fuck up." Shane nodded. "This morning I wrote up a standard petition to overturn the 1.61 and requested your return to duty. It's kinda pro forma when a police officer has been suspended without pay, like an automatic appeal, only I've never seen one get approved before. Guess what? You're the exception." He reached into his back pocket and shoved a fax over to Shane. "Signed by the Big Noise himself." Shane looked at the document. It was as DeMarco said, signed by Chief Burleigh Brewer. "The whole shebang, from application to acceptance, took two hours. Now go figure that."

"I can't," Shane said, staring at the fax in disbelief. The document put him right back on duty with full pay. It didn't make sense in the face of everything else.

"I called Bud Halley and asked him about it. He told me Tom Mayweather walked it through the system personally. However, Halley also told me where they've reassigned you. You're not in Southwest Detectives anymore."

"Where am I?"

"You ain't gonna believe it...."

"Oh, shit. What is it this time, the grain and drain train at the city jail?"

"You've been assigned to the chief advocate's office at Internal Affairs."

"I've been what?!" he said, his voice so loud that Chooch momentarily turned away from the video game he was playing and looked in their direction.

"You report to the tin collectors at the Bradbury Building at eight-thirty A.M. tomorrow."

"That's nuts. I've never heard of an officer awaiting a Board of Rights being assigned to the very division that's trying to terminate him."

"Me neither. But after thinking it over..."

"They want to keep me where they can watch me," Shane said.

"A winnah. Give the man something from the top shelf. You is da new Dark Side kick-me. I guess Chief Brewer doesn't want you running around looking for whatever it is they think you took out of Ray's house. They want you on a tight leash."

The bartender brought DeMarco his new beer. He took three long swallows, then set it down with the others. "All in all, not a good start, Shane, but rigged boards are my specialty. These tin-collecting assholes can be had 'cause they all got target fixation. Just go down there and keep your nose clean. Let me do the grunting and groaning."

As he sat on the barstool, looking at the old defense rep, his heart sank, taking his hopes down with it. He had no choice. He had to go down to Internal Affairs. He'd been ordered, and failure to comply with a direct order was also a termination offense. The only bright spot was that he was still on the payroll. He'd still collect his bimonthly base salary of $2,170.20, plus his ten-year longevity compensation of $60. In return, he'd be working down at IAD, forced to endure the biggest collection of milk-fed assholes on the planet. As he sat there, he decided that he would devote all of his nonworking hours to finding out what was missing from Ray's house.

"Yes! Kick ass!" Chooch yelled suddenly as his game buzzed victory and he was advanced to the next level.

"Don't worry, Shane. I'll unwind this for you. I'll get you off," DeMarco said, causing Shane to look back at him.

"*Factus non verba,*" Scully said darkly.

THE PEOPLE RULE

A S SOON AS Shane got home, he called Sandy. She said she was sorry she hadn't gotten in touch with Thackery, but promised she would. She said she'd had a tough two days.

"What'm I supposed to do with Chooch

tomorrow?" Shane asked. "They've got him sitting in detention all day. He's not even going to classes."

"That guy Thackery is a complete ass," Sandy said. "He's on Chooch for smoking dope? What a hypocrite."

"Not smoking it, Sandy, selling it."

"I was there at the school two months ago when Chooch enrolled. Thackery was just driving out. He put down the window of his crummy, rusted-out van to talk to me, and the smell of old pot was so strong in that thing, I got a contact high."

"Sandy, lots of people smoke pot, okay? It's a sad social truth, but there it is. It doesn't matter what Thackery does in his off-hours. You've gotta call him and set up an appointment."

"Right. Okay, I promise, sugar."

"You promised yesterday."

"This time I pledge it. I *swear* it, okay?" She changed gears. "You go ahead and take him to school tomorrow. Forget Thackery. I'll have already called that snooty headmaster, Mr. St. John. I'll square him away. That guy is always leering at me. Wants to get in my pants."

"You always put things so delicately," Shane said, beginning to wish he'd never met the beautiful raven-haired informant.

"Don't be such a prude. When I get through with St. John, he'll be at Camp Fantasy, pitching a tent in his Jockey shorts. Don't worry about Chooch."

After she hung up, Shane went outside. Chooch was already out there in one of the metal chairs. Shane dropped his tired ass in the vacant seat beside him. They looked out at the still canal, both lost in separate thoughts. Finally Shane jerked his mind off his department problems and focused on the boy sitting sullenly beside him.

"If your mom and I could keep you in school," Shane started slowly, "would you go there and really give it a try?"

"Moot point, 'cause you can't. I already got the scarlet *E* for 'expel.' I'm gone, brother."

"Chooch, I've been thinking about it. You're really smart. You've got a great head on your shoulders. You could be something important in life. You have it in you to be anything you want."

"Like a cop?" he smirked.

"Better than a cop. You could go to college, pick any career. Your mom has money; she'll pay for anything. That's a big advantage for you. It's a chance most guys never get."

They sat in silence, looking at the still canal water, both of them rocking slowly in the old metal chairs.

"I know you're trying to help, man," Chooch finally said, "but it ain't about having a career. Y'know...it's just not what it's about. It goes much deeper than that."

More silence, then Shane turned in his chair to look at the teenager. "Wanna know something?" Chooch didn't answer. "I believe in you, Chooch," he went on softly. "I know that whatever you want, you've got the ability to get it. You've got what it takes. I think you're special."

"That's bullshit," Chooch shot back.

"No, it's not. I've been watching you...how you handle stuff. You've got guts. You stand up. You walk your own trail. That's very rare. It takes strength of character. Most people can't do that." More silence. "Listen. I told you I wouldn't lie to you—not ever. So this is the straight stuff. It's what I see in you, and it's impressive."

Chooch turned his face away from Shane. His breathing had changed. His right hand darted up and brushed his cheek under his eyes. Then he stood up, and anger flared. "Don't fuck around with me. Okay? I can't take any more bullshit. Just leave me alone." He moved quickly into the house.

Shane sat in his garden until the setting sun began turning the still canal bright yellow, then orange and purple, and finally black. After the sun surrendered its hold on the day, a cold evening wind came off the ocean, blowing marine air across the coastline. Shane was getting a chill, so he got out of his chair and walked back inside the house.

"It's fucking forty minutes too early!" Chooch glowered as Shane pulled up in front of the Harvard Westlake School the next morning. There were no waiting lines of foreign cars as Chooch opened the door and dragged his book bag from the front seat.

"I've got a new duty assignment downtown, so I need to get there early. Live with it," Shane said.

"Sure, no problem. Live with it. That's my fuckin' motto anyway." Chooch angrily moved away from the car and sat alone on a bench near the athletic pavilion.

Shane pulled out of the driveway and drove two miles to the Valley Division HQ. He figured if he hurried, he'd be able to get everything done before eight-thirty.

Fifteen minutes later Shane was back in the Harvard Westlake faculty parking lot waiting for Brad Thackery. After ten more minutes the assistant dean of admissions pulled his rusting Ford van into his parking stall and got out. Shane moved to him. "Good morning, sir," he said pleasantly.

"Maybe for you, but it's not a good morning for Chooch. I saw him sitting out front when I drove past. Since I still haven't heard from Mrs. Sandoval, you can just go right back around and pick him up and depart the premises, *ad quam primum*. He is no longer welcome at this school," Thackery said harshly, then added brusquely, "and remove your vehicle from faculty parking. This is a restricted area."

"How do you say that in Latin?"

"I'm through talking to you, whoever you are. Good-bye."

Shane pulled out his badge and held it up for Brad Thackery to read. Thackery looked at it, surprised, readjusted slightly, then with less anger said, "Big deal."

"You're right, it is a big deal, 'specially since your van there is crawling with vehicular irregularities. You wanna put that blinker on? Seems to me it wasn't working when you turned in here."

"I'm about to get it fixed."

" 'About to' doesn't cut it," Shane said. "Put it on, please. I want to check it out."

Thackery glared at Shane. "This is what really gets you guys off, isn't it?"

"Yep. Can't get enough of it."

As Brad Thackery opened the van, Shane moved to his Acura and opened the back door. A black Labrador jumped out and, with his tongue lolling, followed Shane back to the van. Thackery was leaning into the front seat, fiddling with the blinker and trying to get it to work, when the dog started barking and pacing back and forth along the side of Thackery's van.

"Whoa...whoa...whatta we got here?" Shane said with mock surprise. Thackery jerked his head out of the van.

"Get that dog away from me."

"This isn't a dog, Mr. Thackery, this is a drug enforcement officer. His name is Krupkee. It looks like Officer Krupkee's got a noseful. Where is it, boy? What ya got?"

The black Lab had moved to the rear of the van and now had both paws up on the spare tire, which was hooked by a locked bracket to the back of the van. Then the black Lab started barking and pawing at the tire.

"Oh boy, this ain't good, Mr. Thackery. You

wanna give me the key that releases that back tire?"

"No. No, I don't."

"Lemme put it another way, sir. Gimme the key, or I'll pry the fucking thing off with my tire jack. Officer Krupkee just gave me probable cause for a search."

After a long moment, Thackery reluctantly dug into his pocket and produced the key that unlocked the tire bracket. Shane swung it away from the van and looked into the tire. There, attached by magnets to the inside of the tire drum, was a small metal box. Shane pulled it off and opened it. There were about four ounces of grass in a canvas bag and a bottle with a few pills. Shane opened the bag and poured some low-grade pot into his palm.

"This is not good, Mr. Thackery. As a matter of fact, you're under arrest, *regnat populus*." He poured the dope back into the bag. "So you won't get the wrong idea about me and think I'm some overeducated, Latin-quoting blowhard, that's just the state motto of Arkansas. I was stationed there in the Marines. It means 'the people rule,' and the people of Los Angeles don't like this one bit and are about to rule that you go to the city lockup." Shane pulled out his handcuffs, spun Thackery around, and put them on.

"You can't do this," Thackery protested.

"Somebody should tell that to my watch commander. In the meantime, you're gonna sit this one out downtown. Don't worry, I'll call the principal for you and tell him his

130

assistant dean of admissions is gonna be at County Jail riding the pine in the detox box."

"Is this about Chooch? Is that what this is all about?" Thackery's eyes were darting around, hoping no other member of the faculty would come driving in and witness this debacle.

"You bet it's about Chooch. But it's also about you, Brad. If you weren't such an insufferable asshole, I probably wouldn't have gone so far out of my way to knock your dick in the dirt."

"Look, Chooch has problems. Okay? He's got deep emotional difficulties. Besides, he's selling drugs."

"Bet he didn't sell you this crummy bag a' bird food," Shane said, holding up the bag of thin, seed-ridden grass.

"You think this is funny, is that it?"

"It's about as funny as prostate surgery. How do guys like you end up teaching school?"

"What do you want?"

"I want you to cut Chooch some slack. I want you to go to bat for him."

"I can't change the course of events. It's too late. They've already had a faculty meeting about him."

"I'd think the assistant dean of admissions would have a little pull around here," Shane said. "Of course, after this bust, you'll be lucky to be in charge of school bus schedules."

"Look, okay...maybe..."

"Maybe what?"

"If I...if I said to them I'd work with him separately, maybe do some drug counseling or something..."

"I don't think you're exactly the right guy for that, but go ahead, keep talkin'."

"Maybe if I really try, I could get him another chance. Just one..."

"Okay, that sounds more promising. You give him another chance, I give you another chance."

Just then, two other faculty cars pulled into the parking area and slowed as they passed Thackery's van. He was standing there with his hands cuffed behind him. A woman put down her window.

"Is everything okay, Brad?" she asked, looking at the handcuffs.

"We're fine." Shane said. "I'm the magician Mr. Thackery hired for next month's high-school assembly. Just showing Brad here how I do my handcuff escape." Shane smiled and she drove on, not looking too convinced.

"I want immediate results, Thackery. I'm looking for Chooch to get outta that detention hall this morning and back into regular class. If he gets goofy about anything in the future, don't bust him. Call me."

Shane shoved his business card into Thackery's shirt pocket and then unhooked the cuffs. He put the dope and pills in his jacket pocket, gave Brad Thackery back his car keys, then he led Officer Krupkee over to the Acura.

The Lab jumped into the backseat, Shane put the car in gear, pulled out of the faculty parking area, then drove back to Valley Division and returned the dog to the Valley Bureau Drug Enforcement Unit. He shot back onto the freeway and got to Internal Affairs downtown with ten minutes to spare.

12
THE DARK SIDE

THE BRADBURY BUILDING never failed to amaze Shane. He felt that it was the most magnificent building in Los Angeles. Only five stories high, it had been designed in the late 1800s by Gregory Wyman, a draftsman with no architectural degree. It sat bravely on the corner of Broadway and Third while slovenly men leaned forward to piss against her or curled up to sleep, rubbing the grime from their clothes on her magnificent yellow bricks.

Shane pulled into the modern concrete parking structure that had been built next door, took the ticket, then found a spot on the second tier. He rode the elevator down and came out onto a brick patio with umbrella tables that served as a lunch area. It was located directly behind the old building. Along the concrete wall adjoining the patio was the historic fresco depicting the life of an African-American woman named Biddy Mason. The wall chronicled her odyssey, from her birth as a slave in 1810, through her incredible life journey, all the way to her final heroic years of service as a nurse delivering babies in Los Angeles hospitals in 1870.

The fresco had been placed there to show the early African-American commitment to the quality of life in L.A. Shane found it strange that in post—Rodney King L.A., this monument was behind the Internal Affairs building, in a patio where mostly cops accused of misconduct would ever see it.

He pushed through the back doors of the Bradbury, through a section under reconstruction on the first floor, into the building's magnificent covered courtyard. He looked up at the five floors stacked above him. Light brick contrasted with the intricate black wrought-iron railings. They wrapped around the interior hallways that surrounded the open atrium. Polished oak banisters snaked along the top of the ornate black-painted iron. On each side of the building's courtyard were beautiful, antique turn-of-the-century open elevators. They ran on exposed counterbalances that carried the filigreed boxes up and down. They moved slowly, stopping carefully at each floor as if time had not sped up in modern L.A. or had not fallen into desperate conflict with elegance. Over it all hung a glass roof five stories up, supported by black metal grates.

Shane stood there for a long time. He had been here for a week during his last BOR and had learned the rituals of the place. He knew about the waiting-room silence that followed the bustle of echoing voices in the atrium just before the nine o'clock commencement of the boards. He remembered the tense posture of witnesses and police officers as they leaned over the metal railings near the fifth-floor hearing rooms, waiting nervously to testify. There were the subtle, silent signs that were read only by the people familiar with the activity in the building and who spread the word on each board's outcome. The elevator operators watched carefully as accused officers left their penalty hearings, checking to see who was carrying the accused's gun. If it was in the advocate's hand, it meant the officer had been terminated.

The administration of LAPD justice churned relentlessly in the building, leaving bits and pieces of its victims' lives bobbing like scattered garbage in its wake. Like the Tower of London, it was way too beautiful a place for all the beheadings that occurred there.

Shane got on the elevator, rode to the third floor, and moved up to the heavy glass-paneled, wood-frame door of the Advocate Section. After taking a deep breath, he pushed it open and walked inside.

He was back in the narrow, gray and brown space fronted by three reception desks, where secretaries directed business to the twenty advocates seated behind them. Across the hall, on the opposite side of the open atrium, were the investigating officers, known as IOs. They were regular detectives assigned to IAD who did background interviews and took affidavits from "wits." All of Shane's memories of the place came rushing back. From where he was standing, he could see back to the advocates' cubbies located on the far side of the office. The advocates were all sergeants or lieutenants and worked in five-by-five clutter at small desks, cardboard "case" boxes filled with affidavits and IO reports clustered at their feet.

Shane remembered the chief advocate, a tall, vanilla milkshake named Warren Zell. Shane moved to one of the secretaries, a black woman with a remarkable body, and smiled at her.

"I'm Sergeant Scully. I've been assigned here. I'm supposed to report to Commander Zell."

"Hi," she said, "I'm Mavis. Take a seat. I'll tell him you're here."

While she buzzed in, Shane sat and picked up the LAPD newsletter, *The Blue Line,* that was on the table along with a stack of Chief Brewer's newsletters, a glossy white four-sheet called *The Beat*. He assumed *The Beat* was required reading in this political squirrel cage. He was looking down when he heard the female voice that distressed him the most.

"Mavis," the voice said, "can you send all these 301's on the Scully deps out to the subpoena control officer and tell him I need them served as soon as he can get them issued? Also, make sure this charge sheet gets sent to Pam Davis in the District Attorney's Office. They're monitoring his board for a possible murder indictment."

He looked up and saw Alexa Hamilton standing with her back to him, wearing one of her severe, tailored gray suits. Her shapely calves and tight, rounded ass were only a foot from his face.

"Work, work, work," he said softly.

She turned abruptly and, for the first time, saw him sitting there.

"It's not work when you're having fun," she replied.

"Don't forget to subpoena Barbara Molar; she's an eyewitness and supports my statement word for word."

"We always include exculpatory evidence, despite what you think, Scully. This division exists to try and keep the department clean. We're not down here doing hatchet jobs."

"This division exists to destroy hardworking cops so people like you can get an E-ticket ride to the top of the department. You know it. I know it. Everybody on the job knows it. But don't take it from me, go ask any uniform sitting in the front seat of a Plain Jane."

Alexa stood there and tapped her thumb against a file folder. "Y'know, Scully, you mighta been an okay cop, except you've gotta do everything your own stiff-necked, jackoff way. You're always trying to be the smartest guy in the room, always cutting corners and blaming others. This is a division that is set up to defend the rules and mandates of this department. Since you have your head so far up your ass, you only see things through your navel; it's understandable your view is clouded.

That's your problem, not mine." She turned to Mavis. "On second thought, Mave, I'm gonna walk this stuff over to the subpoena control desk personally. Nothing's too good for Sergeant Scully." She turned away and, carrying the paperwork, moved back to her desk behind the counter. Her hips swayed seductively as she walked. Shane felt nothing. She had turned his balls to ice.

The phone buzzed, twice.

"You can go in now," Mavis said.

Shane got up and headed down the long rectangular space between the east wall and the three reception desks. He entered Zell's office at the end of the room.

Seated behind a slab of oak was Commander Zell. He had his jacket off; a huge Glock automatic in an upside-down shoulder holster hung under his arm like a sleeping bat. It is a proven LAPD street-cop axiom that any officer in plain clothes who wears a shoulder rig is, by definition, an asshole. If it's upside down, then he's a puckered, purebred asshole. Zell looked up and pushed a stack of signed papers away as Shane entered.

"Sergeant, don't bother to sit, you won't be in my office that long." It was starting out worse than Shane had expected. "You're under my direct supervision," Zell went on, but while he spoke, he turned his attention to another stack of papers. "I expect you to report for duty at eight-thirty every morning, without fail. You have only half an hour for lunch, so I suggest you bring it. You punch out at five. It's a straight eight. No overtime will be approved. Questions?"

"Well, sir, I have to drop a fifteen-year-old boy at school every morning. I have to get him there by eight-fifteen. Eight-thirty is going to be pretty tight."

"Then here's your solution, Sergeant. You drop him off at eight instead of eight-fifteen." Zell finally looked up, fixing his gaze on Shane, as if to determine what sort of lame idiot wouldn't be able to figure that out by himself.

"Sir, if I might ask, what will I be doing?"

"You're the unit discovery officer."

"I'm sorry?"

"On every case going through here, the accused officer has the right to look at all statements and affidavits taken by our IOs. It's called *discovery*," Zell said, his voice dripping with sarcasm. "In order for the accused to get those documents, somebody has to Xerox the material, or make tape copies if it's a voice or video recording. The discovery officer works at the Xerox machines located on the second floor. There are four machines and some audio/video duplicating equipment. You make copies of everything, including personnel investigations, addenda, and any supplemental findings of proposed disciplinary action. Also include the response of the accused and the reply of the commanding officer, photographs or laser reproductions, rough field-interview notes, chronological records, case summaries, and the department wit list." He was ticking them off from memory, showing off. "Every case folder will tell you how many copies and where they are to be sent. They go out by registered mail to the accused officer's defense rep."

"I'm a Xerox machine operator?" Shane asked. He couldn't believe this was his new job.

"You are the unit discovery officer. Your job is to operate Xerox and electronic duplicating equipment. That's it. That's the job. You're excused."

"Wasn't there a crummier job you could have given me?" Shane asked, anger creeping into his voice.

"If you don't want the job, just tell me."

"Why? So you can hit me with a negligent-duty slip and put me in for insubordination?"

"Then go do what you've been asked to do."

"Yessir."

Shane moved out of the room and walked back down the hall. He stopped at Mavis's desk. "What room does the discovery officer use?"

"Room 256," she said. "It's locked. Here's the key." She handed him a key attached to a square wood block. It reminded Shane of a gas-station lavatory key. Appropriate. He was definitely in the toilet. As he moved out of the Advocate Section into the open corridor, he saw Alexa Hamilton coming back from the ladies' room. She passed him, her gaze straight ahead, as if he didn't exist or, more to the point, as if she knew he was about to disappear.

He punched the button for the beautiful old wrought-iron box. The elevator arrived and he got on. An elderly black gentleman in a dark blue blazer was running the lift.

"You must be new here," the old man said. "Whatchu gonna be doin'?"

"I'm the new discovery officer."

"Boy, good goin'. That sounds pretty darn important."

"Yeah," Shane said sadly. "No doubt about it. I am de man."

13
UNIT DISCOVERY OFFICER

AFTER CALLING Harvard Westlake and leaving a message for Chooch that he'd be late picking him up, Shane spent the morning Xeroxing cases in the narrow one-window office on the second floor. It was the only office that Internal Affairs had rented on two. Except for the occasional secretary who came in and dropped more cases on his stack, he was alone with his thoughts while the Xerox hummed and coughed up copies, passing its white light over the endless pages.

Shane wondered how much longer he should stay on the job. He'd pretty much run out of police department highway. He couldn't believe that the district attorney would ever bring murder charges. That was just being orchestrated by Chief Brewer to put pressure on him. But being terminated by Alexa Hamilton at his upcoming board was a distinct possibility. Except for Bernie Cookson, the judges were stacked against him. He would probably lose his tin and be kicked out, his seventeen-year pension going down the drain with the verdict.

He thought about Barbara Molar, how he wanted to hold her and make love to her, but this was immediately followed by a puzzling feeling of dispirited grief for something he couldn't identify. Moments later he was aware of a thickening depression. As the Xerox machine hummed and kicked pages into a tray, he tried to work it out.

He knew that pursuing a relationship with Barbara was stupid under these circumstances. Beyond that, something else was nibbling at his subconscious. He finally slapped it down and held it up.

It was a simple five-word question.

Why had Barbara married Ray?

What had led her to walk away from him and find solace in the arms of the most brutal cop on the force? She said that it was sweet to see tenderness in such a huge, seemingly brutish man.

Shane had known Ray almost from the day he'd joined the force, and he had never seen tenderness. Ray Molar was buffalo meat. His temper was always close to the surface, hiding there, waiting to explode. So why had Barbara married him? Why had she made such an obviously miserable choice?

With that question came another.

What weakness in her had caused her not to see Ray for what he was? Of course, Shane had also been fooled at first. But he'd had Ray as a partner. Having a kick-ass partner was considered a life-insurance policy in police work. Shane had misevaluated for reasons of his own survival. Why had Barbara been fooled?

His mind left that half-chewed thought and began on another. He had physical desire for her. He had once thought he loved her, but yesterday afternoon at Shutters, she had seemed to be trying to start up their relationship on the heels of Ray's death. He could understand cerebrally why this might be: she was lonely and scared, and Ray had been abusing her. She had come to hate him, but...

Ray had been her husband for twelve years. She had once slept in his arms. Yet his death seemed to hold no consequences for her. Shane had despised Ray, but he had not felt the same way since he'd squeezed off the round from his Mini-Cougar and watched his bullet explode in Ray's head. The picture of that death was on a macabre bulletin board in his psyche. He could not do anything without walking past it. Yet Barbara had no remorse, no guilt, no misgivings. To her, Ray's death was the doorway to her future. *What did that say? What did it mean? Had he been too young, immature, and blinded by lust to see any of her shortcomings back then? Had she changed...or had he?*

Shane looked at his watch. He was surprised to see that it was just a few minutes to twelve. He finished the case he was Xeroxing, then, following instructions, he put the copies in a manila envelope and addressed them to the defense rep involved. Then he put the packet in the OUT basket, where it would be picked up and sent off by registered mail.

He shut off the Xerox, locked the office door, dropped the key with Mavis, and headed out of the Bradbury Building on his lunch hour—make that *half hour.*

Shane wasn't hungry, so he decided to check on his Scientific Investigation Section request. He began to walk the four blocks to Main Street, where Parker Center was located. He needed to clear his mind. He made it a brisk outing, his arms swinging hard, his stride even and quick. When he got halfway there, he ran into another movie barricade. He badged his way through, walking along the sidewalk while wary assistant directors with head-mikes and walkie-talkies clipped on their belts glared at him. He was ignoring their barricades, trespassing on their superiority.

"You're in our shot, sir," one of them yelled.

Shane hurried along. Arnold was across the street with the director, engaged in an animated discussion. There was a lot of gesturing and arm waving. Tourists and downtown office workers stood behind the barricades,

144

holding their cameras at port arms, hoping for a shot while streetpeople angrily cursed this invasion of their living space.

Shane got to Parker Center and moved quickly to the Scientific Investigations Section on the seventh floor. He went down the corridor, hoping to remain invisible. Occasionally somebody would look at him, grab the arm of a companion, and start whispering. Shane could write the dialogue: *"That's him, right over there. Can you believe it? He shot Lieutenant Molar...they used to be partners."*

He got to SIS and asked for the results of his laundry tag analysis. A middle-aged woman with thick, red-rimmed Sally Jessy Raphaël glasses leaned across the counter with the results. "We got lucky. Most of the laundries in the database are local; this one is a ways away, but was still inside the sample area."

Shane looked at the printout. "Mountain Cleaners, Lake Arrowhead," he read aloud.

"That's what the computer says," she replied. Then almost as an afterthought: "I don't know if you missed it, but on the inside of the tag is a date, April tenth."

"Thanks," he said. "You're right, I missed it."

He moved away from the desk with the printout. The address was on Pine Tree Lane in Lake Arrowhead. He left Parker Center for the walk back to Broadway and Third, wondering why Ray Molar was getting his shirts done in Lake Arrowhead, and whether it really mattered.

Arrowhead was a two-hour drive up in the mountains. Shane had been there once or twice before. He remembered that the town sat in wooded splendor, around the ten-mile circumference of a beautiful freshwater lake. The community was picturesque, catering mostly to artists, writers, and L.A. refugees. A lot of old Hollywood royalty had built huge mansions on the lake in the thirties, and some of these houses still existed—out-of-place old European-style homes with their stone walls and slate roofs.

When he got back to IAD, he picked up his key and trudged back down to the Xerox room. He unlocked the door and saw that a new case had been shoved through the mail slot. He picked it up and glanced at it as he walked across the room to drop it on the IN pile. Just as he was setting it down, he saw the name on the face sheet: PATROLMAN I JOSEPH CHURCH.

Shane stopped and looked at the sheet again. Joe Church was the patrolman who had escorted him yesterday morning, red light and siren, to see Chief Brewer. He flipped through the file, reading quickly.

According to the charges, three weeks ago Patrolman Church had been in a Code Thirty burglary car. He had accepted a call on a "hot ringer" in Southwest. A Hoover Street jewelry store was being robbed. It was a "There Now" call. Church had "rogered" the transmission but had not shown up for almost forty-five minutes. His Mobile Data Ter-

146

minal showed him as being three blocks away. When he finally got there, the owner of the store had been beaten almost to death, and was still in the USC Medical Center. The IOs on the case stated that Church claimed he had never received the call, despite the fact that he had rogered it, and all of his communications and times were logged on his MDT as well as in the Communications Center.

Shane dropped the case back on the pile, not attaching much significance to it, except for one stray thought: *Why would an officer whom the chief of police had just personally directed to an IAD Board of Rights be given a special assignment by the chief to pick up and escort Shane to his office?* It didn't make sense. But then, nothing that had been going on lately made much sense.

He turned on the Xerox machine and spent the rest of the day burning copies in the hot, narrow room.

Shane punched out at five-thirty, walked back to his car next door, and headed to Harvard Westlake.

Chooch was sitting alone on the curb. Everyone else had been picked up. He stood slowly, then dragged both his book bag and ass over to the car and got in.

"Sorry. We're gonna have to make new arrangements for the pickup. I can't get back here till five forty-five. I sent you a message. I hope they gave it to you."

Chooch was strangely quiet. He just nodded.

Shane put the car in gear and headed up onto the freeway, back to Venice.

"Did you have some kinda talk with Mr. Thackery?" Chooch finally asked after almost ten minutes of silence.

"No, why?" Shane said, glancing over at him.

"I don't know. He pulled me out of study hall. It was like he was a different guy, wants to be my bud. He said I was gonna get another chance, that he had gone to bat for me."

"I'll bet your mom called and set him straight. Sandy did pretty good, huh? I'm telling ya, you got your mother down in the wrong column, Chooch."

"Yeah... What column is that, the 'Don't bother me, I'm always busy' column? She's had me in boarding school since second grade. Up at Webb School in Ventura, I never even got to come home at Christmas. I was the only kid left in the dorm over the holidays. I was being watched by custodians...had to eat at the headmaster's house. Sandy's some mom, all right. We gotta get her a Mother's Day award."

"People aren't always what they appear to be," Shane persisted. "Your mom has reasons. Her job takes her away a lot. She's trying to give you a great education. She wants you to have a good start in life."

"Thackery said if I have any problems, or if I want to talk, I should look him up," Chooch said, changing the subject. "As if I'd even tell that dickhead which way was due north."

"Look, Chooch, if he's changing his tune, don't hawk a lugie at him."

"He's a prick."

148

"Yeah, maybe. Or maybe he's had a change of heart. If he's trying to cut you some slack, take it."

"And you believe him?"

"Yeah. Yeah, sure, I believe him. Hey, look, Thackery may be okay underneath all that Latin he quotes. Maybe he's just a guy who's scared, like us."

"I ain't scared a' nothin'."

"Then you're the only one on the planet, Chooch. Everybody is scared."

"Were you scared when you shot that guy?"

Shane looked over. He had not discussed the incident with Chooch, and he didn't have a TV. He was foolishly hoping it would never come up.

"It's all over school," Chooch said, reading his look of dismay. "So tell me. When you offed him, were you scared?"

"Yeah. Yeah... I was scared to death. I was shitting bricks."

Chooch sat there for a long moment thinking. "Physical stuff doesn't scare me. I'm not afraid a' getting bombed on or fucked over that way. But"—he hesitated for a moment, his eyes on the road ahead—"sometimes I'm afraid that what I believe in isn't true, that everything I think is true was just set up by somebody to fool me."

Shane nodded. "Yeah, I've been getting some of that myself lately."

"And sometimes, just once in a while, I want to be the most important, instead of the least...." He paused for a long time, his face in a wrinkled frown. "Sometimes I'm scared I'll never have anybody who gives a shit."

They rode in silence.

Finally they got back to East Channel Road. Shane pulled the car into the garage, and they went into the house. Shane closed the door and watched as Chooch dragged his book bag into his room, to sit there with desperate, lonely thoughts that probably matched his own.

14

A.K.A.

SHANE SAT in his living room listening to an occasional siren, which always seemed to come from the east, where the gangbangers held their nightly life-ending turf parties. It was six o'clock and the sun had just gone down. He put his mind back on his problem.

Any police detective worth his salt always started a case by arranging known or probable facts in chronological order. Shane took a piece of paper off the table and began making notations:

1. Late Feb. or early March, Ray Molar gets a job driving for Mayor Crispin.

2. March, R.M. begins not coming home.
3. April 2, Joe Church fails to respond to Hoover St. robbery (related?).
4. April 10, R.M. gets shirts done at Mountain Cleaners.
5. April 14, B.M. gets phone call from mystery woman/tape coming.
6. April 16, 1:30 A.M., R.M. gets home, beats B.M.
7. April 16, 2:35 A.M., R.M. shot (no tape found in house).
8. April 16, 5:17 A.M., T. Mayweather does DFAR (S.S. secure files in IAD possibly accessed).
9. April 16, 6:00 A.M., S.S. threatened by Kono and Drucker, police garage.
10. April 16, Joe Church escorts S.S. to C.O.P.
11. April 16, C.O.P. threatens S.S. with murder indictment. Wants case material returned.
12. April 18, Samansky, Ayers break in and search B.M.'s house (no tape found). Warrant signed by Hernandez, Crispin appointee.
13. April 18, Letter of Transmittal arrives. S.S. suspended. S.S. motive for murder mentioned.
14. April 18, T. Mayweather walks 1.61 appeal through department. S.S. back on duty.
15. April 19, S.S. reports to IAD (DA intends to audit BOR).

He stopped writing and looked at the list. It was his first chronological log. There were huge holes in his time line. Aside from the missing tape, there was Ray's increasingly violent behavior toward Barbara. Also, the list made it even more obvious that there was some kind of link between Ray and the top floor of the Glass House, and that it might have to do with Mayor Crispin. The list directed him to where he had to look next. He needed to find out why Molar had his shirts done ninety miles away. He looked at his watch—seven o'clock. Shane turned on his desk lamp and picked up the phone. He got the number for the laundry on Pine Tree Lane in Arrowhead and dialed. After a few rings, a man's voice came on the line.

"Mountain Cleaners," the voice chirped.

"Yes. Who am I speaking to?"

"This is Larry Wright."

"Mr. Wright, I'm Sergeant Shane Scully, with the LAPD. I'm working a case and I have some dry-cleaned shirts that were done at your laundry. I'm trying to find out who dropped them off."

"I see, well, without looking at the tags, I wouldn't know. They're bar-coded; I'd have to run them through our scanner."

"This case is pretty important. If I got in my car, I could be up there in two hours. I know it's an imposition, but do you think we could make an appointment to meet about nine tonight?"

"No problem. I'm usually stuck here till nine-thirty."

"Great. I'll bring the shirts with me." He hung up and dialed Longboard Kelly.

"Yer tappin' the Source," the surfboard shaper answered. Kelly believed "the Source" was a magical place where great waves came from.

"It's Shane. You think you could come right over and keep an eye on Chooch for a couple of hours?"

"I'm busy crankin' off an eight-ball, dude. After I finish, I could make it."

"You're doing what?" Shane asked.

"I'm on the throne, takin' a shit. Gimme five."

"Great. I'll pay you."

"What for, man? One day, if I get busted, you play the 'Get Brian out of jail' card."

"Right. Only we took that card out of the deck. How 'bout I play the 'Put in a good word for Brian' card instead?"

"Agreed, dude! I'll be right over."

Shane hung up.

He went into the guest bedroom. Chooch was hunched over the desk, doing his homework. Shane had a momentary stab of "parental" gratitude. "It's great you're doing your studies," Shane said proudly.

Chooch looked over at him, and Shane saw that he had a Game Boy on his lap.

Shane's expression of gratitude was replaced with exasperation. "I'm gonna run out for a few hours. Kelly is coming over to be with you."

"Cool. He's kickin'."

"Right. When are you gonna get back to your studies?"

153

"I'm just takin' a break, man. You don't get breaks down at that duck farm where you work?"

"Yeah, I get breaks. I'll be back before midnight."

"Solid."

Shane left the room, got his coat, collected his badge, and grabbed one of the bagged dry-cleaned shirts, which he had hung in the closet. He headed out the back door.

As the garage door was going up, a car's headlights pulled in right behind him, blocking his exit. He put a hand on his belt holster and cautiously moved toward the driveway. As he rounded the back of his car, he could see Barbara Molar's red Mustang convertible. When she turned off her headlights, he saw her behind the wheel, a scarf tied around her hair.

"Shit, Barbara, whatta you doing here?"

"I had to come over. I couldn't reach you. Your machine was off and your cell phone is out of service."

"If they catch us together, *I'm* gonna be out of service," he said quickly.

"Shane, I'm getting phone calls at the house. Spooky calls. I'm being threatened."

"Go park a few blocks away. Lock up. I'll drive over and pick you up."

She nodded and followed his instructions. Shane got behind the wheel and backed the Acura out. He drove up East Channel Street to where Barbara was standing, her arms wrapped around her, shivering slightly in the cold marine air. She had put up the Mustang's top and, he hoped, locked the car. Shane reached over and threw open the passenger door. Barbara got in. He put the Acura in gear and pulled off East Channel to a side street, keeping one eye on his rearview mirror.

"Who's calling?" he finally asked. He could tell she was panicked. Her features were drawn; she seemed even more pale than normal.

"It's a man's voice. He just says, 'If you've got what we want, turn it over, or you'll pay the consequences.' Stuff like that. Then a couple of calls where there was just breathing first, then somebody said, 'Do the right thing, bitch,' and hung up."

Shane pulled to the curb and parked. "That means they still haven't found what they're looking for."

"I'm scared."

"So am I."

She looked at the shirt between them on the front seat. "Is this one of Ray's?"

"Yeah. The laundry is in Arrowhead."

"Arrowhead?"

"You got any idea why he'd have his shirts cleaned all the way up there?"

"None."

"It doesn't make much sense," Shane said. "He was driving the mayor. Arrowhead is two hours out of L.A."

"Maybe the mayor had personal business there."

"Maybe."

"What are you going to do?"

"I was just heading up to Lake Arrowhead to talk to the cleaner. I wanna see what I can find out from the guy. They have customer information on the bar code of this laundry tag." He held up the shirttail with the purple tag attached.

"I wanna go with you. And don't tell me no. I'm scared. I can't go home. Those calls are terrifying me."

"Barbara, the DA is contemplating indicting me for murder. My motive, they think, is that I killed Ray to be with you. If we get caught riding around together, I will be trying to explain it in court."

"Take me with you," she said again. "Please. I need company. I'm shaking."

Kinetic thoughts were buzzing around, bouncing off unanswered questions with pinball energy. Then without really weighing his answer, he just nodded.

"Okay," he said impulsively, and put the car in gear. They headed up the street.

Shane turned right onto Washington Boulevard, which took him to the 405, then north to the 10, which would lead them east toward San Bernardino and Lake Arrowhead.

The road was narrow and winding. His headlights swept across shadowy tree trunks that lined the two-lane highway in the Angeles Mountains. Shane had his eye on the road, but his mind was on Ray Molar.

156

Barbara sat silently beside him. She had started the trip with a lot of chitchat, then had tried to swing the conversation to her future, what she would do with her life now that Ray was gone. Then she made the leap to how Shane was feeling, how he felt about her and about them.

Shane had deflected it all, keeping his answers short. He was beginning to suspect that Barbara had some hidden agenda, but he couldn't yet tell what it was. Maybe it was just his cop instincts that distrusted everything. But something was telling him to pull back—to defend his perimeter.

While she talked, he had been thinking about the night of the shooting: the two critical minutes from the time he'd gone into that bedroom to the moment he had peeled the Nine at Ray. Something in his Letter of Transmittal had stuck in his mind. The department had accused him of inappropriate use of force, of bad judgment, which had escalated the situation out of control. *Had he fucked up? Why had he taken his gun? Had he anticipated shooting Ray? Had he acted out of policy? Was there a way he could have prevented Ray's death?* The only other witness to the event was sitting next to him, so after weighing the consequences, Shane gingerly broached the subject.

"Barb...the night I shot Ray...how well do you remember it? You looked almost unconscious, as if he had stunned you with that blow to the head."

"I remember it all. It's indelible. It's branded in my memory," she said bitterly.

"Do you think I had any other choice but to shoot him?"

"What are you talking about?"

"If I'd called in some uniforms, would it have made a difference?" he asked.

She turned in her seat and looked directly at him. "You mean, if you had called in a 415? Would it have changed things?" she said, using the cop's radio code for a general disturbance, the majority of which ended up being domestic disputes.

"Yeah. What if two blues had come through that door instead of me, Ray's ex-partner, your old boyfriend...do you think it would have changed anything?" He was straining to hear her answer as he drove, straining to evaluate any nuance in her voice.

"Are you joking?" she said, snorting the words derisively. "He was insane." She was incredulous now. "Ray was crazy. *You* know it. *I* know it. He went nuts on spec. Once he snapped, he didn't care what he did or who he did it to. It wouldn't have mattered if Robocop or Pope John Paul himself had come through that door."

"Do you think if I'd held fire that he—"

"If you'd held fire, Shane, you and I would both be dead, and somebody else would have the fucking coffin decorations. You can't be serious."

He looked over at her and could see that she was almost angry about it. Finally he nodded.

"Yeah, okay," he said. "I was just wondering."

She shook her head in amazement, and they remained silent the rest of the way to Lake Arrowhead.

The two-lane highway led into a small, lush, wooded valley and then descended into the beauty of Lake Arrowhead. A-frame houses and log-cabin architecture dotted the roadside.

The buildings on the main street were rustic, the sidewalks narrow. They found Pine Tree Lane, and Shane pulled up to Mountain Cleaners. He and Barbara got out, entered, and found Larry Wright.

After Shane showed his badge, he gave Mr. Wright the shirt. The man walked into the back, leaving Shane and Barbara standing alone in the neon overhead lighting, looking into the area where the finished dry-cleaning hung on a moving conveyor belt. In less than two minutes, Mr. Wright returned.

"Got it." He smiled at them. "These were done for Jay Colter. He lives at 1276 Lake View Drive.

"Then they're not Ray's?" Barbara said.

Shane waved her off, then reached into his pocket and pulled out an old photograph he had brought of himself and Ray when they were both working together in Southwest. The picture had been taken in a bar. They were EOW in plain clothes and had their arms around each other's shoulders, grinning drunkenly at the camera. "Is this Jay Colter?" Shane asked, handing the picture to Mr. Wright.

He looked at the shot and nodded. "Little heavier now, but that's him."

"You know what he was doing up here?"

"Well, I only talked to him once. Seems to me he said he was a builder, or in construction, maybe.... A builder, I think it was."

"Okay, thanks, Mr. Wright. That's a big help."

They moved out of the cleaners and stood on the curb under a streetlight. "What's going on?" she asked. "Jay Colter? Why would he change his name?"

"When we were partnered, Ray told me once that if I ever worked undercover and was going to use an alias, I should choose a name that sounds close to my own. So if somebody calls out to you using your assumed name, you will react to it, instead of forgetting it's your alias. For instance, a good a.k.a. for Shane Scully might be Lane MacCully."

"And Ray Molar would be Jay Colter. But why?"

"Let's go see who lives at 1276 Lake View Drive," he said.

 BADGER GAMES

THEY FOUND the address on Lake View Drive. Shane drove the black Acura slowly past the house. The small cabin-style bungalow was lit up. They could see men moving around inside.

"What do you think they're doing?" Barbara asked as Shane slowed the car but didn't stop. He pulled up the street and turned left at the first intersecting road. He drove half a block up, parked, and turned off the headlights.

"Who are they? What're you gonna do?" Barbara pestered as Shane got his zoom-lens camera out of the trunk.

"Stay here," he ordered, and quickly moved down to Lake View, then crept along the sidewalk toward the target house. He heard something behind him and spun around. Barbara was hovering nearby.

"Go back. This could be dangerous."

"Maybe I know one of them," she said.

Shane realized that it was a good thought, so he nodded, then put a finger up to his mouth for silence. They crept along, slower this time, finally getting to a position of advantage behind a hedge across the street from the lake cabin. Shane put the zoom-lens camera to his eye and adjusted the focus, bringing the small house closer.

Through the front window he could see men moving around, carrying boxes and emptying drawers. He snapped a few pictures with the flash off, hoping that if he pushed it in the lab, he would get adequate resolution in spite of the low light. Through the viewfinder, he could see the men clearly. He didn't recognize any of them.

"What d'you see?" she whispered in his ear.

"They're tossing the place, looking for something, same as at your house," he said softly, handing her the camera. "You recognize anyone?" After a minute she shook her head and handed the camera back.

They continued to watch the house for another twenty minutes. Several times one or two of the men carried a cardboard box out and set it near the back door. Shane used up an entire roll of film, and then finally the men turned off the lights, locked up the house, and carried the boxes down to the little dock on the lake.

Shane moved out from behind the hedge, with Barbara at his heels. He ran in a crouch until he got to the side of the house, in time to see the men load the boxes into a small, old-style, wooden reproduction Chris-Craft, with varnished sides and teak decking. They all jumped aboard, and the boat's engine roared. It pulled away from the dock and sped off across the lake, leaving a white-foam wake that glistened in the mountain moonlight.

"Shit," Shane said, "I was hoping they had

a car parked around here so we could follow them."

He turned and moved back to the house. He tried the doors. They were all locked. Then he took out a pocketknife. He crept onto the wooden back deck that overlooked the lake, and inserted the blade into the sliding glass door. Slowly he pushed the latch up, then slid the door open. He and Barbara stepped cautiously into the small two-bedroom house.

Shane moved to the back hallway and turned on a light. It threw a low glow into the front room and would slightly illuminate most of the rooms in the small house. He didn't want to light up the whole place and call attention to their presence.

"What're we looking for?" Barbara whispered.

"Evidence that Ray lived here or used this place," he said.

"Y'mean like this," she said, picking up a small framed photograph off the living-room TV. It was Ray with his arm around a very pretty dark-haired woman. They were both laughing, holding up glasses of champagne. Slightly out of focus in the background was a small wooden church with a sign that read:

**THE MIDNIGHT WEDDING CHAPEL
LAS VEGAS, NEVADA**

Barbara looked at the picture, and her expression turned dark. "Is this what I think it is?" she asked sharply. "Is this a fucking wedding photo?"

"I don't know." He removed the picture from the frame and put it in his pocket.

They moved through the house. The cottage appeared to be some kind of party pad. Both bedrooms sported huge king-size waterbeds, complete with ceiling mirrors. Shane looked around, opening drawers, searching closets. All were now empty; everything had been removed. When he got to the guest bedroom, he noticed that the closet seemed very shallow, with no hanging rods. He tapped on the back wall. It sounded hollow. He searched around the edges of the closet wall until he found a small kickplate near the floor. He touched it with his toe, and the back wall of the closet opened on a spring hinge. He pushed "the wall" and found that he was in a small, dark area, about six by ten feet. From where he was standing, he was looking through a glass window, directly into the master bedroom.

"Barbara," he called to her, "go into the master bedroom and stand by the bed."

"Okay," she called from the kitchen, where she had been searching the cupboards. She went into the bedroom, and he could see her clearly through the window in the wall in front of him.

"Go to the mirror over the dresser," he said. She walked to the dresser and was now standing only a few feet away, looking directly at him through a one-way mirror.

"Where are you?" she asked.

"In here, in the guest bedroom."

She moved away from the mirror, exited the master bedroom, and in a minute was pushing the wall open and entering the small back closet he had discovered. Shane found the overhead light and flipped it on. The room was empty except for a vacant bookshelf.

"What is this?" she asked.

"Glory hole," Shane said, using the cop term for any opening used for sexual spying. He began looking around the secret room. Finally he pulled an empty bookshelf away from the wall. He found two videotape boxes that had slipped down behind the shelf and had been missed. He picked them up—they were empty. One of the boxes was not labeled, but the other had a name written on the spine:

CARL CUMMINS

"What were they doing?"

"Looks like some kind of variation on the Badger Game. They get a guy up here, have a party, videotape the funny stuff, then blackmail him."

"Ray was doing this? Ray and that girl?"

"I don't know. I'm not sure. Early in an investigation, it's best not to jump to any conclusions," he said. "Are there any Baggies in the kitchen?"

"Yeah, that kitchen is completely stocked," she said.

They moved out of the videotape room and into the kitchen. Barbara found a large Baggie, and Shane dropped the videotape box into it while she held it open. Then he pulled the photo out of his pocket and dropped it in, too. Suddenly they heard the back door open, and froze.

"In there," he whispered, pointing to the pantry.

A breathless moment, then the light Shane had turned on in the back hallway went off. The house was thrown into darkness.

As they crouched in the darkened pantry, Shane slipped his service revolver out of his belt holster and pulled the hammer back. He held the Smith & Wesson .38-caliber round-wheel out in front of him with both hands, using a two-hand Weaver grip. He could hear three, maybe four men conducting a careful search, looking for them. One of the men moved into the kitchen.

"In here, Cal," the man called out. The kitchen lights went on, exposing Shane and Barbara cowering in the back of the pantry. Shane aimed his revolver at the overhead light and put a round in the fixture, shattering glass and throwing the kitchen back into blackness.

Then all hell broke loose.

Gun muzzles flashed in the darkness. Shane pushed Barbara down, grabbed a can off the pantry shelf, and threw it out into the kitchen. It landed on the counter across the room, and where it hit, shots rang out, breaking glass.

Shane grabbed Barbara's hand and pulled her out of the pantry, into the kitchen. He ran full into one of the men, knocking him down, then heard the man's gun hit the floor and slide on the linoleum. Shane dove into the dining room, pulling Barbara. When they landed, two more shots lit the kitchen with their muzzle flashes as the slugs slammed into the dining-room wall over their heads. Shane rolled off his back, came up into a sitting position, and blindly fired all five of his remaining shots into the kitchen. He heard somebody yell in pain, then there were footsteps running. The back door was thrown open. He could hear people fleeing along the side of the house.

"Barbara, you okay?" he whispered.

"Uh-huh," she replied.

Shane got to his feet. His gun was empty, so he knocked open the revolver, tilted it up and dropped the hot brass into his palm, then quickly dumped the shells into his jacket pocket. He pulled his quick-load off his belt and pushed the six-slug package into his open revolver, then snapped it shut. A speedboat at the dock started, and he heard it roar away.

"Stay there," he said, and stepped into the kitchen, his gun out in front of him, combat-style. He moved slowly across the room and finally found the light switch in the pantry. He flipped it on. Whoever he had hit had left about half a pint of blood behind, but somehow had managed to escape. Then he heard a siren's distant wail across the lake.

"These bohunk sheriffs have even better response time than we do," Shane said. "Let's get outta here."

He had dropped the bagged videotape box in the gun battle, and it took him almost half a minute to find it. On his way out of the kitchen, he saw an answering machine sitting on the counter. He grabbed the entire unit and yanked it out of the wall. Then, leading Barbara, he ran out the side door of the house.

The siren was dangerously close. Shane ran up the street, pulling Barbara along. Suddenly he stopped, reached down, and stuffed the videotape box, camera, and answering machine into an overgrown hedge, wedging it way down, out of sight.

Shane and Barbara sprinted to his car. He got behind the wheel, and they took off. As he streaked out of the side street, he ran right into the headlights of the arriving sheriff's car. Shane jerked the wheel, hit the gas hard, and powered past the black-and-white. The sheriff's car spun a U-turn and came after them.

"What're you doing? Why don't you stop? You're a cop!" Barbara shouted.

Shane didn't answer. He had his hands full and his foot on it, trying to take as many corners as he could to get out of sight of the pursuing police unit.

Finally he made a skidding right turn and accelerated down a narrow street. Bad choice. He had picked a residential cul-de-sac and slammed on the brakes. He started to turn around when the sheriff's car squealed in behind them. The two cops were out instantly, crouching behind their squad-car doors. One had a shotgun resting in the window frame.

"On your stomach, assholes!" the shotgun officer yelled. "Do it now!"

"Do as he says," Shane ordered Barbara. He opened the door, dropped his revolver, and kicked it across the pavement toward the sheriff's car. "LAPD!" he yelled.

"On your stomach, now!" the man repeated. Shane and Barbara did as they were told. In seconds he could feel a sheriff's deputy's hot breath on his neck, and cold steel handcuffs on his wrists. They were ratcheted down hard. In L.A. it was what they called an "adrenaline cuff." His hands were pinned painfully behind his back, then he and Barbara were jerked up onto their feet and shoved into the back of the sheriff's car.

16
COP SHOP

THE ARROWHEAD SHERIFF'S Department was wedged in between a gas station and a small country market. The parking lot behind the station had three empty Plain Janes.

Shane and Barbara were unloaded from the back of the patrol car and shoved angrily into the station. The two arresting officers were still burning off their chase adrenaline.

Shane was pushed into a chair at the booking desk while Barbara was taken into another room. Separate interviews were always the rule in any half-decent police department. All cops quickly learned that most criminals never expect to get caught. As a result, they rarely have a cover story. One would tell you he was going to the market to get beer; the other would say they were picking up a sick aunt. Separating suspects to take statements was pro forma.

Shane was pissed at himself for making the same dumb mistake as every deadhead felon he had ever busted. He didn't know what Barbara would say, so he planned to tell them the exact truth.

The Arrowhead Sheriff's Department was in turmoil. Earlier that day they had found a dead body in the lake. From what Shane could pick up, it was so decomposed that they hadn't been able to make an ID. In L.A., a dead body was no big deal, but up here an unexplained death was the kind of unusual tragedy it should be everywhere. Shane watched as the tall, balding, fifty-five-year-old sheriff of Arrowhead made multiple calls to the coroner's office. After five minutes he hung up and walked over to Shane. His nameplate read SHERIFF CONKLYN.

"Sorry to add to your problems, Sheriff," Shane said pleasantly.

"What's your story?" Conklyn asked angrily.

"I'm LAPD. I'm up here working on a case."

The sheriff nodded to one of the deputies, who handed Shane's leather ID wallet to Conklyn. He opened it and looked at Shane's tin.

"If you're a cop, why did you run?" the sheriff said, looking at him critically.

"I'm out of my jurisdiction and I didn't take the time to check with you guys like I should have, so I just decided to get small," he said. "Bad choice. Your guys were magnificent."

"Put away the jar of Vaseline," Conklyn said. "You got a CO we can call?"

"I'd really appreciate it if we didn't have to do that," Shane said. "He's not going to be happy."

"It's a big club. I'm not happy." He pointed to his deputies. "They're not happy. You're up here on Lake View Drive, busting caps, and now I've got lots of unhappy people in houses up there. All of a sudden it's like Mexican New Year."

"My captain is Bud Halley," Shane relented. "He's in Southwest Division Robbery/Homicide."

The sheriff took one of Shane's business cards out of his wallet and went to the phone. He talked softly for a minute, waited, then hung up and dialed another number. The second call was taking entirely too long, and Shane's danger lights started flashing. After another minute Sheriff Conklyn moved back and unhooked Shane's cuffs.

"He wants to talk to you," he said.

Shane went behind the counter and picked up the phone. "Captain?"

"It's Tom Mayweather," the deputy chief said in his resonant baritone voice. "Halley

171

transferred this to me 'cause you're in my division now. What the fuck are you doing in Arrowhead, Scully?"

"Sir, something is definitely not right. Ray had a second house up here and another identity, maybe even a second wife."

"Says who?"

"Sir, a dry cleaner identified his picture and gave us the alias he was using. His picture was inside the house, on top of the TV."

"Scully, you are really pissing me off. Read your fucking badge; it says LAPD. You're ninety miles out of your jurisdiction with Ray Molar's widow, engaging in a gun battle with who the hell knows who. Then you have the stones to try and tell me Lieutenant Molar had two identities and a second wife. He was assigned to the mayor, for God's sake."

"Sir, I—"

"Shut up!" Mayweather said. "Here's what you do. I'm gonna alibi your fucked-up story with Sheriff Conklyn. He'll cut you and Mrs. Molar loose. Then I want you to leave Arrowhead and drive directly to Los Angeles. I want you to park your car in the Parker Center garage, then turn yourself in to the Homicide Division duty officer. Send her home in a cab. I want this all to happen in less than three hours. Are we straight on this, Sergeant?"

"Yes, sir."

"Put the sheriff back on."

Shane motioned to the sheriff, who took the phone, listened for a minute, then nodded. "No problem," he said, and hung up.

Fifteen minutes later Shane and Barbara were back in the parking lot behind the sheriff's station. Barbara rode in the front seat as one of the arresting deputies drove them back to the Acura and let them out.

"Good luck solving your John Doe murder," Shane said pleasantly.

"Want some advice from a fellow badge carrier?" the deputy said.

"You bet." Shane smiled, trying to be as non-confrontational as possible.

"Don't ever come back up here."

"Okay, sounds reasonable." Shane put out his hand, but the cop just looked at it.

"All right, then. Good deal," Shane said, pulling his hand back.

He and Barbara got into the Acura and drove away, staying five miles below the speed limit. Shane kept his eyes on the rearview mirror. The squad car was going to follow him all the way out of Arrowhead. He drove slowly down the mountain, until the black-and-white finally turned off and headed back toward town.

Shane pulled over and parked. He looked at his watch.

"What're you doing?" she asked.

"Giving this guy fifteen minutes to forget about us."

"Only fifteen minutes?"

"Small-town cops have short attention spans," he answered, then added, "I hope." They sat and listened to the motor cool.

"What is it?" Barbara said, noticing a frown on Shane's face.

"Those guys in the speedboat? I was thinking, how did they know we were in the house?" Barbara shrugged. "I think the place is bugged. They heard us searching, then they came back, maybe drifted back to the dock, then jumped us."

Fifteen minutes later Shane started the Acura and turned around. This time he constructed a cover story.

"Here's the deal. We came back to get gas. We only have half a tank." He pointed to the gauge, and she nodded.

He drove quickly through town, made remembered turns, then found himself back on Lake View Drive. He drove up to the bushy hedge, jumped out, and retrieved the videotape box, camera, and answering machine. He locked them in the trunk, then got back behind the wheel and drove quickly out of the mountains, returning to L.A.

17
ELECTRONIC EVIDENCE

USAN AND I can't come to the phone right now, but leave your name and number and, as soon as we can, we'll return your call." *BEEP*. Ray's voice sounded happy and unthreatening. Then there was another beep. "Ray, it's Calvin. Where the fuck are you, man? You gotta call me now." *BEEP*. Then: "Ray, it's Calvin again. The powers that be are asking questions. Don't fuck with love, man." *BEEP*. "Ray, it's Don and Lee. We're on for Saturday night. The Web after dark. Bring the jerseys." *BEEP*. "Ray, it's Burl. Call the special number." Then there were two hang-ups without messages.

Shane and Barbara were listening to the tape in his kitchen. He turned it off after the last message played.

"Burl—that's Chief Burleigh Brewer.... He knows about the house in Arrowhead. Shit," Shane growled. "Ray was the mayor's driver; I guess it makes sense that Brewer would be close to what Ray was doing." Shane was looking down at the answering-machine tape.

"Who are all these other people, and who the hell is Susan?" Barbara asked angrily.

"I don't know.... Don, Lee, and Calvin. I never heard of them, either." He thought for a minute. "There were two cops who braced me in the Parker Center garage at six A.M. the morning I shot Ray. I think one of them was named D. Drucker—maybe that's Don. The other was a Hawaiian guy named Kono. Maybe he's Lee or Calvin. I don't know. 'Don't fuck with love.' And 'the Web'... 'Bring the jerseys'... What's all that?" he said as they traded blank stares.

They stood over the kitchen counter, where the answering machine was plugged in. Finally, Shane changed the subject. "Barbara, look...you gotta go home. I'll drive you down to where your car is parked."

"I'm afraid to go home. I can't take any more of those calls."

"There's a good hotel a few miles south of here, in Marina del Rey. I can't remember the name, but you can't miss it. It's on Admiralty Way. Why don't you go check in there?"

"I get the feeling you're throwing me out."

"I'm not throwing you out. I've got Chooch in the guest room. Longboard is sawing z's on the sofa. It's like a men's dorm around here. Just check into the hotel. I'll talk to you in the morning."

She turned her face up and kissed him on the mouth. When he didn't fully respond, she pulled back and looked at him carefully. "Are you sending me a message, friend?" she asked with an edge in her voice.

"Barbara, let's not confuse this more than it is. We need to focus on what's going on— who's behind this."

"If you promise that you'll let us happen again, once it's over."

"Of course I promise," he said, forcing it. "You know how much I want that." His words hung in the kitchen, bright and empty, like a broken piñata.

"What're you going to do?" she finally asked.

"I'm gonna get this tape analyzed by the Electronics Section at SIS."

"You don't need a voice print. It's Ray's voice, believe me. I recognize it."

"I know it's Ray. I'm more interested in seeing what else is on here. Answering-machine tapes are used, erased, and rerecorded on. Sometimes there are old messages hiding there. I'm gonna see what the ESIS can pull off the erased portions," Shane said, referring to the Electronics Scientific Investigation Section.

"Oh," she said softly. Then she squeezed his hand for luck, and they headed out the back door of the house.

He drove her to her red Mustang, parked a block away. She got out of the Acura and unlocked her car door, then leaned down into his open passenger window and smiled at him sadly. "Why do I get the feeling this is over?"

"It's your imagination, Barbara. It's not over. It's on hold."

She kissed her fingertips and gently put them on his cheek. "Night," she said sadly, then got into the red Mustang and drove away.

• • •

Shane drove back to his house and locked up. He decided not to wake Longboard, who was snoring loudly on the sofa. He turned off the light and moved into his bedroom, stripped off his clothes, and wearing only his Jockey shorts, dropped heavily onto his bed. His head felt like a forty-pound medicine ball, worn, seamed, full of cotton and lead. He looked up at the ceiling, closed his eyes, and fought a wave of intense self-pity: *Why can't I catch a fucking break?*

"When did you get home?" Chooch's voice sounded suddenly, pulling him up from useless thoughts. He opened his eyes and saw the teenager standing in the doorway, wearing a Lakers shirt and baggy shorts.

"I thought you were asleep," Shane said.

"I woke up."

"Well, go back to sleep. You've got school tomorrow."

Chooch didn't move; he had an expression that seemed both frightened and sad.

"What's wrong?"

"Nothin'. It's just..."

"What?" Shane turned on his side and looked at Chooch carefully.

"Sandy called. She wants you to call her first thing in the morning."

"Why? What's up?"

"She didn't say."

"She probably just wants to tell me how she smoked your geek principal."

"She didn't call St. John, I asked her. She said she's been involved in a big deal and hasn't had time to get in touch with him yet."

"Right. Well, okay." He lay back on his pillow. "So I'll call her in the morning."

"That means old Thackery musta talked to you, not her. You made him keep me in school."

Shane looked over at Chooch again, then rubbed his eyes and sat up on the bed. "Let's go outside for a minute. I can't sleep with this fucking headache."

"We could light up, toke some bang?" the teenager said hopefully.

"We're through getting high together. I wanna talk to you."

Chooch shifted his weight uncertainly, then nodded. "Okay, sure."

Shane got up, put on his pants and an old sweatshirt, then the two of them moved quietly past Longboard into the backyard. Shane pulled up chairs, and they both sat under a fruitless tangerine tree, looking out at the still canal. The reflection of an almost full moon wavered on the glassy surface.

"What is it?" Chooch asked cautiously.

"I'm in a lot of trouble," Shane started.

"Trouble's the exhaust of life," the fifteen-year-old said surprisingly.

"The trouble I'm in could get dangerous. Some of the people I'm sideways with could decide to make a play. I don't want you to get hurt."

"I'm not afraid." Chooch smiled. "Got your back, bro."

They were silent for a moment, then Shane continued. "I also think it's time for you to get to know your mother. Maybe you haven't given her a chance."

"I hate her," Chooch said softly. "Let's drop this, okay?"

"You can't stay here. When I talk to her tomorrow, I'm going to make arrangements for her to take you back for a week or so."

There was a long silence. Suddenly some crickets started up in the hedge between Shane's and Longboard's yards. They sawed holes in the silence with their back legs.

"I think it's time you gave your mother a break," Shane persisted. "Make me a promise, give it a week. Just five days."

"You're fulla shit, just like Thackery and all those other dickwads. I thought you were never gonna lie to me. I thought we had a deal."

"I'm not lying to you, Chooch. I'm trying to keep you from getting hurt."

"I'm not stupid. I get what's going on here. I've become a problem, an inconvenience, so you wanna throw me out, simplify things for yourself."

"Just one week, till I can get my problems sorted out."

Chooch got up and started into the house. Shane grabbed his arm to stop him, but Chooch yanked it free.

"Look, it's not... I'm not trying to get rid of you."

"Eat me!" the boy said, defiance and pain shining in his black eyes.

"I care what you think," Shane said. "It matters to me. We need to talk this out."

"You came close. You almost had me fooled, but I got it straight now. I finally got it...nothing's changed. It's just like it always was—I can only count on myself. So fuck off."

Chooch walked back into the house. Shane's head was still pounding. No matter which way he turned, he saw disaster. He didn't know what to do next, so he went inside and wrote a letter to his father.

THE
ARROWHEAD
LETTER

Dear Dad,

I hate to admit it, but I'm really scared. Something big and dangerous is going on, and I have the feeling if I don't figure it out soon, I will be destroyed by it. The answer is in that Lake Arrowhead house. Why would Chief Brewer call a location where Ray was committing some kind of sexual blackmail? Who is Carl Cummins? That name isn't in either the Arrowhead or the L.A. phone book. I need to get the answers to some of these questions fast. I'm running out of time. Why do I feel it all closing in? Dad, I'm losing it. I sense disaster coming. I need to talk to somebody.

I know my problems are the last thing you need right now, but please give me a call.

I love you, Dad, and miss you. I'm scared and lonely. You're all I have left.

Your son,
Shane

18
CLERICAL DIVISION

T HEY PULLED UP in front of the Harvard Westlake School at eight the next morning. It was half an hour before the other students would arrive. Chooch got out, dragged his book bag off the front seat, and walked away from the car without looking back. He hadn't spoken all the way there. He had completely tuned Shane out.

Three times before leaving the house, Shane had tried to get through to Sandy but had reached only her machine. As he pulled away from the school, he dialed her number again.

"Hi, you've reached 555-6979. I'm not in, but you know what to do," announced the recording in her furry contralto voice. Shane didn't leave a third message. He closed his phone and headed back to Internal Affairs.

He pulled into the parking structure adjacent to the Bradbury and used his newly issued employee-parking card. The arm went up, and he found his assigned space on the third level.

He was just getting out of his car when he saw Alexa Hamilton five spaces away, removing a heavy cardboard case-file box out of the trunk of her plainwrap. A few Metro sergeants and special players in the department still had these prized vehicles instead of the hated slickbacks. Alexa's was a new dove-gray Crown Victoria with blackwalls and red velour upholstery. Crown Vics were senior staff vehicles, and hers was prima facie evidence that Sergeant Hamilton had top-shelf department "suck."

She slammed her trunk lid and started carrying the box to the elevators. Shane didn't want to ride down with her, but she had seen him and they were both heading toward the elevators, destined to arrive within seconds of each other. For him to veer off now or pretend he forgot something and divert back to his car would be a chickenhearted admission of weakness, so he kept walking and arrived a few seconds behind her. She had balanced the heavy cardboard box full of case files on her knee so she could push the elevator button with her free hand. She looked over at him with those slanted, exotic chips of laser-blue ice—poker player's eyes that cut holes through him but revealed nothing in return.

"Need help with that?" he asked, hating himself for even offering, the question inadvertently slipping out of him in an anxious attempt to fill the awkward silence.

"Wouldn't that be sorta like asking a condemned man to carry his own ax to the chopping block?"

"Hardy-har," he said sourly. It surprised him that the box was so full. She'd been on the case for only forty-eight hours. "That can't be all me."

"All you. And this is just '92 to '96. 'Ninety-four seemed like a fun-packed year, all those civilian complaints...the second unit-destroying traffic accident coming in April after the first-of-the-month kick down to Southwest Traffic."

"You had to be there."

The elevator arrived and they got in. The door closed, and as they rode down, Shane kept looking into the open box with the morbid curiosity of a freeway rubbernecker passing a fatal accident. All of his mid-nineties career pileups were collected there. He spotted a bunch of his old 7.04 ADAM control cards, which were identification sheets for radio-message logs. It shocked him. She was actually reading his old radio transmissions. He couldn't believe it. He also saw two manila envelopes from the Traffic Division that he assumed detailed the two unit-wrecking collisions he'd had while he was in Southwest Patrol. Wedged down in the side of the box were dozens of 8.49 out-slips, which were like library cards from Records and Identification. She was pulling all of his old arrest reports. The rest of the box was littered with field-interview cards and DR numbered witness statements filed by the IOs working his case. He was staring down into the box with growing dread.

"Jesus Christ, what's with the fucking rectal exam?"

"And you don't even have to grab your ankles," she said, shifting the box away from his stare. She was still balancing the heavy box on her knee as the elevator door opened.

Shane moved out without looking back at her. He had a tinny taste in his mouth as he pushed open the double doors at the back of the Bradbury Building and hurried through. He heard them swing closed behind him, right in Alexa Hamilton's face. She must have been trying to slip in with the file box before the doors closed and mistimed it, because he heard the heavy oak frame hit her hands, which were clutching the leading edge of the box.

"Shit!" she said as the door bounced off her knuckles.

Shane now had his own key to Room 256; he let himself in and turned on the stark neon overhead lights. They blasted a harsh, unfriendly blue-white glare down on the three Xerox machines. He dropped his coat on the back of the chair and glanced at his watch. It was 8:32. Since no deputy chief ever got in before nine, he took a chance and picked up the phone, dialing the number for Parker Center.

"LAPD Parker Center," a cheerful woman's voice greeted him.

"Deputy Chief Tom Mayweather," he said, and a few seconds later got Mayweather's secretary.

"Is he in?"

"Who's calling, please?"

His heart was beating fast. Once he identified himself, if Mayweather was in, he'd either have to talk or hang up; neither was an acceptable choice. What he wanted was just to leave an ass-covering message. "It's Sergeant

Shane Scully," he finally answered, holding his breath.

"I'm sorry, Sergeant, he's at a breakfast meeting."

"Breakfast meeting" was department bull-shit for "not in yet." Shane let out a chestful of air.

"It's really important that I talk to the chief," he lied, laying it on a little.

"I'm sorry," she said. "Can I give him a message?"

"Will you tell him I've been trying to get in touch with him, please? Tell him I was unable to get to Robbery/Homicide last night as he ordered because I fell asleep driving down from Arrowhead. Crashed the car, broke my front fender. It was dangerous to drive when I was that tired, so I stopped in a motel. I just woke up. I have some errands to take care of when I get home, so tell him I'll get in touch with him later."

"I'll be sure he gets the update." She hung up.

Shane hoped the phone call would give him a little cover.

He looked at his IN box and found half a dozen new cases that had been left for him to copy. He started to pull them out, and as he was arranging them in stacks on the worktable, his eyes scanned each face sheet.

He was surprised to see that Don Drucker had made this morning's lineup. Apparently Drucker was scheduled for a full board as well. Under the face sheet was an internal notification slip that informed Drucker's defense rep that his board had just been postponed from April 20 until April 23, as requested. The face sheet had the IAD case number and had been signed by the head of Special Investigations Division, Deputy Chief T. Mayweather.

"What the fuck?" he said softly, thinking, *Why was the head of the division signing these charge sheets instead of Warren Zell, here at IAD?* Then he picked up his phone and dialed the Clerical Division. He asked for and was transferred to a civilian employee who was a longtime friend.

Sally Stonebreaker was nothing like her name...a sparrow of a woman with a Transylvanian complexion, translucent skin, and thin white hair. Shane had met her in municipal court nine years ago. He'd been testifying in a robbery case, and she was getting a restraining order against her ex-husband in the courtroom next door. Al Stonebreaker had beaten her twice and had been threatening her over disputed alimony payments. That same night Shane had looked him up and explained the new rules. The "discussion" had taken place in the alley behind a neighborhood bar and required Al to get half a dozen stitches and some new bridgework. After that, Al Stonebreaker had left Sally alone.

Shane got Sally on the line. Once he identified himself, he could hear a little pause before she went on.

"I'm sorry about what's going on," she finally said. "Ray Molar was some piece of work."

"Sally, I need you to do a computer run. I'm sort of locked off the system now, and I don't want a record of this search anyway."

"Shane, I'm busy right now." She paused, then added, "Besides, they've got new Data-Locks on our consoles and it's real hard to access the mainframe without a case clearance number," she said, trying to shake him. He was already department poison.

"Sally, I need this favor. You've gotta come through for me."

Another long pause, during which he could hear her breathing. "Okay, but only this once. After that, I can't do it again."

"Thanks. I've got an IAD complaint investigation CF number for a Board of Rights on a policeman one in Southwest, named Don Drucker. I need to find out what IAD is trying him for. The number is 20-290-12."

"Just a minute."

He could hear computer keys clicking, then she came back on the line.

"He's been charged under a 670.5 of the PDM," she said.

"What is that? Six hundred codes are like booking and prisoner-escape violations, right?" There were hundreds of numbered codes listed in the five-hundred-page LAPD manual.

"Yeah. Escaped juvenile. Drucker lost him in transit, prior to booking. Gimme a minute to read this," she said. Then a moment later she came back on the line. "Okay. Prisoner was a teenage Hispanic named Soledad Preciado, arrested in Southwest. According to Drucker's

Internal Affairs complaint, he left the arrestee unattended in the back of his squad car while he went into a drugstore. Drucker claims he was having a migraine and needed to fill a prescription, said he couldn't drive with the headache and was getting nauseous. While he was in the drugstore, Sol Preciado got out of the unit and walked away."

"Was this kid, by any chance, a Hoover Street Bounty Hunter?"

"Just a minute," she said, and her computer keys were clicking again. She came back on. "A suspected Bounty Hunter, age fifteen. He claimed he's not in a gang, but he's listed in the Gang Street Alias Index under the name Li'l Silent, so at the very least he's a TG or a known associate." TG stood for "tiny gangster" and was basically a killer in training. Shane knew you didn't usually get a street name unless you'd already been "jumped in the set," so it figured he was probably a full member.

"Can you punch out another name for me?"

"I gotta go, Shane. My supervisor's a great white. All he does is swim and eat. Right now, he's cruising this floor."

"Sally, I need help. I hate to put it this way, but I helped you once, now you gotta do this for me." He could hear her sigh loudly on the other end of the phone.

"Okay, gimme it." She was getting mad.

"A policeman one, his name is Kono. I don't have his first name. Check him to see if he's got an Internal Affairs complaint."

193

He was shooting with his eyes closed, firing on instinct.

"You got a CF number?" Sally asked, frustration in her voice. "It'll make it a lot easier."

"I'm sorry, this is just a hunch. There may not even be a board pending on him."

He could hear keys clicking again, then: "Yeah. Kris Kono. He's got a CF number, 20-276-9."

"No shit," Shane said, his heart beating fast now. He wasn't sure what was tugging on the end of this line, but he'd definitely hooked something. "What's IAD got him for?"

"It's...lemme see..." She was quiet as she scanned the file for a few minutes, then: "It was a gang fight, also in Southwest. Two bystanders got shot. A store owner died. Kono got the BOR 'cause he lost some key evidence. In this case, the murder weapon disappeared from the trunk of his squad car. The case got pitched by the judge at the prelim. The dead store owner's wife complained, and this complaint has a bunch of community affidavits attached. A city councilwoman in that district is on a tear. I process Southwest complaints on my terminal. The division started heating up about six months ago. Gang-related crime is soaring. The community is getting pissed down there."

"Was the Kono blown bust also H Street Bounty Hunters?"

"Yeah...same as Drucker."

"Two more names: Lew Ayers and John Samansky. I think they're operating in Southwest, too."

194

"I can't. I gotta go. I'm gonna get in trouble."

"Just tell me if these guys all worked on the same patrol shift or if you see any other common denominators."

"It's Southwest. That's all I can tell you. Look, Shane, I can't—"

"Okay, thanks, Sally. You've been a big help."

He hung up and sat silently in the Xerox room. His mind was chewing it, looking for the connection. Joe Church, Don Drucker, and Kris Kono were all first-year cops, emotionally distraught over Ray's death, and all had fucked up on cases involving the Hoover Street Bounty Hunters, a Hispanic gang in Southwest Division. Ayers and Samansky were policemen working Southwest, but had searched Barbara's house in Harbor Division, using a warrant supplied by a Mayor Crispin-owned judge. They were also highly emotional over Ray.

He sat in the wooden chair and tried to put it together. *What had he stumbled into? Was this just a bunch of stupid coincidences, or something much more sinister?* His phone rang. He looked over at it as if it were a coiled snake. Finally he picked it up.

"Yeah."

"Chief Mayweather calling Shane Scully," the chief's secretary said.

"Scully just left. He wasn't feeling good. Got the flu, I think. If I see him, I'll tell him the deputy chief was trying to reach him," he said, and after she bought it, he hung up quickly. He grabbed his coat and left the Internal Affairs Xerox room, locking the door behind him. He passed up the slow-moving elevators and hurried down the stairs. In less than a minute he was back in his Acura and driving out of the parking structure on his way to the Records Division on Spring Street.

19
DEN

O N HIS WAY across town, Shane dropped off the roll of film he had taken at Arrowhead. He told the man at the Fotomat that he wanted one set of normal prints and, if they didn't come out, a set with the negative pushed two stops. He was told that pushing the negative could permanently destroy the film, but he okayed it. The man behind the counter told him the film would have to be sent out and wouldn't be ready for six to twelve hours.

Shane drove to the Records Division and parked in the big asphalt lot on Spring Street. He locked the Acura and moved around the front, trying hard not to look at the bashed-in fender. He walked through the door of the large three-story brick building and climbed the stairs to the Criminal Division, where he sat at a table and filled out a records release request.

In order to access Soledad Preciado's criminal offender record information (CORI), Shane had to fill out a right-to-know/need-to-know CORI release form. Those persons defined in the California penal code with right-and need-to-know authorization included the juvenile court, Social Services, and members of the Special Investigations Section, which now, technically, included Shane Scully, its new unit discovery officer. Since it is specifically mandated that automated and manually stored CORI information not be electronically distributed, Shane had to be at the Spring Street building to tender his request in person.

Juvenile records are further restricted by the Department of Public Social Service (DPSS) and can be reviewed only by order of a juvenile court judge or the Los Angeles County Children's Services Department (LACCSD). However, the Special Investigations Division was exempted.... Shane was beginning to view his transfer to Internal Affairs in a more favorable light. Since Sol's case was part of Don Drucker's Internal Affairs investigation and had a Special Investigations CF number, Shane included that number and fraudulently listed himself as the case IO. He handed the paperwork to the clerk, a small, narrow-shouldered man with wispy blond hair combed over a yarmulke-sized bald spot. Shane hoped that the man was too bored to check the request against his badge number.

A few minutes later a manila envelope was

passed over. Shane unwound the string tie, pulled out Soledad (Sol) Preciado's Criminal Records folder, and opened it. For a fifteen-year-old, Soledad had a very extensive yellow sheet. His arrest record included two CCWs (carrying a concealed weapon), one assault with intent to commit, and one attempted murder. He'd been down twice: once for a year at the Pitchess youth camp on the attempted murder, once for six months at CYA on a parole violation. Sol Preciado had definitely been out there flagging with the homies. Shane kept reading and finally came across the incident involving the escape from Drucker's patrol car, which was there by virtue of the department's Alpha Index Criminal History cross-reference system. He scanned Drucker's commanding officer's review. At the end of the page he saw that Preciado had not been originally arrested by Don Drucker. He had been called in later only to handle Sol's transport to Los Padrinos Juvenile Hall, which was all the way across town at 2285 East Quill Drive, in Downey. It was unusual for the arresting officer not to transport his own prisoner. Shane wondered why it had happened. He started flipping back, looking for the original arresting officer's report. He finally found it; Preciado had been arrested on November 12 by Sergeant Mark Martinez. Shane scanned the arrest report.

Sol Preciado, a.k.a. Li'l Silent, had been alleged to be committing multiple assaults outside the L.A. Coliseum (court appearance pending). The crimes occurred at about

12:30 P.M. as people were streaming in for the USC-Oregon State football game. He had assaulted several women, knocking them down and snatching their purses. Events escalated when a man trying to stop him was knifed in the abdomen, allegedly by the enraged fifteen-year-old. Preciado had been apprehended by Sergeant Martinez, a member of the Coliseum Division police unit.

Since Martinez was working a duty station and could not leave, Drucker had been dispatched to the Coliseum to pick up Soledad Preciado, then subsequently lost him on his way to the city jail with the ill-advised stop at the drugstore for a headache prescription. The report said that Preciado had somehow managed to open the handcuffs and escape.

There was a statement by Drucker describing his chronic migraine headaches, which had become unbearable and had caused him to stop for medication. He had listed several police officers who could attest to his medical problem. At the very top of that list was Lieutenant Raymond Molar, whom Drucker identified as his LAPD den leader.

Shane put down the arrest report and picked up the phone on the scarred wooden desk. He redialed the Clerical Division and, after a moment, had Sally Stonebreaker back on the line.

"Aren't you happy it's me again," he said, trying to put a friendly smile in his voice. It didn't work.

"Good-bye, Shane."

"Sally, don't hang up. This will just take a minute. Nobody else can help me."

"You've gotta leave me alone, for God's sake. I can't do this."

"One little, teeny favor. Just one. Take you thirty seconds. Take you fifteen."

"Oh, shit," she groaned, but he knew he had her.

"I just found out Ray Molar was a den leader, and I need to know who was in his den." He could hear a loud sigh for emphasis.

"Okay, but this is absolutely it. You call me again, I'm hanging up."

"Thanks, Sally, and don't get hit by the flower truck 'cause it's on its way."

"Don't send me flowers, just stop calling."

He heard the keys clicking as she entered Ray's name into the computer. After a moment she came back on the line. "He had a den in Southwest. Get a pencil, these are his cubs..."

Shane grabbed a pen out of his pocket and turned over the manila folder. "Go."

"A full pack. There's six: Lee Ayers, John Samansky, Coy Love, Joe Church, Don Drucker, and Kris Kono. Don't call again." And he was listening to a dial tone. No good-bye, no good luck, just a click and a buzz.

But he'd hit the lottery. The connection between all these first-year officers was Ray's police den.

A few years back, the LAPD had instituted an innovative concept called den policing. The department had discovered that it was difficult to go from civilian life into police work. After graduation from the academy, rookies were assigned a den leader to help them make the transition. As civilians, many of them had never experienced the discrimination and hatred that some elements of society aim at its sworn badge carriers. Often, particularly in the first year on the job, officers were totally unprepared for the abuse heaped on them. It was difficult not to respond when someone called you a pig and spit on you or your police car. Many cops ended up losing their tempers and resorting to violence. The idea of a den was to have a veteran officer who had perspective on the problems of police work assigned as a kind of emotional coach to help these rookies through their transition year. Den leaders were not commanding officers or watch commanders; they were not responsible for the officer's performance, only for his emotional stability.

Suddenly Shane could understand why these cops were hovering over Ray's death. He had been their coach; their confidant, their police department godfather. It was a piece of connective tissue that jerked the hostile emotional attitudes of the six officers into focus.

But it still left several more difficult questions unanswered: Why was Chief Brewer using Ray's old den to lean on him, and why were they all facing charges at Internal Affairs? What was the Hoover Street Bounty Hunter connection, and why were these six officers all involved in broken cases concerning that one Hispanic Southwest Division gang?

Shane sat there at the table, deep in thought. After a minute the narrow-shouldered wisp of a man who had given him the folder was hovering again. "You through with that?" he asked.

"Yeah." Shane handed back the folder, with the names of Ray's den still scribbled on the back. The clerk hurried away with it.

Shane was not sure what to do next or where to go. He couldn't return to IAD; he was dodging Mayweather. He didn't want to go home and just sit, taking the chance that the deputy chief would send a patrol unit out there to arrest him.

Finally, because he couldn't think of a better course of action, he decided to check in with DeMarco Saint.

It was not even ten-thirty in the morning when he got there, and DeMarco was already drunk. Shane was standing in the defense rep's living room, watching him struggle to get up off his sofa. He almost made it but fell awkwardly, catching himself painfully by an elbow on the coffee table.

"Whoa..." the defense rep said as he tried once more, this time managing to stumble to his feet. Two young boys, about fifteen, were lounging on the sofa on each side of him, watching the proceedings with glazed indifference.

"The fuck's wrong with you?" Shane asked, looking at his teetering defense rep. "How can you be wasted? It's not even noon."

"Had a few bubblies. Hit me harder'n I

202

thought." DeMarco grinned. "Shane, meet the guys—Billy an' Mark. Guys, meet Shane. They just moved in. Been sleeping under the fuckin' pier. I'm helpin' 'em out."

They looked right through him, no change of expression. He wasn't even a blip on their radar. Anybody in a tie over thirty was in a parallel dimension and didn't exist for them.

"We gotta talk. Let's go." Shane grabbed DeMarco's arm and tried to drag him out of the house. The two fifteen-year-olds rose up to protect their new landlord.

"Sit down!" Shane growled menacingly, and they did.

"S'okay," DeMarco slurred. "Lez go...jus' don' yank on me."

They left the house and walked out onto the sand. It was a bright Southern California day. DeMarco groaned painfully as the sunlight hit him, and he shaded his eyes, wavering badly as he walked. They were twenty yards away from the house when Shane spun him and faced him.

"How can you be fucking drunk, man?"

"Relax, will ya? I was up half the night workin' on your case. Haven't even been t'bed yet. No food...s'why the brews snuck up on me."

"Have you interviewed Barbara, prepared a witness list, contacted Mayweather or Halley to get their sworn affidavits and a copy of the DFAR, sent anything to the subpoena control desk?"

"I... I'm..."

"The answer is no, 'cause I've been with Barbara and you haven't even called her yet. She's gotta be priority one 'cause if she changes her statement, I'm dust. You gotta lock her in with an affidavit, secure her testimony before you mess with the rest of it. Since I know you know that, you've done nothing."

"Hey, Shane...will y'calm down? Okay, just calm down." DeMarco took a step forward and lost his balance and fell down. "Oops," he said, grinning. "Somebody's moving the beach."

"Dee, I was down at IAD this morning. I bumped into Sergeant Hamilton, who is running through my life with spikes on. She's got a box full of every mistake I ever made, even down to my old Patrol Division TAs. She's giving me a fucking sigmoidoscopy, while you're out here getting hammered. We only have eight more days, then we go in front of the board."

"Relax. Okay?" He was trying to get up and not having much luck, so Shane knelt down beside him.

"How can I relax? I'm on the block."

"I don't think Alexa Hamilton really wants to prosecute you. Okay?" He was smiling stupidly.

"That isn't what you said before. You said she'd been in Southwest supervising a patrol watch and came back to Internal Affairs specifically to take my case, that she volunteered for it."

"When I said it, I was trying to duck the case, but now that I have it, I think otherwise."

"She's the queen of the Dark Side. Whatta you mean, she doesn't want to prosecute me?"

"Why d'you think ya won the BOR sixteen years ago?"

"We won because you caught her key witness lying."

"We won 'cause Alexa threw the fuckin' case." He belched and then tried to stand, but again didn't make it.

"She what?"

"She threw th' fuckin' case, went in the tank, intentionally bricked it."

"You never said that before. If she dumped it, you would've told me."

"Hey, winning cases was how I kept my rep hard back then. I din' wanna share the glory. Wha' good's it to win a tough board if the prosecuting advocate throws the fuckin' case? 'Sides, she swore me to secrecy.... Said she'd get busted if I tol'."

"I want facts, Dee. I want the whole story. If you're bullshitting..."

"Not shitting." He sat back and took a deep breath to clear his head, then went on. "She comes to me like two days 'fore the board and tells me the chief advocate himself, the fuckin' Dark Prince, got a statement from Ray that was devastating to your case."

"Wait a minute. Ray was on my side."

"Grow up, man. Ray was on Ray's side. He didn't wan' any part of your problem, and his statement contradicted yours. Since he was your training officer, it was gonna flat fuckin' sink you." He took a deep breath and rubbed his eyes. "Alexa said she wasn't gonna include Molar's affidavit in the discovery material. Said since the DA took Ray's statement personally, he would insist Ray be called to testify, but Zell wouldn't be aware that Ray's affidavit had accidentally on purpose been left out of discovery." Now he was grinning stupidly again. "She said I should object an' get his testimony stricken, because she had failed to include it, makin' Ray's testimony inad... inad..."—he belched—"inadmissible at the hearing. Thas wha' happened."

Shane was confused. It didn't add up.

"Then she tells me she thinks the gas-station attendant was lying," DeMarco continued. "Tells me to polygraph him. She impeached her own fuckin' guy, and he was the best part of her case."

"Why? Why would she do that?"

"Maybe she wants your bod."

"Get up." Shane pulled DeMarco up to his feet.

He stood there, weaving drunkenly. "I'm figurin' there's a good chance she's gonna come across again." He grinned.

"You mean you're sitting around, sucking down beers, waiting for her to throw this case, too?"

"I'm not waiting around. I'm bustin' tail, bud. I'm all over this puppy...."

"Okay, Dee, I'm stuck with you because they fast-tracked my board and nobody else will take it on such short notice. Right now I've got something to do, but I'm coming back, unannounced. You better be fuckin' clear-eyed and sober. Next time I'm here, I want a full review of this case, blow by blow. I want your subpoena list and I want to know who you're interviewing. I want to hear your case strategy."

"Done," he said, giggling slightly, shading his eyes, squinting into the sun.

Shane couldn't believe what he was seeing, couldn't believe what DeMarco had just told him. Alexa, with her box full of his career glitches, was hardly going to throw this board, regardless of what happened the last time. He glowered at the wavering defense rep. "We've gotta get our helmets on. If I catch you drunk again, I'll beat the shit out of you. Don't fall down on me, man." Then he turned, leaving the longhaired defense rep teetering badly in the bright sunlight.

THE BLACK WIDOW

A FTER HE LEFT DeMARCO, Shane sat inside the hot Acura in the beach parking lot with the driver-side door open and called Sandy. Surprisingly, this time he got her; she picked up on the third ring.

"Sandy, it's me."

"Shane, it wasn't anywhere near as bad as you thought. I called the school, and they told me there's no problem. Chooch is back in classes."

"Yeah, no problem. What an alarmist I'm becoming. I need to see you today. We need to work out some stuff. I'll be there in half an hour."

"Today's really shitty for me."

"The whole week has been shitty for me," Shane growled. "You're meeting me at noon."

"Can't. I have a lunch engagement."

"Cancel it." He was pissed at DeMarco but taking it out on Sandy.

"It's not that easy," she hedged.

"Cancel the fucking lunch date. I'm gonna be there at noon." He hung up on her. It was eleven-thirty.

Sandy lived at the Barrington Plaza in Brentwood, in one of two gorgeous penthouse suites. Shane got there in thirty minutes. He pulled up to the overhanging porte cochere and handed the keys for the busted-up Acura to a doorman who had enough braid hanging off his uniform shoulders to lead a Latin American country or the University of Michigan marching band.

"I'll need to announce you, sir," the doorman said, frowning at the bruised Acura parked on his brick entryway, subtracting elegance like a turd on a serving platter.

"Shane Scully for Ms. Sandoval."

The doorman picked up the phone, had a short conversation, then walked with Shane into the lobby and key-carded the elevator for the penthouse level. "You can phone down before you return and I'll have the vehicle brought up." He pronounced the word "vehicle" like an ancient curse.

"Thank you," Shane said. The doors closed and he was alone in the fragrant oak-paneled luxury of the Barrington Plaza elevator, listening to a selection of orchestrated show tunes.

Shane marveled once again at what Sandy had been able to accomplish. When he had met her, he'd been on the job only a little over a year. It was just after he'd been separated from Ray and moved to West Valley Division. The first month in that division he'd been a floater, and because he was a "new face," he had been temporarily assigned to detectives working a bunco scam as an undercover. She had been a top-line L.A. call girl, working an executive clientele. The bunco detectives had been investigating a counterfeit bond trader, and Sandy happened to be balling the guy for a thousand a night. Shane, working UC, had arrested her for prostitution, but then instead of booking her, the bunco squad instructed him to try to "flip" her. He did, and she worked the case for him as an informant. Shane was her contact. She had skillfully pillow-talked the bond trader, allowing Shane and the Valley detectives to expand their investigation. When the bust went down, fifteen bond traders hit the lockup and Shane protected her, managing to keep her from being prosecuted.

During that operation she proved that she had guts and savvy and could be counted on in a pinch. Shane became her friend, and one night, a week later over dinner, she suggested that she might be willing to work for the police if the price was right.

"How much do you guys spend to get a big player into court?" she had asked him. "How much overtime and special duty gets approved to bring down a big vice lord or drug kingpin?"

The truth was, often hundreds of thousands of dollars were spent trying to collar a predicate felon, and sometimes even then they failed to come up with an indictment.

Sandy's proposal was shrewd; it showed her keen business mind. She told Shane she would work any target they pointed her at and charge LAPD nothing up front. Despite the upscale nature of her clientele, she was tired of working one-night stands and wanted to expand her horizons. She had two conditions: if successful, she wanted half the amount of money the department had spent on that criminal investigation in the preceding year, and she would not work a target who had an annual police budget of under a hundred thousand dollars. She said she would trust Shane to divulge the correct amount. After almost a month of negotiating with her over terms and conditions, the department finally agreed.

Sandy proved to be exceptional in this new line of work. She was thorough and totally prepared herself before ever moving in on her target. First, she would study the criminal, research him like a doctoral thesis. If he liked Russian literature, she would memorize passages of Solzhenitsyn. If he was interested in Impressionistic art, she would become an expert on Gino Severini's essays, *From Futurism to Classicism*. Then she would set up shop somewhere in his field of vision. One day Mr. Big would be at his favorite country club bar and he'd look across the room and see a dusky, raven-haired goddess sitting at a table alone, reading an art pamphlet detailing the next Impressionist auction at Sotheby's. A conversation would ensue, and this unsuspecting criminal would find that, lo and behold, he had a soul mate, a drop-dead ten on the libido scale who miraculously liked everything he did, from van Gogh to ocean catamaran racing. She became so tuned in, she could finish his sentences.

Before long they would become intimate. Here, Sandy was on her home field. She was a Hall of Fame sexual acrobat. Mr. Big would think he'd won the quiniela. Then Sandy would slowly begin to work him for information. After sex he'd start bragging. He'd fill her beautiful head with his criminal exploits. She'd coo and tell him he was a genius. Once she had his criminal operation down, she would start looking around for a patsy. She knew that when the cops made the arrest, Mr. Big would know he'd been sold out. He might turn violent from his cell, might figure her for the informant and order her killed. To protect herself, Sandy would look around at Mr. Big's criminal companions for a stand-in who could fulfill this unrewarding role.

Before dropping the dime to the police, she would set up the patsy as the informant. She was careful to always pick someone worthy of execution, so the unsuspecting police department wouldn't put too much time into the scumbag's murder. Once she had selected her patsy, she would begin flirting with him, setting up a romantic triangle. Mr. Big would get furious at the patsy: "Stop hitting on Sandy. I catch you putting the make on her again, I'll drop you where you stand." But Sandy was worth the risk, and she'd work both men into steamy jealous rages.

When the bust came down, it didn't take Mr. Big long to figure out who had fingered him. The patsy would end up strolling the tidal basin in concrete loafers while Sandy sat in the jail visitors' room, crying her eyes red and promising Mr. Big that she would be there when he got out.

Because she always destroyed her targets, and a patsy always died, her nickname in the department was "the Black Widow." Like her namesake, she was a great but deadly piece of ass.

She would then present her bill to Shane for this valuable service, and he would be her bagman for the department's payoff. She was L.A.'s most successful consignment concessionaire. It was a fair deal. If she didn't get the goods, the LAPD didn't pay.

In the beginning Shane was the only cop she would trust to be her intermediary. The cases went down smoothly in court because the tip that led to the bust was always anonymous, so it couldn't be traced back to the department. Naturally, the arresting officers didn't even know about the arrangement. Since Sandy never testified in court or told anybody what she had to do to get the goods, it was, strictly speaking, legal. She was paid as an informant—something police do all over the country. It was a very efficient and profitable deal for everybody.

Inevitably, the feds got wind of her and, in their typical, claim-jumping fashion, moved in. Since their budgets were larger and she could make more money with them, they started poaching on the LAPD, and now she was working mostly federal cases.

The elevator doors opened, and Sandy was standing in the hall waiting for him. Every time he saw her, he was knocked out all over again. It was as if his memory wasn't able to retain her remarkable physical perfection. She was tall, almost five-ten, and had a spectacular, trainer-sculpted body. She had told him once that her mother was Mexican and her father Colombian, which was responsible for her Latin coloring. She had raven-black hair and coffee-colored skin. Her brown eyes twinkled and danced and said "Take me." She was one of the most attractive, sensual women he had ever laid eyes on. Although she was in her mid to late thirties, she could have easily passed for twenty-nine.

She was standing before him, wearing designer heels and a tailored white dress that revealed just enough knee and breast to cause him to lose concentration, but she was never overtly sexy. She was a strange, exotic mixture—classy yet seductive, expensive yet available—and somehow Sandy carried it off with incredible ease.

"Shane, you look tired. I hope you're not doing stakeouts, sleeping in your car," she said, reacting to the circles under his eyes.

"You always know how to make me feel so special," he said darkly as she took his hand and offered her cheek to kiss.

"Come on, stop it, you know I love you. I made us sandwiches." She was smooth, working him now, making him feel important. She was good at it. Men were her business.

The penthouse was huge, beautiful, and all white. White walls on white carpet, with white drapes framing an acre of plate glass. The antiques were all real. A black and goldleaf Louis XV desk and matching secretary unit were on opposite walls; white sofas and European accent pieces immediately caught the eye. Sandy stood in the middle of the entry with her hands on her slender hips, the most exotic decoration in the room by far.

"I think, now that I see you, you need some alcoholic CPR. How 'bout a beer?" She moved into the kitchen without waiting for a reply, got two Amstel Lights, and brought them back, along with the sandwiches on bone china plates. All of it was carried on an expensive antique silver serving tray. She set everything down on the white marble-top table near the windows.

The mirrored glass skyline of Century City twinkled in the clean air blowing in from the ocean a few miles away.

"You have to take Chooch back," he said without preamble.

"I can't, Shane, I told you, I'm on this thing for the DEA. I'm working almost every night. The target is a hitter. I stumble—I'm gone. Honest to God, this guy's a vampire...he plays all night."

"Sandy, I'm going to say this again, 'cause it's important. You need to spend some time with your son. I blew it. I almost got through, but I blew it. Now I'm afraid he's gonna take off, then we're gonna be out there looking for him. He's got some gangbang friends in the Valley; he'll hang with bad company. He's pissed off, ready to run. I'm worried about him."

They sat with the beers and untouched sandwiches between them as Sandy bit her lower lip in concentrated thought. "I know you think I've just dumped him, that I sent him off to boarding school or left him with friends...but I'm trying to make enough money so he can go to Princeton or Yale. I want him to get the best education, maybe be a doctor."

"To begin with, it doesn't matter what I think. It only matters what Chooch thinks. You've gotta show him *you* care. You've gotta make room for him in *your* life, make him feel like he belongs somewhere, like somebody truly gives a shit. Forget about Yale, 'cause the way he's going, he's gonna be doing his post-grad study at Soledad State Prison."

"My plan is to get ten mil in tax-free munis and blue chips, stuff that will grow and throw off cash, then I'm gonna retire and move with Chooch to Arizona—Phoenix, I was thinking—settle down, be a regular mom. I'm a year away, maybe less."

"You don't have a year. You may not have a week."

"Shane, the sting on this drug deal goes down in two days. I'm right at the critical point, creating my exit strategy."

"You mean setting up your dead man," he corrected.

"Boy, are you in a shitty mood. Stop being so contentious. I'll take him once this sting is over. I promise. But I'm not taking him today, or tomorrow.... Maybe this will be over by Monday. Let's shoot for Monday."

Shane got to his feet, without having touched the sandwich or the beer. She didn't beg him to stay, either.

"By the way, who the hell is his father?"

"His name is Carlos Delmonica. I got careless with my pills. He was a drug dealer in Simon Boca's operation, and he's currently a resident of Leavenworth, Kansas, doing twenty-five to life in the federal pen."

"Jeez, no help there, I guess."

"The best thing we can hope for is that Chooch never meets his father. And don't tell him who he is. I don't want Chooch writing Carlos, who doesn't even know he has a son."

"Monday," Shane said with finality.

He started for the door, and Sandy scooped her purse off the sofa table. "I'll go with you. Maybe I can still make my lunch." She picked up the phone and dialed the bandleader with the braided shoulders in the lobby. "Darling, it's Sandy. I'm coming down with the gentleman who just arrived. Be a dear, will you?" She hung up and smiled brightly. "Our cars will be right up. Magic."

They exited into the hall. As she punched the elevator button, a phone rang. Both Sandy and Shane dug for their cells. It was Shane's. He popped it open.

"Yeah," he said.

It was Luanne McDermott, of the Fingerprint Analysis Unit at SIS. "The print lab lifted a set of pretty good latents off the videotape box," she said. "They came back to Calvin Sheets, 2329 Los Feliz, apartment sixteen."

"Calvin Sheets," Shane said, taking a pen and his small spiral notebook out of his pocket. "Spell it *ea* or *ee?*"

"Sheets—*ee*. Also, he used to be one of us."

"A cop?"

"Yeah...got terminated by Internal Affairs six months ago."

"Anything else?"

"That's it."

"Thanks." He closed the phone and tapped the pen on the spiral notebook, deep in speculation.

The elevator arrived at the penthouse level, and he and Sandy got aboard. This time they were listening to an orchestrated version of "Eleanor Rigby."

"I know Calvin Sheets," Sandy said, surprising him.

The doors closed and they rode down.

"You do?"

"He works for Logan Hunter—at least he used to."

"The movie producer?"

"Actually, Logan runs his own independent studio now, Starmax. Calvin Sheets is head of his security."

"How do you know Logan Hunter?" Shane asked, always surprised by the level of people Sandy knew. "Isn't he a big social deal, always doing some major fund-raiser or civic project?"

"Actually, that's how he keeps his reputation. He only works on stuff that will keep him in the press. Right now he's in the paper 'cause he's trying to get a pro football team to come to L.A. He's a football fan like I'm a microbiologist, but it's popular, makes him look good. If it's a news story, he's up for it."

"I hesitate to ask you how you met him."

"I was working Logan for U.S. Customs about two months ago. It went nowhere. He just wouldn't give me any play. One of my few wipeouts. I found out a few weeks later that he's a closet gay. To each his own..."

"What did U.S. Customs want him for?"

"They thought he was smuggling heroin into the country, using film magazines being shipped back from a production he had shooting in Mexico. They thought he was unpacking loads of Mexican Brown in the film lab, but like I said, I never got close enough to find out."

"And Calvin Sheets works for him now?"

"Yeah. And is he ever an asshole. A blister, that one. I'd hate to get caught alone with him in a dark place."

They got to the lobby and stepped out of the elevator. The doorman had already called up the cars; two Spanish-speaking men in white coveralls with BARRINGTON PLAZA stenciled over their pockets delivered the keys and stood by the cars waiting for their tips.

Shane slipped his man a dollar, while Sandy tipped hers five, then rattled some Spanish at him. He smiled and bobbed his head energetically up and down like a sparrow digging for worms. She got behind the wheel of her new bottle-green XJB convertible. They both drove off, heading their separate ways: Sandy in her Jag, to arrange some poor asshole's funeral; Shane in his battered Acura, to pick up her only son at Harvard Westlake before Mr. Thackery threw a shit-fit and started threatening expulsion, *ad summum bonum.*

21
B&E

IT WAS JUST after ten P.M. when Shane left a brooding Chooch Sandoval with Longboard Kelly. He was driving across town to the Bradbury Building, dressed for a burglary in 211 colors: a black LAPD sweatshirt, black jeans, and Reeboks. He had his .38 backup piece snug against his belt. His badge and ID card, picklocks, and penlight were stuffed in all available pockets.

He pulled off the freeway and drove down Sixth Street, right into the hovering helicopter lights of the Schwarzenegger movie. They were back downtown doing night work, barricades in place, assistant directors and klieg lights glaring. He had hoped he would be able to sneak into IAD, rifle the chief advocate's files, and get out unobserved. The last thing he needed to deal with was this fucking movie.

He got stopped two blocks from the Bradbury by a motorcycle cop, now a potential witness who could put Shane at the location. He considered turning around and going home but then decided, *fuck it,* he was running out of options. He had to take the chance.

"Sorry, Sergeant, we're almost on a take," the old motorcycle cop said after Shane badged him. He had outgrown his uniform, which stretched over his belly like a Mexican bandit's faded guayabera.

The LAPD supplied movie companies with police assistance to control crowds and traffic on location, and many of the retired old-timers made some money by working movie gigs. Shane didn't know this officer. He never had many friends in Motors because the officers assigned there were basically "hot pilot" types—attitude junkies known on the job as "mustard cases."

"I need to get to my office," Shane explained.

"Lock up traffic. This is picture," the assistant director's voice came over the motor cop's walkie-talkie.

The officer was in his late sixties and looked slightly ridiculous in his too-tight shirt and worn leather knee boots. He held up his hands as if to say there was nothing he could do. The god of cinema had just spoken. "Sorry, we have to wait for the shot," he said.

"It's a good thing the corner bank isn't being robbed," Shane muttered.

They waited while the helicopter hovered loudly overhead. Suddenly a car squealed around the corner of Spring Street, roared down Sixth, skidded sideways, then disappeared around another corner.

"Cut. Release traffic," the AD said over the walkie-talkie, and Shane was finally waved through.

In L.A., movies had their own hallowed place in the subculture. God forbid anybody should fuck with a unit production schedule.

When Shane got to the Bradbury Building, he was greeted by another surprise. The entire north side of the building was flooded by a huge condor light suspended forty feet in the air from a crane. It lit almost the entire city block.

"Shit," Shane muttered. This was getting ridiculous. He was dressed in black, trying to do an illegal entry while a movie was shooting, and the fucking building he was burglarizing was lit up like City Hall. He had already decided not to use the parking structure, because he was pretty sure that the gate had a common security feature that would read his key card, then time-log it, so he parked in a private lot next to a string of honey wagons and dressing rooms.

He locked the Acura and walked past a line of chattering extras, out onto the brightly lit sidewalk. Hugging the bricks of the Bradbury, turtling his head down into his collar, he tried to hide, feeling stupid and exposed like a cockroach scuttling along a kitchen baseboard.

The building was open, as he knew it would be. Advocates often worked late, so the department kept civilian guards on at night. Usually they slept somewhere on the fifth floor.

He walked into the huge lobby and stood in the atrium. The guard desk was empty. He looked up at the advocates' windows on the third floor. The lights were off. He climbed the stairs, his tennis shoes squeaking on the tile floor. When he got to three, he headed down the corridor and stood for a moment in front of the advocates' offices, looking through the windows, past the reception desks to the cubbies beyond, where any late-working advocates might be sitting. The place looked empty, and the lights were all off. He knocked loudly on the door.

Shane had a cover story ready. If anybody was inside, he was going to abort and say that he had come back to finish some Xeroxing but first needed to pick up his key.

He knocked again, but nobody answered. Everyone had gone home. He looked up and down the exterior corridor, then pulled out a small leather case and removed a set of picklocks.

Ironically, picking locks was a criminal specialty he had learned from Ray Molar. A good set of picklocks contained an array of long, needle-shaped tools and one long, thin, notched metal strip. Shane slid the notched strip into the lock and jiggled it to find the first tumbler by feel. Then the smaller picks slid in behind it. The idea was to fill as many of the lock's keyed openings as possible so that you had enough leverage to turn all the tumblers inside the bolt. It was not as easy as it looked on TV, where some guy would just slide a credit card into a door and, bingo, he was in. It took Shane almost ten minutes before he could turn the lock and let himself inside.

He stepped onto the gray carpeted area just inside the door, then slowly withdrew the picklocks and returned them to the case. He closed the door and locked it from the inside.

He moved down the carpeted hallway between the reception desks and windows, heading quietly toward the chief advocate's office. Shane knew that all of the active IAD cases were in a file cabinet there. He got to the end of the long reception area, pushed open the door to Warren Zell's office, took two steps inside, and stopped to adjust his eyes to the low light.

He had stood right in this same spot yesterday, when Zell had informed him that he was IAD's new Xerox machine operator.

He saw the file cabinet at the far end of the room. As he moved to it, he prayed that the cabinets weren't locked. He didn't want to spend any more time there than necessary. As he crossed the room, he took the small penlight out of his back pocket, turned it on, and stuck it in his mouth, gripping it between his teeth. The narrow light hit the top of the metal cabinet, reflecting the beam off its burnished gray finish. He put his hand on the top drawer handle and tugged on it. It slid open. The sound of the little metal rollers filled the room.

He looked down into a file crammed full with case folders; each one had a yellow tab with the officer's name and CF number. He cocked his head to aim the light on the tabs and, working alphabetically, quickly went through the cabinet. In the middle of the top drawer, he found a tab marked L. AYERS. He pulled the file out and opened it. Inside was a single slip of paper with the typed words:

He looked in the second drawer for Joe Church, the second name on the list, and found a file for him as well. It contained the same slip, indicating that the contents had been sent to the secure files over at Special Investigations Division in Parker Center. He glanced at several of the other case files in that drawer and found that none of them had been relocated, only Ayers and Church.

He knelt down and opened the bottom drawer, where he figured he would find Samansky's file, if there was one. It was right in the middle of the drawer, also empty, except for the same note.

What the fuck is this? he thought as he began looking for the Drucker and Kono files. He found both folders empty; the same note was in each. Coy Love didn't have a case pending. He was the only one of Ray's den not facing a Board of Rights.

Shane closed the drawer and stood up. He was just taking the penlight from between his teeth when he heard a gun cock behind him.

"Don't move," a woman's voice said. Then the lights were switched on.

He turned and saw Alexa Hamilton framed in the doorway, a black automatic gripped in both hands, her arms triangled out in front of her in a shooting stance. "You sure are one rule-breaking son of a bitch," she said.

"I'm just trying to—"

"Shut up, Scully! Where's your piece? Where're you packing?"

"Huh?" His mind was spinning, looking for a way out.

"Turn around. Put your hands behind your neck."

"Come on—this Dirty Harriet thing isn't working. I'm assigned down here, same as you. Put the gun down."

"Do what I say, asshole. Do it now!"

He turned his back to her and assumed the position; she quickly patted him down. She removed his clip-on holster, took a step back, and put it on the desk.

Shane assumed she didn't cuff him only because she didn't have her handcuffs handy. She was dressed in a blouse and jeans, her hair was slightly mussed, and he guessed she'd been working late, then fell asleep on the sofa in the back of the advocates' section. He'd awakened her when he'd broken in.

She shifted her gun to her left hand and held it on him while she picked up the phone, locked the receiver under her ear, and dialed three digits. "This is Sergeant Hamilton...requesting a Code Six Adam at 1567 Spring Street, third floor. I'm in the chief advocate's office. Notify the responding unit that they will be transporting a police officer under arrest to Parker Center, and notify Chief Mayweather, head of Special Investigations, to call me at 555-9878." She listened for a moment, then hung up the phone.

"You've gotta hear me out before you do this."

"It's done, Scully. You've just been yanked."

"I wasn't looking at my file—"

"I don't wanna hear it. I'm prosecuting you, so we're not having an ex parte conversation. Just button it till the backup gets here."

Shane was down to his last chance. She would either have to shoot him or listen to him, but he was not going to just stand there, mute, waiting to be arrested.

"Ray Molar was supervising a den of six guys. Five of them have cases going through IAD."

"Shut up. I don't wanna hear another word outta you."

"All of their case files are missing. They've been relocated to the secure files at SID. Why? I've never heard of that before, have you?"

"I said be quiet."

"Alexa, I need you to listen to me. Those files are missing because they contain dangerous information."

"Those files could be missing for a lot of reasons."

"Only the files on the guys in Ray's den are gone," he said incredulously. "Why only those guys?"

"I don't care. It doesn't matter. The chief advocate can relocate files anywhere he wants. They're his. Maybe he knows what a loose cannon you are, figured you'd pull this dumbass burg."

"Ray has a second home in Lake Arrowhead," Shane went on. "He had a second identity up there: Jay Colter. The house is owned by a real

227

estate company, Cal-VIP Homes. I don't know who owns the company yet, but I have a search being done by the Corporations Commission. When I was up at Ray's Arrowhead house last night, I caught four guys cleaning the place out. After they left, I broke inside."

"So, you're averaging one illegal entry a night. This some kind of sideline for you?"

"Listen to me, will ya?" He was getting impatient. He told her about the one-way mirror, the glory hole, and the videotape box with the name Carl Cummins on it.

"None of this ties to anything," she said. "You're rambling, Scully."

"What're you talking about? A lot of it ties together. Ray's old den had some kinda deal going with the Hoover Street Bounty Hunters, possibly to blow arrests and let them off. Chief Brewer was on his answering machine at the party house. I can play the tape for you if you don't believe me. I think maybe even the mayor, who Ray was driving, is somehow involved."

"In what? Involved in *what?* You think it's some kinda buy-down? Some bullshit collars-for-dollars scheme?" she asked, referring to a situation in which a criminal shares his take with the arresting officer in return for a chance to walk. "Why would the chief of police and the mayor of L.A. be involved in some two-bit street hustle like that? You're delusional."

"I don't think it's a buy-down. I think it's something else, something much bigger. I got called into Brewer's office yesterday. He threatened me with this ridiculous murder charge, told me he thought I stole a videotape out of Ray's house, and if I gave it back, maybe all my problems would go away. If Ray was videotaping sex parties, maybe this Cummins character or somebody else was getting blackmailed, and if I lean on him hard enough, maybe he'll tell me what's going on. That is, if I can find him." He *was* rambling now, his own voice sounding desperate to him.

"This is weak shit, Sergeant—delusional and paranoid."

"Gimme some time. I've only been working on it for two days. Whatever is going on, it's sure got the top floor of the Glass House worried. They're threatening me with a murder indictment to get some tape they think I have."

"They're threatening you with murder because Ray's wife was your eighty-five. You used to date her, and my IOs say, like the stone-ass moron you're proving to be, you're still actually seeing her."

"Eighty-five" was police slang for girl-friend. Shane ignored it and went on: "All of these IAD cases involve the Hoover Street Bounty Hunters. Some ex-cop named Calvin Sheets is involved. His fingerprints were on the Carl Cummins videotape box I found up at Ray's house in Arrowhead."

When Shane mentioned Calvin Sheets, suddenly Alexa's body posture turned rigid.

Her jaw clenched and her expression darkened. "Calvin Sheets is now head of security for the Starmax movie studio," he continued. "It's an independent studio owned by Logan Hunter, who U.S. Customs suspects of drug smuggling."

She was looking at him differently now. So he took a wild guess, trying to reel her in. "You know Calvin Sheets."

For a minute, he didn't think she was going to answer him.

"Another advocate, a good friend of mine, terminated him," she finally said. "He was a rogue officer, a dirty sergeant. How was he involved with Ray?" Shane had *finally* piqued her interest.

"I'm not sure. I've got his voice on that same answering-machine tape from Ray's house in Arrowhead. He said, 'Don't fuck around with love.' At first I thought they were talking about love in the romantic sense, but now I know they were talking about Coy Love."

He waited for her to respond, but she didn't, so he went on. "I'd like you to explain to me why my case jumped over the Shooting Review Board and went straight to a BOR, and why the district attorney is setting me up for this bullshit murder charge, when I have an eye-witness who backs me up."

"Barbara Molar is a shit witness. She's the motive for the murder. I should've punched your ticket sixteen years ago."

"Okay, since you brought that up, why didn't you?"

Her ice-blue eyes were sparking anger. "Why didn't I what?"

"You threw my board sixteen years ago. Why?"

"Who told you I threw it? That's ridiculous."

"DeMarco told me. He said you impeached your own witness and withheld Ray's sworn affidavit."

Now they could hear men's voices downstairs; they echoed in the hollow atrium. The backup unit had arrived. The elevators were shut down for the night and, after a minute, they heard footsteps marching up the tile stairs.

"You might have me on this low-grade B and E, but I'll get you for throwing that Board of Rights sixteen years ago," he threatened. "DeMarco will testify that you gave the case away. You'll probably be getting your own CF number down here. Give you a look at this division from the other side."

"I wish I'd never laid eyes on you," she said sharply.

He could see the beginning of indecision in her eyes. She was a career cop, high on the lieutenant's list.

There was a rattling at the front door of the Advocate Section.

"Anybody in there?" a cop's voice called into the office.

"What's it gonna be, Sergeant?" he asked. She stood frozen, holding her gun in one hand. Finally she lowered her weapon, turned, and walked to the door, then opened it.

Two uniforms moved in. Shane could see

them through Warren Zell's open office door.

"It's okay, Officer. My mistake," he heard Alexa say. "It was just one of our sergeants. He works here."

To punctuate the point, Shane pulled out his badge and flashed it at them.

"Sorry for the call," she said. "If you could do me a favor... Cancel my Code Six A and ask Communications to cancel my call to Deputy Chief Mayweather."

The cop nearest to her touched his shoulder mike and started broadcasting a Code Four, which was a stand-down. Both uniforms turned and left. Alexa closed the door and walked back to where Shane was standing. "We're even. Get outta here," she said angrily.

"Not until you hear the rest of it," he said softly. "And not until you tell me why the hell you threw my board sixteen years ago."

22
EX PARTE COMMUNICATION

THEY WALKED DOWN Third Street, through the glare of the movie lights, and settled on a small, dingy bar called the Appaloosa, two blocks south of the Bradbury. The proprietor had made a half-assed decorating attempt at a Mexican motif: table candles with corny glass sombreros, badly painted pictures of Appaloosas with stoic Mexican cowboys or dusty regal hombres from Santa Ana's army looking across prairies or valleys, their heads held high, reeking Hispanic nobility.

"That fucking Schwarzenegger movie is driving me nuts," she said as they slid into a cracked vinyl booth and waved at a Mexican waiter wearing a dirty white coat about the same color as the gray linoleum floor. Mariachi recordings hissed and popped through a bad speaker system. The place was a refried dive.

"Scotch and water," she said.

"Two," he added.

The waiter left and they sat there, each waiting for the other to start. She was pushed back on the ruptured red vinyl seat, as if she were trying to get as far away from him as possible.

"This is your party," she finally said.

"I want to know why you threw my board."

"Ancient history."

"I wanna know, just the same."

"I wanna know why Christie Brinkley can't keep a husband. It's a mystery. Leave it at that."

"You threw my board sixteen years ago, and now you volunteer for this one?"

"I didn't volunteer. I was ordered. I've been out of Internal Affairs for ten years, running a patrol shift down in Southwest. I wanted to stay in the field, but because of you, I ended up getting called back by Tom Mayweather to handle your board. Don't ask me why."

"Tom Mayweather?"

"Yeah. Heard of him?" Cutting sarcasm now, laying it on with a trowel. "He's head of Special Investigations Division. Read your department administration list."

"I heard you volunteered."

"Look, Scully, for whatever it's worth, you don't even remotely interest me anymore. I'm gonna try your BOR in seven days because the Glass House wants me to. Then I'm going back to Southwest Patrol, where I can actually do some honest-to-God police work."

"Why would Tom Mayweather pull you back to handle my board?"

"If I tell you what I think the reason is, it'll just piss you off."

"I'm already pissed off."

"Because I hold the record. I'm the best advocate they ever had down there. I only lost your case and a few others in the time I was in that division. Mayweather wanted the best, so he ordered me back. If that seems egotistical and self-serving—tough. That's what I think."

"You know what I think?"

She didn't answer, but sat staring at him with those remarkable laser-blue eyes.

"He pulled you back because you tried me before. Sparks flew back then, and he knew it would piss me off. He's trying to pressure me to turn over that videotape he thinks I have. He thought putting you on the case would up the stakes." He paused while the waiter set down their drinks and left.

234

"That's your take, because you always put yourself at ground zero," she said. "To everyone else, you're marginal business, just another dumb mistake that needs to be handled in due course. This has been fun. We've had our one drink. Meeting's over, see ya." She took a long swallow, then set the glass down and started to leave.

"Hey, Lexie, I'm not through yet."

"I don't go by 'Lexie,' asshole. The name's Alexa."

"I don't go by 'asshole,' Alexa. The name's Shane."

They sat in silence for a moment.

"So, why did you throw my board?"

"You won't get off that, huh?"

"It's pretty unusual. You're the best advocate down there, the Black Witch of the Division, yet you intentionally let me slide? I want to know why."

"Because I knew Ray Molar was using you. In the years I'd been at IAD, I'd seen a handful of probationers take violence beefs for him...guys he'd handpicked out of the Academy and teamed up with. It became pretty obvious what was happening. He was busting heads and holding court in the street, then getting you dummies to take the heat for him if complaints came down. It was starting to piss me off. Then, when Ray gave the chief advocate that bullshit statement behind my back, saying that you had emotional problems and that he'd been worried about your mental stability, I sorta lost it. Furthermore, I was sure my key wit, that gas-station attendant, was dirty. Ray musta threatened him to get him to say he saw you beat that kid, because he flunked the poly I gave him. The case was an air ball, so I called DeMarco and told him where the holes were."

Shane sat there for a long moment and looked at her. She seemed different, somehow softer, more vulnerable. Maybe it was the low light, or the scotch, or maybe it was what she'd done for him sixteen years ago at some risk to her own career. But he was being compelled to view her in a different way, so he sat there, turning dials, trying to regain some focus on her.

"You just throw cases if they seem wrong to you?"

"Listen, Scully, I know you think Internal Affairs is a sewer full of ladder-climbing politicians who don't care how many cops' careers they wreck."

"And it's not?"

"No, it's not. Don't you think we're drowning in all the politically correct bullshit that goes through this division? The Gay and Lesbian Alliance gets pissed because some cop gets tough trying to bust a two-hundred-pound angel-dusted bull dyke who's brandishing a hammer. The arresting officer ends up putting the bracelets on but has his head opened up in the process. Instead of filing a resisting-arrest charge on the hammer-wielding debutante, the cop gets accused of gay bashing. It's a big news story. Lots of angry meetings in West Hollywood. The *L.A. Times* does a blue-death dance on the front page, and our fearless leaders dump the whole thing into our basket....

"Or some gangbanger caught standing over a dead body with a smoking MAC-Ten accuses the arresting officer of beating him in the station I-room. The EMTs are called, and the banger doesn't have a mark on him. But the special-interest groups take it to the press—racial violence, forced confessions, cops on the rampage. It's a big deal, and everybody knows all the banger is doing is getting back at the cops who busted him. It's total bullshit. My own IOs are telling me the board won't float, but the perp's a minority. The Glass House and the mayor fold like deck chairs, and the whole mess is back in my office.

"After a while you start to sort out the really bad ones, maybe drop a few key pieces of manufactured evidence overboard, impeach one of your own lying wits if you have to, lay back a bit, try and even things out so good cops don't end up paying the price for somebody's political agenda.

"Then along comes a Rodney King, where the cops were dead wrong, and you gotta go to war, kick some ass. The police need policing. A department without self-investigation is bound to become corrupt."

She drained her drink, the ice cube clinking on her teeth. She set the glass down hard on the table, telling him the lecture had ended. "Is that all? Can I go now?"

"Tell me about Calvin Sheets."

"I told you. Calvin was terminated by a good friend of mine, a current advocate named Susan Kellerman. Susan and I were both sergeants in Southwest Patrol, and I recommended her for Internal Affairs. She's not there two weeks and she gets Calvin's board. He was threatening her life with anonymous phone calls all during the investigation, but she couldn't prove it was him. She called me and asked what she should do. I took a ride out to Calvin's house and gave him a heads-up talk. It wasn't pleasant."

"What happened?"

"I just said it wasn't pleasant. Okay?"

"Did Susan tell you everything about his case?"

"In detail. As a matter of fact, I got so mad at Sheets, I worked it for free. Did some IO work in my off-hours to help her."

"What was he charged with?"

"He was shift commander on the Coliseum detail and was keeping bogus time sheets. He had officers listed as 'on duty' who weren't even there. They were kicking back salary and overtime to him. It was a mess—more than ten cops involved. His whole shift was signing their own arrest reports 'cause Sheets wasn't around. On top of all that, he was off working a second job at the movie studio, doing security work."

"For Logan Hunter."

"Yeah. The cops on his detail called him Dream Sheets because he was so tired when he finally got to the Coliseum, he would just sleep in his office. He was running the slop-piest PED team I ever saw. His Prostitution Enforcement Detail at the Coliseum was watching the games while the hookers were running wild. There were more blow jobs going on in the parking lot than at a swingers' convention. The Coliseum Commission was enraged. We had dozens of letters from those guys. Calvin's board took two days, and Susan got his tin. Eight of the ten cops he was super-vising got terminated with him. Two rookies survived but were given six-month mandatory suspensions. It was a disaster for the city. Calvin called me up after he got termi-nated...told me he would pick a time when I wasn't looking and pay me back with interest. I can hardly wait for him to try. Total sleaze."

Shane sat across the table, absentmind-edly twirling a red swizzle stick between his fingers.

"Stop playing with that, will you? It's making me nervous."

He put the stick in the ashtray. "Doesn't any of this seem strange to you? Add what I have to what you just told me, and it starts to reek. All these Internal Affairs cases, Ray's den and the H Street Bounty Hunters...a banger named Sol Preciado was doing assaults at the Coliseum; Calvin Sheets was failing to supervise his PED team down there, his fingerprints were on that videotape box, in an Arrowhead house where I think prostitutes were screwing guys that Sheets and Ray were black-mailing..."

"You've gotta connect the dots, Shane. You haven't done that. It's called police work."

"I know, but don't you think a lot of this is damn strange?"

She sat looking at him for a long moment. Finally she nodded her head slowly. "Drucker's case is going to a board tomorrow."

"No, it's not. Mayweather just got an extension pushing it back to the twenty-third. If you're so concerned about policing the police, why not work on this?"

"Because I'm on the other side of *your* case. I'm prosecuting you. How on earth can I help you?"

"I won't tell if you won't." He grinned.

"Tell you what, tomorrow I'll ask a few questions, just for the hell of it."

"I think we should talk to Sol Preciado. He's a witness in Drucker's case. Why don't we go out to juvie and sit him down."

"When were you planning for us to do that?"

"Now. Let's do it now. You've got an advocate card; the jail warden won't question it. Let's get him in an I-room at juvie hall and play 'I've Got a Secret.' Bluff him, see what he knows."

She sat looking at him, not answering or reacting to the suggestion.

"If we get nothing, I promise I'll leave you alone." Then he added, "You won't have to see me again till my board."

"We've gotta get one thing straight first,"

she said. "I want an unequivocal promise that you're not gonna use what I just told you about your old BOR against me."

"Alexa, I was never gonna use that. You may think I'm an asshole, but at least I'm an asshole with principles. You did me a favor. I won't forget it. Whatever you decide now, as far as I'm concerned, nothing happened back then."

"Okay, then let's go do some jailin'," she said.

They each took a car and followed each other all the way out to the juvenile jail in Downey.

Trouble was, once they got there and asked that Sol Preciado be brought to an interrogation room, they found out he was no longer a guest of the city. Earlier that afternoon a door had been mysteriously left open in the back of a court transport vehicle and the fifteen-year-old gangbanger had escaped again.

Shane and Alexa took the creaking elevator back down to the lobby and walked out of juvenile hall into the harsh Xenon lights of the parking lot.

"This kid has more jailbreaks than Dillinger," she said.

"They pushed Drucker's board back to get time to arrange for this. They let him go so he wouldn't be around to testify," Shane said. When she looked over at him, he added, "I'm telling you, it's been like this ever since I shot Ray. Somebody is pulling strings, making shit happen. It's been orchestrated better than the Philharmonic."

"You're being paranoid," she concluded.
"I'm being framed," he corrected.

23
CROSSROADS AND CROSSFIRE

"I'M MAKING ARRANGEMENTS for you to go back to your mom on Monday," Shane said.

They were sitting in his backyard chairs, Chooch with his feet up on the low picket fence, leaning way back, trying to look as though he couldn't give a shit. "Make any arrangement you want, but I won't be here on Friday," Chooch snarled. "You can go quakin' about it with the cave bitch all you want, don't matter, 'cause I'm gone."

"You think that I'm dumping you, that I don't want you here, but you're wrong. I'm telling you the truth, Chooch. I feel shitty about this."

No response.

"Tell you what. I should be clear by the end of next week. Whatta you say you and I get outta town, go do something together."

"What're we gonna do? Score some tasty together? Do some jay?" He was smirking now, letting Shane know he was back on the other side.

"I told you no drugs. How 'bout a weekend at Disneyland?" Shane said. "We'll stay at the hotel there, ride the Matterhorn, Space Mountain; do the Log Ride, all that stuff."

"You think I'm some little kid? You can't bribe me with a trip to Disneyland."

"You ever been to Disneyland?" Shane asked.

Chooch shrugged, not answering.

"If you've never been, you don't know what you're turning down. And if you wanna score some tasty, there're girls all over Disneyland," letting Chooch know he understood rap lingo.

But Chooch said nothing.

"You told me once that you wanted to be the most important instead of the least. And I get that, man. I really do. But lemme ask you something. If I let you stay here, knowing that I was in some real danger and that you might end up hurt, what kinda guy would that make me? And how important would you be to me if I just flat disregard your safety?"

"Whatever... You're gonna do what you wanta."

"You want me to understand, to care about your problems, but you don't want to understand or care about mine."

"Is this gonna take much longer?"

"You're going to Sandy on Monday. Sorry you and I can't talk about it."

"You say you're in danger, that someone's gonna ride on you? And I'm supposed to believe this?"

Now it was Shane who didn't answer.

"Well, I don't. Okay? I see it as total doo-rah. You're a fuckin' liar."

Shane got up and moved toward the door. Before going in, he turned and talked to Chooch's back. "There are defining moments in a man's life, Chooch. You're at one. You can deal with this like a man, or you can run from it like a kid. If you run—if you take off and go hang with a buncha street bravos, you're gonna regret it."

" 'Cause why? You're gonna get me booked on a juvenile court detaining order?" he said, surprising Shane that he knew the exact document, and further proving he'd been hanging with some very unsavory people.

"You're at an important crossroad. Read the signs carefully before you choose what direction you want to go. You're fifteen. Nobody can tell you what to do anymore, certainly not me. You're gonna make your own decisions, no matter what Sandy or I say. You're almost a man now, so you stop getting the juvenile discount. But you also gotta pay adult rates—be careful."

Shane went inside and undressed for bed. It had been a strange night. He had left Alexa not knowing what she would do, or whether she believed any of what he had told her. Then he had come home to this draining conversation with Chooch. He lay on his pillow, looking at the cracked ceiling, wondering where it was all heading.

In his wildest imagination, he never would have expected what happened next.

• • •

Shane heard something outside the house.

It woke him.

He didn't know whether it was part of a dream or someone in his yard. He lay still, his heart pounding, his senses tingling; then he rolled out of bed and crept slowly to the dresser, where he had put his gun. He retrieved it, snuck out of the bedroom, padded down the hall in his underwear, and checked the guest room. Chooch was asleep in the bed next to the wall, so Shane went back up the hall.

He wasn't two steps into the front room when a machine gun opened up, blowing out the entire front window. Glass rained in on him, taking part of the drapery with it. Shane dove for the floor as the machine gun kept firing, stitching holes in the wall behind him, breaking plaster, shattering pictures. He worked his way toward the front door on his stomach.

Another burst from a second gun came through the side window. Nine-millimeter slugs tattooed the living room's east wall. He was pinned in a deadly cross fire. Shane rolled over and sat up, firing blindly out the broken side window with his .38. Then he heard a car start in the alley.

Chooch ran into the living room, and Shane launched himself at the teenager, taking him down seconds before another barrage of bullets screamed just above their heads, breaking a lamp and turning an end table into splinters.

Shane pinned Chooch under him, protecting the boy with his body.

"Let's go. Let's get outta here!" somebody shouted.

A car door slammed; an engine roared. There was the chirp of rubber and then the sound of a car speeding away.

"Stay here. Stay down," Shane ordered Chooch. He wormed his way out the front door, slid down the front steps on his belly, and rolled behind a low wall. He didn't want to risk sticking his head up until he had a chance to check out all possible lines of fire. He strained to hear in the dark, to identify any warning sound, trying to be sure all of them had left. Then he rolled up and scooted back on his ass until he could feel the side of the house against his shoulder blades.

His neighbors were starting to shout: "What's going on!?" "What the fuck's happening?!" "Call the police!"

Shane couldn't remember how many shots he had squeezed off, so he flipped open the cylinder...three cartridges left. He snapped the revolver shut and got to his feet, quickly making a lap around the house. He ran into Longboard in the backyard and almost shot him.

"Get back inside, Brian," he ordered.

The surfboard shaper turned and ran back into his house.

After Shane was certain the house was secure, he went back inside.

"Let's go," he said to Chooch.

"Where?"

"You're going to your mother's. You can't stay here. Get your clothes, now! Meet me in the garage. We're outta here!"

They could hear sirens approaching, way off in the distance.

"Let's go. I don't wanna be here when the cops arrive. Move it!"

Shane grabbed his clothes out of the bedroom and, not waiting to put them on, bolted for the garage. He was already pulling the Acura out when the teenager arrived, carrying his shirt, shoes, and pants; Chooch jumped into the passenger side. The police sirens were now only a few blocks away.

Shane shot up the alley behind the east canal, made a left away from the water, and floored it. Miraculously, he didn't choose the same streets as the arriving squad cars. Five minutes later they were on the freeway, both clad only in their undershorts, heading toward Barrington Plaza.

Chooch sat quietly in the passenger seat, shaken by the experience. Finally he looked over at Shane.

"I thought it was bullshit," he said.

"Now you know," Shane answered, but he hadn't been prepared for the ferocious machine-gun attack. He had never imagined that somebody would stand outside his house pouring lead into his living room. His hands were shaking; he was glad he was gripping the steering wheel so it didn't show.

"Who were those guys?" Chooch asked.

"They ride down on you with fucking machine guns...."

"I'm not sure. Bad cops, I think."

When he looked over at Chooch a second time, he saw a strange expression on the boy's face, too complicated to read.

They got off the freeway at Sunset. Shane found a dark spot and pulled to the curb so they could change into their clothes in the car. Then they drove around the corner and pulled in at Barrington Plaza. Shane badged the doorman with the braided shoulders. Sandy was standing in the living room wearing a silk robe belted around her slender waist. Her hair was tousled. She looked composed but concerned, an actress playing a scene.

"I can't believe it," she said after Shane filled her in.

"This isn't going to be a discussion, Sandy. You're taking Chooch."

"My God, who do you think they were?"

"I'm not sure, but I have a few hunches." He stood there, feeling a wave of fatigue. Then he looked at Chooch, wearing the same strange expression Shane had seen in the car. In the better light of Sandy's apartment, it looked a little like regret, or maybe it was guilt.

"Okay, here's the deal, Chooch..."

The boy jerked to attention and faced Shane.

"Disneyland, next weekend. You stay here till then, and I'll be back for you. It's a promise."

Chooch nodded.

As Shane moved to the door, he heard Chooch call his name, and he looked back. "I'm sorry," the boy said. "I thought you were lying, but I was wrong."

THE POLICE BILL OF RIGHTS

WHEN SHANE GOT BACK to his house on East Canal Street, it was sunup. Five black-and-whites and a crime-scene station wagon were blocking the street. He edged the Acura past them and pulled into the garage.

There were ten cops standing in his living room. When he entered, they turned, clearly surprised to see him.

"Where the hell you been?" Garson Welch asked. The fact that the old detective had been called out on this told Shane that he was still a murder suspect in the criminal investigation surrounding Ray's death.

Welch had been given this call because he was investigating Molar's shooting and this machine-gun attack was most likely connected. The old detective looked at Shane with his basset-hound expression and tired brown eyes. "We just put a bulletin out on you."

"I had something personal to take care of," Shane said.

"What the fuck *was* this?" Garson said, pointing at the destroyed wall where Crime Section techs were busy digging 9mm slugs out of the plaster and bagging them as evidence for a ballistics comparison later. That is, if they ever found the weapon, which was right up there with the odds on Shane's next promotion.

Shane was sure that the machine guns were illegal street sweepers: AK-47s, maybe MAC-10s, most likely taken from the vast array of confiscated weapons held in the Firearms and Ammunition Section's secure property room, destined for eventual burial at sea.

"Who did this?" Garson asked.

"Don't know," Shane said. "The lights were out, and I was flat on my stomach eating carpet."

"Okay, let's go. You got an appointment at Parker Center."

"Shit...do we have to do that again?" Shane asked. The remark was greeted by a flat stare.

Shane was taken from his house and again made the early-morning ride across town to the Glass House. Garson Welch stayed quiet as they drove. He had the case but didn't want it. As far as Welch was concerned, the brass at Parker Center could ask the questions. They pulled into the parking garage next to the huge lit police building, then rode the elevator up to the ninth floor. This time Shane found Deputy Chief Tom Mayweather standing in the hallway waiting for him, looking very *GQ* in his black pinstripe suit, white shirt, maroon tie, and matching pocket accessory. His bald head was gleaming, his handsome face theatrically troubled. He didn't say anything but motioned Shane down the hall. Garson Welch stayed in the lobby, glad to be out of it.

Shane followed Mayweather into his office. The room was not as large as Chief Brewer's by half but had a picture window with a Spring Street view. The shelves were littered with Mayweather's old basketball trophies, game balls, and team photos, along with the more standard police memorabilia: his Academy class picture, civil-service awards, and plaques attesting to his superiority as a police officer.

Mayweather stepped behind his desk, using the large, light oak piece of furniture as a barricade to separate them and define their roles. Shane stood while Mayweather sat in his tan executive swivel chair. The overhead ceiling spot kicked white light off his shaved head.

"You are an amazing piece of work, Sergeant," the deputy chief finally said.

"Thank you, sir."

"I wasn't complimenting you. Why the hell didn't you come back from Arrowhead and report in here, as instructed?"

"I left you a message."

"Right...the 'I had an accident/fell asleep at the wheel/stayed in a motel' message, left with my secretary at eight-fifteen A.M." He shook his head in wonder. "You must think I'm one stupid son of a bitch."

"How would you like me to respond to that, sir?" Shane was getting mad now, wanting to fire back but on tender ground professionally.

Mayweather leaned back in his chair, the knife-sharp creases in his pants now visible over the desktop. "Take off your gun and hand me your badge. You're suspended from duty without pay pending your Internal Affairs Board of Rights."

"Don't you have to write up a 1.61 before you can suspend me?"

"Consider it written."

"The Police Bill of Rights really seems to have its limits where I'm concerned, doesn't it?"

"The 1.61 will be in your hands before nine o'clock. Take off your gun and give me your badge and ID card."

Shane removed the clip-on holster from his belt, then pulled his badge and ID in the brown leather fold-over out of his pocket.

"Put them on the desk, please," Mayweather commanded.

Shane did as he was instructed. "Now what?"

Mayweather seemed puzzled by the question, so Shane added, "Doesn't the district attorney show up about now with a murder warrant and cart me off to the lockup?"

"You really have an active imagination."

"I didn't imagine the nine-millimeter machine-gun slugs in my living-room walls. Chief Brewer has been threatening me with a murder indictment. Since you're not doing that, something else must be happening. Maybe you just want to leave me on the street without my gun and badge, where I'll be easier to get at?"

"You are a sick, paranoid man, Sergeant Scully. There are other ways to view what just happened."

"Let's hear."

"I think you're involved with the wrong people, vice or drugs...some other street action. You were taking a 'patch' and you took too much." A "patch" was police argot for a payoff to a cop for letting a crime happen, differing from a "buy down," which was a bribe to turn an arrestee loose or book him for a lesser crime. "People you thought you had fooled, or had under control, got tired of paying and threw you a party," Mayweather added.

"You surprise me, Tom," Shane said, using the deputy chief's first name to show he had lost respect for him. "The word in the department is you're a good guy, a smart guy, but what's happening here right now, between us, isn't smart at all. If you really don't know what's going on, then you're being used— played for a patsy. Either way, it marks you."

"I see." Mayweather seemed to consider this, sitting still, thinking, his big trophy-filled office and black Armani pinstripes dissing Shane—making him small. Then the deputy chief seemed to make up his mind and sat upright. "Get out. Check in every day with Captain Halley. Go home and leave this alone."

"Go home? Should I sit in the window?"

"That will be just about enough of that. Go home. Stay put. If you know what's good for you, you'll stop making trouble."

"You can suspend me, but you sure as hell can't tell me not to work on my own defense. Somebody made a big mistake. They thought I took something out of Ray's house and they overreacted. Now they're pretty sure I don't have it, but Chief Brewer leaned too hard and got me looking in the wrong places. Suddenly I have too much of it and have to be neutralized. Whoever's behind this had one easy shot and missed. I won't be stumbling around, half asleep in my undies, next time. It's gonna be much harder."

Shane turned and walked out of the office without looking back, leaving his badge, gun, and career in police work behind.

Once again, he was stranded downtown without his car. He didn't trust anybody enough to ask for a lift, and as a suspended officer, he couldn't check a slickback out of the motor pool...so he walked four blocks east to the Bradbury Building and waited in the parking garage for Alexa Hamilton to arrive.

25
PRINT HIT

SEVEN THIRTY-FIVE A.M. Alexa pulled the gray Ford Crown Victoria into the parking structure and parked in her spot. She was early, as usual, getting a jump-start on the day while DeMarco slept late.

She got out of the car, dressed for success in a dark charcoal pantsuit tailored to her trim, twenty-three-inch waist. She was carrying another cardboard box full of files, her bulging, faded leather briefcase hanging from a strap over her shoulder. She headed toward the elevators and stopped when she saw him standing next to a concrete pillar in the shadows of the huge, underlit parking garage.

"You shouldn't be here," she said.

"I know, I should be in a slumber room at Forest Lawn."

She walked toward him now, closing the distance, stopping two feet away. He could smell her perfume. He'd never thought of her as wearing perfume.

"What happened?" she asked. "The chief advocate called me at six. He said somebody shot up your house."

"Shot up... My house was massacred. I got enough lead in the walls to go into strip mining. On top of that, I got suspended this morning by Mayweather. He took my gun, badge, and ID, kicked me loose. So I'm back on the street running around, a moving target. It's been way too entertaining. I was expecting to get hit with a murder one indictment, but for some reason it didn't happen. I guess things were bound to slow down sometime."

"The warrant's coming. The writ got signed. I saw it yesterday. Looks like they're holding it in reserve.... Let's go back and sit in my car," she said unexpectedly.

They walked to her car. She put the box in the backseat, then they both slid into the Crown Vic and closed the doors.

"Look, I don't understand what's happening. I agree, something's going on. I don't get it myself...but I'm compromised here," Alexa said with some anxiety.

"Lemme see if I got this straight," he said. "I've been threatened by Chief Brewer and most of Ray's old den. Somebody blew the shit out of my living room, Mayweather just suspended me, I got a murder warrant pending, but we're worried *you're* 'compromised'?"

She sat quietly, deep in thought. He sensed there was something she wasn't telling him.

"What is it? You know something else," he said.

Finally she opened her briefcase and pulled out a sheaf of papers.

"Those are the missing files from the Chief Advocate's Office. On my way in this morning, I stopped by the Office of Administrative Services. They supervise the Officer Representation Section at Parker Center. I have a friend down there. She pulled the duplicates on all missing case folders from the discovery files and made copies for me."

Shane took the missing files and looked through them. "Jesus, look't this, it's just what I thought. All of them involve Hoover Street Bounty Hunters. Lee Ayers was beefed by a store owner just like Drucker; slow response to Code Thirty calls. Kris Kono is also accused of a slow response. Joe Church failed to Mirandize a banger after a street homicide. The case got pitched." He looked up at her and, for the first time, saw indecision on her chiseled face. "Why would Ray's old den be kicking gangsters loose?" he asked.

"I don't know, but it's not my case. You're my case. I'm supposed to be prosecuting *you*."

"Well, excuse me," he said, anger filling the space between them.

"Look, Shane, I just said I agree you may have stumbled into something, but—"

"But you don't wanna see your career go in the bucket with mine."

"What do you want me to do? If I start messing with this, they're going to pull me off your case. The district attorney will file against you anyway. It won't change anything."

"Yes, it will, because you'll be doing the right thing. Alexa, I'm down to just you. Nobody else in the department will even talk to me. With no badge, I'm locked out. I can't even access the computer system."

"And you want me to sacrifice myself for you?"

"All that righteous shit you were giving me last night, the Rodney King speech about IAD policing the police, kicking ass when there's corruption—that was just bullshit. Sounds good, but what you really meant is, as long as you can do it without hurting yourself or putting yourself in jeopardy."

"That's not fair."

"Then help me."

"I can't help you. I'm prosecuting you. Don't you get that?" She sat in the car, glaring at him. Shane wondered how it happened: this woman he had despised so recently now seemed like the only chance he had left.

"I'll resign from the department, okay? I'm gonna get terminated anyway, so I'll save you the trouble. I'll send a letter of resignation, and then you won't have to prosecute me. You won't have this monumental ethical problem."

"Don't resign," she said softly.

"Why not?"

"Because...just because."

Then her beeper sounded, and she pulled it out of her purse. She looked at it, then quickly put it away.

"What is it?"

"Prints and Identification. I dropped off one of those empty folders from Zell's files. They're calling me back."

Shane didn't say anything, but he thought it was a good move to see whose fingerprints were on those empty file folders. He was surprised he hadn't thought of it.

She pulled her cell phone out of her brief-case and dialed a number. "This is Sergeant Hamilton, serial number 50791. I got paged to this number. I have a fingerprint request, number 487, April twenty-third," she said, reading off a slip of paper from her purse.

They sat in the still air of the parked Crown Vic as she waited. Then: "Okay...right. Okay, I've got it." She hung up and put the phone back in her purse.

"What?" he asked.

Indecision was tightening her lips, bending them down. "I've been a cop for seventeen years. It's all I ever wanted to do," she said sadly.

"Alexa, whose prints were on the file? They weren't Commander Zell's, right?"

"Zell's were on there, of course. But there was another set, fresh ones."

"Whose were they?"

"Why is the fucking head of Special Investigations Division personally clearing active case folders out of the Chief Advocate's Office?"

"Mayweather?" Shane said.

They sat in the Crown Vic, both realizing the answer was obvious. Mayweather had been doing damage control. There was no way she could ignore it, he thought. Mayweather was actively involved. The deputy police chief was personally emptying sensitive files because he didn't trust anyone else to do it. Shane looked at her and waited. Would she finally admit he was right? Whatever was going on, it was frightening and went straight to the top of the department.

26

ALEXA HAMILTON sat in the Crown Vic for another minute, saying nothing. Then she opened the door and stepped out, retrieving her box of files from the backseat. She kicked the back door closed with her foot and stood looking over the roof of the car at Shane, who had also exited the vehicle.

"I don't know what you expect me to do," she said, her voice ringing in the cold, empty structure.

"I don't, either," he said. "If the district attorney files that 187 warrant, I'm going to be sitting this out in jail. I've got a lot of ground to cover, six cops to check out."

She stood there, reluctant to stay, unable to go. The heavy box was balanced on her slender knee. "What're you gonna do?" she asked, finally sliding the box up onto the trunk so she wouldn't have to hold it.

"On the tape in Ray's Arrowhead house, Don and Lee left a message. It said, 'We're on for Friday night, the Web. Bring the jerseys.' I don't have a clue what that means, but it's Friday, so tonight I thought I'd tail Drucker or Ayers, see what and where the Web is."

She listened but said nothing.

"Then I've gotta find out about Cal-VIP Homes...research who owns that company."

A car came up the ramp in the garage and pulled past them.

"I can't stand around here talking to you. Give me your cell phone number. I'll call you," Alexa said impatiently.

"When?"

"*When I'm through.* I've got six affidavits scheduled for today, starting with Bud Halley at eight-fifteen this morning. I've gotta go to the Patrol Division and dig out your old TA reports, then over to the Traffic Coordination Section and pull the reckless-driving sheets. You sure busted your share of city vehicles."

"You can't be serious?"

She pressed the alarm activation button on her car key, and the Crown Vic chirped loudly, cutting him off, ending the argument. Then she pulled the file box off the trunk and headed away from him toward the elevator. He watched as she stood in front of the elevator, balancing the heavy box; then the door slid open and she stepped inside. Just as it started to close, she stuck her foot out and stopped it.

"Meet me at the Appaloosa after work, five-thirty. We'll follow Drucker and Ayers together." Before he could answer, the door closed, taking her from view.

Shane spent the morning getting himself settled. He rented a room in a building called the Spring Summer Apartments, picking it because it cost only two hundred for one week. It was also within walking distance of the Bradbury.

The room was small but clean. He sat on the faded blue bedspread and dialed Budget Rent-a-Car. He reserved a Mustang from the rental agency located a few blocks away on Third, and walked over to pick up the car.

As he started down Third Street, he could see signs posted on telephone poles and buildings that notified residents and store owners that there would be no parking permitted on Saturday, by order of the LAPD, as a motion picture would be shooting on these streets. Schwarzenegger, no doubt.

When he got to Budget, they showed him to a red Mustang convertible, a year or two newer than Barbara's but totally unacceptable for a tail job. He turned it down in favor of a dull-brown four-door Ford Taurus.

He drove the Taurus back to the Spring Summer Apartments, parked, went back up to his room, and checked in with the Corporations Commission on his request for a printout of corporate ownership of Cal-VIP Homes. He was informed by a cold female voice that his request was in line but had not been processed yet. Maybe sometime after noon. He gave his cell phone number to her, stressing the urgency, and the woman promised to call back.

He hung up and sat in the room, feeling restless and caged. After pacing for almost half an hour, he called the Electronics Scientific Investigation Section (ESIS) to check on Ray's answering-machine tape analysis. He got a clerk there, somebody named Boyd Miller, who told Shane that ESIS had picked up fragments of old voices on the tape.

"Some of this is kinda jumbled," Miller said. "On one message, our best fragment sounded like 'If this is Susan Burbick or Burdick, we have your...something.' I couldn't make out the rest."

"Anything else?" Shane said, writing it down.

"No. That's it. You want to pick this up or shall we send it back to your office?"

"Hold it for me. I'll pick it up."

He hung up and sat there for several moments before reluctantly calling Barbara Molar at her house. He got the machine, so he tried her new cell phone. After he identified himself, she brightened.

"Hi, stranger. How you doing?"

"Terrible. How 'bout you?"

"Well, actually, pretty good. It's nice you finally called. I was worried."

"Have you ever heard of someone named Susan Burdick or Burbick?" he asked.

"What do I get if I say yes?"

"You get to find out if Ray was actually married to her or not."

"Oh...well, I'll have to think about it. I'll look in Ray's address book. How 'bout we get together for a drink, talk it over?"

"I can't, I'm meeting someone at five."

"Don't play hard-to-get with me, Shane. I don't like being dumped."

"Neither did I," he said softly, and hung up.

He sat in the transient apartment with its chipped, broken bathroom fixtures and fly-speckled wallpaper and wondered what to do next. Finally he got the number for the Arrowhead Sheriff's Department, called, and asked for Sheriff Conklyn. After a few minutes the tall, middle-aged sheriff was on the phone.

"Sheriff, it's Sergeant Scully. Remember me?"

"Whatta you want?" He was angry now, or maybe just impatient.

"When I was up there, you had a murder, a body you pulled out of the lake and couldn't identify. I never heard if it was a man or a woman."

"Woman."

"You ever ID the corpse?"

"Nope, still a Jane Doe." There was a sliver of interest in his manner now.

"Check out a woman named Susan Burdick or Burbick. I don't know which. I also don't have an address, but maybe you can get a line on her through her marriage license. I think she was married to Ray Molar using the name Jay Colter. They tied the knot at the Midnight Wedding Chapel in Vegas six months ago. If that checks, you could get a dental match and maybe pin it."

"Why do I get the feeling I'm doing your foot-work?"

"Hey, Sheriff, I'm trying to help you. If you don't wanna ID your icebox cases, don't bother with it."

"But if I do, you'd probably be interested in who she is and where she came from."

"I'm a curious guy."

"Okay, this will probably take a day or so. Call me back."

After he hung up, Shane drove back to the Fotomat to pick up the Arrowhead pictures. He was told by the clerk that they had to push the negative four stops to get an expo-sure. Shane opened the envelope and looked at six grainy snapshots of the men inside Ray's house. He could see most of their faces but didn't recognize any of them. He wondered which one was Calvin Sheets. Since his camera was in the Acura back in Venice, he bought a new Canon with a zoom lens and some film. He was loading the film when his cell phone rang. It was Sandy.

"Chooch ran away," she told him straight out.

"I was afraid of that."

"You've gotta find him."

"How'm I gonna find him, Sandy? All I can do is put a 'runaway juvie' out on him, and he's gonna get arrested. Then you'll be fooling around with the LACCSD—that's children's social services. If they find out what you do for a living, they'll take him away from you. Then he's gonna be a ward of the court."

265

"Well, what can we do?"

"I don't know. I'll try and find him, but I don't even know where to start. It's not going to be easy."

But it was easier than he thought. As soon as he hung up from Sandy, his phone rang. It was Chooch.

"I'm in a phone booth over by UCLA, the Texaco just off the freeway on Sunset," the teenager said. "I gotta see you."

"On my way." Shane got into his rental car and headed back to West L.A.

27
DEAL

H E WAS SITTING on a low wall that framed the perimeter of the Texaco station one block west of the 405. He seemed small sitting there, diminished by events, his head down, staring at the sidewalk as if the answer to his life might be hiding in the scrub weeds growing between the cracks.

Shane pulled the rented Taurus into the gas station and tapped the horn. Chooch got off the wall, moved to the car, and slid in, pulling the door shut. He sat there, silent, looking like he'd lost something he couldn't replace.

"Your mom's worried."

266

"Yeah. Okay, let's go," he said.

"You had lunch? There's a good place in Westwood, over by UCLA. Got subs and a great deli."

The boy shrugged, so Shane put the car in gear and headed that way.

The place was called the Little Bruin. Shane and Chooch got a booth in the back surrounded by chattering college students and lunch-break shopkeepers. Chooch ordered the special; Shane, pastrami on rye. They both had Cokes.

"I thought we had a deal. You were gonna stay put, and I was gonna try and get my stuff settled, get back to you by next weekend at the latest."

Chooch was looking out the window at the passing traffic so he could avoid Shane's eyes. "I been thinkin'," he said. "I know it's like a problem all the time havin' to have somebody look after me, but like you said, I'm a man. I make my own choices now, right?"

"Right."

"So, if I moved in with you, you wouldn't have to baby-sit me anymore or have Longboard come over and sit. I don't need to be supervised. I'm sorta beyond that. Like you said, right?"

"Yeah, I guess," Shane said. "But I got guys shooting up my place. We'd have to get Kevlar jammies."

"You're not sleeping there, either. I'll go wherever you go."

" 'Cept I'm not your legal guardian. I can't make that choice for you. Sandy has to."

"Yeah, well, the thing is, Sandy and me, we're not gonna happen."

"You sure of that?"

"Yeah. I'm sure. It didn't work."

"You gave it a whole nine hours."

"You know what she does for a living?"

Shane didn't know how to answer that. "Do you?" he finally said.

"Yeah. She's a hooker. I found her trick book. She has over fifty guys in there. It lists what they like, what kinda sex." He was having trouble talking about this, watching the traffic out the window, studying the street with manufactured interest.

"She's paying for my school and shit by fucking guys. She's a whore." He turned back, and Shane could see the anger in the boy's black eyes.

"Chooch, your mom—"

"Yeah?"

"When I first met her, she was young, alone in L.A. She made a bad choice, but she doesn't do that anymore. She's an informant for the police department. Federal, as well as LAPD."

"How does that pay for anything?" he challenged. "The private school and that penthouse."

"She dates guys that law enforcement wants to bust, works 'em for information, then sells it to the cops. She does real well. She's trying to save up enough to retire, live with you in Phoenix, be a regular mom."

"Some real mom."

The waitress, a college girl in shorts and a

UCLA T-shirt, delivered their lunches, set down silverware wrapped in paper napkins, and left. Shane unwrapped his knife and fork and put the napkin on his lap while Chooch continued to look out the window, brooding.

"Whatta you want, man?" Shane finally said. "It is what it is. I can't change it; neither can you. You've gotta move past it."

"Easy for you. I got nobody now. Least you've got somebody you can talk to."

"Yeah? Who's that?"

"I found all the letters you write to your dad. They were in the desk drawer in the living room. I was looking for paper for my homework."

Shane put down his half-eaten sandwich. Chooch watched him closely, focused on him hard.

"You shouldn't read other people's mail," Shane said softly.

"You write them but you never send 'em."

"He's sick. They were downers. I didn't want to distress him. I don't want to talk about this with you. It's not right you reading my private mail."

They sat in silence for a moment, then Shane's cell phone rang, interrupting an awkward moment. It was the guy at Parker Center checking the Cal-VIP Homes with the Corporations Commission.

"Go," Shane said, grabbing a pencil.

"Spivack Development Corporation, Long Beach, California, owns Cal-VIP and paid the real estate taxes on the Arrowhead address you gave me."

"Anthony Spivack? That Spivack Development? The big corporate developer?"

"It just said Spivack Development, 2000 Lincoln Ave., Long Beach, California."

"Thanks," Shane said, and folded the phone.

"I can't go back to Sandy's place. I won't do it," Chooch protested.

"Okay, okay, I'll work out something. But I've gotta call and tell her you're okay."

"Fine. I don't care. I just don't wanna go back."

"Okay. We can try, but I can't promise that's gonna stick."

They sat quietly in the booth and ate their sandwiches. Chooch, still deep in thought, only picked at his.

"Shane," he said, and Scully looked up at him. "Did she ever tell you who my father was?" The question had been waiting there building up pressure, needing to be asked.

"Yeah," Shane said, "but she didn't want you to find out who he was."

"Because he was one of those guys, one of the crooks she plays to the cops?"

"Chooch, come on..."

"I wanna know. Was my old man a criminal?"

"She'll have to tell you. She made me promise, but it's not really gonna change anything, because he's not coming back for a long time."

"He's a crook...I know it. Some legacy, huh? No wonder I get into so much trouble."

"Hey, Chooch, criminal behavior isn't genetic. You don't pass it on, father to son, like blue eyes and freckles. You can make whatever you want of your life. It's up to you. Your father's mistakes are his. Everybody gets to make their own."

"That's what you keep telling me," the boy said. Then he gave Shane a rueful smile. "And you don't ever lie, right?"

"Right," Shane said. Then without really knowing why, but realizing it was the right thing to do, Shane finally unburdened himself of something he had kept hidden for years. "You wanna know why I never mailed the letters?"

Chooch nodded.

" 'Cause I don't know where to send them."

"It says Florida."

"I don't know where he is, or even who he is. I was left at a hospital. 'Infant 205,' in 1963. I got named by City Services. It's silly. I write the letters when I need to get my thoughts down. And my father..." He stopped, unable to finish for a second. "My father is an idea I can talk to."

"Somebody you wish you had, who can be whatever you want him to be," Chooch said, knowing exactly what Shane meant, feeling all the same things...the loneliness, the disenfranchisement, the emptiness coming from the same hole in their personal histories.

"Yeah." Shane's voice was husky.

"I wondered why you agreed to take me. That's why."

"I don't know why, Chooch. I don't know what I was looking for."

The waitress came to the table and asked them if they wanted anything.

"Yeah," Chooch said. "But I don't think you've got it in the kitchen."

Shane smiled. "Let's get going. I've got an errand to run. You want, you can come with me."

He paid and they left the Little Bruin and headed to the brown Taurus parked at a curbside meter, dazed by what had just happened.

"Thanks for telling me about your dad," Chooch finally said.

"I won't tell about your dad if you won't tell about mine," Shane said.

"Deal," Chooch said, and smiled. They got in the car and left Westwood, both wondering what this strange new connection held for them.

28
CONNECTING THE DOTS

THE FIFTEEN-STORY steel-and-glass building on Lincoln Boulevard was named the Two Thousand Building by a large monument sign that marked the entrance. Under that in gold letters:

A SPIVACK DEVELOPMENT

It was also on top of the building in five-foot-high lit letters, leaving no doubt about who owned the place.

Shane and Chooch parked in the underground garage, got out, and moved to the elevator, taking it up to the management floor at the top of the building. They exited into a huge architectural lobby decorated in monochromatic colors, dominated by too many sharp edges and angular lines. Steel-and-glass furniture dotted the interior. Futuristic recessed lighting laid down a cold blue-white glow. A huge gold sign behind the receptionist again announced that this was:

SPIVACK DEVELOPMENT
CORPORATE HEADQUARTERS

Shane left Chooch by the elevator and approached a striking, unfriendly white-blond receptionist who looked cold enough to have been delivered with the furniture. Shane opened his wallet and took out his police business card. Since he didn't have his badge, the business card was the best he could manage. He was hoping it would get him past the blond goddess who was guarding the floor, stationed behind her huge, semicircular, two-inch-thick green glass desk, like a turret gunner.

"What's this regarding?" she asked, speaking coolly, not intimidated by his card or manner.

"Police business," he replied.

"Mr. Spivack isn't here. Perhaps someone else can help you?"

"How about Calvin Sheets?" Shane said, wondering if Logan Hunter's head of security was also working for Spivack.

"He's down at the city council meeting with Mr. Spivack. Sorry..."

"The Long Beach City Council?"

She ignored his question and smiled an icicle at him. "Would there be anybody else...?"

"Coy Love."

"We don't have a Coy Love."

"I'm not doing too well, am I?"

"Sometimes if you make an appointment in advance, it works wonders." Freon.

"I may just have to get a search warrant and start emptying everyone's desks.... Do a couple of body searches."

"Anything else?" She had grown tired of him.

"Pamela Anderson Lee wouldn't happen to be around, would she?"

"Just left." But at least this earned him a smile.

He picked up his business card, tucked it into his wallet, then took a Spivack Company brochure off the glass desk and walked across the lobby, the ice-blonde watching him all the way. He retrieved Chooch, got into the elevator, and went down. He left the teenager in the lobby, then found the staircase to the basement. It took him five minutes to find the service utility room. Inside was a huge gray panel box with a dime-store lock that took Shane less than thirty seconds to pick. Now he was looking at a startling array of colorful wires. "Shit," he said, then slowly went to work unraveling the building's complicated alarm system.

"I wonder where the city council meets. Probably city hall," Shane said as they settled back into the Taurus. He picked up his almost fried cell phone, called Information in Long Beach, and got the address for city hall on Front Street just before the phone quit.

They drove away from the Two Thousand Building and, with some help from a gas-station attendant, found Front Street. The huge domed city building loomed two blocks ahead....

As they pulled up the street, they could see quite a demonstration in progress—thirty or forty pickets were congregating around in front of city hall. It was a strange mixture of people. Some were old men in American Legion uniforms, holding duplicate hand-lettered signs that read:

VETERANS AGAINST LONG BEACH LAND-FOR-WATER DEAL

Other pickets carried more traditional union placards:

AFL-CIO OPPOSES NAVAL YARD WATER SWAP
THEY GET THE DOUGH, WE GET THE HOSE

Others protested with:

**GIVE US JOBS, NOT SOBS
SPIVACK-EVACK—WE DON'T WANT
YOU HERE
WE SAVED THE WHALES—YOU
SAVE OUR JOBS!**

Shane and Chooch had to park a block away in a city parking lot and, after locking up, moved across the shimmering, heated asphalt to where the demonstration was taking place.

"What's going on?" Shane asked a tough-looking woman with inch-long hair wearing a plaid shirt and carrying a sign that read:

**BEACHFRONT FOR H_2O?
OUR CITY COUNCIL SUCKS!**

"These idiots are trading the Long Beach Naval Yard to Los Angeles County for a bunch of fuckin' water rights," she growled.

"Naval yard? I thought the navy shut it down years ago."

"Yeah, they did, and now we're giving it to L.A."

"Isn't it federal property?" Shane persisted.

She shot him a withering look. "Where you been, buddy? This is all over the fuckin' news."

"I don't have a TV," Shane answered.

"It was leased land. Now Long Beach's gonna trade it for some dumb water rights."

Shane moved past her and, along with Chooch, climbed up the steps and entered city hall.

The Long Beach Municipal Building was a large brick structure that had been built in the forties. It had a high, two-story rotunda, now overflowing with TV news crews who had set up there for a press conference.

"I'm gonna try and find this guy Spivack," Shane said to Chooch. "Stick close, okay?"

"Got it."

Shane moved past the news crews but got stopped at the door to the City Council Chamber by a uniformed Long Beach police officer.

"Sorry, we're maxed out. Fire regs," the cop said.

"LAPD, I'm working." He handed the cop his business card.

"Okay, Sarge, but it's a madhouse in there."

"He's with me," Shane said, indicating Chooch; then they entered the meeting hall.

The council room was a theater-sized, cavernous hall with a sloping floor and raised dais. The room was packed. They could hear a contentious argument being staged over microphones:

"How the hell can you say that the property can't be used by Long Beach?!" a woman yelled from the floor. "I worked at that yard, I was an employee of the Metal Trades Council for thirty years. I thought we were being reamed in '94, when the government closed the only profitable shipyard in the navy. But that's nothing compared to what's going on here. You're taking a huge city asset and trading it for chump change!"

The crowd shouted its approval. The president of the city council banged his gavel for order, then replied, "To begin with, the yard was closed in '94 because it was badly situated, too close to the big refitting yard in San Diego. What's going on here now is *good* for the city of Long Beach. Mr. Spivack is going to clear all the old military buildings off the site, regrade the property, and develop it. Okay, it's going to be ceded to the city of L.A., but I might remind you that the shipyard borders L.A. on the north and Long Beach on the south, so it's contiguous with them as well as us."

"Who cares? I'm not talking about geography. I'm talking about jobs!" the woman fired back, to a chorus of cheers.

The city council president was prepared. "Long Beach residents *will* get the jobs because the yard is much closer to our main workforce than to L.A.'s. There'll be hotels, shopping malls, restaurants—all employment for Long Beach citizens. And we don't have to float bond issues or construction loans to develop the site. We won't have to pay for its construction; L.A. will. But we will get the major work benefits, plus much-needed water from L.A."

Shane was looking for Anthony Spivack somewhere down front, not paying much attention to the argument going on between the Long Beach City Council and its angry residents. He had the Spivack brochure open to a picture of the CEO. Spivack was a heavyset man with a thick head of close-cropped, curly gray hair. The woman at the mike raised her voice in response, cutting through the background noise with electronic shrillness. "And who, may I ask, gets the municipal tax revenue on all this commercial property, Mr. Cummins?"

Shane spun around and looked up at the president of the Long Beach City Council. He was a slender, hollow-chested man with horn-rimmed glasses, identified by a plaque in front of him on the elevated dais:

CARL CUMMINS
PRESIDENT, LONG BEACH
CITY COUNCIL

"Son of a bitch," Shane said.

Chooch looked at him. "What is it?"

Just then, some kind of disturbance seemed to be taking place in the back of the hall. A chant began: "AFL-CIO... Tony Spivack, you must go."

About thirty protesters had broken into the hall and were trying to march down the aisle, carrying placards. The agitated audience soon picked up the chant.

Carl Cummins started banging his gavel, trying to regain order. "We can't conduct this hearing under these conditions!" he said, screeching it into his mike, getting loud boos and electronic feedback. "The discussion period on City Resolution 397 is concluded. The board will retire to chambers to take its vote. We're adjourned." He angrily banged his gavel and rose.

The chorus of boos grew louder. Suddenly people in the front rows stood up and started throwing fruit at the stage; pulling oranges and plums out of carry-bags, brought in anticipation of this demonstration.

Carl Cummins and the nine other members of the city council bolted from their chairs as they were pelted with fruit, making a hurried exit from the stage.

The pushing and shoving was getting increasingly intense in the auditorium, threatening to turn into a riot.

"Let's go!" Shane said, grabbing Chooch. "Stay close to me. Hold on to my belt."

He felt Chooch grab hold of his belt in the back, and then Shane pushed through the melee to the fire exit on the same side of the room that Carl Cummins and the city council were using as a retreat. By now most of the frightened council members had left the stage.

Shane got to the fire exit, but it was guarded by another Long Beach cop. "Sorry. This is an alarmed fire door," the policeman said.

"Long Beach Fire Marshal," Shane bull-shitted. "I'm authorized to open it under Regulation 1623. Excuse me."

He handed the startled cop his official LAPD business card and jostled him, hoping he couldn't read it in the commotion. In that moment of hesitation, Shane pushed down on the silver bar and opened the door. The alarm bell sounded. People were panicking as fruit continued to fly. Shane pushed past the Long Beach cop, dragging Chooch into the hot sunshine.

Up ahead, he could see a black limousine waiting with several chase cars. Then Shane spotted Anthony Spivack beside the limo. With him were several of the men Shane had photographed in Arrowhead. He assumed one of them must be Calvin Sheets. The people with Spivack started piling into cars. Carl Cummins arrived with one of the other council members and jumped into Spivack's limo. Like the last politicians leaving Saigon, they slammed car doors and squealed away from the angry mob pouring out of the doors behind them.

"Stay with me!" Shane said, trying to get an idea which direction the fleeing cars were headed while simultaneously sprinting for the Taurus, parked almost a block away.

He and Chooch finally reached the car. Both were out of breath as they jumped in. Shane put the car in gear and sped across the lot, cutting between parked cars. He bounced over the curb, shot out onto Front Street, and took off heading south, after the speeding limo and its four chase vehicles.

"What's going on?" Chooch asked.

"Some of these guys were in the house up in Arrowhead," he said, fearing he couldn't catch up with them.

Shane had lost sight of the cars but was now driving along a frontage road that bordered the Long Beach Airport. On a hunch, he turned into one of the executive terminals, past an open bar-arm at the end of a ramp, driving out onto the tarmac that bordered the runway. As he sped along past a row of FBOs (flight base operators) that lined the west side of the field, several ramp attendants and cargo loaders started screaming and waving their arms at the brown Taurus. Shane just ignored them, racing past parked Lears and Gulfstreams.

He thought he saw the black limo in the distance parked near a large Sikorsky helicopter, idling with the rotor turning slowly.

He drove around more executive jets—transportation necessities of the megarich.

Finally he could see the helicopter more clearly. Spivack and Cummins were getting into the idling chopper with the rest of the men from the Arrowhead house. He was close enough to the helicopter to read SPIVACK DEVELOPMENT on the side door as the huge green-and-white nine-passenger Sikorsky lifted off.

Shane got there half a minute too late. He watched in frustration as the chopper hovered for a minute a few feet above the tarmac, then the rotor changed pitch, and the helicopter streaked away, climbing to the north. Soon it was just a speck in the bright blue cloudless sky.

TAIL JOB

A T A FEW MINUTES before five in the afternoon, Shane was back inside the Appaloosa, watching a cockroach trying to hide under the molding that framed the tabletop, one feeler reaching out, tentatively tapping the Formica. He was in the same cracked vinyl booth in the back, nursing a Coke grudgingly supplied by the same greasy-coated Mexican waiter. "Das all chu gonna haf?" the man said.

"Yep," Shane said. "Working." The waiter left. Shane kept a wary eye on the barricaded cockroach and while "Malaguena" played through ruptured speakers, he was thinking about Chooch, whom he had left ten minutes earlier at the Spring Summer Apartments with the TV blaring. Shane had convinced Longboard to stop by the Venice house, get Chooch's book bag with his homework assignments, take it to the apartment on Third, and stay with the boy until Shane got back. In return for this service, Shane had given up his Lakers-Trailblazers tickets for the weekend. He made a mental note to call by six to make sure Longboard had gotten there okay.

Surprisingly, with trouble and chaos swirling around his own life, Shane found himself worrying about Chooch's back homework assignments as well as his emotional well-being.

Something about this newly found concern for someone else's future seemed to settle his own emotions in a way he couldn't understand. Underneath the boy's grumbling and bitching about the extra supervision, Shane suspected that he appreciated the concern. Earlier in the hectic day, when Shane had turned around unexpectedly and caught Chooch staring at him, the expression on his face was one of wonder. It said more than any words could convey.

Perhaps Shane could work out something more permanent with Sandy. She had her hands full right now with the DEA, but after that, she'd change teams and be on to some other predicate felon. He, on the other hand, was in the checkout line. If he didn't end up in prison or the grave, he was certainly through being a cop. Once he was off the force, he could devote more time to Chooch, stop farming him out to Longboard. Chooch didn't know who his father was, and although Shane couldn't fill that role, he sure as hell could be a big brother. Then he looked up, and she was coming through the door.

Alexa stood backlit in the late-afternoon sunshine, holding her briefcase under her arm, the shoulder strap tucked inside. She let her eyes adjust to the cavelike darkness of the windowless bar-restaurant. Finally she spotted him and moved across the room, her hips swaying seductively with the motion.

She slid in and smiled wanly at him. "Our spot," she said dryly.

"If it is, we've gotta either train these cockroaches or start killing them." She looked puzzled, so he lifted the sugar shaker, and the eight-legged German roach took off like a shot.

She let out an involuntary feminine squeal, then returned to form, slapping at it bare-handed and missing. The roach dodged, shooting across the table as Alexa slammed her palm down again—the only thing she hurt was her hand. The roach went off the end of the table, hit the floor, and was gone.

"Sign him. Good broken-field run." Shane smiled.

She checked around the perimeter of the booth, looking for relatives, then glanced at Shane. "Strong survival instincts. We should take lessons."

He took out the Arrowhead pictures he'd had developed and slid them across the table to her. "Know any of these guys?"

She went through them while he waited.

"Yep. All of 'em. This one is Calvin Sheets." She pushed a picture over and showed it to Shane. It was of the medium-built man with the ash-blond hair, setting a box down at the back door. Shane realized he'd been right, that Sheets had been the man standing with Tony Spivack at the limo.

"This is Coy Love," she said, sliding another photograph over to Shane, who could see why you wouldn't want to "fuck with Love." He was large, over six feet, with a huge, jutting jaw and a cruel, angular face. He had a thin, lipless mouth, straight as a ruler.

"These other two guys were cops on Calvin's Coliseum detail. They both got terminated with him on his bullshit time-sheet hustle." She pushed those shots over. "Lon Sherwood and Carter something, I can't remember his last name."

She looked up, and the waiter was back, hovering like a dragonfly over a lake, waiting for her order.

"I'll have what he's having."

"Chu makin' my day." He left, grumbling.

"Cummins is president of the Long Beach City Council, and I found out Spivack Development Corporation owns Cal-VIP Homes." Shane filled her in on the Long Beach City Council meeting; the dispute over the transfer of the naval yard to L.A. for water; the chase through Long Beach trying to catch Sheets, Spivack, and Cummins; and their eventual helicopter escape. She was holding her briefcase on her lap in both hands, ready to strike in case another cockroach took off on an end run around the Mexican condiments.

"You had a busy day," she said.

"I won't ask how your day went, for fear it'll severely depress me."

"I hope DeMarco is staying busy, 'cause I'm getting good prima facie stuff," she said, needling him.

"Don't worry about DeMarco. The Saint's all over this. He says with what he has, we'll probably want to to file a civil action."

"Good. 'Cause I'd heard he'd become an

286

alcoholic—a blackout drunk—and that's why he pulled the pin."

"Don't worry about Dee. He's kicking ass."

Blackout drunk? I'm fucked, Shane thought.

She looked at her watch as the waiter set down her Coke and left. "I ran both Drucker and Kono through the Office of Administrative Services at the Personnel Group," she said. "Drucker just got reassigned from Southwest to Hollenbeck. He's working street patrol—day shift. Kono has a worrisome nickname. They call him Bongo. I'm hoping that's because he's of Hawaiian ancestry, and not because he beats people like a drum."

She picked up her Coke and drained it. "Thirsty," she apologized. "Anyway, Kono's still in South Bureau, but now he's working day watch in University Division. That means we're going to have to split up if we want to follow both guys." She glanced at her Timex. "We better get moving. Day watch breaks in forty minutes. Which one a' these raisin cakes do you want?"

"Ladies first."

"Chivalry always knocks me out," she said drolly. "Okay, since he's closer, I'll take Drucker."

He put some money down on the table for the two Cokes, and they both stood.

"Let's communicate on a tactical frequency," she said. "One of the high ones nobody uses. Organized Crime is on tac ten, and that division doesn't have much going now. Let's use that."

"I don't have a police radio; my car's in Venice. I'm using a rental."

"You really bring it all to the table, don't you, Scully," she said sarcastically.

He needed her help, so he let it go.

"We can pick up a handset at IAD. I saw a whole bunch of them in a box in the IO's section," Shane suggested

She nodded. "We better move it, or they'll both be EOW before we get there."

The University Division station was an old concrete four-story building located on South Adams Boulevard, near USC. Shane left the Taurus in the only available spot he could find, half a block up the street. He fed the meter, moved away from it, and sat on a bus bench across from the station. From there he had an unobstructed view of the station parking lot. He had on an L.A. Dodgers cap, pulled low over his eyes, and a dull green-and-brown camouflage windbreaker he had picked up that afternoon at a surplus shop downtown for fifteen bucks.

Shane felt invisible and ready for action: Mr. Brown-and-Green in his camo jacket and dirt-brown Taurus. He had the police handset in his lap and was watching as the day watch started streaming out in civilian clothes, on the way to their private vehicles. It was 5:45.

"Six to Five. Target D is in motion." He heard Alexa's voice coming over the radio on tactical frequency 10. They had chosen their radio code numbers in the parking lot outside the Bradbury while doing a quick equipment check. He picked up his handset.

"Copy, Six. I'm still parked and waiting."

"Roger that," she said. "Target D just left Hollenbeck, heading up onto 91. He's westbound."

"Roger. Standing by on tac ten." He laid the radio on his lap and sat on the bus bench waiting for Kris "Bongo" Kono.

Officer Kono was one of the last ones out the station side door. He was dressed in jeans and a T-shirt and was carrying a duffel bag. He sprinted to his car, obviously late. He jumped into a blue '76 Camaro with racing stripes and a primered left front fender, then pulled quickly out of the lot, burning rubber.

Shane was caught leaning. He was half a block away from the Taurus and late getting back to it, fumbling to unlock the door as the Camaro made a sharp turn out of the parking lot. The 455-cubic-inch engine and blown mufflers on the muscle car roared angrily past and sped up the street.

"Shit," Shane said, finally piling into the Taurus and starting it up. He found a hole in traffic and pulled out, already dangerously behind. He watched, frustrated, as the Camaro went through the intersection up ahead on the yellow light. Shane tried to make up ground, spinning his wheels, chirping rubber, trying to get around slower traffic. When he got to the cross street, the light was against him, so he leaned on his horn and broke recklessly through the intersection against the red light, causing an eastbound truck on Atlantic to slam on its brakes. The angry traffic started screaming at him, blaring their horns and flipping him off.

As Shane shot through the red light, he could see the blue Camaro one block ahead, speeding through another light on the yellow.

"Slow the fuck down!" Shane yelled at the Camaro as he was forced to stop at the second light, trapped behind a row of cars, unable to get around them. He could see the Camaro a block ahead, turning right, heading up onto the 110.

"Come on, come on, come on..." Shane begged the five-way light that was trapping him. Then it turned green, but an old woman in a rusting Subaru was making a cautious left, blocking traffic, afraid to go. "Come on, lady. You got the fuckin' right-of-way!" he shouted at his windshield.

"Six, I'm on 91, heading west, passing Olive," Alexa's voice announced. Static, then: "Six, do you copy?"

Shane had his hands full as the woman finally completed her turn. He was flooring it, illegally passing a city bus on the right, shooting past the line of traffic, hanging a right, going up the on-ramp. His tires squealed on the sun-hot asphalt.

He hit the 110 going way too fast for the flow of rush-hour traffic that loomed before him on the packed freeway. He had to hit his brakes to keep from plowing into the right side of a Ford Escort, startling the two hard hats inside.

"Six, this is Five. Do you copy?" Alexa's voice persisted. "Six, you are Code One. Copy, please." Code One was a command to respond and was given only when a unit did not answer a radio call and was perceived to be in difficulty. It was imperative to respond to a Code One, if at all possible.

Shane impatiently snapped the radio up off his lap. "I copy. I've got my hands full, for Chrissake. Gimme a minute." He threw the radio back down on the seat and managed to get around the Ford Escort. He couldn't see the blue Camaro anywhere. "Fuck!" he said, but kept heading west on the 110, going as fast as he could, dangerously passing cars, trying to make up lost distance, driving on the right shoulder, getting angry horn blasts from a whole line of drivers.

"Six, Target D is transitioning to the 710. I'm making that freeway change now." Alexa's voice, pissing him off, was cool and in control. *Fuck her.*

Shane was sweating. A river of perspiration ran down under his arm, slicking his shirt and rib cage. People around him were screaming through their car windows as he passed them on the shoulder illegally. He was running out of room, so he veered back into the right lane, forcing the Taurus between a sixteen-wheeler Vons Grocery truck and a green Chevy van. Both drivers yelled obscenities at him. The grocery truck blew its heavy six-tone air horn, scaring the shit out of Shane, but he forced his way in, now catching a glimpse of the blue Camaro in the far left lane. Kono was transitioning off the 110 to the 105.

Shane was fucked. He slammed the heel of his hand on the steering wheel. He was fenced off by four lanes of bumper-to-bumper traffic and was pushed helplessly along by the slow flow, past the 105 transition, heading uselessly in the wrong direction. The tail was completely blown. He snapped up the radio.

"Five, this is Six," he said.

"Roger," she said.

"I lost K. He was on the 110. I got trapped, missed the transition. He's southbound on the 105, running clean." Shane waited for Alexa to curse him out or belittle him for losing his man. But she didn't do either.

"Okay, I copy," she said. "My guy just left the 710 at Ocean. We're down by the water. I'll talk you in."

"Roger that, coming your way," he said, feeling like a complete rookie.

For the next ten minutes she was silent, then: "I'm Code Six at 2300 Ocean Boulevard. Take the 710 to the end of the freeway and turn left. I'm in a gas-station parking lot."

"Copy that," he said.

It took him another ten minutes before he pulled up Ocean Boulevard and saw Alexa's gray Crown Victoria parked in a Texaco station across the street from a vast piece of fenced property.

Razor wire ran for miles in both directions.

He could see two big gates, each with a private security guard. The sign over the drive-through arch had been torn down.

Shane pulled into the darkened gas station, parked near the Crown Vic, got out, and slid into the front seat next to Alexa.

"Sorry, I got totally jammed on the 110."

"It's okay," she said. "All roads lead to Rome."

"Huh?"

"Your boy just pulled through that gate five minutes ago. A blue Camaro with racing stripes and a bondoed front fender, right?"

"Yeah."

He looked through her windshield at the five-hundred-acre piece of land across Ocean Boulevard next to the bay. On the east side of the property, the buildings were still standing, but to the west there were piles of rubble where the structures had already been knocked down. It looked a little like pictures of Berlin after the bombings in '45.

"Is this place what I think it is?" she asked.

"Yep," he said softly. "The Long Beach Naval Yard."

CHOIR PRACTICE

THE SUN SET slowly and magnificently over the Pacific Ocean. Scattered clouds that were strung across the horizon in steel-gray formations suddenly turned deep purple, riding above the dark blue sea like a colorful celestial armada until the sun was gone and night claimed its final victory.

Shane retrieved his new camera from the trunk of the Taurus, grabbed the heavy lens and some film, then walked with Alexa along busy Ocean Boulevard, across the street from the old naval yard. They were both looking for a good place to climb the fence. With cars streaking by in both directions, they picked a hole in the traffic, sprinted across the busy four-lane street, then continued west, looking through the fence at the property beyond.

There were security lights located inside the old naval yard every block or so, illuminating sections of the torn-down facility. This part of the huge yard had already been completely razed. Behind them, on the east end of the property, the surviving naval buildings loomed.

Shane reasoned that they had a better chance of getting inside unobserved if they went west, where there were no structures left standing and, hence, nothing to steal and less need for security.

"Where do you want to try?" she suddenly asked.

He pointed to a place up ahead where the razor wire had come down, making it possible to get over the fence without ripping their hands and clothes.

"With all this traffic on Ocean, we'll be spotted; somebody's gonna call it in," she said. "Let's try over there." She pointed to the far end of the property, where the fence seemed to turn a corner and head south toward the bay.

There was a huge lit structure looming down there that Shane didn't like the looks of. "Except, what the hell is that?" he asked, pointing at it, but she didn't answer.

They kept walking and finally got close enough to see that it was an active Army Reserve post, with its own entrance located at the far end of the naval yard. A bunch of weekend warriors were standing around in the parking lot, milling in front of the post HQ.

"Okay," she said. "You're right. Let's go back and try your place."

They returned to the spot Shane had seen, and then waited for the line of traffic to pass. Once the light down the street turned red, Shane touched her arm.

"Now," he said.

He and Alexa hit the fence simultaneously. It was an eight-foot-high chain-link; Shane scrambled up and over fast, surprised to see that they hit the ground on the other side at about the same time.

They sprinted away from Ocean Boulevard as the light down the street turned green and the headlights of the approaching cars came toward them. They crouched in the dark unobserved as the traffic streamed past on the far side of the fence.

"When Drucker and Kono went in, you sure you couldn't see which way they turned once they got inside?" Shane asked.

"They were stopped by the plastic badge guarding the east gate, but once they drove through, I lost 'em. I was half a block away, across the street. I didn't want to chance getting spotted."

"If they went in there, then they're probably still on the east side of the property," Shane reasoned.

"Probably."

They took off along the paved road inside the fence, this time heading east, back the way they had just come. The two-lane base road they were on was identified by a sign as COFFMAN STREET.

They were both struck by the vastness of the old shipyard. Shane had heard about the property ever since he was a kid growing up in L.A., but he'd never been down there before.

"This place is huge," he said, stating the obvious as they quickened their pace, doing a speed walk. "No wonder those people at the city council hearing were pissed. This place has gotta be worth billions of dollars. Prime waterfront, right on the border between L.A.

and Long Beach; the *Queen Mary* is half a mile from here, Fisherman's Village a stone's throw away."

She nodded but said nothing.

They were coming to a part of the yard that had not been demolished yet. They began passing huge covered docks, once used to refurbish naval vessels. Faded signs hung on every kind of structure, from wood-frame officers clubs and enlisted-personnel mess halls to poured-concrete warehouses and five-story-high covered sheds. They passed blast foundation plants; the compressor boiler plant loomed next to an air compressor building; then some hazardous-waste staging areas. There were mammoth towers leaning against a dark sky, marked COLLIMATION TOWER and PUMPING STATION TWO. Neither Shane nor Alexa had a clue what they were used for.

They passed the old naval credit union building, the sheet metal shop, and the asbestos removal headquarters, which was part of the current demolition operation and consisted of a flock of portable trailers.

The property was beyond anything that Shane had ever imagined. Now they were at the end of Coffman Street, where it turned into Avenue D.

Up ahead they could see some bright light streaming out of a huge warehouse. They were moving slowly now, trying to hug the shadows created by the occasional street-lamps.

They finally got close enough to see ten or twelve cars parked in front of a huge lit warehouse. Shane and Alexa could see the open loading door with a sign overhead that read:

**BUILDING 132
MACHINE SHOP—
PIPE AND COPPER**

They crept across Avenue D and found cover behind a two-story-high cylindrical tank. When they looked around the rusting tank, Shane and Alexa could see directly into the mouth of the warehouse through the raised loading door.

A party with more than thirty people was going on inside. Some tables had been set up full of food and buckets of beer. Men and women were dancing on the cold concrete floor, which was lit by lights from two gray police plainwraps that had been pulled inside. Both Crown Vics had the doors open; stereo music was coming from the car radios tuned to the same FM station.

Shane was looking through his telescopic lens at the partyers. "Most of these guys are cops.... I know some of the girls. I busted a few when I was in West Valley Vice."

"Hookers?" Alexa asked. "Gimme it."

He handed her the zoom-lens camera, and she squinted through the eyepiece, panning around inside the lit building. "You're right, it's a regular coyote convention in there," she murmured. "Those are Beverly Hills pros—thousand-dollar girls—Angelica DeBravo, Deborah Kline, Donna Fleister, plus the rest of our police-department cast of characters." She was referring to Ray's den: Joe Church, Lee Ayers, John Samansky, Don Drucker, and Shane's blown tail, "Bongo" Kono. Calvin Sheets and Coy Love were not there, but the other guys he'd photographed up at Arrowhead were. Alexa identified them as ex-cops terminated from "Dream" Sheets's Coliseum detail. Then she caught her breath. "Shit—don't like this," she said, her eye pinned to the camera viewfinder.

"What?"

"There're two guys from the mayor's staff in there—his legislative assistant, Mark somebody, in the suit by the door; and Rob Lavetta, his press-relations guy, the one standing next to Drucker." She handed the camera back to Shane, who took a picture of both men.

The party was in full swing, everybody drinking beer and dancing to the music, although "dancing" was a conservative description of what was going on. It was more like a group grope in 4/4 time. Dress was optional, with the thousand-dollar girls opting for maximum exposure.

Shane wanted to photograph everyone, keeping a mental count of whom he had already shot and whom he still needed, waiting for the right moment when the dancers would spin, giving him a good angle of one or both. When he finished, he sat next to Alexa, leaning back against the rusting cylindrical tank.

"They oughta put these shots in the departmental brochure," he finally said. "We'd end our recruiting problem."

Alexa volunteered a slogan: "Not just long hours and cold coffee. Police work—a changing profession."

"Whatta you wanna do?" he asked.

"I don't know...." She winced, then pulled something out from under her. It was a sign she'd been sitting on. They both read it:

ABRASIVE TANKS
MAINTAIN 50-FOOT SAFETY
PERIMETER

They both looked up fearfully at the old rusting tanks they were hiding behind. Then Shane realized that his hand was in something wet, pulled it up, and looked at it.

"Shit," he said, shaking it dry.

"Let's move back, get outta here," she said.

Suddenly they heard laughing nearby. A man's voice: "You're on. Let's do it."

Shane and Alexa cautiously leaned out and looked at the party. It had now spilled out of the huge building; people were standing around the back of one of the cars parked outside, while Drucker pulled two cardboard boxes out of the trunk. He ripped them open and started handing out shirts to everybody.

"What the hell are those?" Alexa asked.

"The jerseys," Shane replied.

Black football jerseys with red numbers and letters on the back that read:

The shoulder trim was done in a pattern resembling a red spider web. The cops started moving in a pack up the street with handfuls of beer and their arms draped casually around the hookers.

"I gotta see this," Shane said.

He and Alexa followed from the shadows, staying at least a hundred yards behind the group, which was drinking and grab-assing its way along Avenue D until finally they came to the old base athletic building and adjacent field. Shane and Alexa found themselves at the far end of the old field, the grass long dead from lack of water.

Someone had brought a football, and after more drinking and groping, a very fundamental game of tackle ensued. Slow, looping passes drifted to giggling hooker wideouts who gathered the spirals in without too much interference. The playful tackles were short on violence but long on rolling around on the ground and piling on. The beer kept flowing. The game looked to Shane like a hell of a lot of fun.

"How do you get a jersey and a place in the lineup?" he wondered.

"You don't want in that game, Shane. You'd get tired of all the AIDS testing."

He nodded and smiled. He realized it was the first time she'd used his first name.

They watched for quite a while and finally decided that everybody was so drunk, this was where the evening would end. They backed out, got over the fence, and returned to the gas station.

"I hate spiders," she said once they got to their cars.

"So the jerseys are football, but is this place the Web?"

"I don't know, must be," she said. "But I can tell you this much: these cops are having choir practice with first-string girls and two guys from the mayor's staff." "Choir practice" was an after-hours police drunk, usually in a park or some deserted place.

"Gimme the film," she said. "There's an all-night drugstore half a block from my apartment. I'll have the proofs back in two hours."

He hesitated, then unloaded the camera and gave her the two other exposed film containers.

They got into their respective cars and started to pull out when Alexa sounded her horn. Shane rolled down his window. She leaned across her front seat, talking through her passenger window. "For whatever it's worth, I believe you. Something big and shitty is going on here. I'm in."

"Thanks," he said gratefully. Then she waved at him and drove off. It had been more than a week, and she was the first one.

31
THE PITCHES MOTION

SHANE WAS on the 405 on his way back from Long Beach when he saw the transition ramp for the Santa Monica Freeway. He wondered whether DeMarco had been working on his case or whether he'd spent the day drinking and listening to rap. He decided to find out. He put on his blinker and made the turn onto the 10. Seven minutes later he was standing on the bike path outside DeMarco's house.

He hesitated a moment, almost afraid of what he would find. Finally he pushed open the gate, walked up to the front door, and knocked. One of DeMarco's new surfer roommates opened the door. He looked right through Shane and, without saying a word, stepped back and let him in. The boy was wearing surf trunks with no shirt and had an athlete's build. The eyes were where the problem was: empty, hollow tunnels of distrust.

"DeMarco around?"

The boy didn't seem to want to waste even one syllable on Shane. He jerked a thumb in the direction of the hallway, then flopped back down on the sofa, where his buddy was lounging with the TV remote. MTV's *Real World* was on the large Sony. Two teenage girls were on the screen arguing about their gay male roommate's new rottweiler, who apparently was shitting all over their London flat. One of life's smelly little problems. Shane moved through the hall and knocked on the end door. His defense rep called out angrily: "What?!"

Shane pushed the door open and looked in. For the first time, Dee was hard at it. He had law books and police department manuals open on the cluttered desk in front of him, his half-glasses perched on the end of his nose. He was a blue and gray vision in a faded LAPD sweatshirt and jeans. He had taken his long gray hair out of the knot in back, and it now hung on his shoulders, Cochise-style.

"How's it goin'?" Shane asked.

"Don't you wanna give me a Breathalyzer first?" he groused.

"Come on, Dee, gimme a break."

The defense rep leaned back in his squeaking swivel chair and swung around to face Shane. "Basically, it ain't getting any better," DeMarco said.

"You talkin' about the 1.61 Mayweather sent through this morning? I haven't seen it yet. I haven't been home."

"Copy right here," DeMarco said, picking up a fax and waving it at Shane. "But it's worse than just the 1.61. I found out this afternoon that Donovan McNeil, the only friendly face you had on your judging panel, is no longer able to attend the hearing." DeMarco rooted around his paperwork, found another fax, and held it up. "He's been transferred as of yesterday to the command chair at Administrative Vice in Central Division. Big fucking job. And since that transfer is effective immediately, it has been determined by the Special Investigations Division that, under these extreme circumstances, he does not have the time available to serve on your board. He's been replaced. I guess these Dark Side pricks finally found out you two used t'sling bait together."

"Who'd we get this time? The chief's brother-in-law?"

"Nope. The chief's old driver, Leland H. Postil."

"Fuck," Shane said. "Don't we still get to throw one out?"

"Yeah, they gave me two choices. The other was Peggy York, former head of IAD. In your absence, I chose Postil."

"Things can't get much worse," Shane growled.

"Wanna bet? Check this. I've been trying to restrict Alexa Hamilton's demands for your personal background file. It's full of a buncha unsustained complaints, CO's tardy slips, ridiculous stuff that every cop gets the minute he starts hooking up scumbags and dealing with this nitpick four-hundred-page LAPD Manual. The stuff in those background files is always just unproved bullshit, but it looks bad if you string it out in front of a board hearing."

Shane was pissed. "Old, unsustained complaints can only be used *after* the board convicts, *if* they convict, and then it can only be used as part of the penalty phase of the hearing to help determine past history and state of mind," he said.

"I see you've been reading Section 202," DeMarco said.

"I sleep with the fucking thing, for all the good it's doing me."

"Well, buddy-boy, once again, the powers that control the Special Investigations Division have ruled against you. Alexa filed a Pitches motion to overturn that section of the Police Bill of Rights. The panel granted her motion, and the package went over to her at four this afternoon."

They sat quietly in the room. Finally DeMarco got up, went to a small refrigerator in the corner of the office, and pulled out a beer. "You want one?"

"Dee, you've gotta stay off the Bud Lights. Okay?"

"Fuck you. I'm through listening to that shit from you." He ripped the tab off and took a swallow.

"I'm hearing around that maybe you have an alcohol problem," Shane said. "I hear that's why you pulled the pin."

DeMarco looked at him and smiled, then took a long fuck-you swig. "I won't even favor that with an answer."

"Look, Dee, I'm into something here. I think I've got the mayor tied into a blackmail scheme to trade billions of dollars' worth of property from Long Beach over to L.A. Ray and his den were blackmailing people in

Arrowhead so this would happen, most notably Carl Cummins, who's president of the Long Beach City Council. I followed some guys out there to the old naval yard. I've got—"

"You got shit," DeMarco interrupted, slamming the beer can down on his desktop. "Maybe if you'd stop running around, accusing all these high-profile guys of bullshit crimes, we wouldn't be facing all this administrative flack. We wouldn't be losing the Pitches and all our other motions."

"But—"

"No! Don't 'but' me. Ever since I took this fucking case, you've been accusing me of not trying. The reason we're getting hosed here, buddy, is that you have proceeded to piss off the chief of police, Deputy Chief Mayweather, Ray's rookie den, and everybody in between. Add to that the fact that you're acting like you're fucking guilty. What kinda asshole breaks into Warren Zell's office and goes through his files?"

"Who told you that?" Shane asked.

"It's all over the department that Alexa Hamilton caught you in there, you dumb shit!"

Shane stood there, feeling slightly dizzy and stupid as hell. *Had Alexa lied? Had she told the department what he'd done?* "I... I don't see how—"

"On top of all that, you're about to get arrested for first-degree murder," DeMarco interrupted. "I got a call from the warrant control desk today. They wanted to know if you were here. They've been checking your house and said you're not living there. I think you'd better get in touch with them—turn yourself in."

Shane spun and moved out of the office, back into the hall. DeMarco followed him through the living room and out the front door.

"If you run, you're making a huge mistake," DeMarco said, standing in his doorway, peering over his half-glasses at Shane on the sidewalk.

"What else can I do, huh?" Shane answered. "I got nobody but me. If I get arrested, I'm gone without a ripple. Nobody will try and find out what's happening here. If I don't figure it out, I'm gonna go down in front of this rigged murder case." Then he turned and walked up the path. When he arrived at the parking lot two doors away, he got into his car and pulled out onto the highway.

He decided to go up the coast and cut across town on Sunset, afraid that DeMarco might call the cops down on him. He tried to get his head clear and to organize the facts. But one thought kept coming back.

Why would Alexa tell about his break-in at Zell's office? Shane could end her career with the information about her throwing his old BOR. Something had to be wrong.

Less than an hour ago, Alexa had said she believed him.

Now Shane needed to decide if he could believe her.

THE MONEY SHOT

IT WAS TEN-THIRTY when Shane got back to the 110, heading downtown toward the Spring Summer Apartments. His pager buzzed. He pulled it off his belt and read the printed message on the LED screen:

911 to IAD
A.H.

A.H.—Alexa Hamilton. She wanted Shane to go to the Bradbury Building immediately. He wondered what she wanted, or whether he should even trust her. Maybe the warrant was there and she was drawing him in so he'd be served and end up spending the night in jail. He picked up his cell phone, dialed her cell number, and got a not-in-service recording. He tried her apartment, no answer. Despite his suspicions, he had almost no choice. He had to take a chance on her. He knew the switchboard at the Bradbury was closed, so he fumbled in his pocket for the number of the Spring Summer Apartments. He dialed and after a minute got Longboard Kelly on the phone.

"Yeah," the surfboard shaper said softly.
"It's Shane. Everything okay?"
"Yeah." Again, a whisper.

"What's wrong? How come you're whispering?"

There was a long moment, then: "Chooch is asleep."

"Look, I've gotta go run an errand on my way home. It's only a few blocks outta the way. Are you guys cool?"

"Yeah."

"See you in about an hour. If that changes, I'll call."

" 'Kay," and then Longboard was gone.

Longboard Kelly sounded strange. He was usually a nonstop talker. Shane wondered whether he and Chooch had started toking together. He almost called back, but then he had to change lanes to make the off-ramp on Sixth Street. In a few more minutes he was downtown.

It was just before eleven and Schwarzenegger was back.

"Sorry, absolutely nobody gets through on Sixth. We're shooting a big stunt," the motorcycle cop said. "Back up, go four blocks over to Wilshire."

"I gotta get to Spring and Third," Shane said.

"Can't. It's inside the restricted area. You'll have to park it here and walk. This area has been posted for three or four days." The cop was another old-timer, a forty-year veteran, in his mid-to late sixties. He was standing on Spring Street, behind his yellow barricade, glowering in his knee boots and dark blue shirt with its thirteen hash marks, each one representing three years of service. The entire eight-block section from Wilshire to Seventh had been closed. There was a helicopter sitting in the middle of Sixth Street; klieg lights and a condor had the buildings lit up almost like daylight. Stunt people were milling about. A Brinks armored truck was parked in the middle of the street, near a camera on dolly tracks. The director and some assistant directors were pointing at extras with briefcases, directing them where to stand.

"When are you guys gonna be outta here?" Shane said darkly.

"Don't know," the motor cop replied. "But we got special permission tonight for this big shot, 'cause we had to land the bird in the middle of the street and then do the chase with the armored car down Spring. It's some lash-up," he said proudly, eager to display his film expertise. "We're using Tyler mounts on the camera ship to photograph the stunt exchange from the picture bird to the roof of the speeding armored truck. Arnie is gonna be on top of the moving truck, do the fistfight with the stunt captain while they're heading down Spring. Then Arnie jumps and catches the bar under the picture chopper and does the car-to-helicopter exchange. We cut, rerig, and the stunt double hangs there on the fly-away. It's a money shot," he said proudly. Everybody in L.A. talks the talk. Arnie had to be Schwarzenegger. It never even occurred to the bragging cop that half of downtown L.A.

was ready to strangle this entire cast and crew.

Shane got out of the car and started to move past the barricade, toward the gathering of assistant directors and stunt people standing near the idling helicopter.

"Hey, you can't just walk through here, buddy. It's restricted," the cop warned.

"I'm not parking here and walking a mile."

"You gotta go around. This is a danger area. Nobody can be in there who's not cleared or been to the stunt safety meeting."

"Sarge, I'm on the job. I gotta get to Internal Affairs at the Bradbury." Shane dug into his pocket, pulled out his last business card, and handed it to the cop.

"You got a badge?"

"Left it at home. I was out on a boat when I got the call."

" 'Cept you could a' got this card from anybody," he said suspiciously.

"When did you stop being a cop and start being a movie PA?" Shane was getting pissed. He started around the barricade, and the old cop reached out and grabbed Shane's arm just as an assistant director came running up.

"What's the problem, Rich?" he asked the motor cop.

"Guy says he's a cop. Wants t'drive through." He handed Shane's card to the assistant director, who looked at it.

"We're still a bit away from the shot," the AD said to Shane. "Lemme see if I can set this up. Hang on." He turned and ran back to the group of men huddled near the armored car, handing the card to a tall man in a safari jacket. The man looked at the card, then up the street to Shane, and nodded.

The assistant director waved his arm at Shane to come ahead. The motorcycle cop was pissed off and didn't look at Shane as he moved the barricade.

Shane got back in the Taurus and pulled up the street, right into the activity of the movie set. He was trying to get around the idling helicopter when a man stepped out from the group by the armored car and motioned him to stop, then leaned in his passenger window, smiling.

"Hang on a minute," he said.

Suddenly Shane felt something cold and hard press on the left side of his head.

"Howdy-do," a low, soft voice said with a country twang. "Y'all wanna slowly get out of the car?"

Shane tried to look back, but the second man had positioned himself to the left of Shane and behind him, pointing the gun through the driver-side window, placing it against the left side of his head. Shane didn't have to see the gun to know what it was.

"This is pretty dumb, whoever the fuck you are," Shane finally said.

"Hey, dipshit, we been lookin' all over for you. You're the dummy. I sent you the nine-one-one. We was down here anyway, and you stumble right on in here, nice as can be."

Then the man with the gun suddenly shouted at the man in the safari coat.

"Dom," he yelled. "What if, when Arnie leaves the car, we stage Sandra's abduction like this. Lookee here." Then he opened the door to the Taurus. "Out," he growled at Shane. "We're gonna get in that chopper. You're sitting in the back right side."

"You're gonna kidnap me in front of all these people?"

"This ain't a kidnapping, it's a rehearsal," he said. "You're gonna be Sandra Bullock. Don't fuck with me, pal. You make trouble, I'll clock you and carry you over. It'll look like blocking to these idiots." Then he pulled Shane out of the car, led him twenty feet to the helicopter at gunpoint, and shoved him into the back. Shane saw that it was Calvin Sheets.

Waiting in the helicopter was another piece of muscle Shane had never seen before. He was holding a gun low, out of sight. Shane settled in, and the man's cold eyes never left him. Calvin looked back down at the director, who shouted, "Yeah, maybe that could work, Cal. But I gotta deal with this first."

Calvin shouted back, "Hunter just called. We'll be back in half an hour, if that's okay."

"Go ahead," the director shouted. "We're an hour away, but we need the chopper back by eleven."

Calvin waved, climbed into the helicopter, and motioned to the pilot, who revved up the motor.

They lifted up off the pavement, hovered, then veered over the street and climbed away from the movie company.

Shane looked out the window and saw the fully rigged and lit street with the hundred or more movie people who had just witnessed his kidnapping without realizing it. They became miniatures as the chopper rose.

"So this is a Logan Hunter film," Shane said.

"Huh?" Calvin shouted back over the roar of the chopper.

"Forget it," Shane said.

Then the helicopter turned north and flew toward the mountains, picking up altitude, leaving the L.A. basin far behind.

33
THE HAT

I'M GONNA PUT her down in the Valley of the Moon," the pilot yelled over the rotor noise. "I'll call the house; they can meet us there."

Calvin responded with the okay sign. They were flying low, streaking through the San Bernardino Mountains, following a river-cut canyon about fifty feet off the ground. Occasionally Shane could see the moon shadow of the helicopter against rock outcroppings of the granite cliffs on the west side. Suddenly the helicopter rose and veered right, then flew around a mountain peak.

"Arrowhead Peak!" the pilot yelled at Sheets, pointing at the pinnacle, acting like a tour guide instead of a fucking kidnapper.

They skirted the mountaintop and cleared the east face. Shane could see Lake Arrowhead shimmering off in the distance directly ahead. A few miles closer was a smaller body of water five or six miles west of Arrowhead, which Shane remembered was Lake Gregory.

The helicopter streaked low, skirting the shore of Lake Gregory, until finally they were hovering over the appropriately named Valley of the Moon...no trees, no rocks, just acres of brown dirt.

The helicopter engine picked up rpms as it hovered. Out of the window below, Shane could see a late-model Land Rover streaking along a dry riverbed, its headlight beams bouncing against the ground. The pilot pointed to the black four-wheel drive racing toward them, and Sheets nodded.

They found a flat spot in the center of the riverbed, and the pilot lowered the chopper until it was just a few feet above the ground. The black Land Rover came to a stop a few hundred feet away. Dirt flew out in every direction, sandblasting the shiny new vehicle, pitting its ebony surface. Then the helicopter touched down its skids. The pilot didn't kill the engine; the turbine whined and the rotor flashed overhead as Sheets and the man sitting opposite Shane opened the door.

"Out!" Sheets commanded. Shane looked out of the helicopter at the desolate terrain, wondering if he was going to get a seat in the Land Rover or become an eternal resident of the Valley of the Moon.

Before he could protest, he felt cold steel on the back of his head as Sheets pushed the weapon against his skull. Shane didn't move.

"Just gimme a reason, and I'll put one through your wet wear."

"This hard-ass routine you got ain't working, Sheets."

"You know who I am?"

"Everybody in Southwest knows you. You ran the French embassy in the Coliseum parking lot."

"Get the fuck out," Sheets snarled.

"Calm down," Shane growled, but he got out of the chopper before Sheets could sucker punch him. He ducked his head reflexively as the rotor spun safely above him and the silent man. Sheets got out last, and they pushed him toward the Land Rover. Dust was flying, getting into everybody's eyes.

They scrambled to the SUV, driven by a shorthaired, bullnecked man. Before they could get the Land Rover turned around, the helicopter revved its engine and lifted off, pelting them with sand and destroying what was left of the paint, starring the back window near Shane's head with a flying rock.

"Shit. Fucking guy..." Sheets said, glowering at the chopper as it spun around and flew away, hurrying back to Spring Street, Arnold Schwarzenegger, and the money shot.

Shane was glad to be in the SUV, moving out of the Valley of the Moon. The fact that they were taking him anywhere gave him some hope. If he was being brought here to be disposed of, they probably would have gone ahead and chilled him in this desolate valley.

Calvin Sheets sat next to the bullnecked driver, looking out the front window, the .38 snubby still in his right hand. The silent man from the helicopter sat in the backseat next to Shane, never taking his eyes off him.

They raced along the creek bed in four-wheel drive, bouncing through rain ruts, and after five tire-pounding minutes, shot up onto the paved highway. The driver shifted out of four-wheel and sped past a weathered sign that identified the road as North Drive.

Soon they came to Bay Road, which Shane knew went all the way around the perimeter of the Lake Arrowhead shoreline. He watched the shimmering lake appear and disappear, peeking out from behind buildings and trees as the Land Rover sped around the lake, finally turning onto Peninsula Road, making a left onto Long Point.

They pulled up to a dock at a deserted camping area. Shane could see a man with his left arm in a sling standing next to the same classic reproduction Chris-Craft inboard that had delivered his assailants to Ray's dock two days before. The varnished sides glistened against soft teak decks.

Sheets went through his rough-guy routine again, poking at Shane with the gun. "Let's go, asshole," he growled. Shane got out of the Land Rover and moved ahead of the ex-LAPD sergeant, toward the boat.

Now he was struck by another gruesome possibility: maybe, instead of a dirt nap, he was about to go swimming with a forty-pound anchor. He didn't have much time to worry about it, though, because as he stepped up to the boat, the man with his left arm in the sling stepped forward as if to help him aboard, then, unexpectedly, threw a right hook, knocking Shane back against Sheets. His vision starred; he bit his tongue; his mouth filled with blood.

"Cut it out, Marvin," Sheets growled. "Rich, get the lines."

"Motherfucker," Marvin said, snarling at Shane, who was trying hard to clear his vision. The blow had landed high on his cheek. His eyes started watering badly. This was probably the guy who stopped his bullet and left the two pints of blood on Ray's linoleum floor.

"You know what they say, Marv. The kitchen is the most dangerous place in the home," Shane said.

"Fuck you," Marvin growled.

Rich untied the boat as Marvin got behind the wheel and turned the key; while the engine burbled and growled, they all took a moment and listened like teenage boys to the throaty rumble of the blown 257 flathead. Shane was pushed into the enclosed backseat of the boat, which was separated from the front by a teak deck and a second chrome windshield. He found himself wedged in tightly next to Sheets and the silent man named Rich from the helicopter.

Marvin angrily slammed down the throttle with his good hand caught the wheel, and the boat roared away from the dock, picking up speed as they headed across the lake in the shimmering light of a three-quarter moon.

Shane could see Arrowhead Village twinkling across the water, about half a mile to the right. Finally Marvin slowed the boat and turned the wheel. Ray's party house and dock were ahead, about a hundred yards away. Seconds later they were slowing down, and Shane could feel the heavy inboard bumping softly against the wood dock.

"Out," Sheets ordered, again jamming the pistol in Shane's ribs.

They walked up onto the porch. The door was unlocked and they went inside.

Coy Love was waiting in the living room. Shane had only seen his picture, and the photo didn't begin to capture the essence of him. At least six foot six, he towered over all of them, wearing a blue windbreaker and jeans. His thin, lipless mouth, oversize head, and stringy, muscled neck dominated an overpowering physical presence. He stood Lurch-like and speechless until they all got inside and closed the door. "This doesn't have to end badly," he said. His voice was rough—hard and dusty, like boots marching through gravel.

"That's good news," Shane replied.

"I want to show you something," Love said. "Follow me." He turned abruptly and led them through the hall into the master suite.

The lights were all on in the room. Shane tried not to look at the mirror, which, he knew from before, fronted the hidden room with its glory hole. A small suitcase was open on the bed, and it was full of cash. The used bills were stacked and banded. As soon as he saw the money, Shane was sure that he was being videotaped.

It seemed that Coy Love was in charge, which momentarily surprised him, because Love had been only a rookie patrolman when he'd been terminated. Sheets had been a sergeant, a watch commander. Yet Sheets seemed content to stand in the background and do his funky gun-poking routine while Love ran the show. Shane figured the shift in roles was primal— the law of the jungle. Love was more dangerous and brutal and, therefore, the alpha male. "Don't fuck with Love" the message machine had said. Love was the hammer.

"We need to come to terms," Coy Love said, his bloodless lips stretched tight across tombstone-shaped teeth.

"Good," Shane said. *A one-word answer— keep it thin; don't volunteer anything.*

"That's yours," Love said, indicating the cash in the suitcase on the bed. "A hundred grand in tens and twenties."

"Lucky me. Did I win the lottery?" Shane asked.

"Yeah, you were down to your last ticket, and then you got lucky, hit the number. If you start acting smart now instead of just running around like a hard-on with dirt for brains, then maybe there's another suitcase like that one in your future."

"I like this so far."

"We got some rules that go with giving you this hat." Police terminology for a bribe.

"Rules? Okay."

"One. You go home, you sit in your house, and you stay there."

"Trouble with my house is, it's full of nine-millimeter federals. The Major Crimes dicks have been digging them out of the walls like fruit seeds."

"That was a mistake. We apologize."

"I accept." Shane was beginning to think that maybe he might actually get out of there alive.

"Two. You stop messing around in Long Beach. Stop going to the naval yard."

"No problem there. I didn't like it much anyway."

"Three. Whatever you think you've figured out about Mayor Crispin or the top floor of the Glass House—forget it."

"Okay...it's forgotten."

"Let me explain to you why you are being offered this hat instead of a plot at Forest Lawn."

"Okay."

"Since you shot Ray, you have been in the press a lot. We're trying to keep a low profile.

You get to live as long as you play ball." Love moved around Shane, forcing him to turn sideways to the mirror while keeping his own back to it. This was definitely being videotaped. Shots of Shane Scully taking a suitcase full of cash. Damning evidence if he ever changed his mind. On the plus side, it also probably meant the murder one charge wasn't coming. If the DA had what he needed, these guys wouldn't be doing this.

"Okay, since we're playing ball, I assume I'm the catcher," Shane said.

"That's what you are. You just caught a break. If you're smart, you won't catch a bullet."

"I'm gonna be smart. I'm gonna just take my suitcase of untraceable cash and go home and sit in my bullet-riddled living room until you tell me it's okay to come out."

Love closed the suitcase, snapped the clasps, and handed it to Shane, spinning him slightly so that he was looking more toward the glory hole. Love kept his back to the bedroom mirror the whole time.

"Is that it?" Shane asked. "Is our business concluded?"

"Not quite yet. Come in here." Love moved out of the bedroom and back into the living room. Shane followed him, carrying the suitcase, thinking the hundred thousand in small bills was surprisingly light. Sheets, Marvin, and Rich stayed behind him.

In the living room Coy took a videotape box off the TV, opened it, slid the tape into the

VCR, then turned his frightening, bloodless smile on Shane.

"I think it's important that you do not mistake kindness for weakness," Love said as he grabbed the remote off the TV and turned the set on. He punched PLAY.

Suddenly Shane was looking at Chooch and Longboard Kelly on the videotape. They were tied to wooden chairs in Shane's rented apartment on Third Street. He recognized the faded wallpaper and frayed blue drapes. Both Brian and Chooch had silver duct tape across their mouths. A man was offscreen holding a shotgun, the barrel of the weapon sticking about an inch into the frame.

Shane felt his guts tighten into a knot. Bile instantly flooded the back of his throat. "He's a fifteen-year-old kid," he protested weakly. "Brian Kelly is just a surfboard shaper. He doesn't know shit."

"You go home and stay quiet for two or three days. Then, if everything goes right, you get them both back. Otherwise, I'm gonna put these cowboys on the ark," Love said.

On the tape Chooch was struggling against his ropes. Longboard looked dazed and had blood on the side of his head.

"Seen enough?" Coy said, and when Shane nodded, he turned off the TV and handed Shane a set of car keys. "There's a department car parked in the driveway. Take it back and leave it in the motor pool at the Glass House. Then take a cab home and pull the grass up over your head."

Shane took the keys and the suitcase and walked on wooden legs out of the house. They all followed. There was a gray Crown Victoria with blackwalls in the drive. He got behind the wheel, started the car, and pulled out of the driveway. The headlights swept across the four ex-cops as he backed into the street, turning right. He was operating on autopilot...his mind on the sickening video images of Chooch and Brian tied to the chairs.

He drove down Lake View Drive, the black suitcase full of cash jiggling on the seat beside him. He took the correct turns from memory and found himself back on I-7, heading out of Arrowhead toward L.A.

As he drove, he could picture Chooch's black Hispanic eyes staring out at him from the recesses of his memory. He remembered the boy's swarthy, handsome features as he sat in the Little Bruin deli in Westwood, looking out at the traffic, his gaze averted so Shane wouldn't see his pain.

"Do you know who my father is?" the boy had asked. *"Did Sandy ever tell you?"* Hurt and longing in the question.

Shane had wanted to fill the void in Chooch's life, just as he had wanted to fill it in his own. But he had been slow out of the blocks and running two steps behind, a clown in swim fins, flapping along, heels down while the rest of the field breezed past him.

Almost without thinking, he picked up his phone and for the second time in twenty-four hours asked Alexa for help.

By the time he got to the San Bernardino Freeway, he had explained to her in detail what had happened and what was on the videotape. "I'll meet you at the Spring Summer Apartments," she said. "Maybe we can pick up something there."

An hour later he was back in downtown L.A. He found a spot at the curb on Third Street, across from his rented room. He could see Alexa's gray Crown Vic at the curb across the street. He quickly got out of his borrowed car and hurried into the building, afraid of what he might find in the cramped rented single on the third floor of the dingy rooming house.

34
THE THREE-FLUSH RULE

HE FOUND HER kneeling by the toilet in the bathroom, wearing latex gloves and brushing black granite powder from her field-investigation kit onto the toilet handle with a fine bristle brush. Every detective and patrol officer carried a crime-scene investigation kit in the trunk of his or her car.

"You got gloves?" she asked, glancing back at him, not bothering with a greeting.

"No," he replied woodenly. Alexa reached into her open kit and pulled out an extra

326

pair. "I'm gonna need a set of elimination prints from you. We've also gotta get a set of Chooch's and Longboard's from somewhere."

"Right," he said, and looked around the bathroom. "You get anything yet?"

"Hard to tell. A lot of this is junk, smudged or overlapped. I got a partial palm off that kitchen chair, where somebody must've grabbed it by the back and carried it. I think, from what you described on the phone, the videotaping took place in the center of the living room. They moved the chairs back to the kitchen, but there are fresh indent marks on the living-room carpet. I marked 'em with chalk, so don't step on 'em. I'm gonna take pictures. I emptied the kitchen trash into a towel in the sink, but I haven't gotten to it yet."

Shane moved out of the bathroom and looked at the small living room. "You try the TV?" he called out to her. After a minute she came out of the bathroom with a yellow four-by-five fingerprint identification card in her hand. She leaned down on the dining-room table and labeled a partial print she had just lifted off the toilet flush handle.

"We'll never get a print run with these," Alexa said. "They're mostly partials and smudged. The best we can hope for, if we even catch these perps, is maybe a match on a few of the basic Galton classifieds—maybe connect up on some of these ridge endings. The loops, arches, and whorls are pretty smudged."

"Chooch used the TV; maybe the remote has a set of his you can use for elimination," he said.

She took the channel changer, holding it by its side, and started dusting it, dipping the brush into the glass vial of black powder, then softly brushing the fine camel-hair bristles across the remote, looking for graphite residue that would indicate the oil of a fingerprint. She found a few good latents on the underside of the channel-changer, then took the clear tape out of her field kit and lifted the prints, stuck them on the card, and pressed them down, labeling the back of the card, "Channel Changer Right Index and Middle Finger."

While she worked, Shane moved through the apartment. There were no signs of a struggle, no blood, but lots of dirty black powder. She had been working there for quite a while and had left graphite everywhere—on the doorjamb at shoulder height, where somebody might lean with a palm, against the wall, on the cupboard doors, on the countertops.

Shane put on his latex gloves and began, halfheartedly, poking through the trash collected on the towel lying in the deep kitchen sink. He found a cardboard roll about an inch in diameter and plucked it out, using a pen from his pocket. Then he saw an empty bag of M&M's. Longboard was an M&M's freak. He pulled it out as well and took both items back into the living room. He handed the cardboard roll to Alexa. "Looks like the core from the roll of silver duct tape," he said.

"I saw that, too," she said. "We can try, but there's so much gummy shit on it, I doubt we'll lift anything." She took the powder and brushed it on the cardboard core, but as predicted, it was too sticky. Powder clung everywhere, turning the core graphite black and revealing nothing.

He told her about Longboard's candy addiction, so she went to work on the M&M's wrapper.

"Was there anything on the videotape you can remember that might be helpful?" she asked as she brushed the surface of the wrapper.

"No," he said. "Except there was a shotgun in the side of the frame...a riot pump. Looked like an Ithaca."

"Department issue." She said what he'd been thinking. "I don't think we're gonna find anything. If those guys were cops, they wouldn't leave evidence behind. They were probably all wearing gloves and picked up or flushed everything."

"Speaking of flushes, did you check the trap in the toilet?" he asked.

"No," she said, looking up. "I always hate that job, but I guess we oughta give it a try." She finished with the M&M's wrapper, lifting three good prints. "We're gonna need wrenches to get to the toilet trap," she said.

"I'll go see the manager."

"Don't bring him in here," she said sharply.

"Don't worry, I'm not a total idiot," he snapped back, then went down to the front desk, rang the night bell, and got the manager out of bed.

"Trouble with the toilet," Shane lied to the bleary-eyed man, who looked as if he hadn't shaved in two days. Rumpled, tired, and angry, he glowered at Shane from under the harsh light above his desk.

"Shit," the man said.

"You got a pipe wrench? I used to be a plumber. I can clear it for you."

The manager looked at him and computed the odds that Shane might break his toilet against the cost of calling a regular plumber. Money won... South of Main Street, it usually did. The manager moved into the back room and returned with a toolbox.

Shane took it up to the third-floor apartment. He closed the door and put on his gloves, then he and Alexa moved to the bathroom and removed the commode. He took off the porcelain top and plugged the flush valve with toilet paper. Then they began to remove the metal elbow from the back of the toilet.

One of the little-known truths about modern plumbing is that it takes at least two, sometimes three flushes to completely get rid of a bowl load. On more than one drug raid, the perps had flushed the dope with the cops coming through the door, not bothering to repeat the procedure, then were shocked to learn that two or three grams of cocaine remained in the water in the elbow and trap. Liquid samples had rolled up more than one drug dealer. The Drug Enforcement teams called it "the Three-Flush Rule."

They got the elbow off, and toilet water spilled onto the floor. Shane kept from kneeling in it by squatting as he worked. The elbow looked pretty clean, so he went after the trap, which was below the elbow and was there to keep larger obstructions out of the plumbing lines until they dissolved or softened.

"The things one learns in law enforcement," he muttered as he finally got the trap out and took it to the sink, emptying the four-inch cylinder into the basin. The last thing out was fat, round, and dark brown. It landed on the white porcelain like a turd on a wedding cake. The object had a shiny gold band around it.

"Cigar," he said triumphantly, picking it up with his latex gloves. It was a three-quarter-smoked panatela. The gold band said DOMINICAN REGAL.

"I think this is what's commonly called a clue," she said, smiling. "We have us a cigar smoker." She was holding out an evidence bag.

He dropped the mushy stogie inside the glassine pouch, then washed his gloved hands.

Five minutes later they had replaced the toilet fixture, taken the living-room crime scene photos, and were sitting on the cigarette-burned sofa, trying to figure it all out.

"There was no forced entry, so Longboard must have just let the guys in. If they were cops, they probably just flashed a potsy," she said.

"Maybe." His mind was circling a worrisome thought, but he pushed it aside. "Coy Love told me to go home and wait for two or three days. That means whatever it is they're worried about, it goes away after that."

"Makes sense," she answered.

331

"He also said to forget about the Long Beach Naval Yard and Mayor Crispin."

She nodded, but said nothing.

"These guys aren't gonna turn Longboard and Chooch loose, are they?" he blurted, putting the distressing thought into words. "They're gonna kill 'em."

"Probably," she said. "They'll hold 'em for leverage in case you get restless, but once this is over, they can't leave a kidnapping charge and two vics on the table."

"Shit," he said, rubbing his eyes. "I've fucked this up so bad. It's always like...if I knew yesterday what I know today..."

"Shane, I think we need to tell his mother."

"Yeah. I guess I've been putting that off." He looked at his watch. "It'll be sunup in an hour. Sandy is having sleepovers with some DEA target. She won't be there till sometime after eleven. I'm whipped, but I can't sleep here. How's your place sound?"

"I got a couch you can use," she said, then gathered up all of her stuff and stood in the doorway, looking at the dusted room. "If we leave it like this, you're gonna forfeit your security deposit."

"Fuck it. Let's go."

They closed the door and locked up, heading downstairs. Shane deposited the toolbox behind the counter without ringing the night bell, and they walked out into the street.

"I gotta drop this department car back at the Glass House. I don't wanna disobey any of their instructions. Follow me, then later we can go to Sandy's in your car," Shane suggested.

"My car's at home. I was with a friend when you called. I had him drop me off here. I figured we'd use your car."

"Then who owns that plainwrap?" he said, pointing to the gray Crown Vic across the street. "That's gotta be department issue. No civilian is gonna buy a stripped-down gray sedan with no air and blackwalls."

They moved across the street and looked through the windshield of the locked car. They could see the telltale wires hanging down under the dash, identifying the recessed police radio.

"Yep," she said, "but it's not a detective car. No coffee lids on the dash."

She was right. Since detectives had to do lots of stakeouts, they drank gallons of coffee. The cars were department-owned, so the cops had no pride of ownership. The common practice was to peel the plastic lids off the Styrofoam Winchell's cups and throw them up onto the dash. Shane had never been in a detective's plainwrap that didn't have half a dozen or more plastic lids up there. If the motor pool ever cleaned the interiors, the old, wet rings from the tops stained the dash and remained behind as a permanent testament to the practice.

"Staff car?" he said hesitantly.

They both walked around the Crown Vic, looking through the windows. It had beem immaculately cleaned. All the cars in the staff motor pool were automatically washed and vacuumed once a day by inner-city gangsters dressed in jailhouse orange.

Alexa took out her cell phone and punched in a number. After a minute she got the Communications Center.

"This is Sergeant Hamilton, serial number 50791. I found one of our plainwraps parked in a bad spot. It's a 548E," she said, giving the radio code for a vehicle parked illegally across a driveway. "It should be moved. Could you give me the officer's name so I can contact him to move it?" She listened, then said, "City plate, DF 453." Another wait, then, "Thanks," and she closed the cell, a troubled look on her face.

"Shit, I don't even want to ask," he said.

"It's a Triple-O staff car," she said.

Triple-O stood for the Office of Operations, which reported directly to the chief of police. Shane remembered that the administrative staff of the Office of Operations contained about five men and women, all captains and above. The office acted as an adviser to the chief of police and exercised line-of-command oversight in all divisions. In short, Operations was Chief Brewer's right hand.

"It could have been left here because of the movie," she said hopefully. "Triple-O handles press relations."

"You packing?" he asked.

"Yeah, of course."

"Gimme it. Mine's gone. I've been losing guns faster than winos' teeth."

"What're you gonna do?"

"Break into this thing. I don't wanna fuck

around with the lock, standing on a street corner. Lemme have it."

She dug her Beretta 9mm out of her purse and handed it to him. He dropped the clip and handed it back, then tromboned the slide to make sure the chamber was clean. He held the automatic by the barrel, looked both ways for potential witnesses, then broke the side window of the car, shattering glass onto the maroon velour upholstery.

"Dominican Regals are expensive smokes," he said. "I don't know many line cops who can afford ten-dollar cigars."

He opened the door, leaned inside, and started rummaging around. The ashtray was clean. He opened the glove box. There were three objects inside: the departmental registration, indicating that the car was indeed the property of the Los Angeles Police Department; an L.A./Long Beach Thomas street guide; and in the back of the compartment a sealed Baggie containing three fresh Dominican Regal cigars.

THE COURTESY REPORT

T HE UNOFFICIAL NOTIFICATION of a crime to a civilian was known in police work as a courtesy report.

Shane had revealed Sandy Sandoval's identity to Alexa over breakfast in her neat duplex apartment on Pico, two blocks east of Century City. He had slept fitfully on her living-room couch, and now, marginally refreshed, they left her place and drove across town. It was Saturday morning, and Barrington Plaza loomed, a tower of sunlit granite.

Shane pulled up, and Alexa badged the shoulder-braided bandleader who announced them, then keyed the elevator. Show tunes from the Boston Pops serenaded their arrival at the penthouse level. It was eleven-thirty A.M.

"So this is the famous Black Widow Nest," Alexa said, looking at the magnificent hallway on the eighteenth floor.

Most of the LAPD knew about her and knew that Shane had once been the Black Widow's handler, but her real name had been in the possession of only two Special Crimes detective commanders. Shane had deliberated hard before telling Alexa. In the end, it was the fact that Chooch's life was involved that made the decision for him.

Shane rang the doorbell to Sandy's penthouse

apartment, dreading the job of telling her what had happened. He was sweating, but it was flop sweat, cold and clammy as wet clothing.

The mahogany door opened, and Sandy was standing there in a tailored black sheath that fit her size-four frame like a second skin—skin that was dusky, the color of dark sand; her eyes, golden-brown amber; her long raven tresses swirling around her shoulders with planned abandon. A single strand of pearls dangled with fuck-you elegance. She was dressed to party. She stood in the doorway, a questioning look on her gorgeous face. Then she shot a quick glance at Alexa.

"What is it? This is a terrible time, Shane. I'm bushed, I just got home."

"Chooch is gone," Shane said. "He's been kidnapped."

"I...I thought you said you had found him," Sandy finally stammered, her liquid amber eyes losing focus, clouding like a fighter hit too hard.

"He's been kidnapped, Sandy. By men who are trying to stop an investigation. I'm afraid..." He stopped. "I think by cops," he finished.

"Cops?!" she said, and involuntarily her hand went up to her mouth.

"This is Sergeant Hamilton. She's my—" He looked over at Alexa. *What exactly was she? His department prosecutor? His only believer? His nemesis? What the hell else was she?*

"I'm Shane's partner," she said, answering his question and filling the void.

Sandy spun abruptly and headed back into her apartment. Alexa and Shane followed.

She walked slowly ahead of them, fluid as a dancer, her hips swaying seductively. Shane would have preferred a more leaden gait. Even in the face of this news, she radiated sexual grace. When she turned and faced them, he saw distress bordering on hysteria in her eyes. Instantly his heart went out to her, and guilt overwhelmed him.

"Why? Where did it happen?" she asked.

"An apartment on Third Street, a safe house I was renting. I guess they followed the sitter over from my place in Venice. I can't think of any other way they could have found him," Shane said.

"We aren't exactly sure who," Alexa said. "But it appears to be high-ranking police officers who are calling the shots."

"You should go to the chief. Go to Burl. Tell him what you suspect."

When Alexa hesitated and looked at Shane, Sandy sank down on the sofa. "You're telling me you think Burl's—"

"We don't know exactly who is involved," Shane said. "But it goes way up. Maybe all the way to the mayor. It involves Logan Hunter, Tony Spivack, and the Long Beach Naval Yard."

"The 'why' is easier to understand. They took Chooch to keep us from continuing an investigation into it," Alexa said.

Sandy looked down at the white plush pile to hide her devastation.

"Sandy... I'm sorry. I'm really sorry. I didn't see it coming. If I could change this, I—"

She waved this away with her slender hand, sat absolutely still for a moment, then looked up. Her expression had hardened, the vulnerability had vanished. "How can I help? There must be something we can do." He watched in fascination as she tucked the loose strands of panic away, grabbed hold of her plummeting emotions, pulled hard, and darted up quickly, climbing hard, like a kite in a strong wind.

"Do you know any of these girls?" Alexa asked as she reached into her purse and handed over two packets of pictures from the party at the naval yard. Sandy spread them out on the white marble coffee table. She picked up a small antique magnifying glass with a carved ivory handle and examined each picture.

"I know one or two of these girls," she said, looking at them slowly, studying the shots, separating out the pictures of the two girls she knew. "Scarlet Mackenzie is the red-haired one. This one here—this blonde—changed her name from Gina Augustina to, what the hell was it... Avon Star. Used to have black hair. I think some of these others used to work with Madam Alex until Heidi took over the L.A. market. They all work the executive trade."

"What about the men? We know a lot of them are cops," Alexa said.

Sandy looked through the pictures again but shook her head. "To be honest with you, I'm not working much with LAPD anymore." She shoved the pictures of the two girls she knew toward Alexa, never once looking over at Shane. "I only know these two."

"These girls might know what's going on," Alexa said. "We need to find somebody who can help us, somebody who can tell us who took Chooch."

Sandy studied Alexa for a moment, then looked back at Shane. "I'm going to have to shut down this thing I'm doing for DEA. I'll tell 'em I need two days, that my brother got sick in Connecticut." She got up, moved to the phone, then punched in fourteen or more digits, which Shane knew was probably a number for a satellite beeper that the feds all used now.

After she finished, Sandy hung up and returned to the table. She sat down and looked at them, biting her lower lip. "Maybe I could convince Scarlet to duke me in with this crowd."

Duke me in, Shane thought. Sandy was even beginning to talk like a cop. It was definitely time for her to get out of the business.

"I could call Scarlet, say I just got out of a bad marriage and want to get back on the stroll. Nobody knows what I've been doing all these years. I haven't seen these two girls in ages."

Shane had to get out of there. He was starting to feel trapped. He got up abruptly. "Here's my beeper number," he said, giving Sandy one of his cards. "It's on all the time."

Alexa took out a pencil, wrote hers down, and handed it to Sandy.

"Okay," Sandy said. "I'll check back with you tomorrow. I should be able to get in

340

touch with her by then. I'll set something up. If she knows anything that will help us get Chooch back, I'll find it."

"Good," Shane said.

They all walked to the front door. Sandy seemed cool and in control again. After she opened the door, she looked hard at him, and Shane knew he had to say something.

"I was trying to do you a favor when I took Chooch," he said. "It didn't work out, and I'm sorry."

What she said next was very strange. "You weren't doing me a favor, Shane, I was doing one for you."

He saw the dark, strange look again, and then her amber eyes opened for a moment and he was seeing her uncovered core...a self-loathing and sadness deeper than he could have ever imagined. Then the look was gone, replaced in a heartbeat by shrewd cunning and the cold gleam of sexuality. She closed the door, and he found himself looking at brown mahogany, the exact color of her eyes and almost as hard.

36

S AND J

IT WAS NOON, and they were back in Shane's borrowed Crown Vic. Alexa had turned on the police radio, and they were listening to staccato radio calls detailing the menu of violence and death, all of it described numerically in a flat monotone: "One X-ray twelve. A 415 at 2795 Slauson. Handle Code Two." Human carnage was a day-and-night routine.

"I don't know what the next move is," Alexa admitted.

Shane looked over at her. He knew what he was going to do, but it was a felony and he didn't think he should confide in her, for fear she'd hook him up on the spot.

But she was good, and she read the look in his eyes. "Let's hear what you're planning," she said suspiciously.

"You don't want any part of it. I'll drop you home."

"Lemme guess. You wanna go pick up Drucker or Kono or one of Ray's other hamsters...then go give them some S and J."

S and J stood for "sentence and judgment." Cops used to call it "holding court in the street." Either way, in this case it would be kidnapping and assault, both Class A felonies.

"Right idea, wrong guys," he said. "Kono

342

and Drucker are small players; they may not even know what's really going on. I think they're just getting envelopes."

"It doesn't matter, 'cause we aren't going to kidnap and threaten anyone. That's a bonehead play." She stared hard at him in the dim light. He didn't look back. "Who, then?" she finally asked, her curiosity boiling over.

"You're gonna hate it." And then for some unknown reason, he told her.

After he had finished explaining his idea, she sat silently in the car for almost five minutes. The police radio underscored their separate thoughts, broadcasting misery while each of them pondered the personal cost if his dangerous plan went wrong.

Shane knew he had nothing more to lose. Any way he looked at it, odds were, he was headed to prison, where as a cop in the joint, he would last about as long as ice cream on a summer day.

Alexa, on the other hand, was only on the edge of this. She hadn't been put in play yet. Nobody except Sandy knew she'd been helping him. She could still go home and sit it out, saving her career and maybe her life.

He finally looked at her and saw those chips of blue staring out the front window, her brow furrowed in stubborn concentration, frustrated and confused like a fifth-grade algebra student.

For Shane, it was only about Chooch. It was his fault the boy was gone, and if he had to end his own life behind the secure perimeter of Vacaville State Prison, at least it would be for trying to put this mess right. Deep down he had formed a fraternal attachment to Chooch Sandoval. He couldn't exactly explain why, but it had happened.

Then he felt Alexa's weight shift on the seat beside him. He looked over at her. She had turned to face him.

"Okay," she said slowly, "I'm in."

The marina was strangely quiet for a Saturday afternoon. Shane thought the boat was a ketch or a yawl—whatever the hell they called them when the second mast was taller than the first.

"Schooner," Alexa said, reading his thoughts perfectly. The stern of the fifty-five-foot sailboat carried the boat's name.

"*Board and Cord*—cute name for a sailboat," she said.

He assumed she was thinking it stood for the wood of the hull and sail lines, so he set her straight. "It's a basketball expression. Means a bank shot off the backboard and through the net."

"Oh." She smiled. "In that case, he should have called it *Cheap Shot.*"

They were parked in the lot next to the slips at D Dock in Marina del Rey, looking out the front window of the car at the boats tied up forty or fifty yards from them, baking in eighty-degree sunlight. Both were wearing drugstore baseball caps and wraparound sunglasses—a minimal disguise.

"I heard he's down on this thing every weekend," Shane said, focusing a new pair of binoculars he'd found under the seat at the boat's portholes, looking for movement inside. "He's probably sleeping late."

Shane shifted his field of vision, concentrating on the yachts to either side of Mayweather's schooner. It appeared that most of the boats around the *Board and Cord* were empty.

"You sure you want to do this?" he asked. It was hard for him to believe she was about to risk her career and maybe even her freedom for Chooch Sandoval, whom she didn't even know. Of course, he had completely missed the point, so she set him straight.

"You claim I didn't believe what I said about keeping the job free from corruption, that I didn't want to risk it when the chips were down, and maybe there's some truth there. This is hard for me, I admit it, but these guys are committing crimes. They're kidnapping children. So, if I know this is happening and I walk away, that makes me as guilty as they are."

"Still, we're talking about committing a Class A felony."

"Shane..."

"Huh?"

"Shut up, will ya? Let's go roll up this shitwrap."

She opened the door and got out of the car. He followed her to the concrete path.

"I hope he's here. I wish I knew what his POV looked like," she said, changing the subject so he wouldn't pursue it, looking out at the

345

twenty or thirty parked cars in the marina lot.

"Listen, you've gotta hear me on this," he said, turning her around, holding her arm as he talked, feeling the tight muscles in her biceps. "This means a lot to me—Chooch has become important—Brian, too, but Chooch... Chooch and I, we...it's like he's the piece of me that got lost growing up. It's hard for me to explain exactly, but I'm never gonna be able to pay you back."

"No shit, Sherlock." She smiled, then turned and moved off toward the slips.

They walked quietly along the concrete path and down onto the dock, light-footing it. They had already decided how they would do it, and as they got to the stern of the boat, Shane found some cover one boat away as Alexa moved up to the cockpit.

"Hello, anybody there?" she called out. "Anybody home? Chief Mayweather? Request permission to come aboard."

The back cabin door opened, and Deputy Chief Thomas Mayweather stuck his gleaming black head out. "Yes?" he said. "What is it?" He had on a striped polo shirt and white pants.

"You alone, sir? It's Sergeant Hamilton, IAD. I need to talk to you."

"My wife and kids will be here in an hour. What is it, Sergeant?" he said impatiently.

"It's about the Scully prosecution, sir. I've got a big problem, but I don't think we should talk about it out here. May I come aboard?"

"Okay." There was some hesitancy in his voice, almost as if he smelled deception. He came out of the cabin, reached up, and helped her down into the cockpit, then into the main salon. Once they were inside, he closed the rear hatch.

Shane had been hiding, lying flat on the dock one slip away. Now he got up and moved around until he was standing behind the schooner. They had planned to take Mayweather in the main salon, where they could control the capture and not be observed. Shane knew that he had to be very careful getting aboard. Mayweather would feel the sway of the boat if he rocked her when he stepped on.

Shane slowly lowered himself down and hung his feet carefully over the deck, gradually getting his footing on the upholstered cockpit seat. But to his dismay, the moment he put all his weight down, the boat shifted with the load, and a few seconds later the salon door flew open. Mayweather glared out at him.

"Permission to also come aboard?" Shane said stupidly.

"What the fuck?" Mayweather blurted.

Then they both heard Alexa chamber her 9mm behind the deputy chief. The sound froze Mayweather.

"Assume the position, asshole," Shane snarled, switching to street demeanor. They would have to take him out in the open. Shane moved farther onto the boat.

Deputy Chief Mayweather glanced back at Alexa in the middle of the salon, holding her gun, glaring blue ice over the barrel.

Shane was unarmed and presented Mayweather's best avenue of escape. Suddenly the deputy chief charged. Shane had been ready for it and had already screwed his heels awkwardly into the padded seats for traction.

Mayweather was coming at him fast, lunging from the cockpit. Shane swung a right hook, missing the shot, bouncing his fist off the top of Mayweather's head. The ex-UCLA point guard was fast, his quickness and athleticism on full display. He grabbed Shane's legs and took him backward over the rail onto the wooden dock. While Shane clutched him tightly and held on for all he was worth, Alexa clamored off the boat and screwed the barrel of her 9mm into the deputy chief's ear. She pulled the hammer all the way back; the gun "snicked" dangerously in the still air.

"It won't be pretty," she warned him.

Mayweather stopped struggling. Alexa grabbed her cuffs off her belt and hooked him up. Shane got untangled and yanked the deputy chief to his feet. A few people on the next dock turned to look at them.

"You people are fucking crazy! You have any idea what you're doing?" Mayweather protested.

"Do you?" Shane replied.

Three minutes later they had pulled him off the dock, past some startled onlookers, then pushed him into the trunk of the Crown Vic with his own socks stuffed into his mouth.

They drove fast, up the 405, back to the Bradbury to pick up a videotape unit. Then they headed out to a deserted spot Shane knew about in the Pavia Aqueduct of the L.A. River.

THE ULTIMATE FIELD INTERVIEW 37

THEY PARKED the Crown Vic off the road in Glendale where the 134 and 5 freeways intersect, then helped a stunned and blindfolded Thomas Mayweather down the paved concrete levee that bordered the riverbed. Their hard leather shoes fought for traction on the forty-five-degree slope. They finally got the deputy chief to the floor of the wash, where a narrow trickle of water flowed down a spillway cut into the center of the paved concrete riverbed.

Black metal drain caps, thirty feet in diameter, each with two triangular cutouts on the top, faintly resembled the heads of huge black cats. Glendale taggers had completed the impression by spray-painting the metal with white noses, eyes, and whiskers.

They moved in single file, in broad daylight, under the leaden stares of the painted drain covers. Shane led the way along the wash, under several bridges, until they got to a huge metal drainage pipe, tunneling deep into the side of the hill. As they entered the mouth of the seven-foot-high sewer, they could hear things slithering and rustling in the inky darkness ahead of them. When they had gone far enough so that there was only a dim residue of sunlight from the tunnel's mouth behind them, Shane stopped.

"This is good enough," he said, and spun Mayweather around.

The deputy chief started to gurgle and wheeze around his sock gag, but Shane paid no attention. He knew there was a ladder about where they were standing that led to the surface a few hundred feet above.

Shane had been in this sewer drain two years before on a tip that it contained the body of a dead rape victim, a ten-year-old child. He'd found the girl's mutilated corpse in the tunnel, her blond hair and tiny body caked with mud and covered with feasting rats. He had had nightmares about it for a month afterward. He never caught her killer.

Shane found the ladder, more or less by feel. He uncuffed Mayweather's right wrist, dragged the disoriented deputy chief over, and hooked him to the ladder with both hands behind his back through the metal rail.

"Gimme the nine," he said to Alexa. She handed it to him, and he stuffed it into his belt. Then they set up the video camera. It was a Sony compact with a sun gun on the front. The telescoped tripod was fitted neatly into the bottom of the video carrying case. Mayweather, blindfolded and terrified, harrumphed and squirmed at the ladder. Shane secured the camera on the tripod, then turned on the sun gun. The single beam of harsh light hit the deputy chief in the chest. Shane adjusted it until it was right in Mayweather's face, then stepped forward and yanked the blindfold off the startled deputy chief.

"Welcome," Shane said softly, making his voice loony but also cold and hard as a steel blade.

"Scully?" Mayweather said, blinking his eyes frantically. Shane knew his prisoner couldn't see much, forced to look directly into the bright light.

"*Mr.* Scully! Let's have some respect for your host."

"You're gonna go away forever," Mayweather said angrily. "This is the most outrageous thing I've ever heard of. You're history. You'll both rot in jail for this. Sergeant Hamilton, you're smart, there's still a chance for you. Just turn me loose, I'll do what I can—"

"Shut up and *listen!*" Shane said. "If I don't get exactly what I want, this is where you check out, Tom."

"You can't possibly be serious."

"Hey, asshole, *think about it!*" Shane screamed, performing now, trying to sound demented and out of control. "You think I'd pull this if I weren't desperate? You've got a fucking life-ending problem here!"

Mayweather's eyes darted around right and

left, then back to center. All he could see was the blinding light of the sun gun and occasionally Shane's silhouette as he paced. Bathed by the intense glare, his pupils had closed up like a Main Street junkie's.

"You screw up down here, Tommy, and you're on the lobby wall." A place just inside the huge double doors at Parker Center where they put pictures of all the dead policemen, under a huge gold emblem of the department and the letters EOW—end of watch.

"Now, here's how it goes. You tell me everything. I already know a lot, so if you even leave out one little shred, I'm gonna... I'm gonna park a nine between your eyes." Adding a little insanity into his routine, some Mel Gibson *Lethal Weapon* madness.

Street cops had to learn to play different roles to get confessions. "Loose-cannon homicidal maniac" was a favorite. Trouble was, once you'd seen the show, it rarely worked twice. Shane didn't think Chief Mayweather, with his shelfful of basketball trophies and high-profile sports background, had ever spent much time on the street. He probably went right from the Academy to Press Relations or the Chief Administrative Staff. Hopefully, he would be disoriented and frightened enough to buy the act.

"You wouldn't dare kill me. You wouldn't dare," Mayweather said, but he sounded now as if he was trying to convince himself, not Shane.

"You don't think I'll kill ya; watch this,

asshole." He pointed Alexa's Beretta at the wall beside the deputy chief's shaved head. He aimed it wide so that the shot would ricochet off the concrete a few inches from Mayweather, then fly harmlessly up the tunnel, into the dark. But he wanted the bullet to be close enough for Mayweather to feel its draft.

Shane fired the gun. The echo of the 9mm pistol was deafening in the enclosed space. Chief Mayweather actually yelped when the gun fired. The slug hit inches from the side of his head, throwing plaster and dust in all directions, then whined away up the tunnel into the dark. Speckles of blood suddenly appeared on Mayweather's face where some flying concrete chips had hit his left cheek.

"Shit, Alexa, this thing pulls right," Shane said, keeping it loony and loose.

"Whatta you doing?" she shouted. "Are you nuts? Stop it! You can't kill him.... *You can't!* I don't wanna go down for murder!" Picking up her cue perfectly, she turned on the camera without having to be told. Shane heard it whir softly behind him, and just like Coy Love, he stayed to the side, out of the frame.

"Okay, okay... I won't. You're right—you're right. Jesus, what's wrong with me.... It's just... Ahhh, fuck it! This guy is *going!*" Shane pointed the gun at the chief and pulled the hammer back. The metallic *click* echoed in the silence.

"Don't, Shane. Please!" she shouted, in standard Actors Studio over-the-top fashion.

Mayweather was too panicked to spot their bad performances.

"Please...please stop him. Don't let him shoot me," the deputy chief begged Alexa. This was a new Tom Mayweather; no longer the officious police commander, this one was shitting his pants, pleading for his life.

"How can I stop, Tommy? You're such a hopeless prick. I can't believe all the worthless shit you've been pulling, starting with screwing me for Ray's death, going all the way up the penal code to double felony kidnapping."

"What're you talking about?" he said, his lips quivering, blood beginning to run down the side of his face where the cement chips had cut him, staining his collar.

"What I'm saying, Tom, is I want answers. Don't you get it? *I'm fucking pissed off!* I'm through taking your *shit.* You don't walk away from a bad FI down here. You get buried in this fucking wash!" Shane was taking time on his performance now, first working on his loony sound, then screaming, making it unstable and completely out of control.

"Look, I don't know what's going on," Mayweather blurted.

"Come on, you think I'm a fucking moron? You're the deputy chief, *asshooole,*" he said, dragging the word out, leaning on it. "You're Burl's guy. You think I'm gonna believe that? You took all those files outta Zell's office. Your fuckin' prints are all over the folders." He was pacing madly back and forth, strobing the floodlight, keeping his head turned from the lens but throwing a moving shadow against Mayweather and the sweating concrete tunnel wall. The effect was eerie.

"I just get money. I don't ask questions. I do what I'm told." His voice shook badly.

"Is that how you can afford that shiny new sailboat?" Shane asked.

"I... I... Yes."

"And you know what? You know what? You know what I'm feeling?" He was rolling his words around like marbles in a tin dish. "I'm thinkin' you and Brewer and Ray and his whole fuckin' den are just *scum-sucking pieces of shit!* You sold out the fuckin' job for a fuckin' sailboat."

Mayweather was breathing through his mouth now. His fear was so pronounced, he'd forgotten to swallow; drool started coming out the right side of his mouth, running down his chin. He was close to snapping. Close to the edge of temporary insanity.

"Hey, Shane, calm down, for Chrissake. Whatta you doing?" Alexa said, seeing the dangerous change in Mayweather, not wanting him to snap and start babbling. "The man wants to talk—why don't you let him?"

"Tom, you gonna talk?" Shane said, sounding a little more in control. "You talk, maybe you could live to go sailing again.... Maybe— just maybe. But I need answers, man. I can't take no more shit! I can't... I just fucking can't." A little insane exasperation.

"Let him talk, for Chrissake," Alexa persisted. "Go ahead, Tom. Just tell us."

"What...what is it you wanna know?" His voice was close to tears.

"I wanna know what's going on with the H Street Bounty Hunters. How come Ray's den was letting those bangers run free in Southwest?" Alexa asked.

"I don't know."

"This is just more fucking *bullshit!*" Shane screamed, and cocked the gun again.

"No, no... Please... Please stop it. What I'm saying is, I know they're being allowed to rob down by the university." His words tumbling out now... "The gangbangers were told to do whatever they want from Exposition Boulevard to the freeway, and the police would look the other way."

"Down by USC?" Alexa said.

"Yeah, the old University Division."

"Why?"

"I don't know. For the love of God, I'm telling you all I know, I swear it."

"*Why* are those Gs being told it's okay to caper south of Exposition?" Alexa continued.

"I don't know. I don't... All I know is Brewer, once when I asked him, said that he wanted to drive the crime stats up in that part of town."

"The chief of police wants to drive the crime stats *up?*" Alexa asked from the darkness behind the camera. "Why? His job performance depends on driving the stats *down.*"

"I don't know. It's all he said."

"Tommy, this is all fucking, runny yellow *bullshit.*" Shane shoved the gun out in front of him, right into Mayweather's face, the barrel pressed against his right cheek.

"Shane—NO!" Alexa shouted.

"Stop it," Mayweather sobbed, his eyes bugging, straining to get away, the cuffs rattling against the metal ladder. "I don't know—I swear it! All he said was he was trying to increase the number of uncleared crimes in that section of the city. Molar's den was setting it up, running it. They transported the H Street bangers after the arrests and turned them loose. Sometimes they blew the busts by not reading the Miranda or by losing evidence." He was glistening with sweat under the floodlight. Shane didn't answer, but recocked the gun. The sound echoed menacingly in the concrete tunnel.

"Scully... Calm the fuck down," Alexa ordered.

There was a moment when all Shane could hear was the three of them breathing. Then Alexa moved out from behind the camera.

"Stop him.... Make him stop," Mayweather pleaded. Tears were suddenly running down his cheeks.

"Tell me about Calvin Sheets," Alexa said. "He worked the Coliseum detail down there. He was letting hookers and petty thieves run wild. Was he part of it?" She was taking over "point" on the interview because Mayweather had begged her. She probably seemed like his only chance. Shane let her have him, taking a step back.

"I don't know why, but yes, I heard Sheets was in on it."

"So that's why all Ray's den members have cases going through IAD," Alexa reasoned. "But why send them to full boards where they'd be tried in the open, in public hearings? The chief could have disposed of the charges on his own, in private, under Section 202."

"Because the community down there was getting pissed. Their shops were being held up, people beaten or killed. They were filing complaints. That city councilwoman, Alicia Winston, is making a big fuss, her and Max Valdez. They want the bangers stopped, so the chief sent all those cases to open boards to appease the community. The panels were gonna be rigged. I was in charge of picking them. The officers were all gonna be acquitted or get modulated penalties—days off without pay, but no terminations. If that happened, they'd get envelopes to make up the difference. Burl wanted to control the timing of the boards so they wouldn't fall one on top of the other."

"And that's why Drucker's board was just postponed?" she asked.

Mayweather now seemed uncomfortable. He shifted his weight, averted his eyes.

"Something wrong with that, Tommy?" Shane asked, stepping in again. "Did I get that wrong? *Spit it out!*"

"Uh...uh...uh...please...please...make him... I'm trying to..." the deputy chief said inarticulately.

"Was Li'l Silent making trouble?" Alexa persisted. "Did he want something that you couldn't give, so you couldn't trust him on the stand in Drucker's case? Was he shaking you down?"

"Look, I've told you all I know."

"Are we ever gonna see Sol Preciado again?" Shane asked softly. "Or did Li'l Silent break jail and dive into a pit full of lye?"

Mayweather licked his lips and said nothing, but it was as good as a confession.

"How did you ever get to be a deputy chief?" Alexa said softly.

Mayweather was sobbing heavily now, standing there, psychologically stripped, cuffed to the ladder and sweating like a field hand, his chest heaving, tears streaming down his handsome face. "My dad was a cop, y'know. He was a uniform in Lake Falls, Illinois. When I went to UCLA to play ball, he used to save up, come to the games.... He loved watching me play. He was proud.... He was...he...he..." Mayweather was so lost and out of control, he couldn't get the words out.

Shane closed his eyes. He didn't want to hear this man's bullshit story.

"When I didn't make it in the pros, I wanted to make my dad proud...so I...so I..."

"Shut the fuck up, or I'll kill you just for being a pussy," Shane shouted, not performing now, truly pissed.

"You kidnapped a boy named Chooch Sandoval. With him was my next-door neighbor and friend, Brian Kelly. I want them back. If I don't get them back, you die."

"Honest, honest... I know nothing about that.

I told you, I know nothing about any kidnapping."

Shane took the cold barrel of the gun and again laid it up against Mayweather's cheek and held it there. The man's eyes got wide, trying to look down to see it.

"Why should I believe you?" Shane asked softly. "Make me a believer, Tom."

"Sol Preciado is dead," he whispered. "They let him out of that jail-transport vehicle, then took him out and shot him. That makes me an accessory before the fact in a first-degree murder. You think I'd confess to that with a tape running and withhold information on a kidnapping?"

Shane took a deep breath and a moment to get level, turned away, then shut off the videotape and sun gun, packing up the camera. Alexa reached out and uncuffed Mayweather. Shane could barely see him but knew the deputy chief would not make trouble. He was beaten.

"Go home, Tom," Shane said softly. "Think about what you've done, the lives you've hurt or destroyed. Not just mine or Sol Preciado's, or Chooch Sandoval's or Brian Kelly's, but all the shop owners who had their brains kicked loose or were murdered. Think about all the old ladies who got knifed or beaten for their welfare checks so you could have that pretty new sailboat. If you believe in God, you better start working on a good excuse, 'cause you're gonna need it."

He turned and, carrying the video box, walked out of the tunnel with Alexa.

When they were outside, he paused and handed her gun back to her. They could hear Tom Mayweather splashing around in the tunnel, slowly making his way out.

"You wanna drop him somewhere?" she asked.

"Let the prick find his way home. Maybe some H Street gangster will pick him up and finish the job for us."

They scrambled up the concrete incline and finally got back to the car. Shane locked the video box and tape in the trunk. Tom Mayweather's confession was obtained illegally and under duress. It would be useless in court but would surely keep him on the sidelines. The last thing the deputy chief wanted was to see it on the six o'clock news.

They sat in the front seat of the Crown Vic for a long moment, both changed by what they had just done.

"That was brutal," Alexa finally said. Shane nodded, and she added, "What now?"

"What now? We've just pulled off a pretty successful kidnapping and felonious assault," he said. "Wanna try your hand at forced entry and burglary?"

A BEGINNING?

SHANE DIDN'T WANT to attempt a B&E in broad daylight, so they went back to Alexa's apartment to wait for the sun to go down.

He felt dirty and tired as he sat on her snow-white sofa. Mayweather's confession had darkened his mood, driving his spirit down without producing Chooch.

Shane had always considered police work a noble calling, where Blue Centurions defended the public, upholding society's laws. The slogans reverberated in his mind: *Protect and Serve; Reverence for the Law; Integrity in Word and Action.* His oath made seventeen years ago while holding his head and right hand high now seemed hollow and meaningless. *"I recognize the badge of my office as a symbol of public faith and I accept it as a public trust to be held so long as I am true to the ethics of police service."*

Years on the job had shown him that police work was a flawed occupation at best, its participants on a narrowing, cynical path toward destroying the very thing they had pledged to uphold. Mayweather's crimes made Shane as dirty as if he had committed them himself.

"Is it okay if I take a shower?" he asked Alexa, hoping that maybe a long, hot soaking would wash the feeling away.

"Sure," she said. "I was just thinking the same thing, but you go first."

Shane heard a sadness in her voice that matched his own. He got up and walked into the bathroom, closed the door, and looked at himself in the mirror. The face staring back at him was tired and craggy and didn't resemble what he'd come to expect. The change worried him. He stripped off his shirt, pants, shoes, socks, and underwear, then turned on the shower and waited for it to get hot. Shane stepped in and stood under its steaming spray. He looked up at the nozzle, his eyes squinting as the spray bounced hard off his face and hot water filled his mouth. He was dirty in places it could not reach.

"You want, I'll do your laundry. I'll throw it in the machine with mine," he heard Alexa call from outside the bathroom.

"Good. Thanks. I tossed 'em next to the sink," he shouted back. Then, through the frosted shower door, he saw her step into the bathroom, retrieving his clothes. He turned his back, pinching his eyes shut, trying to blank out his troubled thoughts, when, almost before he knew what was happening, the frosted glass door opened and Alexa was in the shower with him, standing there naked, the steam turning her beautiful body slick with its moisture.

"Move over, you're hogging the spray," she said.

"What're you doing?" Shane's mind was doing flip-flops.

"I feel... I feel..."—she stopped, then looked up at him—"like I don't exist...like I don't even want to."

"Me, too," he said softly.

"I thought if we..." She stopped. "Bad idea..."

Shane didn't say anything, just took her into his arms and held her. As her wet body slid up against him, for the first time in days he felt the tension disappear; the knot in his stomach released as they stood locked in a cathartic embrace. They remained like that for a long time—holding each other, feeling each other's comfort and warmth. Then Shane felt his desire for her swelling and pushing between her legs, proving that he was still alive, still a man; perhaps all his failures of the past week could somehow be forged into a new beginning. He desperately wanted to start over. Then he felt her clutching him, pulling him closer, and was overtaken by a desire for her that was so intense, it brought tears to his eyes. "Is this right?" he said, asking for absolution, permission, and maybe directions all at the same time.

"Shut up," she whispered.

And then they were caressing each other in the steaming shower, Shane's mouth covering hers, his body pushing her back against the wet tiles on the wall of the small shower, kissing with abandon, feeling each other's warmth. Suddenly she pulled herself up, wrapping her arms around his neck, bringing her legs up around his waist. While she clung to him, he entered her, slowly at first, then thrusting more deeply. As her moans of pleasure washed over him, he felt changed and reborn.

Shane didn't know how long it lasted; time, in that small place, had become endless. They were in a wet cocoon of human ecstasy, and then he heard her cry out as he released inside her. She kissed him hard on the mouth, her breath mixing with his in the steaming shower.

Shane finally set her down, and they remained under the hot spray in a desperate embrace, almost afraid to let go, afraid to return to their individual fears and loneliness. Finally she took the bar of soap and began to wash his back, his arms, lathering him in erotic places. After she was finished, he did the same for her. They held each other in a sweet fragrance of body and soul. Shane felt different, stronger, more alive.

He looked down into her laser-blue eyes, which now seemed softer and filled with caring.

"Now we can start over," she said, putting his exact thoughts into words.

Later she made dinner and they sat at her kitchen table. She was wearing a white terry-cloth robe; he was wrapped in a towel.

After dinner she handed him his clothes, fresh from the dryer; they felt soft and were still warm as he put them on. When he walked into the living room, he noticed that there was renewed energy in his stride and a spring in his step.

They said very little, but as they locked her front door and headed to her car, she reached out, took his hand, and squeezed it.

THE HOT PROWL

H E WAS BACK in the parking lot, studying the fourteen-story steel-and-glass building in Long Beach. They had waited for the sun to go down. It was 8:05 on Saturday night, and they were still using the staff car Shane had been given up in Arrowhead. Across the street, roof letters announced Spivack Development Corporation in five-foot-high blue neon.

"I feel like Bonnie and Clyde. Do you have this effect on everybody?" Alexa said. She was sitting in the Crown Vic next to Shane, putting on a pair of latex gloves so she wouldn't leave her prints behind, both of them feeling a sense of awkwardness from the passionate lovemaking they'd engaged in a few hours before.

"Y'know, you're the last person I would ever have thought I'd be pulling a second-story job with," he finally said. She ignored it.

"You said you were here before. Did you scout it? You got a way into this place?" She was all business, putting that memory out of reach, taking the binoculars out of the glove box, unwinding the strap and training them on the building.

"Look, things have changed. We both know it," he said softly.

"Yes, but... Shane, it's dangerous. We have to be either cops or lovers. We can't be both. You've seen what a mess that turns into when it happens.... For now, we gotta do the job."

He knew she was right and finally nodded.

"So, did you scout it?" she asked again.

"Yeah...we can get to the roof by way of the fire stairs. Go down through a special staircase up there for the helicopter pad. It leads right down to Spivack's floor. The fire doors have interior bolt locks except on the first floor."

She nodded. "Y'know what pisses me off?"

"Ummmn," he answered, putting on his own pair of gloves.

"These binoculars piss me off—Bushnell 16x35s with a waterproof case. I worked Southwest Patrol for three years with a cracked pair of six-power prewar Lens Masters with one side out of whack. Couldn't focus the right eyepiece, asked for new binocs ten, twelve times, was told it wasn't in the budget. And here, in this staff car, they leave 'em under the seat like throwaways."

"Yeah, and we don't get sailboats, either."

She didn't answer but continued to focus the binoculars on the building. "You think we try for the roof? Go up through the fire stairs, pry the lock up there, then go down one floor, hope the interior doors aren't wired?"

"You're a fun date," he said, finishing with his gloves, snapping the wristbands while she lowered the glasses.

"Spivack builds shopping centers and commercial real estate all over the place, right?" she said.

"Yeah, malls, sports complexes, city buildings—anything where you've got high budgets and low administrative supervision costs."

"Tony Spivack, Logan Hunter, Chief Brewer, Mayor Crispin, and Ray Molar—quite a five-man team," she said.

"With Tom Mayweather still at point guard. Seems pretty obvious they stole this land in Long Beach—the naval yard—to build something. Hotels or a huge resort would be my guess. It's right on the bay...."

"Why would Logan Hunter be part of it? He's a movie guy."

"I don't know. He likes press...maybe it's gonna be his new studio, with a theme park like Universal's...call it the Web. Lotsa rides, lotsa fuzzy cartoon characters greeting you at the gate in chipmunk costumes. Who the fuck knows?"

"Let's go," she said. "This isn't gonna get any easier the longer we wait."

They got out of the car and moved across the parking lot.

"If we get stopped, flash your tin," he said.

"Always *my* tin, *my* gun."

"You collected mine already, remember?"

"Stop bitching," she said, but they were both smiling.

Strange how that can happen, in the midst of losing Chooch and Brian. Despite feeling devastated in the face of that loss, he had first had a moment of uncontrolled sexual passion with her and now he was grinning like an idiot, adrenaline driving his emotions, skewing his senses while keeping his vision bright...both of them acting like kids snatching a pie off a bakery-shop windowsill.

They got to the side of the building and began walking around it, looking for the fire door. There were several private security guards inside. Shane and Alexa could see them in the lobby looking out through the glass at them.

"Gimme your hand," he said.

She immediately reached out and took his, strolling lazily beside him, putting her head on his shoulder. They looked like two lovers going nowhere special, nuzzling and feeling it again: a new sense of closeness.

Shane was acutely aware of her perfume, and in that moment, while they were pretending to be lovers, he felt something strange and confusing and powerful stir inside him. The feeling was undeniably strong but totally inappropriate in the middle of a hot prowl, so he bundled it up, stowed it on a top shelf in the back of his mind, slammed the cupboard shut, and saved it for later. He turned his thoughts instead toward the fire door coming up on the left.

She took her latex-gloved hand away from his and tried the door. It was locked.

"I have keys," he said, removing his little leather pouch of picklocks.

"No way," she said, looking askance at the burglar tools.

"Stand back. I'm not as good as Ray was, but I'll have this open in a sec." He went to work on the lock while she turned and watched the terrain behind him, making sure no slow-moving Long Beach patrol car came upon them unexpectedly.

After a moment he manipulated the last pick in the lock and felt it hook down into the tumbler inside the door. He was ready to turn the knob. "Okay, all set," he said.

She turned back to him. "What about the alarm?" she asked.

"What about it?"

"Won't it go off when we open it?"

"Here's the way I have this figured," he said. "If there's an alarm on this door, then when I open it, it will damn sure go off. If there isn't one, then my thinking is, it won't."

"Asshole."

"Of course, if it rings, we need to fall back and think up a new strategy. I'm not good with alarms; I haven't had time to perfect that talent yet."

"Let's go. Do it," she said, and watched breathlessly as he put his hand on the knob.

He felt the lock turn and then pushed the door open.

Nothing!

They ducked into the dimly lit concrete stairwell and closed the exterior door.

"That's amazing," she said. "Why wouldn't they have this door rigged?"

"They did. I unplugged it yesterday afternoon when I was here. The unit box is in the sub-basement." He smiled while she glared. "Come on, lighten up. I wanted you to experience the whole thrill."

Then he turned and ran up the stairs, taking the first flight two at a time.

It took them almost five minutes to get up to the roof, then they were standing in the reflected glow of the five-foot blue letters while Shane went to work on the roof door.

"This leads right down to the lobby on the top floor," he said.

"Is this alarm unhooked, too?"

"I hope so. The panel was a little confusing down there. I had to straight-wire a lot of shit."

"So you *are* an expert on alarms."

"Ray always said the picks are worthless if you set off alarms."

"Some probation training you got."

He finally had the door open, and the two of them went down the one flight to the fourteenth floor. The interior door to the helicopter stairs was unlocked, and in another minute or so, they were inside the steel-and-glass offices of Spivack Development Corporation. The only thing missing was the blond ice goddess behind the reception desk.

They moved through the lobby into the back, where they found themselves in a long, narrow hallway decorated with artistic schematics of past Spivack developments. Huge hotels and major airport buildings hung in stainless-steel frames. The renderings were crisp line drawings with pastel watercolors. They passed out of the corridor into a huge drafting area. "I wonder where Tony Spivack lives," Shane said.

After a few more minutes of searching, they found his office, fronted by a vast secretarial area and a set of mahogany doors with ANTHONY J. SPIVACK engraved on an antique silver plaque. Shane turned the doorknob and pushed it open. They entered an ornate, palatial office: red carpet, embroidered drapes, and a mixture of furniture styles; French armoires and steel-and-glass tables populated the room. Shane moved to the immense plate-glass window that overlooked the city of Long Beach. He could see the domed city hall and, way off to the west, the *Queen Mary* sparkling with lights. Beyond that, he knew, was the Long Beach Naval Yard, which was magnetic north because everything pointed to it.

"We've gotta go through his files, see if we can find the project drawings," he said, still looking out the window, struck by the view: the shimmering Pacific Ocean beyond a ribbon of moonlit sand.

"Shane, look at this," he heard her say.

He turned, and she was no longer in the office.

He found her standing in the adjoining conference room. There was a magnificent 1:16 architectural model on a ten-foot-long side table. It covered the entire tabletop and was ten by five feet. Shane approached the huge model and saw that it was the architectural layout for the five-hundred-acre Long Beach Naval Yard project.

The plaque read:

THE WEB
A NEW CONCEPT IN
ENTERTAINMENT

The centerpiece of the development was a football stadium with two rings of luxury suites. It was perched on the property, a big concrete oval, its escalators arching away from the perimeter like eight long spider legs. It dwarfed everything. Engraved over the stadium's modern entry was a tiny sign:

THE WEB

"The L.A. Spiders. A football team," Shane said. "Sandy told me Logan Hunter was trying to bring an NFL franchise to L.A."

"This is about *football*," she said, appalled, sounding exactly like every housewife in America.

"It's really not about football, it's about real estate." He studied the rest of the development. The thirty or more architectural models placed on the site plan were beautifully made and exquisitely detailed. They dotted the five-hundred-acre site. There was an amusement park with roller coasters and Ferris wheels; five luxury hotels, each one next to the water; shopping malls and restaurants. Little catamarans were stuck in the "water," racing along motionlessly up on one pontoon, their tiny sails billowing orange and red against aqua-blue plaster waves.

Shane was trying to put it together. "Okay," he said slowly, using her words. "It's called police work.... Connecting the dots... Ray Molar and his den blackmail the Long Beach City Council with hookers at the party house in Arrowhead. A video festival occurs that forces Carl Cummins and the embarrassed city officials of Long Beach to give the naval yard over to L.A. and Mayor Crispin in return for some bogus water rights. The mayor gifts the property to Spivack in return for Spivack's promise to develop it for the city of L.A. as a home base for a new sports franchise. Spivack funds the actual physical development in return for the property. Logan Hunter gets the NFL to award L.A. a new football franchise, and everybody, from top to bottom, gets silent ownership in the deal and walks away multimillionaires."

"And the H Street Bounty Hunters were just a fun idea that got included for ethnic diversity?" she said.

"Okay, that's a wild piece. I don't have that connection yet, but I like the rest of it."

"Could be..." She sounded less sure.

"I remember reading once that the real money play on these sports franchise deals is the land, not the team. These guys get billions of dollars' worth of land from L.A. for free in return for financing the project and building this thing. Most of the public doesn't bitch, 'cause they don't care about the land; they want the team and a class A stadium to go with it. Sure, you end up with a roomful of environmentalists and hotheads protesting, but it's on page ten of the Metro section.... Nobody gives a damn about them because pro football is coming back to L.A.!"

"They can do that? Just give the land away?"

"Yeah, happens all the time. Years ago the city of Anaheim gave Georgia Frontiere hundreds of acres around Anaheim Stadium to get her to move the Rams there. Then, even when she carpetbagged the team off to St. Louis, the land was still hers. The O'Malleys were given Chavez Ravine for Dodger Stadium—the city condemned it, moved out all the Hispanics who lived there, then gave the O'Malleys the property, free and clear, in return for building Dodger Stadium. That way they wouldn't have to try and float a bond issue."

"Do you mind if we get out of here?" she said. "This is all quite fascinating, but I'm not as comfortable doing hot prowls as you are."

"One more thing first," he said, and moved out of the conference room and over to Spivack's desk. He opened the center drawer and took out Tony Spivack's appointment calendar while Mrs. Spivack and two dark-haired children eyed him suspiciously from behind a silver frame on the corner of the desk.

He opened the leather-covered book and started flipping pages.

"What're you doing?" she asked.

"Wanna see if he's in town. Last time I saw this shitbird, he was flying off in a green and white helicopter." Shane flipped the calendar to April. "Here it is; Sunday, April twenty-sixth, Miami Beach, NFL, eight-thirty A.M."

"Lemme see that," she said, and he spun the calendar toward her.

"Alexa, he's in Miami Beach right now, meeting with the NFL at eight-thirty tomorrow morning. You likin' my theory any better?"

They moved out of the office, but she stopped at the secretary's desk and looked around at the slips of paper that Spivack's secretary had pasted up neatly on a bulletin board: lots of yellow Post-its, reminders, important numbers and addresses.

"I thought you wanted to leave."

"If we're gonna do this, let's do it right," she said, still looking. "I worked as a secretary once, during a summer vacation in college. You keep the boss's temporary numbers up near the phone if he's traveling." She reached up and pulled a Post-it down. " 'Coral Reef Yacht Club.' That sound like Miami to you?" she asked.

"Take it. Let's go," he said.

Seconds later they were on the roof, then back inside the concrete fire stairs; a few moments later they were in the Crown Vic and gone.

BACKGROUNDING

"D on't worry, I'll get us there." It was just after ten P.M. and the last flight to Miami had departed LAX, so Shane drove to the Long Beach Airport. He found the executive jet area and drove along Executive Terminal Row until he found a busy-looking FBO called Million-Air Charters. He pulled into the parking lot next to the mostly glass one-story building, then he and Alexa got out.

"Private jets cost big money," Alexa said

"I've got a hundred thousand in small bills, but we're gonna look like drug dealers, so get your tin ready."

He opened the trunk and retrieved the suitcase with Coy Love's cash bribe inside. They walked into Million-Air Charters, and Shane plunked the leather bag down on the counter.

"We'd like to charter a jet to Miami," he said.

The girl behind the counter was young but no dummy. She took one look at Shane and Alexa's off-the-rack clothes, stole a quick peek at their fourteen-dollar Timex watches, and knew these two were not customers.

Alexa pulled out her LAPD identification and laid it on the desktop. "If you need to talk to a manager, this is police business. We're with the Drug Enforcement Task Force and we have got to get to Miami before morning."

Shane snapped open the suitcase and spun it around, revealing the stack of cash.

"Confiscated drug money," Alexa explained. "We'll need you to receipt it for us." All bull-shit, but comforting words when a civilian is looking at a suitcase full of used bills.

"Let me talk to Mr. Lathrope," she said.

Mr. Lathrope wanted to be called Vern; he had hunched shoulders, wireless granny glasses, and hair that had the general shape and texture of a number-nine paintbrush. He looked at the cash and Alexa's badge speculatively, then made a few calls. His weary attitude said he didn't like them, but business was business. "I can have two pilots here in half an hour, then I'll put you in 868 Charlie Papa," he said to Shane.

"What's 868 Charlie Papa?" Shane asked, showing total ignorance of jet charters.

"Tail number. It's the white Gulfstream Three with green stripes," he said, nodding his head toward the window where three or four executive jets were parked.

Shane didn't know a Gulfstream 3 from a palomino pony, but he nodded anyway. " 'Bout how much is that gonna run?" he asked.

"It's fifteen each way, thirty for the whole trip. We won't charge you for hangar time up to five hours; after that, the ground rate is one-half the hourly."

"Not giving us much of a break here, are you, Vern?" Shane said.

"Our prices are competitive. Make as many calls as you want—check it out. However, if you're interested in an opinion, it is a bit unusual to be getting paid with used bills out of a suitcase."

Stalemate.

Shane moved to the sofa, put the open suitcase on his lap, and began counting out stacks of banded cash. Each packet had fifty twenty-dollar bills in it. Shane counted out thirty stacks, snapped the suitcase shut, then walked up and handed the money to Vern Lathrope, who couldn't get his right eyebrow down from the middle of his forehead.

"I usually have a brown paper bag for transactions like this," Shane said as he shoved the cash over.

Shane and Alexa sat and waited on the expensive calf-leather couches, now clients of Million-Air Charters. Shane made two calls to Sandy, but she didn't pick up and her answering machine was off.

Half an hour later two young pilots in uniforms led Shane and Alexa to the Gulfstream 3 that Shane now realized was the biggest plane sitting on the flight line.

"Vern didn't like taking used cash, but he sure didn't mind renting us the most expensive piece of iron he had," Shane groused.

They stepped on a small rectangular red carpet before climbing the ladder and entering the jet. Then the copilot quickly rolled it up and stuffed it in a luggage compartment, with a "so much for that" smile on his face. He climbed up the stairs and pulled the door up after him. A few minutes later the Gulfstream jet, with Shane and Alexa and nine empty seats, was out on the end of the Long Beach runway, waiting for the tower to green-light the takeoff.

Shane found a beer in the refrigerator and brought one back to Alexa, who had kicked off her shoes and was reclining in the seat.

The plush interior was heavily scented with the smell of English leather. Rich, polished burlwood glistened in the Trivoli lighting. There were Baccarat crystal glasses in slots over a full bar.

"Okay, Shane and Alexa," Bob, their friendly pilot, said. "We're cleared for takeoff, so we're gonna do our thing now. Anything we can get you along the way, we're on channel three on the intercom."

"Thank you," Shane said to the empty cabin.

"I think you have to pick up a little receiver first," she said, smiling at him.

"For thirty grand, Bob can come back here when I want to talk to him." Then he kicked off his loafers and put the seat back. He had chosen to sit across the aisle from Alexa, facing backward so he could look at her.

Suddenly the plane was hurtling down the runway, its wheels coming up immediately on takeoff, climbing fast. They flew out over the ocean, then the pilot made a slow turn and headed east.

Shane and Alexa sat in the luxurious executive jet, sipping imported beer while the plane climbed to altitude and the lights of Long Beach gradually slipped away below the starboard wing.

"I'm gonna try to get some sleep," she said, putting her head back and closing her eyes.

Shane could smell her perfume again; it drifted across the aisle like a carefully thrown net.

"Mayweather's dad was a cop in Illinois," she said unexpectedly, without opening her eyes. "I didn't know that."

"Yeah," Shane said. "Just another grunt in a blue suit, out there hookin' and bookin' assholes for the city."

"My dad was a cop in Hartford, Connecticut," she said, her eyes still closed. "He was a patrol cop but never made sergeant. Couldn't take tests. He froze every time he went up for the exam."

"Oh," Shane said, trying to picture her father. What must he and Mrs. Hamilton have been like to have produced this iron-willed yet exotic-looking creature?

"Did you have brothers or sisters?" he asked, hoping she would open up. After a long moment:

"Two brothers." She started slowly, then it seemed important for her to tell him more. "I was the youngest. My mom died in childbirth. For a long time I thought that was my fault. We had pictures of her all over the house. It was like a shrine. My brothers and I, we tried to imagine what it would have been like to have her around. I used to wonder if she was in heaven looking down, mad at me for causing her death, so I tried to make her happy by doing all the chores: cleaning up after Dad and my two brothers, doing dishes, washing clothes, trying to take her place but knowing I never could." She stopped, the memory somewhat painful, then went on. "Dad remarried when I was fifteen, and we got Karen, who was nice but kind of distant. It was like Dad's three kids were some sort of mistake that she was forced to accept in the deal. I went to college on a track scholarship at UCLA—sprints and hurdles. I was there about ten years after Mayweather, but they still talked about him on Bruin Sports Radio, particularly during Bruin basketball games. He was a big deal, even years after he graduated. They all said he should have made the pros, but he ended up on the police force instead...."

"It felt shitty watching him plead and beg down there.... Somebody special that everybody looked up to turns out to be a self-centered shitball. Down there in that tunnel, I lost something. I don't know why it should affect me, but it does."

He was looking at her, wondering if she was ever going to open her eyes.

"Is that enough personal history?" she said, shining her blues at him again.

"Are you mad at me for some reason?" he asked. "You seem pissed off."

She sat still for several moments.

"Yeah... I guess I am. I wanted this career, wanted to believe in it. I wanted Mayweather to be stand-up. I actually liked him once. Respected him. Life is full of disappointments. I'll get over it. I wanted Santa Claus to come down the chimney with toys made at the North Pole especially for me."

He studied her, his dark, intense eyes trading her amp for amp.

"But just so you don't get the wrong idea, Shane, I don't think it's your fault this is happening. You just got put in the soup. You didn't ask for this any more than I did. It happened to you, and I'm in this with you because to do anything else is unthinkable."

There was a long silence. He was trying to think of the right thing to say. Finally he just smiled.

"Thank you," he said.

"You're welcome."

They didn't speak again until they landed.

Before he closed his eyes and tried to sleep, he glanced over at her. Her shoes were off, feet up on the seat facing her, those restless ice-blue lasers sheathed now. She was breathing rhythmically, sleeping peacefully.

He tried to picture her as a child, a little girl wondering if she'd killed her mother during her own birth, carrying that burden around with her. Just as he'd carried the idea that he had not meant enough to his own parents to have them hold on to him even for one day. He'd been left at the hospital like trash put out by the back door.

He had often tried to picture his parents.... Who were they? Did they go to college? Were they just teenagers who got careless and conceived him in a drive-in movie and decided to run? Were they hicks from Alabama, driving a pickup and drinking sour mash from a jug, with no money to raise him? Was he part Jewish or Italian or Irish? Did his mom and dad ever think about him and feel bad about what they'd done?

Why had they left him without even a first name pinned to his shirt?

He'd spent his life struggling to move past it, struggling to overcome it, finally using Chooch as a way to pull himself up, until he discovered that Chooch had become more important to him than the whole tired problem that had been weighing him down in the first place.

Alexa had been struggling, too. Internal Affairs was the perfect place for her. Weeding out the bad ones, making another house clean, all the time looking up, wondering if her mother hated her...wondering if she was good enough to be forgiven.

He admired her for it, but it also made him sad.

The sound of the huge jet engines hypnotically hummed in his ear. *I wonder if, despite all that's happening, I'm actually beginning to feel something important for this woman.*

Then Shane Scully, whose first given name was Infant 205, finally closed his eyes and went to sleep.

Shane dreamed about Chooch. The boy was on a vast beach, flying a kite over the ocean, but the kite was all black and dipping dangerously, diving toward the surface before straightening up again. Each time it seemed to get lower and lower.

"Shane, help me!" he was yelling. "It's going to crash!" Shane was moving toward him, but the faster he ran, the farther away Chooch seemed to be. If Shane didn't stop the kite's wild flight, he knew it would all end in disaster.

41
THE LAST DOT

MIAMI WAS BAKING in heat, the temperature in the mid-nineties, the humidity intense. They walked down the steps of the Gulfstream 3 into an invisible wall of moisture. A rent-a-car arranged by the FBO in Miami was waiting for them—a bright yellow Thunderbird. Shane signed for it; then, after locking the suitcase containing the rest of the money in the trunk, he got the map of Miami out of the glove compartment and looked for the Coral Reef Yacht Club. It was a large piece of property marked on the map in orange, located east of Highway 1, south of the wealthy town of Coral Gables.

"You navigate, I'll drive," he said to Alexa, getting behind the wheel.

The car was a hardtop, and somebody had been chain-smoking in it. The unpleasant smell of old tobacco hung over them, wet and onerous. The air conditioner needed Freon and put out a stream of tepid air. They pulled out, and she directed him to Seventh Avenue, which turned into Cutter Road.

The sky was that special tinsel-blue that you can only get in Miami, where the land is so flat that no pollution can stay trapped above the city, instead blowing across the state, dissipating in the ocean breeze, leaving Miami glistening in bright sunshine and mirrored glass architecture.

Clouds floated by intermittently, huge white formations of indescribable beauty moving slowly across the flat horizon like whipped-cream galleons.

The Coral Reef Yacht Club was just down the road from the U.S. Department of Agriculture's Plant Introduction Station. The yacht club sat on man-made levees and fronted a dredged ocean cut that was enclosed on three sides. Nestled among this lush marine setting were clusters of old Florida-style buildings made of coral bricks, with overhanging eaves. Boats of all shapes and sizes were moored at dock fingers in front of the exclusive club.

Shane pulled through an open gate with a guardhouse but no guard. The parking lot was jammed; he finally found a spot way down by the docks. There were several news vans parked a hundred yards away, by the main building.

Shane and Alexa got out of the Thunderbird and moved up a crushed-gravel drive, where they found a man leaning against one of the mobile units, having a smoke.

"They inside?" Shane asked vaguely.

"Yep. It's going down right now."

"Yeah? The...uh... NFL owners' meeting?"

"No. The owners' meeting was in July. This is the new team announcements," the man corrected, taking a closer look at him.

"Right, that's what he meant," Alexa said; then they moved past the man into the yacht club.

There was a large hall off the entry called the Trophy Room, and it was packed. There were a dozen news teams—network as well as local Miami stations—with cameras and mikes marked CNN, ESPN, and WNS (World News Service). There were also radio and print media. Close to two hundred people were milling about in the room under exposed beams and slow-turning paddle fans.

Without having to discuss it, Shane and Alexa separated. If one got thrown out, the other probably wouldn't. They took up positions on opposite sides of the room.

There was an NFL banner behind a makeshift stage. All around the room were yachting trophies and pictures of past commodores of the club, smiling out of their lacquered frames, wearing their captain's hats with too much braid on the visors. The room was elbow to elbow. Shane's cop mind noted that they were dangerously over the fire regs.

Up on the stage, a man was droning on. Shane tried to catch the flow of his remarks:

"...as they said...which, of course, made us very sure we had embarked on the right course as far as that program was concerned..."

Shane looked around for Tony Spivack or Logan Hunter, whom he remembered as a slim, somewhat handsome blond man from pictures he'd seen in the newspapers.

"...So, Don and Fred, who will be speaking to you in a minute, took all of those factors into account. These decisions, at their core, are difficult at best, because community pride is always involved. That's why we have been so deliberate on this issue."

Shane waited, crushed in between a florid-faced man in a Hawaiian shirt and a news crew from WKMI-TV.

"...That having been said, I'd like to present, with great pleasure, our very own commissioner of the NFL, Mr. Paul Tagliabue."

There was a smattering of polite applause. Shane was scanning the podium now. There were twenty-nine men and two women seated in leather club chairs behind the main speaker. He was beginning to recognize some of the faces from TV or the sports pages: Wayne Huizenga, owner of the Miami Dolphins; Alex Spanos of the San Diego Chargers; Jerry Jones of the Dallas Cowboys. All the owners of the thirty-one NFL teams were up there.

"Thank you, Lee," the commissioner said. "Okay, now for the moment we've all been anticipating. We have, as you all know, decided to award three new expansion franchises to three deserving cities: Houston, Los Angeles, and Oklahoma City. We have picked three facilities and ownership structures to be the homes of these new franchises. In Houston, we are proud to announce that we are awarding the NFC expansion franchise to the syndicate headed by Keith Fowler and Martin Fisk."

There was a gasp from the room, and then a whoop went up from the back of the hall. Shane turned and looked as the two men went up onto the stage.

The Houston winners had named their new expansion team the Houston Blaze and were holding up uniform jerseys and doing their photo op as news crews swarmed.

Shane looked over at Alexa on the far side of the room, just as a gray-haired man with a belt buckle the size of a small serving platter stepped to the mike and started throwing out Texas homilies:

"Now that we got this here thing safe in the corral, guess it's time ta wash off the war paint and throw us a shindig," he said. "We're set up like pigs in a mud bath over at the Four Seasons Hotel, so y'all come on over and help us raise the roof." He went on to thank half a dozen people.

Shane finally spotted Logan Hunter. He was dressed in a tan suit tailored to his wispy frame, without one sag or wrinkle. He had an abundance of too-blond hair and was wearing a mint-green shirt with no tie. There was something exotic in his carriage. Logan Hunter wore his millionaire film-mogul status like imported cologne; it wafted around him. He was boyish and, except for the wrinkle lines around his eyes, would have appeared to be in his mid-thirties instead of the fifty that Shane had read he was.

"In L.A. we had a terribly difficult choice." The commissioner was now back at the mike. "We had two competing franchises—one from Bill Kaufman, who proposed a restoration of the L.A. Coliseum. Bill has made a wonderful presentation, showing how that grand old lady could be brought up to millennium standards. And I've gotta say, a lot of incredible thought went into that plan. The other group, headed by Logan Hunter and Tony Spivack, have proposed a fresh site, a new development at the now-deserted Long Beach Naval Yard, which has recently been ceded to the city of L.A. I'm pleased to add that the mayor of Los Angeles, Clark Crispin, is with us today, and I'm going to let him announce the winner of the new L.A. expansion franchise. Clark...?"

A door opened at the side of the room, and Clark Crispin came onto the stage. Shane had seen him at many official L.A. gatherings and had even worked his security detail one weekend during his second election campaign. He was tall and angular, and when he smiled, his face always radiated warmth. He was dressed in hit-man black, his Armani pinstripe relieved by a festive red tie.

"Thanks, Paul. What a day for L.A. We, of course, have missed having a pro team in our city since you took the Raiders back north, Al." He smiled at Al Davis, who barely returned it. "Or since Georgia moved my beloved Rams to St. Louis and won a championship..." She smiled warmly, but there seemed to be a definite "fuck you" in the mixture.

"So now we have a new opportunity. Will it be the Coliseum, with Bill Kaufman, or the Web, with Tony Spivack and Logan Hunter? The envelope, please," he said, grinning, and there was a mild groan in the room.

"It is my honor to announce that the new Los Angeles AFC expansion franchise, and soon-to-be Super Bowl football team, will be the L.A. Spiders, playing at the Web. Tony? Logan? Come on up. Tell us how it feels."

Suddenly, as the two of them made their way to the stage, a side door opened and ten Spiderettes, dressed in their new black and red minicostumes, came onto the stage. Music played through a speaker system as they began to dance, waving black and red pom-poms. The crowd loved it.

The TV crews were circling, gunning footage, and then as the music stopped, the girls fell back, and Logan Hunter went to the mike.

"Thank you, Clark. Well, who would've thought this day would come?" More cheering and applause.

"Please," Shane said derisively under his breath; then the nickel dropped, and he knew what the missing piece was.

"I'm delighted we're going to be bringing football back to L.A.," Logan Hunter said. "We're going to deliver a top-flight product. We'll spare no expense to build a first-rate franchise at the Web. If you buy season tickets today, we'll guarantee you a spot in the stands when we kick off in our new stadium in the fall of 2001. We're gonna be up and ready. We break ground tomorrow. Tony, you wanna say a few words?"

Spivack, who had just put on a new Spiders football jersey over his suit and tie, came to the mike. "I don't have much time to talk. I better get back and grab a shovel if I'm gonna meet Logan's date."

There was a ripple of laughter.

"Commissioner Tagliabue...one question!" Shane shouted. "How come you didn't choose the Coliseum? That's a national historic landmark, built for the '32 Olympics.... Plus, the people with businesses in that neighborhood count on Coliseum events to survive."

The room fell silent. Spivack stepped back and handed the mike to Paul Tagliabue. "There were other factors involved. It was a complicated decision," the commissioner said. "We don't want to get into that right now."

"Was it the high crime stats down there?" Shane persisted, rolling the idea up to the stage like a live grenade.

"The growing crime rate around the Coliseum certainly entered into our decision," he said. "But there were many factors. We'll have a question-and-answer session after the announcements are concluded. Now, moving on... We come to the last franchise, in Oklahoma City—"

"Why do you suppose crime in that neighborhood rose so dramatically?" Shane was pulling the pin now.

A police officer appeared at his elbow. "May I see your pass, sir?"

"Don't have one," he replied.

"Whatta you doing here?"

"I'm a mental patient. We sorta wander around."

"Not funny. Let's go." He led Shane out of the room, walking with a firm grip on his elbow. They moved past Alexa, who was standing next to a WMI Radio team. She caught his eye and smiled as he was ejected from the room.

Once they were outside, the cop glowered at Shane. "You can leave, or you can take a ride with me. Your choice."

"Why don't I just leave..."

"Why don't ya," the cop said.

Shane walked to the yellow T-bird, took a piece of paper out of his pocket, and wrote Alexa a note. He shoved it under the car, got behind the wheel, and rolled over the note, then drove out of the parking lot, up the winding driveway, and parked on the street outside. He sat in the front seat in the oppressive heat, with the lousy air conditioner blowing a foul tobacco smell, until he couldn't bear it any longer. He got out of the car, threw his coat off, and looked down at his sweat-soaked shirt. He tried to get cool under a Japanese banyan tree while he contemplated what he had just learned. It was maddeningly simple once you had all the pieces:

The NFL wouldn't put a team in an area where violent crime and prostitution were out of control, so they awarded the franchise to Logan Hunter and the new entertainment/stadium complex being built at the old Long Beach Naval Yard. That was the last dot. He didn't know what he was going to do about it, but after ten days of eating everyone's exhaust, Shane had finally caught up.

For the first time since this all started, he actually knew what the hell was going on.

HALF AN HOUR LATER she came out of the Coral Reef Yacht Club and, shading her eyes with a four-by-five card, stood amidst milling news crews.

Shane could see her from the road, a slender figure standing defiantly in the entryway, looking toward the empty space where the yellow T-bird had been parked.

Shane had just tried to get Sandy on the phone again, but with no luck. He folded his cell and watched from the road, three hundred yards away, as Alexa walked uncertainly to the empty parking spot, reached down, and picked up his note. Then she turned and headed toward the main road, quickening her pace when she saw him, walking out the main gate and approaching the car. She frowned when she saw Shane's sweat-plastered shirt.

"Did you decide to take a swim?"

"I can't handle this steam bath they got down here." She nodded and handed him the card in her hand.

"What's this?"

"Logan's having a barbecue. He borrowed Elton John's house to celebrate. I'm invited. I can bring a guest, but I'll be damned if I'm showing up with a guy who looks like he's been playing in the sprinklers."

"I'll stop on the way and buy a new shirt. Let's go." They got into the T-bird and drove off.

They actually made two stops, first at a drugstore for deodorant and a razor, then at a small department store, where Shane bought a new white shirt and Alexa bought a simple cocktail dress. After he washed up and shaved in the employee bathroom, Shane felt 50 percent better.

He walked out and got into the idling T-bird, joining Alexa in the lukewarm stream of tobacco-scented air. "That looks good on you," he said, glancing appreciatively at the way the short pale blue dress fit her trim, athletic body.

"Thanks," she said noncommittally.

They drove up Cutter Road, back toward Coral Gables.

The beautiful Japanese banyan trees hung overhead, strobing leafy shadows across the T-bird's hood. They turned right on Casuarina Concourse and drove east, toward the water.

Elton John's house was not hard to spot. The press was already there. Shane turned into the winding drive and waited in a long line of cars while the guests showed their numbered invitations and were checked off a list.

"By the way, I'm Whitney Green, WMI Radio. Whitney does the noon show and couldn't make it."

"How the hell did you get invited?"

"I promised Whitney's husband, Don, I'd have a drink with him later."

"Yuck."

"Double yuck. You haven't seen him."

They pulled up to the man checking invitations. Alexa leaned across Shane and handed over her engraved card. "Whitney Green and guest," she said as the security guard wearing a tailored blazer checked the invitation, then nodded. Two valets opened both doors. Shane and Alexa got out as a man in a red jacket ran up, jumped into the car, and pulled away.

As they joined a line of people heading up

the drive toward the house, they could hear a band playing. They walked under a large balloon arch stretched across the driveway, done in red and black Spiders football colors, with a large sign that read:

L.A. SPIDERS 2001

Waiters in white coats circulated with trays of champagne and hors d'oeuvres. The grounds were magnificent. The huge Florida antebellum house stood at the end of the drive like a turn-of-the-century dowager; lace curtains and wicker chairs framed a sloping porch.

"Do you get the feeling that winning this franchise wasn't much of a surprise to Mr. Hunter?" Shane said.

"Even Martha Stewart couldn't lash this together in two hours," she agreed.

They got to the house and climbed the wooden steps, moving inside.

People were clustered in the magnificently furnished living room, but the flow of the party was being directed through the house and into the backyard, where the bar and the band were set up.

Shane and Alexa walked under more slow-moving Florida paddle fans out onto the veranda and stood for a moment on the back porch, looking out at the sparkling aqua-green water of Biscayne Bay.

There was a huge hundred-foot yacht called *Rocket Man* moored at the concrete dock. Palm and banyan trees hung over the grassy lawn. The twenty-piece orchestra was dressed in white tuxedos.

"Some barbecue," she said.

He nodded, but his eyes were wandering, checking out guests.

"How do you want to do this?" she asked.

"The play's at any base."

They moved down and joined the line at the bar. Four or five mannequins dressed in Spiders football uniforms, complete with helmets, had been set up in different parts of the yard in the Heisman Trophy pose. When they finally got up to the bar, Shane ordered a ginger ale; Alexa had a glass of Evian with a lime twist. Just as Shane was turning away, the bartender smiled. "Cigar to celebrate the franchise, sir?" and held out a box of Dominican Regals.

"Got anything else?" Shane asked, looking down at the box suspiciously.

"Mr. Hunter owns this company, so we only have Regals."

"In that case, give me one." He took a cigar, and they moved away from the bar, stopping a few feet away, looking at the panatela identical to the one they found in the toilet trap at the Spring Summer Apartments.

"You don't really think Logan Hunter was at your little fleabag on Third Street, supervising that videotaping and kidnapping...?"

"No. But somebody who works for him was, and as far as I'm concerned, this stogie ties him in directly."

"That's theoretical, not evidential."

"Fuck evidence. I'm way past worrying about that."

As Shane moved toward the house, Alexa grabbed his arm and pulled him back. "We gotta worry about that. We're hanging out a mile here. We gotta get something worth taking to the DA, or we're dust."

"Yeah, sure."

"I'm not kidding, Shane. I'm in this with you, but you've gotta run everything past me first."

"I think we oughta find Mr. Hunter, invite him to a quiet spot in the garden, and have a little talk," Shane said, changing the subject.

"*Find? Invite?* Define your terms."

"I'm gonna kidnap the little prick, stuff this stogie up his ass, and make him smoke it rectally until he tells me where they're holding Chooch. It worked with Tom Mayweather."

"We got lucky with Mayweather. That doesn't mean we can throw a bag over Logan Hunter in the middle of this soiree and get away with it."

"Sure it does. All we've gotta do is find a good quiet interview room before we take his statement. Don't worry, you don't have to do it. I'll pick this daisy. Believe me, he's gonna tell me what I want to know."

"Shane, he's got forty security guys here, most of them packing."

"If you wanna wait in the car, go ahead...."

"Shit! You are one stubborn son of a bitch," she said angrily, but he just looked at her for a long moment and nodded. "Let's stop arguing and do it, then," she relented.

They moved slowly around the party, looking for an appropriate spot. Shane recognized one or two of the girls they had photographed at the naval yard. They were dressed in slinky evening gowns, wearing hostess tags and escorting the press. Shane thought the main house looked too crowded. The gardener's shed was too close to the pool. Finally they found themselves down by the dock, where the hundred-foot yacht was tied to the wharf. There was a rope across the boarding ramp that warned: OFF LIMITS.

Shane removed the rope and they walked up onto the fantail of the yacht, where they were screened off from the party by the huge triple-deck superstructure.

"Some barge," Alexa said as she looked inside the main salon.

Shane had already tried the door and had his picklocks out.

"Not again," she said.

"Unless you can find a key, this is the best I can do." He worked for a few minutes while Alexa stood on the fantail, out of view of the party on the grassy lawn. They could hear the band playing an instrumental selection of Elton John hits. The music was mixed with the low murmur of party conversation.

Shane got the door open quickly and looked back at her. "I'm getting better at this, refining my technique," he said.

"I'll add it to your charge sheet."

"I'm gonna find a nice quiet place below. Why don't you see if there are keys in that thing?

We may need to make a fast exit," he said, pointing over the rail at a small red-hulled Scarab speedboat tied to bumpers against the side of the yacht.

"How'm I supposed to get down there?" she complained, looking over the rail at the Scarab ten feet below.

"Climb over the side, stand on the rub rail, then lower yourself down. Lotta people keep the spare ignition key in the engine compartment, hanging on a hook. Lift the cowling and take a look."

"The nautical equivalent of the back-door flowerpot?"

"Exactly."

He paused inside the main salon while she pulled up her short dress to climb over the side. Her toned, shapely legs were straddling the rail. She glanced up and caught him staring. "What're you looking at?"

"Nothing," he said too quickly, then ducked inside. He heard her drop down into the small boat as he moved through the magnificent yacht. Beautiful antiques and silk fabrics adorned the classic interior. He went below to the crew's quarters.

A few moments later he found the engine room behind a pair of soundproof double doors. It spanned the whole width of the boat. He turned on the lights. White-painted machinery glistened in the strong bluish neon. A hook, used to winch up heavy equipment so it could be worked on, hung between two large 2300-horse Caterpillar engines. Shane found a coil of rope on the engineer's bench, stowed it nearby, turned off the lights, and left.

When he got back to the rear deck, he found Alexa with a strange expression on her face. "You find the key?" he asked.

"Yeah, it was there, right where you said." She held up the ignition key.

"What's wrong, then?"

"I think I just saw Sandy. I went off the boat for a minute. I was trying to spot Logan Hunter...and I think I saw her with Calvin Sheets, walking up the path. She didn't look too happy about it."

"Sandy must've hooked up with her friend Melissa," Shane said. "Got herself invited to this party. But how the hell did she get all the way to Florida in ten hours?"

"Logan Hunter has his own jet," Alexa volunteered.

Shane nodded and walked out onto the fantail. "Let's see if we can find her."

They moved off the boat, rejoining the party, then walked along the carefully manicured path across the lawn, toward the house. Shane and Alexa were both scanning for familiar faces. Shane spotted Tony Spivack with a group of men and women, still wearing his quarterback jersey. He saw Coy Love over by the bar and grabbed Alexa's arm, turning her away.

"What?"

"Coy Love."

They got to the path that Sandy and Calvin Sheets had taken moments before, then started down it. The path wound around and finally ended about a hundred yards from the dock, down by a chauffeur's stone house on the east side of the property. The two-story stone house was connected to a six-car garage and separated from the rest of the property by a stand of mango trees. As they moved around the side of the house, they heard moaning. Shane stopped and looked at Alexa, who raised her eyebrows. They couldn't determine the nature of the sound yet, so they stood by the house and listened. Suddenly they heard a hard slap, and a woman cried out in pain. Shane recognized the voice.

Alexa pulled her Beretta as they moved toward the front door. Shane, without a gun, felt vulnerable and exposed. He paused by the back door.

"Okay," he whispered. "Standard SWAT kick-down. I'm going right—on three. One...two..."

Then he stepped back, kicked the door, and dove inside to the right, sideways and low. He hit the floor and was unable to see the room as he rolled, but he heard Alexa dive in behind him, going left and yelling, "Freeze, asshole!"

Then two shots blasted from the opposite side of the room. Shane finished his roll and came up behind a couch. The bullets thunked into the wall over his head. Alexa rolled to the left, then fired twice. Her first shot took Calvin Sheets high in the chest. He flew backward and hit the far wall, leaving a streak of blood on the white plaster as he slid down.

Shane came up in time to see Don Drucker move into the room, pulling his gun. Sandy was darting right just as Drucker fired. She passed through his sight and was hit in the back, screaming in pain. Shane watched in horror as the bullet went directly through her abdomen, exploding out the front, leaving an exit wound the size of a softball. Sandy looked down in abject terror as blood and stomach contents streamed out of her, staining her light-green cocktail dress. Then she slumped to the floor, groaning.

Drucker turned his gun on Shane, who dove right just as the rookie cop fired. Shane felt the 9mm whiz by, inches from his head. He heard Alexa's gun discharge twice more, then Drucker flew out of Shane's field of vision and hit the floor. It was quiet for a second, but as Shane came up, he could see Drucker lying on his back, his mouth gaping open, dead. Alexa had hit him in the center of his forehead.

She was still low against the wall on the left side of the door, grim-faced and sweaty. Suddenly they heard footsteps on the path.

"Bolt the door," he ordered.

Alexa slammed it shut and threw the latch while Shane checked Drucker and Sheets. "These two are history," he said.

Shane snatched up Calvin Sheets's Smith & Wesson and tucked it away in his belt, then moved to Sandy, who was lying in an expanding pool of her own blood. It was widening beneath her, staining her dress a dark crimson, soaking the sides around her waist. He knew instantly that she probably wouldn't make it. The wound was fatal; she was already shivering, turning cold as her blood left her.

"Sandy... Sandy...it's me. Can you hear me?" he said, kneeling beside her.

When Sandy looked up, her face had lost its shape; her eyes were dimming as blood pumped out of her onto the tile floor. "I know...where... Chooch...is... Calvin told me...after we...we had sex and...and...he told..." She was shaking badly, struggling for breath. "Then... Clark Crispin came...seen my file...knew I was... Black Widow..." She started to choke, blood flowing from her mouth now, running down her chin.

"Shit," Shane said. "Let's get you outta here, to a hospital."

"No..." she said as he tried to lift her. "No... Please...listen. In Arrowhead... Sheets said...they're holding him there..."

Sandy's strained words were overwhelmed by a heavy pounding on the front door.

"Open the fucking door, Cal! Open up!" Coy Love shouted.

"Give that asshole something to think about," Shane barked. Alexa turned and fired her fifth shot through the bolted wood door.

"Shit," they heard Coy say angrily from the porch outside.

"Shane...you've gotta listen..." Sandy whispered.

When he looked back down at her, she seemed smaller than she had just a moment before, as if she were losing volume, a pint at a time.

"Shane...you get him back...you take...take care of Chooch..." she rasped.

"I'll get him."

"He's yours... Shane...yours and mine." She was almost whispering now, her voice so small that he had to bend down to hear her.

"I was wrong..." She reached up and clutched his collar, pulling him down closer. "I didn't think you'd want him.... I wanted him but couldn't raise him.... You gotta do better." Her voice was so weak now, he placed his ear almost on her lips to hear. "He needed...his father... It's why... I made you take him... It's why...it's why... I..." And then she was looking at him, but her gaze had turned empty. Her heart had stopped beating. Those flashing black eyes went dead and stared up at him, damp and blank as licked stones.

Shane slowly lowered her to the floor. When he looked up, he saw Alexa staring at him from the door.

"Shane, we've gotta get outta here," she said.

Suddenly, Coy Love's face appeared at the window. Then his gun came up, aiming at Shane, who snatched Calvin's .38 out of his belt and fired twice just as Alexa peeled her last two rounds at the ex-cop. The window shattered as four bullets hit Coy Love, blowing him backward into the brush outside the chauffeur's cabin.

"Let's go!" Alexa screamed, and Shane got to his feet.

They could hear more voices screaming outside. They found the back door and threw it open. It led into the six-car garage. A black Lincoln Town Car was parked inside. Shane grabbed the keys off the pegboard, then he and Alexa jumped into the car; he started the engine, pulled the garage-door opener off the visor, and pushed the button. The door opened while Alexa was digging into her purse for a spare clip. She jammed it into the grip of her Beretta just as he floored the Lincoln, hurtling out of the garage and onto the driveway.

Armed men in black suits blocked their path but scattered as he plowed through them.

Out the front window, he could see security men running at them from several directions, all digging under their coats for weapons. Shane yanked the wheel and bounced the car up over the curb and onto the newly sodded front lawn. They shot across it, taking the direct route to the front gate, tearing up chunks of grass before finally bounding back over the curb onto the main driveway.

With four men chasing them on foot, they sped out the front gate, Alexa holding her gun at port arms. The Town Car skidded onto Casuarina Concourse, then a mile and a half later rounded the corner onto Cutter Road. Soon they were speeding under the leafy banyan trees, heading toward the airport.

"Get Bob at the flight center. Tell him we gotta get moving."

While Alexa turned on her cell phone and

dialed, Shane got a Miami all-news radio station. It had been only five or six minutes, but the story was already breaking.

"Our field news team covering the plush NFL party Logan Hunter is throwing at Elton John's Coral Gables mansion has reported a shooting," the announcer said. "We're still awaiting more details, but as we have it so far, several people have been gunned down. A man and a woman are identified as the shooters and have fled the scene in one of Elton John's personal vehicles. Stand by as we get more information."

Shane let Alexa off at Million-Air Charters, then parked the car around the corner and up the street in a dense growth of oleander bushes, out of sight of the road. He wiped their prints quickly, using his old shirt, not forgetting to do the back of the rearview mirror, the place most car thieves miss. Then he walked around the corner and met Alexa. They entered the office and found Bob in the pilot's lounge, filing his FAA flight plan.

"Ready to go?" Bob said. "That was quick."

"Can't afford the hangar time." Shane smiled, but the grin felt wide and shiny and about as genuine as an Amway salesman.

"Be right out," Bob said.

They quickly boarded the plane, this time without waiting for the red carpet. Shane and Alexa sat in tense silence as the two pilots finally got aboard, shut the door, and smiled warmly. "We've got a slight tailwind for a change," Bob said happily. "Should get us back

408

in four and a half hours or so." He settled into the right seat and wound up the engines.

Moments later they were rolling down the runway, taking off, leaving Miami and four dead bodies behind.

Shane sat stoically in the cabin, unable to deal with his thoughts. Alexa reached over and took his hand. "You okay?" she asked. "What did Sandy say to you?"

"Nothing," he answered. He couldn't tell her yet, couldn't quite admit it to himself.

His mind went back almost sixteen years, recapturing a memory long forgotten: it was his second summer on the job, right after the first arrest Sandy had arranged on the Valley bond trading case. They'd gone to dinner several nights later, to celebrate. Sandy had made her pitch to him, offering to work for the police as an informant. They'd had too much to drink, and in the car outside her apartment, he had shucked her out of her dress, then in awkward, thoughtless passion had entered her. There had been no tenderness in the coupling, and surely no love. It had been pure sex for him, raw and unadorned, an act he thought held no consequences. For Sandy, it was like a handshake to close their new deal. He had been just twenty-two years old.

The next morning he had felt cheap and ashamed of himself. She was a prostitute, and since he had always demanded more from his intimate relationships, he had never made love to her again. Instead, they'd gone into business together. Over the years he had managed her informant's career, making her rich while getting his share of class A busts in the bargain. The drunken romp in the backseat of his car was all but forgotten.

All these years later, the consequences of that mindless act had finally come due. If what Sandy had told him was true, she had changed his life forever with her one dying sentence.

Then he remembered what she had said in the doorway of her Barrington penthouse two days before. It had made no sense then, but now it spoke volumes: "You weren't doing me a favor," she had told him solemnly. "I was doing one for you."

43

DEAD END

THE ROAD WAS DARK and winding, and he was going too fast, overdriving his headlights.

"For Chrissake, slow down. We're gonna die on one of these curves," Alexa barked at him.

Shane momentarily lifted his foot off the gas and then, without realizing it, slowly sped up again, impatient to get there.

They had turned off the car radio because he and Alexa had just been named as the shooters at Elton John's Florida home and were now dominating every national newscast.

Somebody at the party in Florida had made them, probably one of the ex-cops from Sheets's old Coliseum detail. They were the subjects of a national manhunt. Shane knew it was only a matter of time before their sleeping pilot would get up, turn on his TV, and see the story. He would inform the police that Shane and Alexa were back in L.A., thereby narrowing the manhunt.

The national news story was snowballing, becoming as big as when Andrew Cunanan shot Gianni Versace, each broadcast digging deeper into their pasts. Shane was now being described as a rogue cop prone to violence. His moment of self-defense when he protected Barbara and himself from Ray's insanity was now being called the cold-blooded murder of an exemplary police officer that launched a coast-to-coast crime spree. The news media was having a party with Alexa's involvement, calling her his Internal Affairs prosecutor, accomplice, and partner in crime. Her Bonnie and Clyde joke had come true.

Shane had chosen to take the back road up to Arrowhead. They were on I-18, known as "the Rim of the World Highway," heading through the mountain town of Snow Valley. There were patches of snow visible at the highest elevations, distant reflections glimmering faintly in the moonlight.

Shane took another turn too fast, and the tires on the Crown Vic screamed in protest.

"For Chrissake, Shane, slow down!" she repeated, then reached out and switched on

411

the police-band radio but got only static. They were too far up in the mountains to get anything, so she turned it off.

They slowed down to drive through the small town of Running Springs. At Crest Park Drive they took 173 along Burnt Mile Creek and finally dropped down into Lake Arrowhead. Shane knew the route to Ray's house and quickly found his way there.

He drove slowly past the party house on Lake View Drive. It looked dark inside. If they were holding Chooch and Brian, he reasoned, they would probably try to make it look deserted. Shane turned the car around before parking it. He wanted no cul-de-sac mistakes this time.

Shane had found a sporting goods store in South Central on the way in from Long Beach. The owner-manager made it a point to mind his own business as Alexa bought a box of FMJ 9s and Shane a box of .38 hollow points. She had changed back into the clothes she wore to Miami: jeans, tennis shoes, and a turtleneck. Alexa pulled her handcuffs and reload case with the extra clip out of her purse and slid them into her belt with her cell phone. Then she and Shane got out of the Crown Vic and moved down the street toward the Arrowhead party house.

As they approached, his heart was beating fast. Shane knew he had to do this just right. He couldn't take a chance that Chooch would end up in a cross fire as Sandy had. He pledged to rescue Chooch and Brian, or die trying.

The problem right now was that Shane and

Alexa couldn't get backup. If they showed their faces in any police station, they'd be arrested on the spot. Nobody would listen to them, and Chooch and Brian would simply become part of the untold history of the new L.A. football franchise.

They were across the street from the house, crouched down behind the low hedge, looking at the property carefully. "I hate to say this, Shane, but that place looks empty. No cars out front, nothing," she whispered.

"They use a boat to get here. A Chris-Craft inboard."

"Okay, let's go, then," she said.

They moved like shadows across the street, their guns out in front of them, staying low as they went.

They got to the side of the house, creeping through the old rosebushes, trying to ignore the thorns. When they were within view of the dock, they could see that there was no Chris-Craft tied there. They made their way to the back porch, where, after checking the windows and seeing nothing, Shane shimmied up under the porch rail, then wormed his way across the deck on his stomach. Alexa covered his approach, her gun at port arms, looking right, then left, scanning the area, straining her night vision.

Shane was finally at the sliding glass door. He looked into the living room but could still see no lights or movement inside. Then he knelt, taking out his pocketknife, and pried open the door as he had done before. He motioned for Alexa, who came quickly and lightly up onto the porch, using the steps on the far side.

They entered, breathing the stagnant air of an empty, shuttered house. They went through the place efficiently, moving fast—Shane going one way, Alexa the other, no longer creeping silently but throwing open doors SWAT-style, training their guns through the thresholds, calling out to each other.

"Master bedroom and bathroom clear," he heard her call from the back of the house.

He threw open the guest bedroom and was looking at another empty room. "Guest room clear," he shouted. Then he made his way to the secret room. He pushed the door open, hoping—praying—that Chooch would be there, alive, waiting. But the room was empty.

"Kitchen and pantry clear!" he heard her shout from the back of the house. Then she yelled, "We're secure!"

The entire house was empty.

They met in the living room and looked at each other. Shane's face was pulled tight. "You think they got here ahead of us and moved him?" Shane asked.

"No. There's no sign of anybody having been here. No garbage in the kitchen trash. Nothing. This isn't the place."

"Sandy said he's in Arrowhead," Shane protested.

"But not here. He's someplace else...."

"Alexa, we've gotta find him." His voice was thin. Even he could hear it screeching in the still house.

"I wanna find them, too. It's how we get out of this. But ever since Miami, you've been different. You're not right, Shane. You're not thinking straight. You gotta calm down." And then she asked softly, "What did Sandy tell you? Whatever it was, your face dropped when she said it."

When he didn't answer, she took a guess. "Did you used to sleep with her?"

He still wouldn't answer.

"He's your son, isn't he?"

When he looked up at her, his expression told her it was true.

"Okay. But you've still gotta calm down, okay? Calm the fuck down. We can figure this out, but we gotta think it through."

" 'Kay," he said softly.

"All right. You said they owned an old boat—that they used a boat to get here. *Who* owned it?"

"I don't know. It's not really old. It's a reproduction of one of those classic Chris-Crafts with two windshields like they used to make in the thirties or forties."

"Maybe there's a dealer...."

"Shit, that's gonna take forever. They know we talked to Sandy in the chauffeur's house and that she got the location out of Calvin Sheets. That's gotta be the reason they were hitting her, trying to find out how many people she told. If they know Sandy knew where Chooch was, they're gonna move him. He won't be up here anymore."

"We've gotta take this one step at a time,"

she said evenly. "Let's start with the phone book. There's one in the kitchen." She walked away from him, into the kitchen, turned on the light, and grabbed the Arrowhead directory. Then she started looking in the Yellow Pages, under "Boat Dealers." "Here. Butterfield Boats, an authorized Chris-Craft dealership."

"It's nine o'clock at night, Alexa. They're closed."

She was already flipping to the *B*s in the white pages. "Leo Butterfield, Lake View Drive. Can't be too far from here. We can call him or pay him a visit. Connect the dots.... What's it called?"

"Police work," he said dully. "Our faces are all over TV. We'll probably do better on the phone."

"Okay. Who makes the call, you or me?" she asked.

"The head of the department up here is a guy named Sheriff Conklyn. Let me.... Let's hope these guys don't go fishing together."

Shane had pulled the phone out of the kitchen four days ago, so they returned to the one in the living room. He dialed the number and after a minute a woman answered.

"Mrs. Butterfield? This is Sheriff Conklyn at the substation. I need to talk to your husband," he said.

"Just a minute." Her voice sounded puzzled.

So far, so good. She didn't seem to know Conklyn personally. Chances were her husband didn't, either.

"This is Leo Butterfield. What is it, Sheriff?" a baritone voice said.

From his tone, Butterfield didn't seem to know Sheriff Conklyn. "Mr. Butterfield, sorry to bother you at home, but I'm trying to run a trace on a classic reproduction wooden Chris-Craft. You deal in that line of boats, I understand."

"That's right."

"I can't be too specific, but I'm looking for somebody who lives up here who may have bought one of those classic designs in, say, the last two or three years."

"We got a few of those boats on this lake. It's a rare item. They're beautiful, but not for everyone. I service most of them myself."

"Can you give me the owners' names from memory?"

"Think so... Let's see... Carl Nickerson bought one last June...."

Shane made a writing sign in the air, and Alexa grabbed a pen.

"Carl Nickerson," Shane said. "Go on."

She jotted it down on the back of the phone book.

"Bert Perl has one...."

"Bert Perl," Shane repeated, and she wrote it down.

"Logan Hunter," Leo said. "The movie producer."

"Logan Hunter," Shane said, and Alexa closed the book and looked up.

"Does he have a dock? Where's he keep it?" Shane asked.

417

"It's the old mansion on Eagle Point Drive on the Shelter Cove side. The one built by Clark Gable in the forties, looks like a Transylvanian castle."

44
THE CODE SIX MARY

THEY PARKED off the road and got out of the car. The house was down by the water, two blocks away.

Shane and Alexa walked down Mallard Road to Eagle Point Drive, where they found the public dock that accessed Shelter Cove. They walked out on the wooden float and stood on the blue and white platform, looking back across the moonlit waters to the huge house that loomed majestically against the distant snowcapped mountains. Its slate roof was glistening in silver light, its four roof turrets, each crowned with metal spikes, punching holes in the cloudless sky. The twenty-thousand-square-foot mansion had been designed in the forties and resembled a medieval castle, complete with stone arches and dormer windows.

The lights were on downstairs, and from the distance, across the cove, they could see occasional movement inside. From time to time people passed in front of the first-floor leaded-glass windows. Parked on the grass, near the water, was the same Bell Jet Ranger that had brought Shane up to the lake after he'd been kidnapped in front of an entire movie company on Spring Street.

Tied to the dock was a classic reproduction wooden Chris-Craft.

"Sandy told me that Logan Hunter was a closet gay. This must be his getaway house. Good place for slam-dance weekends."

"Boy, do I hate this layout," she said, still studying the mansion carefully. "The house sits on high ground, acres of grass all around. Porches and too many windows... Tactically, we're fucked."

"Come on...don't be so negative. We lickety-split across the lawn, slip through an open window, find Chooch and Brian, make the rescue, bust ass, and we're gone—zim, zam, zoom."

"Shane, we need backup."

"Who did you have in mind, the Power Rangers?"

"If Chooch Sandoval and Brian Kelly are being held here and we get them out, they make the kidnapping case for us, and we're halfway off the hook. If we get caught, we're dust anyway. I think we need to call in a Code Six Mary." She was referring to the LAPD radio designation for officer assistance required due to extreme militant activity. "We'd have to time it right, but once we know Chooch and Brian are there, let's just dime ourselves out, let Sheriff Conklyn sort the frogs from the princes."

"What if Chooch and Brian aren't here," he said, "and we don't get killed, but arrested? Then we're sitting in jail, trying to talk our way out of four killings in Florida."

"No plan is without some operational deficiencies."

He shot her a withering look.

"Okay, let's go in, scout it, then back out to a safe spot and do a nine-one-one," she said, revising her idea.

He thought about it for a long moment, then said, "I'd rather take it one step at a time and see what develops. But, either way, I think we should tee up the Code Six Mary before we call it in."

"Good idea...but how?"

"Gimme your phone."

She handed the cell phone to Shane. He got Information, then called the Arrowhead Sheriff's Department. After asking for Sheriff Conklyn, he was transferred, then got the tall, balding man on the phone. "Guess who?" Shane said.

"I don't have the faintest idea...."

"Turn on your TV. I'm starring in every newscast."

"Shit... Scully?"

"I'm looking for you to take me in, Sheriff. I want you to make the bust. You'll be famous. It's probably at least good for a shot or two on Oprah, but I have a few conditions...."

Conklyn paused, and then Shane heard a

click, so he knew the rest of the conversation was being T and T'd—taped and traced.

"Why me?" Conklyn asked.

"If you're tracing this call, it's just gonna come back to a cell station in Arrowhead. I'm up here now, but I'm not quite ready to turn myself in yet. I want you to make the arrest because I've got problems with some of my brother officers in L.A. and I don't want to stop a stray bullet by mistake."

"Not to mention all the dead bodies you left in Florida."

"There's a story that goes with that, Sheriff. Extenuating circumstances."

"If you're smart, Scully, you'll tell me where you are now. Otherwise, this will go down hard."

"I want you to call Bud Halley, my old CO in L.A. He's a good cop. Tell him what's going on. Tell him I need to see him and to get his ass up here."

"Where are you, Scully?"

"Stick by your phone. I'll let you know." Shane hung up and looked at Alexa.

"Pretty good," she said, nodding. "He'll have his flak vest buttoned and be ready to roll."

They moved off the dock and skirted the water's edge until they got to a wire fence that went ten feet out into the lake and separated the castle's property from its neighbors. Shane climbed out on the fence, U-turned around the end post, then came back toward shore, and dropped off onto the sand inside the grounds.

After a minute Alexa repeated the maneuver, landing on the sand beside him.

They crept away from the shoreline and ran up toward the house, both silently cursing the full moon as they sprinted under its silvery glow. They hurried across the vast expanse of lawn, then hugged the wall, moving around the castle house slowly. They could see a row of ground-level windows throwing streaks of light out across the dew-wet lawn. They moved in that direction. Once they got to the windows, Shane dropped to his stomach and looked through a narrow glass pane into what looked like a huge billiards room.

"Uh-uh," he whispered, rising again and moving on. Alexa followed quietly in his footsteps.

On the south end of the house, he found the ground-level window he was looking for. When Shane glanced inside, he saw that it opened into a basement laundry room. He took out the .38 S&W and tapped loudly on the window with the gun butt.

"Whatta you doing?" Alexa hissed. "Why don't we just ring the fucking doorbell?"

"If somebody's down here, I'd rather find out now. Better to be outside than trapped down there in the basement. I'm gonna break the glass. If we get a ringer, get small."

She nodded, then watched as he slammed the gun butt hard into the pane, breaking it. The sound of tinkling shards hitting the cement floor froze them. They lay prone on the grass for several long minutes, waiting.

Nothing.

Shane reached through the glass, unhooked the latch, and swung the window open. They slipped into the laundry room and dropped onto the basement floor. Once inside, they could hear the faint sounds of opera music playing upstairs.

"Okay, let's work our way through this place, starting with this side, then moving east," he whispered.

She nodded, and they opened the laundry-room door and found themselves in a narrow, concrete-walled corridor with a vaulted ceiling. The corridor had no carpet, windows, or wall decorations. They crept along the tile floor, trying to keep their shoes from echoing on the polished surface. They checked doors as they went, mostly storage rooms and a basement bathroom. Then they were back at the poolroom Shane had seen from outside. The room was medieval in design, with old lances and shields on the walls. Two full, man-sized suits of armor on stands stood guarding a pair of double doors.

Movie posters hung on every wall, each one featuring a well-known Logan Hunter film. A red felt pool table loomed like a mahogany crypt in the center of the huge rectangular room.

They slipped out of the poolroom through a side door, still heading east. Shane and Alexa found themselves transiting through a part of the basement that was beginning to resemble a dungeon—bars and studded steel doors, ornate metal hinges with brass church locks. At the end of the center hall was a wooden door with a small, eight-by-ten-inch barred window set at eye level. Shane looked through the bars into an even narrower, underlit hallway. The door was locked. He reached in his pocket for his picks.

"What would we ever do without those?" she quipped.

It was a simple two-tumbler lock, designed more for looks than function. He got it open quickly. The door creaked ominously as he pushed it wide.

They crept down the three-foot-wide stone-block hallway. The first door on the right was unlocked, so he pushed it open and found that he was standing in a replica of a medieval torture chamber, replete with fourteenth-century stretching racks, wall restraints, and steel wall hooks holding every imaginable kind of leather apparel.

"This kink is into S&M," Alexa said.

Shane felt a chill go through him and prayed that Chooch and Longboard had not been subjected to a dose of that madness.

He passed through the dungeon toward a door on the far side of the room, opened it slowly, and found a hallway that ran farther underground. It stretched for about forty or fifty feet on a gentle slope. At the end of the corridor was another large wooden door with metal trim and steel studs.

"Hold my back," he said, then ran down the concrete tunnel. When he got to the end, he tried the door. It was unlocked.

He pushed it open and found himself looking

at Chooch and Longboard. They were blind-folded, gagged, and handcuffed to pipes in a small room that contained three giant water heaters. Shane ripped the blindfold off Chooch, then pulled the wadding out of his mouth. "You okay?"

"Shane," the boy said; tears started flowing from his eyes. "I knew you'd come...."

"Shhhh..." Shane said. As Brian *umph*ed behind his gag, Shane checked Chooch's handcuffs before quickly turning and removing Brian Kelly's blindfold and fishing the gag out of his mouth.

"Shit, am I glad to see you," Longboard said weakly.

"You guys okay?"

"I guess," Longboard said. "Frickin' scared, but okay."

"Stay quiet. I'll be right back. Gotta get a key for those cuffs. They look like standard LAPD issue."

Shane sprinted back up the ramp to the dungeon room, where Alexa was guarding the hallway.

"They're down there. They look all right. I need your cuff key."

She reached to her belt, pulled it off, and handed it to him.

Shane hurried back to the heater room and unhooked both sets of cuffs.

"How many guys are here? How many guns?" Shane whispered.

"There's about four guys who are packing," Brian said.

"Shane, that movie producer is here," Chooch said. "He owns the place."

"That kink didn't put you on any of those tables up there, did he?" Shane asked.

"No. They just cuffed us to those pipes," Brian said. "Seems like we been here almost two days."

"Okay, listen up. We're on our way out. There's a woman with me. She's an LAPD sergeant. Once we're out of this dungeon, I'll go first, she'll bring up the rear. Stay close. Don't make any noise. What I want to do here is just disappear. I don't wanna fight our way out." Shane's words echoed softly against the walls of the stone room.

He led Brian and Chooch up the corridor, rejoining Alexa. Silently they retraced their footsteps out of the dungeon and back into the connecting hallway. Shane paused by the door, looking into the billiards room. It was still deserted, so he pushed the door open and they headed out across the tile floor, past the suits of armor, and back to the laundry room at the far end of the house.

They slipped inside; then Shane locked the door and turned to Alexa. "You're first. Once you're out there, scout both sides. We need a good exit line."

"Got it," she said.

He put his hands around her slender waist and lifted her up to the open window. She grabbed the ledge and shimmied out. She was amazingly light, which surprised him. Her intellectual weight had become so huge, it didn't seem possible that her physical weight was only 115 pounds.

Next he lifted Chooch. Once the boy was out of the window, Shane turned to Longboard and cupped his hands. "Hop aboard. You're outta here."

Longboard stepped in, and Shane boosted him out the window. Then Shane grabbed the ledge and pulled himself up and out onto the wet grass.

The cold, moist lake air filled his nostrils as he regained his feet and looked at all of them.

"Somebody just pulled in. They're in a truck in the drive. There're people in the big front room now. They'll see us moving across the grass," Alexa said. "Our best bet outta here is that speedboat. We need keys, but if they aren't in the boat, we could get trapped down there on the dock, out in the open."

"Don't need keys," Chooch whispered bravely. "I'll hot-wire it. Car theft is my Vato specialty."

"Okay then, that's the plan," Shane whispered. "Alexa, you look for the keys. If they're not aboard, Chooch, you get it going. Brian, you're on lines. I'll hold the back door and lay down cover fire if we get spotted. Everybody straight?"

They nodded, their faces grim.

"Okay—let's do it."

They slipped away from the house, staying close to the west side of the property, moving like shadows against the fence line.

They finally got to a spot where, in order to

427

reach the dock, they had to make a final dash across an open stretch of moonlit lawn. They huddled down in the dark and checked the house. There were a few people visible in the windows. Nobody was on the porch.

"This is as good as it's gonna get. Let's go," Shane whispered.

They started running in a group. They moved fast and low, across the open area, but quickly spread out. Alexa, the sprinter, took the lead, with Shane a few steps behind. Chooch and Longboard were losing ground. They all finally reached the pier and headed out to the dock.

"Who's out there?!" a male voice yelled from the house.

"It's blown. Move it! Move it!" Shane shouted. He was out on the small dock, standing by the ramp leading down to the float, motioning to Chooch and Longboard, wind-milling his arms, trying to get them to go faster. They ran by him heading for the boat.

Now all but Shane were on the boat.

Alexa was looking for the keys when Chooch and Longboard got aboard.

"No key in the ignition," Alexa shouted. She was pulling the engine cover up, looking for a key on a hook inside, when the first shot rang out. The bullet pinged off the top of the concrete piling next to Shane's head, then whined angrily away into the night.

Shane, still holding his position on the dock, fired blindly up at the house. He couldn't see anyone, so he popped only one cap—firing for effect—turned, and ran to the boat.

Chooch was under the dash pulling out ignition wires, and Longboard ducked down low in the backseat. As Shane jumped into the boat, two more shots rang out from the sloping lawn. One of the bullets thudded into the boat's hull. Alexa pulled her pistol and returned fire.

"Save your rounds!" Shane yelled. "Unless you can see 'em, don't fire."

Suddenly the boat engine started, and Chooch backed out from under the dash. Longboard came up from his hiding place and started throwing off lines.

They could now see two men running down toward the dock. Both stopped halfway out on the wooden pier, aimed their pistols, and fired down from a position of advantage. Shane felt a bullet tug at the sleeve of his sport coat. He dropped into the seat behind the wheel and slammed the throttle all the way forward.

The Chris-Craft roared away from the dock amidst a hail of gunfire. He heard Alexa's Beretta bark near his left ear, then the distant sound of return fire from the dock.

"Shit," she said, and dropped onto the seat beside him. He glanced over at her, alarmed.

"I took one," Alexa said, looking at her side. She couldn't see the blood in the moonlight because of the dark turtleneck.

"How bad?" Shane shouted over the roar of the engine.

She pulled up her shirt and checked the

wound. "Looks like a through and through. The right oblique. Just drive. If I start fading, I'll let you know," she shouted.

They heard two more shots, but they were distant popping sounds. One bullet ricocheted off the metal windshield, and then they were out of range.

Longboard and Chooch were lying prone on the backseat. "Did we make it?" Longboard asked tentatively as he sat up.

Shane looked back at the dock, a receding structure in the distance.

"They're out of range," he said. All of them had wide smiles on their faces. It was a well-known police axiom that nothing is more exhilarating than being fired on without serious result.

The little speedboat streaked across the lake, its metal-tipped bow parting the moonlit water, leaving a frothy, expanding wake behind them as they headed toward the lights of Arrowhead Village two miles away.

"We've gotta get to a place where Sheriff Conklyn won't panic making the arrest. Someplace out in the open. I don't want one of his trigger-happy deputies ruining this perfect rescue," Shane shouted to Alexa over the wind and engine noise.

"How 'bout the main dock in town?" she suggested. "It's open from all sides. He can make an arrest easily there."

"Good idea," Shane agreed. She pulled out her cell phone to call, but before she could dial, the odds abruptly changed.

It was coming at them low and fast across the water, its rotor blade flashing streaks of reflected moonlight. The blue and green helicopter was ten feet off the surface, approaching quickly. By the time they heard it, it was way too close. The throaty roar of the speedboat's engine had camouflaged its deadly approach.

The Bell Jet Ranger swept low across their speeding bow. Two men leaned out the open door with police shotguns aimed down at them, and seconds later the men let loose.... The teak deck and left windscreen were peppered with buckshot. Exploding safety glass flew back in pebble-sized pieces. Chunks of pellet-riddled teak flew up, caught the air, and were whipped away over their heads.

Shane jerked the wheel right, to change the angle, taking away the Bell Jet's point-blank line of fire. Now the speedboat was heading west, away from the town. The chopper banked, its engine whining as it turned, and in seconds it was behind them again, closing in. Two more blasts from the shotguns, and the rest of their windshield was gone.

Shane felt sharp pain on his ear and cheek where several pellets from the widening shot pattern had nicked him. Blood started running down the right side of his face. He spun the wheel again.

Alexa turned and was now facing back. She had her knees on the leather seat; her body was prone across the center deck. She had her 9mm Beretta in both hands, aiming up at the approaching helicopter. She took her time

431

sighting. "Slow down, you're bouncing too much!" she shouted.

Shane eased the throttle back, slowing the boat and subtly drawing the chopper in closer. Then, sighting carefully, she fired twice. Suddenly the chopper veered right and pulled up fast, exposing its belly. She fired again. The pilot, feeling the hits, banked the helicopter away. He pulled back to avoid further gunfire, but was now also way out of shotgun range.

Her shots had not disabled the Bell Jet Ranger.

Shane sped up. The chopper paced along a hundred yards to the right, skimming low across the water, tracking the speedboat from the side at about forty miles an hour.

The boat was bouncing badly, hitting the larger chop in the center of the lake. The waves slammed against the varnished hull, throwing water wide to each side.

"Don't shoot! Don't waste rounds—we're pounding too much!" Shane shouted. "They can't reach us with those twelve-gauges—save it for when they come in close."

Alexa nodded as they sped across the center of Lake Arrowhead, the chopper flying sideways now, the nose aimed at them. Four faces were staring out from behind the bubble-glass windshield.

Shane was headed toward Blue Jay Bay.

Alexa pushed redial on her phone. A moment later Shane heard her shouting at Conklyn. "Sheriff, it's Alexa Hamilton. I'm with Shane Scully and two others. A male Caucasian and teenage Hispanic. We're Code Six Mary in a speedboat heading across Lake Arrowhead, taking gunfire from a helicopter above us. We're at Blue Jay Bay. We need help. Get here fast, or notify the coroner." She threw the phone down on the seat without waiting for a reply, then aimed her gun at the tracking helicopter.

They streaked past a sign marking Village Point, then past two poles planted in the lake that warned:

SHALLOW WATER—SANDBAR

"Shit," Shane said. He was going almost forty. If he went aground at that speed, they would all end up as part of the dashboard. He pulled the throttle back, slowing to about twenty. The helicopter veered again, vectoring toward them. They could see distant flashes of fire from both shotgun barrels, then heard the slower sound of the blasts. Simultaneously the varnish on the side of the boat exploded and turned chalky white as the pellets tore holes in it.

The body of water narrowed abruptly ahead; they were running out of lake. Shane saw Totem Pole Point coming up on the right, marked by a hand-painted sign. Suddenly they were in the narrow and unforgiving waters of Paradise Bay, heading for the mouth of Little Bear River.

"Fuck," Shane said. If he turned back now, he would be forced to slow way down to make the turn in the narrow inlet, making them vulnerable to a withering shotgun attack. So he eased back on the power, cutting his speed to ten miles per hour, then headed up the narrow mouth of the river. Occasionally he could feel the boat hesitate as it scraped bottom.

The helicopter came in close now, making another pass. Two men were leaning far out of the door of the chopper. Alexa fired three more times. One of the men screamed, his voice faint and distant, barely audible over the racket of the competing engines. Then the man tumbled out of the helicopter door and splashed into the shallows below.

Shane could see the end of the ride coming up ahead. A sandbar was stretched across the narrowing river. He sped up momentarily so he could run the heavy boat up onto the sand.

The Chris-Craft shot up onto the bar. He felt the sand scraping beneath, heard the propeller pin shear. The engine screamed as the propeller flew off. As soon as the boat slammed to a stop, it leaned right against its bottom, white smoke and a high-rpm whine coming from the exposed shaft.

"Out! Out! Get out!" Shane shouted, and yanked the .38 out of his waistband. He trained it on the helicopter that was now hovering and watching, waiting for them to run away from the grounded speedboat, where they would be easy to pick off.

"Stay put. Use the boat for cover!" Shane yelled. They all huddled behind the beached hull, keeping the Chris-Craft between them and the chopper. The overheating inboard engine finally coughed and quit.

Then the nose of the Bell Jet Ranger dropped and, like a bull in an arena, made its deadly charge. Shane unloaded the .38 as the chopper streaked over them. He could hear the shotguns firing, in a steady *ka-boom, ka-boom, ka-boom!* He knew they were using police-issue, Ithaca pump-action 12-gauge riot guns. As the shots continued, the engine compartment on the beached boat blew open...the last shot hit the exposed gas tank.

The next thing Shane knew, he was flying through the air, the sound of the exploding gas tank ringing in his ears. He landed ten feet away and saw that Alexa, Chooch, and Brian had also been blown off their feet by the blast.

Shane had been nearest the tank, and he now realized that his clothes were on fire. He got up and made a stumbling run for it, then dove into the shallow Little Bear River. While he was rolling in the water, trying to extinguish the flames, the helicopter turned back and made a low pass at him. He was now sitting upright in the middle of the shallows, an easy, stationary target, when the shotguns started again. The first pattern went wide, turning the river water to the left of him foam white with the pellets. In his peripheral vision, he could see Alexa splashing across the open ground toward him, limping slightly, favoring her right side. She was slamming her last clip into the Beretta, chambering it as she ran.

The helicopter flashed over her now, getting closer to him. As it went over, she peeled the full clip straight up into the belly of the chopper, hitting the Bell Jet Ranger with all nine shots.

Shane didn't know what the hell she hit, but it was certainly something vital, because the helicopter immediately began spinning on its axis, wobbling around like a slowing top, going out of control. Then it slammed, nose first, into the water and went down fast.

Shane got up out of the river, his burnt clothes steaming in the cold night air. He joined Chooch, Longboard, and Alexa at the water's edge. They looked out at the spot where the chopper had crashed. The engine housing and rotor were all that was still above water. There had been no explosion and no attempt by anyone to get out. Then it disappeared, sinking quickly.

"Fuck you," Shane said softly to a bubbling spot in the water where the helicopter had been.

A few minutes later, while they were still watching the Bell Jet's last air bubbles rising to the surface, exploding trapped air, they saw the black-and-white Hughes 500 approaching, coming in low over the lake. The belly-light on the sheriff's chopper snapped on, and they were caught in its blinding glare. Shane and Alexa immediately threw down their guns and assumed the position, placing both hands behind their heads. Shane instructed Longboard and Chooch to do the same.

They were all standing out in the open as the sheriff's helicopter hovered overhead, churning up rocks and river water. "On your stomachs. Facedown on the ground!" they heard Conklyn's voice shout over the bullhorn.

All of them proned-out on the sand and waited.

It was only moments before the first squad cars arrived. They drove off the road, their tires squishing on the wet river sand, their cherry-colored bar lights flashing. Then, as patrol officers swarmed them, the police chopper landed.

"Watch it, she's been wounded," Shane said as sheriff's deputies cuffed Alexa and dragged her to her feet. They ignored his instructions and pushed her roughly toward the squad cars. Shane was cuffed and pulled to his feet, then found himself looking at the jacked-and-flacked Sheriff Conklyn. "Glad to see you, man," Shane said.

"What the fuck? What chopper? She said there was a chopper shooting at you...."

"There was," Shane said, nodding to the spot in the river where the Bell Jet Ranger had gone down. "But you're gonna need to come back with divers, a crane, and some body bags if you wanna see it."

Shane watched as Chooch and Longboard were roughly cuffed, then put into squad cars. "They're victims. You don't need to throw them around like that. They were kidnapped," he complained, but Conklyn didn't seem to care.

"You're really some kinda jerkoff, Scully.

This is a quiet town. Every time you come up here, I gotta throw a fucking cherry festival." Conklyn pushed Shane toward the squad car. "I can hardly wait to hear this one."

"Right," Shane said softly. "But you better send out for pizza, 'cause it's a long and complicated story."

EXCULPATORY EVIDENCE

POLICE MISCONDUCT is defined under Section 805 of the LAPD Manual and falls into one of four categories:

1. Commission of a criminal offense
2. Neglect of duty
3. Violation of department policies, rules, or procedures
4. Conduct that may tend to reflect unfavorably upon the employee or the department.

After their arrest, Shane, Alexa, Chooch, and Longboard Kelly were taken to the Arrowhead substation. Alexa's bullet wound was stitched up and bandaged by EMTs in Sheriff Conklyn's office. Then she was returned to a holding cell.

A pissed-off Bud Halley arrived at two A.M. and reluctantly did Shane's DFAR. They were in one of two windowless FI rooms.

After he heard it all, Halley leaned back in the wooden chair and glowered. "Shit, Scully, I'm supposed to believe that the mayor of L.A., the Super Chief of our department, and one of the largest developers in the state of California, along with a dozen or more sworn or terminated LAPD personnel, are involved in murder, blackmail, kidnapping, fraud, and a buncha other criminal misconduct," Halley said, looking at Shane through tired eyes. He didn't want any part of it. This was the ultimate red ball.

Shane had asked for Captain Halley for three reasons: One, with Tom Mayweather sure to get indicted, he was Shane's most recent CO. Two, the captain was well respected in the department, and Shane needed a trusted "rabbi" as his advocate. And three, he knew that Halley was deeply religious, with a highly developed sense of morals and ethics. Underneath all the police bullshit, he was a stand-up guy. If Halley could be made to believe Shane's story, he would come aboard, regardless of the consequences.

Shane had started his DFAR talking about the kidnapping of Chooch and Longboard, finally convincing Halley that they had been hit over the head, tied up, videotaped, and abducted from his Third Street apartment. They had then been taken to Logan Hunter's mansion in Arrowhead and held there for two days by current and former LAPD officers.

Shane, Alexa, Chooch, and Longboard all volunteered to take lie-detector tests, and after Halley agreed, Conklyn rolled a big, new Star Mark polygraph machine into the FI room. One by one they were given the test, and one by one they passed.

Shane could see the building frustration in Bud Halley's hazel-green eyes as night turned to day.

By ten o'clock the helicopter had been pulled out of the Little Bear River. Inside were the remains of the pilot, as well as Logan Hunter and Joe Church. Kris Kono had been found in the shallows with Alexa's 9mm slug buried deep in the Hawaiian officer's chest.

It was all exculpatory evidence, further sustaining Shane's statement.

Alexa and Shane described the events that occurred in Miami, starting with their attempt to rescue Sandy Sandoval and ending with the attack by Drucker, Love, and Calvin Sheets. Alexa handled their escape from Elton John's Biscayne Bay estate, then Shane explained about Ray's Arrowhead house and how Molar had been blackmailing the Long Beach City Council so Los Angeles could get control of the naval yard. Halley listened, took notes, and groaned as the scope of the corruption grew larger, reaching all the way up through the chief of police to the mayor's office.

Halley kept the startling events under wraps as best he could, but of course Logan Hunter's death had leaked out. News crews from L.A. were arriving in vans and helicopters. The newsies were already picking up other shreds of the story, sharking for details, sensing that much more was at stake.

"I don't know what to do with this," Halley admitted to Shane and Alexa after he'd heard it all. They were no longer being kept in holding cells and were seated in Sheriff Conklyn's office. He had promoted them from suspects to witnesses.

Out the window they could see a small TV uplink antenna farm being constructed on the vacant property across from the police station.

"I'm gonna call in Erwin Epps," Halley finally said, referring to the Baptist minister and political activist who had just been elected head of the L.A. Police Commission. "Under Section 78 of the city charter, the board of commissioners has the power and responsibility to supervise, control, and regulate the department." Halley quoted the section from memory.

"Good idea," Shane said.

Shane asked for and was given a chance to talk to Chooch. The boy was staying in the Arrowhead Motel with a sheriff's matron. Shane was driven over and let himself in.

Chooch was watching the news, his legs stretched out on the bed. He snapped off the television as Shane came through the door.

"Man...can you believe the coverage this is getting?"

"Chooch... I wanna talk to you about your mom."

"I know about Sandy...it's on the TV." His voice was guarded.

"I'm sorry you had to hear it that way. I wanted to tell you, but they wouldn't give me a chance until now."

Chooch nodded, his black eyes showing little. "I'm sorry she's dead," he said. "I didn't want that to happen.... I just wanted her to..." He stopped, then shook his head in frustration. "You know what I mean." He looked up. "You and me are the same, Shane. I got nobody, same as you." The way he said it, Shane couldn't tell what he was thinking. Chooch, like Shane, had become good at hiding his emotions.

"I want you to know something—something important about your mother."

"That she loved me?" the boy said, but his tone said he found it hard to believe.

"Yeah, she loved you, and she died trying to save you. She gave herself up for you, Chooch."

Chooch got up off the bed and moved to the window, his muscular body silhouetted in the morning sunlight streaming past him into the room.

"You were the one who saved me," he said softly.

"I never would have known where to look if your mother hadn't gotten that information for me. She gave up her life to get it."

There was a long moment, then finally Chooch turned and faced Shane. "I want to cry for her.... It seems like I should. Am I being an asshole?"

"No, Chooch. I just wanted you to know.

442

Whatever you feel about Sandy, in the end, when it counted, she was there for you."

Chooch nodded; suddenly his eyes filled, and he moved quickly to the bathroom and closed the door.

At two that afternoon, Chooch was picked up by the Child Protection Section of the Social Services Department and whisked away. Shane was back at Sheriff Conklyn's office and found out about it an hour after it happened. They said that since Chooch had no mother or father, he was being remanded to Juvenile Hall.

Shane knew he couldn't claim Chooch without a DNA test, and that would take time. Besides, the more he thought about it, the more he was beginning to suspect that Sandy had lied about his being Chooch's father. It was just what she would do—just like her to say that to get Shane to look after Chooch once she was gone. Either way, he couldn't get a DNA analysis up in Arrowhead, so it would have to wait until he got back to L.A.

Three hours later, Reverend Epp arrived and conferred with Bud Halley. He was a tall, dignified African American in his fifties who had tremendous credibility in the black community and had been put on the L.A. Police Commission to help deal with the charges of racism that had plagued the post—Daryl Gates department.

The two devout Christians listened all over

again as Shane, Alexa, and Longboard Kelly retold their story.

Slowly, over a period of hours, it became distressingly clear to both Captain Halley and Reverend Epps that much of what Shane and Alexa had been describing was undoubtedly true.

The two tired sergeants were finally allowed to move into the Arrowhead Motel to get some sleep. They had rooms right next to each other but were too exhausted to even say good night.

One by one, other members of the L.A. Police Commission quietly arrived in town. They had decided to hold their meeting in the Arrowhead Lodge, away from the sheriff's department and the hovering press corps.

At the end of their first meeting, after Shane, Alexa, and Longboard had retold their stories, Sheriff Conklyn got a district judge to issue a search warrant.

On Monday evening they broke the front-door lock and entered Logan Hunter's lakeside mansion. What they found in his office files pretty much confirmed everything Shane and Alexa had been saying.

At ten o'clock on Tuesday morning, Reverend Erwin Epps chaired a meeting in his Arrowhead Lodge hotel room. Shane and Alexa were both present, along with Captain Halley, Sheriff Conklyn, and the entire seven-member L.A. Police Commission.

"I think we now have to consider Section 79 of the L.A. city charter," Epps said gravely.

444

Then he took that bound document out of his briefcase and opened it to a paper clip marking the section.

"Let me read this to refresh you: 'A simple majority of the Police Commission is necessary to enact the provision of Section 79, which grants the commission the right to *appoint,* as well as to *remove,* the general manager of the department. However, the chief of police shall only be removed under the terms and conditions in city charter, Section 202.'" He flipped to that section and read the paragraph pertaining to the removal, suspension, or demotion of sworn police officers, then:

"I think we need to instruct the head of the Internal Affairs Division to draft a resolution to suspend the duties of Chief Brewer and bring him up on administrative charges. The head of IAD should further notify the district attorney of the possibility of criminal misconduct."

Shane couldn't help a small smile thinking of the panic that "resolution" would bring to the vanilla features of Commander Warren Zell.

The news was leaking from Lake Arrowhead to Los Angeles, and, little by little, shreds of it were showing up in the press and on TV.

The case went further into frenzied hyperspace when Tom Mayweather's body was found in the main salon of his boat anchored off Avalon Harbor in Catalina. He had put a police-issue shotgun into his mouth and blown his head off.

The subpoena control desk at Parker Center

445

was flooded with paperwork issued by Warren Zell and the fifteen IOs he had assigned to the case. John Samansky and Lee Ayers, the two surviving members of Ray's den, had hired criminal attorneys and were both clamoring to cut a deal.

Samansky won that ugly contest and became the department's star witness against Chief Brewer, Tony Spivack, Mayor Clark Crispin, and the surviving officers. The district attorney petitioned the department for the right to sit in on the upcoming BORs under Section 21.2 of the L.A. city charter—a sure sign that criminal charges would be forthcoming.

One day after Logan Hunter's helicopter was fished out of the river, Mayor Crispin was arrested at the airport on his way to a "vacation" in Mexico.

Chief Brewer staged a press conference after his subpoena was served. He denied any wrongdoing had taken place and promised a victory in court. Nevertheless, at the district attorney's request, two detectives from Special Crimes were assigned to his house, and he was ordered to remain at home, pending further investigation.

A day later the district attorney finally filed murder one charges against them all.

Alexa and Shane had been released, then went back to L.A. and watched the rest of it on her TV, since he didn't have one. She had cooked a remarkably good Italian dinner for them, and after they had two glasses of red wine, Shane was lying on the sofa in her anally neat living room, watching Dan Rather talk about him. Alexa was in the kitchen doing dishes, hoping her mother was watching over them all.

Shortly after the news ended, an investigator from IAD knocked on the door to pick up the files Alexa had gathered for Shane's BOR. The IO notified her that she was no longer the advocate prosecuting Scully's case.

"What case?" Shane asked, coming up off the sofa like a Harrier jet. "You mean, after all this, they're still planning to terminate me?"

"Just because you two turned this department upside down doesn't mean your unnecessary use of force on the Molar shooting goes away," the IO said. Then he took the four crammed case-file boxes and left.

"When will it end?" Shane growled.

"Shane...you'll prevail at that board. With all this going on, believe me, their case won't stick."

He looked at her and again felt something stir inside him. She saw it in his eyes. "I know, but this time let's wait," she said. "Let's not do anything again until all this calms down and we know if it's real, or if we're just pulsing 'cause we're glad to be alive."

"It's real," he said. But she was right, now was not the time.

Shane had heard that Chooch was being held under IDC—Intake and Detention Control— at Juvenile Hall. So he called Captain Halley and had Chooch moved to PNP—USCMC, which was the patient-not-prisoner section of the Juvenile Detention wing of the USC Medical Center. They were talking about assigning him to a foster home.

Shane slept on Alexa's couch, and the next morning, after she cooked him breakfast, he had her drop him off at the police impound garage, where he reclaimed the rented Taurus he had left on the movie set the night he got kidnapped. Then he drove down and gave blood at the USC hospital. He couldn't see Chooch, by order of the district attorney, who was still interviewing him as a witness, so Shane found an old friend named Ellen Webb, who worked in PNP as a nurse. He gave her his blood sample number and asked her to get a match from Chooch.

"How come?" Ellen asked, brushing a wisp of honey-blond hair out of her eyes. "According to the news, he's Hispanic."

"His mother was, but I think I may be the father."

She looked at Shane for a long moment and smiled. "Can't keep the little head from controlling the big head?" she said playfully, so Shane stuck his tongue out at her and left.

He had one more stop to make before he went home and slept for a year.

The freeway was crowded, and he was locked in bumper-to-bumper five o'clock traffic. He finally got to the end of the 10 and found himself back on the Coast Highway. He didn't have his badge, so this time he had to pay for parking. He left the Taurus, walked onto the bike path and up to DeMarco's house.

For once it was quiet out front. The blond beach ornaments were all gone, off playing with somebody else's mind. Shane passed through the gate and walked up to the front door. He tried to look through the front window, but the blinds were pulled and he couldn't see anything. Finally he reached into his back pocket and fished out his trusty collection of picks. The lock was an old brass Yale and was a bitch to open, but after five minutes he turned the tumblers, went into the house, then closed and relocked the door behind him.

He stood in the living room, looking around, remembering his trip here two weeks days ago.... He had stood in this very same spot, watching DeMarco play with his speakers while Snoop Doggy Dogg spewed race hatred. It seemed as though that had been in another lifetime. He walked softly through the place, looking into each room. No one was home, so he entered the office at the end of the hall, walked across the room, then sat at DeMarco's desk. His defense rep's case material was sitting there in one half-filled file box. DeMarco had been on Shane's case for almost ten days, and as Shane went through the material, he was surprised by the lack of evidence he'd collected to support Shane's position. The defense rep hadn't yet received all of the discovery items, and there wasn't even a copy of Barbara Molar's statement. There was a half-hearted, half-full spiral notebook.... It was all damned puny compared with the mountain of stuff that had been carted out of Alexa's house.

He finally stopped looking at the case files, leaned back in the chair, and waited.

An hour later he heard the front door open; DeMarco was talking to someone. He heard a young boy's laughter, and then the music came on. Shane waited for a minute, then got out of DeMarco's chair and continued silently down the hall, into the living room.

What he saw didn't surprise him as much as it sickened him. On the living room sofa, DeMarco Saint and one of the fifteen-year-old surfer boys were lying in a romantic embrace. They were both naked.

"What a total shitbox!" Shane said.

DeMarco snapped his head around and glowered up at Shane. Then he scrambled up into a sitting position and grabbed for his underwear. The boy made no move to cover himself. Instead he remained lounging on the sofa, glaring his indifference.

"You didn't get thrown off the job for drinking. You got thrown off for pedophilia," Shane said.

"Nobody ever proved anything," DeMarco said, now reaching for his beach shorts.

"I should've seen it. First you turn me down, then a day later, all of a sudden, you're taking on my case. Mayweather got you to do it, didn't he? He wanted somebody on the inside of my defense. He wanted to find out what I was up to. He knew about this thing you've got for underage boys. He could've still filed criminal charges and gone after your pension. He forced you to reconsider."

"That's nonsense," DeMarco sputtered as he got his shorts on and rose to his feet. He was flushed, his complexion a ruby red. Sweat was slick on his skinny white chest.

"Nonsense?" Shane said reflectively. "I only told one person that I went to the Long Beach Naval Yard. Two hours later I'm kidnapped and taken up to Arrowhead, and Coy Love knows about it. The person who told him was you!"

"Whatta you...whatta you...gonna..." DeMarco's lower lip was quivering.

"Do?" Shane finished the sentence for him. "I'll show you." He grabbed DeMarco's arm and jerked him off balance. As his defense rep fell forward, Shane swung, landing a left hook square on the side of Dee's face.

DeMarco went down in a slump and began to weep. The naked teenager was on his feet now, his hands up, fists balled.

"Don't try it, Jocko. I'll make fucking hash outta you." Shane walked to the door, then turned. "By the way, Dee, you've got a subpoena coming. I'm putting you in the mix." Without saying another word, he left.

Shane drove back to Venice. The incident hung with him and poisoned his mood.

He worked hard to shift his thoughts and finally tried to contemplate his future. He thought about his life, about Chooch, and whether he was truly the boy's father. Shane had been looking for a deeper meaning in his life. Chooch had begun to fill that emptiness.

In the past two weeks, Shane had had two big surprises, both from unexpected places. Chooch had been one; Alexa, the other.

He was paralyzed with fear that the blood test would prove that his one intimate moment with Sandy would turn out to be just what he'd always believed it to be—a mindless mistake—instead of what he hoped it was now, a chance for a different kind of future. He parked the Taurus in the garage at his Venice house on East Canal Street, walked past his ruptured Acura, and went into his kitchen. Longboard had slipped a note under the door:

Shane,
I got some cold beer and steak.
I'm tapping the Source.
You're invited.
Longboard

He put the note on the counter and slowly walked through the house, taking stock of his minimal emotional and physical existence: the furniture—remnants from broken love affairs; the bullet-riddled plaster walls in his front room, reminders of his fragile mortality. He picked up a pen and paper, then went outside and sat in one of the old rusting metal chairs.

He looked out at the setting sun just dipping below the horizon, dragging the last vestiges of the day across the shallow channels like a burnt orange memory.

He was in a new place, starting a new chapter in his life. He was not sure where he was going or how long it would take to get there, but for the first time in a long time, he was looking forward to the journey.

Then he uncapped the pen and wrote a long, personal letter to Chooch.

THE NEWS VULTURES were on the sixth floor of the Bradbury Building, leaning over the rails, blowing white streams of cigarette smoke into the huge glassed atrium. The ancient wrought-iron elevators went up and down, making unhurried stops, measuring each trip with a tailor's precision.

Shane was seated in the witness room on the fifth floor because he didn't want to stand out in the corridor and be pestered by news crews asking about the whole breaking Long Beach story. The NFL had just rescinded the L.A. Spiders' franchise along with the Web, and the Coliseum was now the likely choice to get the nod.

Burl Brewer was awaiting trial in County Jail,

and the LAPD had a new chief named Tony Filosian, from New York. A short, round man who wore huge pinkie rings and spoke with a Brooklyn accent, he showed up for work in a shiny suit and was instantly dubbed "the Day-Glo Dago," but he seemed like an excellent choice because of his background of turning around troubled departments.

Barbara Molar got off the elevator and walked down the hall. Shane saw her through the window. He hoped she wouldn't come into the witness room, but when she saw him, she smiled and quickly came through the door, her blond hair shining, smile radiant, dancer's calves flexing as she took a chair next to him in the empty room.

"Boy, talk about a cluster fuck," she said, opening the conversation in typical in-your-face Barbara fashion.

"Yep, it's assholes on parade," he said, not showing her much.

"I'm here to back you up. I did the IO interview last night. I've been out, so I stopped by and signed it this morning on my way over."

"That's good. Thanks."

"So who's your new DR?" she asked. "I heard you canned DeMarco Saint."

"I'm gonna try my own board," he said.

"Is that smart?"

"I've been getting that question a lot, so I'm beginning to wonder." He smiled at her.

She fished a cigarette out of her purse, lit up, and started smoking in the small room.

Shane wished she wouldn't; he'd never completely gotten over his desire for cigarettes.

"I figured I know the case better than anybody," he went on. "Since the department didn't want to give me more than a four-day postponement, I figured, what the hell…"

"Right. What the hell," she said. "Are we finally at a place where we can talk about the future?" she asked, smiling through the smoke.

Shane thought it'd be bad timing to piss her off just before she was going to testify. On the other hand, the IO had told him that she'd backed his story in her deposition, and he knew she pretty much had to stick to her statement.

He turned and faced her. "Y'know, Barb, I don't think we're gonna get a chance to see that happen." He watched her as her expression turned sour. "I've got some new responsibilities," he continued. "I took a blood test to see if I'm Chooch Sandoval's father. I'm expecting the results today. Then I'm picking him up and taking him home for the long weekend. We're gonna talk it out. After that, who knows? I may decide to raise him. I mean, if everything works out."

"Y'know, Shane, our timing was always pretty damn shitty, but you're not giving this a chance. Now that Ray's gone, it can work. And a kid? You wanna raise a kid?"

"Well, yeah, I sorta do," he finally said. "He and I hit it off."

"Kids are a drag," she said, stubbing out her cigarette. "Ray and I never wanted kids. You

455

never said anything about wanting kids...baby-sitters, homework, car pools... You can't be serious?"

"Listen, Barbara, thanks for being there for me."

"Yeah. Well, I'm gonna see if they've got coffee. See you inside." She got up and left.

Over and out.

Then Commander Van Sickle arrived, and a uniformed police officer announced the commencement of the Scully Board, in hearing room one.

Shane walked out of the witness room and entered room one. It was the largest of the hearing rooms, and there were news crews in all the available chairs in the back. Internal Affairs Boards were public hearings, so there was no way of keeping the press out. They would have to suffer through his clumsy presentation of the defense.

The room was rectangular, with large arched windows that streamed in sunlight and backlit the three-man judging panel. The two sworn and one civilian panel members were seated in leather swivel chairs at a long table at the head of the room. The American and LAPD flags decorated opposite ends of the stage. A court reporter was in a chair off to the side.

Warren Zell was prosecuting the case for the department, and there were four IOs clustered around him. Shane was alone at the defense table; his one assigned investigating officer was still out, taking statements and collecting last-minute depositions. Hopefully he would be back by noon.

Commander Van Sickle opened the proceedings. "Sergeant Scully, are you ready to proceed?"

"Yes, sir."

"To start with, I'm going to read you your rights, from the Police Disciplinary Manual. Okay?"

"Yes, sir."

"You have the right to appear in person and present a defense to the charges against you. You have the right to be represented by a department defense representative. You may produce witnesses to testify on your behalf, including character witnesses. You may cross-examine witnesses testifying against you. You have the right to testify in your own defense. You have the right to be present when board members examine your personal history and records. You also have the right to have all sworn testimony at this hearing reported and transcribed by a hearing reporter. You shall be entitled to a copy thereof." He looked up. "Do you understand your rights?"

"Yes, sir."

"This board has been convened to determine if unnecessary and escalating force was used in the fatal shooting of Lieutenant Raymond Molar. There are five counts of misconduct, all listed in your letter of transmittal."

The door in the back of the room opened, and Alexa Hamilton walked into the hearing. Everybody turned to look at her. She was wearing a tailored black suit coat and skirt over a white silk blouse. A red scarf decorated the collar.

"Excuse me, Sergeant Hamilton. You've been replaced as the advocate on this case," Warren Zell said. "I thought you'd been told that."

"Could I have a moment with Sergeant Scully, Commander?" she asked the board chairman.

Commander Van Sickle heaved a sigh and nodded. She moved briskly across the room and sat down in the empty chair beside Shane, resting her purse on the defense table. She leaned in to whisper to him.

"Since I can't prosecute you, I'd love to defend you," she whispered in his ear.

"Are you serious?"

"You can choose anybody in the department below the rank of captain; the last time I checked, that included me. I know this case from top to bottom. I prepped it for ten days. I know where every piece of bullshit is. Warren Zell is a mediocre administrator and a worse trial advocate. Just say the word, and I'll kick his vanilla-milkshake ass."

"Alexa, will you please represent me?" he whispered softly.

"Honored."

"If you're through with your little discussion?" Van Sickle asked with irritation. "I'd like to get started."

"And I'd like to notify the board that I'm taking over as Sergeant Scully's defense rep," Alexa announced.

"I'm afraid you can't do that," Zell said, rising to his feet. "She's a member of the Advocate Division and, as such, is prohibited from acting as a defense rep."

"To be precise, I'm currently assigned to Southwest Patrol," Alexa said. "I was brought back to try this one case. Once I was replaced as the advocate, I was immediately reassigned to my Southwest Patrol commander, freeing me to fulfill Sergeant Scully's request that I represent him."

Commander Van Sickle looked over at Zell.

"It's completely improper, sir," the chief advocate protested.

"But not outside of department guidelines," Van Sickle said. "Sergeant Hamilton is accepted as defense rep."

"I'd like a recess for fifteen minutes to get my files on this case out of my car and up here into the hearing room. I reproduced the entire case history and have been working on it all night. Maybe you could get a few officers to help me? There's a bunch."

They adjourned, then reconvened fifteen minutes later. For the rest of the day, Alexa shredded every piece of evidence that Zell put forward.

The board had been scheduled to go for two days, but by five o'clock that evening, Commander Van Sickle had heard enough.

"If you have something substantive to add that will make your case, would you put it on

459

now, Commander Zell? Otherwise, I'd like to entertain a motion from Sergeant Hamilton to dismiss this case."

"Sir... Due to obvious circumstances, this case has been fraught with monumental difficulties."

"This case should never have been brought here in the first place," the commander scolded. "It should have gone to a Shooting Review Board, which would have resulted in a finding of appropriate use of force. So, unless there is some statement or evidence to the contrary, I'm suggesting that this board immediately dismiss the proceeding. And let Sergeant Scully get back to work."

Alexa so moved.

He stood in the parking lot outside of the Bradbury Building and waited for her.

She came down at about six-thirty, carrying a stuffed briefcase and a box of paper supplies. He took the box and walked her to her car in the adjoining parking structure. They stopped at the trunk of her Crown Vic, and he put the box inside.

"I have something that belongs to you," she said. Then she reached into her purse and retrieved his badge, gun, and ID.

"I want to get to know you better," he said awkwardly.

"We killed half a dozen guys together...what does it take with you?" She smiled and then saw that he was serious, so she nodded her head.

"I'm free most evenings unless I'm on night watch."

"Tonight I'm barbecuing dinner for Chooch. I'm picking him up at the Med Center and we're going home. We'd love to have you join us."

"No...that would be wrong. You should do this one alone."

"Tomorrow night, then?"

She nodded, and he stood there in the garage, not sure what to do. Then he reached out and took her hand.

"Are you going to kiss me?" She smiled.

"Probably not good form for the accused to kiss an advocate in the IAD parking garage...."

"But it's okay for him to kiss his defense rep," she said.

So he took her into his arms and kissed her. The electricity that he felt again surprised him. It made him feel warm inside. His breath got short, his legs weak.

They finally separated, and she looked up at him. "Wow, you're a good kisser."

"Let's find another verb," he said, grinning.

Then he turned and left her standing there, looking after him, a smile on her beautiful, exotic face.

THE
LETTER TO
"CHOOCH"

Dear Chooch,

I told you once that you were an adult and that you were in charge of your life.

A man makes his own decisions but is also forced to live with the quality of his choices.

Your mother wanted a lot for you. She wanted to see you grow up to be strong, valuable, full of integrity and vision. Unfortunately, wanting something isn't the same as achieving it, but her heart was in the right place. Everything she was doing, she was doing for you. I know that's hard to envision when you're spending Christmas vacation alone in the prep school dorm, but I believe she wanted the best for you.

Sandy had parts of it right, but maybe she didn't have the whole deal figured.

Now she's gone. She died in my arms, asking me to take care of you. Making me promise that I would.

Even before that moment, I've been wanting you in my life, but I've also been wondering if I'm the right person to attempt it. Is it fair for me to mess up, when you've been given so little up to now?

And, of course, in the long run, as an adult, it should be your decision anyway. These questions have been on my mind. Since you've come to mean a great deal to me, I want you to carefully

465

consider my offer to move in and live here, before you give me your answer.

I'm not skilled at sharing. My life has been about grabbing and holding. It's a long way from the back door of the community hospital to this house in Venice. It doesn't represent much wealth or status, but it's the best I could do, and I feel blessed to be here.

You asked me once if I knew who your father was, and I told you that you would have to find out from your mother, that she had sworn me to secrecy. She once told me that your father was a criminal, a drug dealer that she had helped to put in jail.

Before she died, she told me why she had asked me to take you for this month. She said she felt it was finally time for us to get to know each other.

They say that things are never the way they appear, and I guess in this case that is certainly true. Sandy loved pulling all our strings, and now we're both faced with her last request.

I know the responsibility of looking after you goes much deeper than advice or guidance or suggestions to do your homework. It's about being a worthwhile role model. I'm not sure I can do that well.

Sandy had dreams of glory for you; she wanted you to go to Princeton or Yale, to be an attorney or a doctor. I have different goals. I want you to be a man of substance. I want you to know how to be a good friend and how to love without reservation. I want your word to be your bond.

So, Sandy and I have different goals now, just as we did when she was alive.

If you decide to take a shot with me, I will try hard to make this part of your life enriching. Can't say we won't argue or that I won't be wrong, but I can promise I'll try to always be honest with you.

Chooch, it's a much shorter journey we're on than it appears to be at its beginning. You can accept this ride or flag down another. It's all choices. It always will be.

> *Love,*
> *Your father,*
> *Shane*

He heard the door open behind him and sat quietly on the metal chair. After a moment he heard footsteps coming across the grass. Then Chooch sat in the metal chair beside him. He was holding the letter and looking out at the still water. The three-quarter moon was coming off the horizon, hiding behind a drifting cloud, lighting its lacy edges. They sat in silence and watched it float slowly by.

Shane was almost afraid to speak; his heart was beating fast in his chest. "So, whatta you think?" he said softly.

Chooch sat looking at the still canal, his face strangely set, breathing deeply. Then he dropped the letter on the grass, reached out and took hold of Shane's shoulder, and squeezed it.

"I want to stay here," he finally said. "This is where I belong."